About the Author

Born and educated in Evesham, En
of his professional life in the Royal
captain. After early tours as a fighter pilot and flying instructor, he
qualified as a fast-jet test pilot, eventually to become chief test pilot. In
an extraordinarily varied working life, travelling widely, living and
working in the middle east, the USA, Germany and the UK, he has since
been college vice-principal, hospital director, and magistrate. Also a keen
yachtsman, he uses this broad background to good effect, bringing
colour, depth, and dramatic action to his writing, which will draw you
into an 18th century plot where injustice demands revenge. 'An American
Exile' is the first of the *Jack Easton* novels which follow the adventures of
the eighteenth century stonemason from his transportation to Maryland
through the last decades of British colonial rule in America.

Ron Burrows makes his fiction debut with this gripping and unusually
atmospheric historical drama. His second novel, Fortune's Hostage,
published 2009 (ISBN 978-1-84549-381-3), continues the series, and is
available through Amazon and good bookshops.

An American Exile

RON BURROWS

Published 2007 by arima publishing

www.arimapublishing.com

ISBN 978 1 84549 217 5

© Ron Burrows 2007
(Reprinted 2009)
All rights reserved

Printed and bound in the United Kingdom

Typeset in Garamond 11/14

Swirl is an imprint of arima publishing.

arima publishing
ASK House, Northgate Avenue
Bury St Edmunds, Suffolk IP32 6BB
t: (+44) 01284 700321

www.arimapublishing.com

For

My family

- and for my old buddy,

Lt Cdr Walt Lawrence USN
1943 – 1990.

Acknowledgements

I gratefully acknowledge the help and advice received from the following individuals and institutions during the writing of this book:

The College of Southern Maryland, La Plata, Md.,
St Mary's College, St Mary's City, Md.,
The volunteers and guides of Historic St Mary's City,
The administrative director of the Weems-Bott Museum, Dumfries, Virginia,
The staffs of the Portland Museum and the Tophill Library, Portland, Dorset,
Lara Doran and Richard Franklin of Arima Publishing.
Sally Campbell and my daughter, Sonja, for proof reading my first draft,
And my wife, Caroline, for her advice and patience, and for putting up with my absences, both mental and physical.

Prologue

Dorset, England, September 1750

An owl's piercing shriek brought Andrew White out of his dozing with a start. It took him only a moment to clear his head and remember where he was as he raised his capped head above his cover and quickly glanced about, his apprehensive face catching the pale half-light of a waning moon. The creature's sharp eyes had most likely spotted him, he thought, and for a short time he worried that other eyes had seen him lying in the scrub and might even now be lining up their sights. But he saw nothing untoward, and reproaching himself for nodding off, he brought his focus again to the object of his earlier attention – the pier not a hundred yards to his front. The furious activity on the stony promontory continued unabated, its participants still apparently unaware of his presence. He exhaled a sigh that combined relief with resignation - his lonely hours of dreary observation had already taxed him to the point of tedium, but he braced himself to wait much longer yet.

Hidden in the shadows of the woody undergrowth behind him, his tethered horse flicked its tail and let out a single slow breath that might have been an echo of his own weary sigh. White's ears pricked up at the faint sound, his senses now fully reawakened. Above the gentle lapping of the surf and the rattling of the shingle in its constant ebb and flow, he could hear the muted voices on the pier drifting on the air. Further off, in a slow lament of the early hour, a distant church bell struck four. While in the bay, etched out darkly against the moon's shimmering reflections on a somnolent sea, a brig under full canvas continued slowly on her course, the long tenuous line of her wake still linked to the pier as if reluctant to let go.

Then a heavier rustle in the vegetation nearby almost made White's heart stop. He froze, holding himself quite still for a long moment, his dark uniform hidden by the camouflaging vegetation making him all but invisible to human eyes. But then slowly, so as not to give himself away, he turned his head in the direction from which the sound came. 'Let's hope that this is Hayes returning at last - and that he's got the captain and some men with him,' he thought. But he could not be sure it was this friendly presence that now approached. Perhaps he had been spotted after all and was even now being stalked? His anxious eyes searched the dark backdrop of the trees as the sound of stealthy movement grew closer. He heard a murmur, but still saw nothing but shadowy greyness in the dim light. Then the rustling stopped abruptly, and for a moment silence descended as with bated breath he waited, his eyes and ears straining until they ached. Then, through the shadowy gloom came a whispered call:

'White! Are you there?' It was the voice of Captain Middleton.

'Over here, sir!' White replied, with manifest relief.

Two uniformed figures approached out of the darkness, bending low as they trod. The stocky form of Captain Middleton was unmistakable even as a dark shape in the moonlight, as was the willowy figure of Hayes following awkwardly and rather nervously behind. Both reached White quickly and squatted at his side.

'I came as fast as I could,' the captain said, breathlessly. 'We had to get the off-duty watch out of their beds and open up the armoury. Are we in time?'

'Their brig set sail about fifteen minutes ago, captain, but we'll catch the shore party and the contraband on the pier if we're quick about it.'

'Did you get the vessel's name?'

'No sir. Sorry sir, it was too dark.'

'Pity. How many men?'

'I counted about twenty; it's a large load and it'll take them some time to shift it. They're loading up their wagons now.'

The captain lifted his head above the cover and surveyed the scene. Illuminated in the moonlight, his sharp face looked intense as his calculating glances moved quickly to and fro. He fell back on his haunches, his features firm-lipped and contemplative. His companions waited expectantly for a pronouncement.

'Hmm!' he uttered in an uncertain tone. 'I could only raise eight men, so we're outnumbered two to one, but its worth a try,' he said at last. 'Smyke's taken the others to Ringstead Bay on that tip-off he received, so we shan't see them until morning.' His forehead creased as if something had suddenly occurred to him. 'Didn't he want you two with him?'

'No, sir,' White replied, looking slightly irked. 'He said he didn't need us - perhaps he thought he already had enough subalterns,' he offered unconvincingly. 'So I decided that I'd show Hayes around this part of our patch instead. There was always the chance that we'd spot something going on. And …well, we just stumbled upon the brig making her approach. I thought it too good an opportunity to pass up, sir, so I sent Hayes back for you.'

The captain nodded, but his thoughts were already apparently elsewhere. White continued nevertheless:

'Mr Smyke will have my guts for garters if he gets to know we came off on our own, sir,' he said uncertainly. 'He doesn't seem to like us taking initiatives!'

'Quite right too!' The captain's tone became stern as he rose again to inspect the pier. 'You can't be privy to everything that's going on White! You could have blundered into an official operation - and totally wrecked it!'

Middleton dropped down onto one knee; his tone had been mildly rebuking but his features softened. 'Anyway, well done on this occasion,' he said with an appraising glance, 'but don't come out on your own again without my authorisation! And this'll have to be our little secret - we wouldn't want Mr Smyke getting the idea that we're doing things behind his back, would we?'

'No sir,' returned White, relieved.

'No sir,' echoed Hayes, still looking ill at ease.

With another quick inspection of the pier, the captain beckoned both men to draw closer.

'Now listen!' he whispered urgently. 'I've left our little posse hidden in the trees. They're well armed with muskets and pistols, and I've brought enough for us to carry four pistols each – two for our hands and two for our belts! We'll divide the men between us and form up under cover in a line – uh, over there,' he said, casting his gaze and pointing his finger towards the moonlit tree line directly above the pier. 'Then, at my signal, we'll rush the wagons, making as much racket as we can, firing high to scare them off. I just want to teach them a lesson and there's no way we can capture the lot! With luck, they'll scatter, leaving us to pick up a few stragglers - and the contraband of course.' Middleton flashed a meaningful glance at his attentive listeners. 'Now, it'll be vital that they don't get time to think, so get your men to stagger their fire. We'll have to fill the gaps with pistol shot while they reload so as not to give the smugglers time to regroup - if they realise that they outnumber us, they'll turn the tables for sure and give us an unpleasant time. Understood?'

The two subalterns nodded silently.

'Right then,' the captain said firmly, 'follow me. We'll brief the men!'

The activity on the pier meanwhile had continued at a frantic pace, and the large pile of contraband unloaded from the now distant brig had already been reduced to half its original size. A chain of men, bending under the weight of their burdens, carried casks and boxes on their shoulders towards two horse-drawn wagons standing on the shoreline. The first of these looked fully loaded and ready to depart up the steep and rutted track that led up through a sandy ridge towards the trees; its driver was already perched on his driving seat, reins in hand. The loading of the second wagon was now briskly underway with every man working as if driven. But one stood apart from the rest, urging the others on.

'Come on lads! We're running late,' he whispered impatiently to a group of men struggling by with heavy casks upon their shoulders. 'The Revenue might well have had their notice drawn elsewhere tonight, but the stuff still has to be in Pettigrew's cellar before daybreak - or there'll be hell to pay!'

But it was not long before a shrill whistle and the sharp crack of a whip punctured the night air and the wagons began to move upon their way. Some of the men put their shoulders to the wheels to speed them up the gritty track; others half walked, half ran behind. But just as the last man was leaving the pier, a hoard of shadowy figures leapt out from the tree line in full cry and charged down upon them under a barrage of blazing musket and pistol fire. As the flintlocks struck, the powder ignitions lit up the night in a peppering of brilliant flashes, the explosions seeming to come from such a wide arc of view that a regiment of soldiers might be descending. Taken so completely by surprise, the smugglers had no time to think about returning fire, and someone from the wagons screamed an expletive. Panic erupted immediately as twenty men bolted for their lives in all directions, their racing feet splashing and crunching noisily in the surf and shingle as they scrambled along and up the beach in a wild bid to escape.

With so few officers, however, the momentum of the assault could not be sustained at its initial frenzied pitch, and it began to falter as the musketeers stooped to reload. The hiatus was covered skilfully by some pistol fire from Middleton, White and Hayes who pressed on regardless, despite some of the smugglers taking the chance to turn and loose off a few shots of their own - if wildly aimed and ineffective in their fright. Before they could regroup, however, a second musket volley from the customs' men lit up the darkness with renewed fury, and in the face of the renewed assault, those who had thought of resistance instantly thought better of it.

The officers' charge now took up a new line, focussing on the abandoned wagons, with Middleton directing the thrust so as to divide the fleeing gang in two, deliberately forcing a smaller contingent back down the beach towards the sea. In the moonlight, the splashing of these escaping feet along the waterline threw up a telltale marker of phosphorescent foam and Middleton called his men to concentrate on this group, allowing the rest to scatter into the gloom and run home in panic to wonder at their escape. Aided by the steepness of the beach, the captain's charging posse swooped down upon their quarry with relative ease, while the smugglers waded with leaden legs through the clinging surf, sliding and stumbling in the loose shingle, until they fell, exhausted.

The hapless cohort was thus quickly rounded up and marched back to the pier where the customs men, astonished by their own success, sat guarding them and the contraband until dawn when Middleton's call for reinforcements was eventually answered. If they were in high spirits at the beginning of their watch, morale was higher yet after a modest sampling of the booty they had so neatly captured.

As Captain Middleton later reported to the satisfied members of his supervising Customs Board, the operation represented a further victory under his new leadership in the renewed campaign against smuggling in the region. It was indeed a feather in the captain's cap; but he chose not to mention the relative failure of the rather larger planned operation in Ringstead Bay led by his deputy, Smyke, the same evening. Nor did he inform the Board that his own success was largely due to a lucky accident and the initiative of his junior officers White and Hayes. Thus was the burgeoning reputation of the ambitious captain in his new appointment further enhanced; but his recent successes would come at a terrible cost.

Chapter One

The sight of a lantern moving with such apparent purpose in the high ground was unusual so late at night, and so its progress had drawn the attention of three men walking on separate but converging paths through the dark folds of the land below. All three had glanced warily at the light as they crept silently in the moon's shadows, tracking its path in case it posed a threat. But they need not have been concerned, it was not a riding officer on patrol but a returning mariner striding out along the Ridgeway who was the unwitting subject of their scrutiny.

The seaman had followed a well-trodden path from the harbour at West Bay towards his home in the downs above Melcombe, climbing the contours until attaining his present height some six hundred feet above the sea. He now walked on easier ground along the middle section of his journey where the gradients are gentler. Here, the path becomes uncertain in its direction in navigating a gully, and in darkness this final winding incline is difficult to follow. A rising moon had begun to be of some assistance to the seaman, but descending into a shadowy undulation not yet penetrated by the moon's oblique rays, he had needed to tread carefully, holding his lantern at arm's length to be sure of his footing. At last, breathing heavily from the demanding pace he had set himself, he reached the crest and once more came out into the open, breaking out again into the moonlight as the path came over the top. The moonlit panorama that unfolded before his eyes stopped him in his tracks and stilled his breath as he marvelled upon it. Although he must have gazed upon the scene countless times before, it had never been like this. Above him, an infinite void glittered with a million pinpricks of starlight in a sky so clear that it felt as if he could reach out and touch the most distant of galaxies. Hovering a hand's width above the horizon, a brazen moon hurled its white light upon a sparkling sea, which glittered with such bright intensity as to cause him instinctively to raise his hand to shield his dazzled eyes. Then, adjusting to the brightness, he let his hand fall, and against the shimmering backdrop once again revealed, he saw a coastline etched in such dark contrast that every crag and fissure, every inlet and outcrop of its topography could be traced in intricate detail.

Directly in the centre of this dark outline, the jagged beak-like form of the Isle of Portland reached out from Dorset's southern shore five miles into the English Channel, pointing as if something of great interest lay over the horizon. This Isle, however, was not a true island at all; it was connected to the mainland by a narrow isthmus, the Chesil bank, a long curving sliver of stones piled high by powerful currents to make a natural breakwater for the bay formed in its lee. The embankment swept northwards from the Isle in a graceful arc, gradually turning north-west to run parallel with the mainland shore, creating a lagoon over eight miles long. The walker's gaze idly traced its familiar outline to the dim edges of moonlight where it faded into the gloom in the direction from which he had come. His breath had calmed now and, with weary reluctance, he made to walk on, but just then a glint of light emanating from the shadows of the ground below caught his eye. The flash had been so brief that he might have imagined it; certainly it was not a lantern, but he thought it could have been a reflection of moonlight from something of human manufacture, and he was curious as to what might have been its cause. Scanning the dark terrain below for some moments, he waited expectantly and in vain for a repeat of the phenomenon; but eventually he tired and turned once more upon his way. Had he stayed there a little longer he might have caught further indications of the men who still watched his light from the moon's long shadows, walking on their convergent paths. And it might also have been possible for him to predict that their routes would meet at an isolated mansion house standing on the rising ground above the long lagoon.

It had taken the three men some hours of careful walking to approach their rendezvous from the villages of Weymouth and Wyke, and they had paused to watch the unusual light with heightened interest. One of them had been so curious that he had taken out his eyeglass to inspect it more closely, not realising that the moon's reflection from its lens had all but given him away. But now seeing the lantern moving eastwards again, its carrier apparently indifferent to their presence, the men once more resumed their pace. Their converging paths wound through a rich and gently undulating landscape of small fields painted by the moonlight into eerie shades of grey, in which silent sheep, moon-white on a charcoal background, moved about unhurriedly like ghostly apparitions. The night was still, so deathly still, that for each man only the sound of his own breathing reached his ears; no rustle of creatures in the hedgerows, nor even a whisper from the gentlest zephyr in the thinning branches came to cloak their quiet progress.

The last to arrive at the rendezvous was the tallest of the group; his lumbering stride was recognised immediately against the chalky whiteness of the approaching track by the two men already waiting there. These two stood hidden in the shadow of an old yew tree watching the man come closer as the moonlight picked out his mean and pointed features. His dense eyebrows seemed joined in a continuous line above his prominently hooked nose; heavy side-burns descended from his officers' cap and curled around his fleshy cheeks almost reaching the corners of a mouth which seemed set in a permanent pout. In the pale light, the hirsute adornment fashioned his face into an ugly mask, made yet more sinister by the dark pits of his deep-set eyes from which two tiny white glints of moonlight reflected. The waiting men stepped forward from their concealment into the light to be revealed to his advance.

'What's this all about?' the tall man called in a gruffly whispered voice as he came upon them, leading the pair back into the shadowy cover of the yew tree. In this isolated place and at this god-forsaken hour, there was not much need for lowered voices, but the stillness seemed to demand it.

'You should know!' the younger of the two men retorted. 'The bloody Revenue got six of my men the other night, and we lost the whole sodding consignment!'

The young man's grey-haired companion shook his head derisively.

'Lucky I was already underway, Mr Smyke, or they'd have got the brig too,' he added testily. 'You were supposed to have kept them occupied!'

Smyke shifted his weight uneasily as his expression changed from affront to consternation. It seemed to take a few seconds for him to marshal a response, his eyes meanwhile glancing at the pale façade of the mansion house that stood just a field's width away through a gap in a line of stunted and wind-bent trees.

'I had almost the entire unit with me in Ringstead Bay all night,' he said at last, his voice taking on the tone of one piqued by an unfair accusation. 'It must have been a West Bay unit,' he protested.

'It was your new boss, Middleton,' said one of the men, emphatically.

'It can't have been!' came Smyke's incredulous reply. But then he saw from the two men's robust expressions that he must be mistaken. 'Oh Jesus!' he muttered under his breath, and he sagged visibly.

'My sentiments entirely,' said the old man, simply.

All three then turned their gazes as if by a common instinct towards the house as if expecting a comment from that direction; it remained dark except for the dim crimson glow of a candle flickering behind the curtains in one of the seven upstairs windows.

'And Mr Pettigrew was not pleased, as you will no doubt soon find out,' continued the old man, in a sort of proprietary tone.

The skin of his face weathered and stretched by a life at sea, the old man looked gaunt by comparison with the late arrival whose overbearing figure physically dominated the group. In unconscious retreat, he stepped out from the cover of the yew and moved over to an opening in a nearby dry-stone wall and stood alone, silently thoughtful, gazing up at the façade. The moonlight caught the untidy strands of steel grey hair dangling from his crumpled tricorn hat and glinted off the brass buttons of his mariners long navy barathea coat. After a while, the others moved across to join him, propping themselves against the wall to watch for the signal that would release them from their waiting. The young man was of stocky and muscular build, and he had a certain aggressive poise about him as if looking for a fight. His common face, framed by a shock of unruly black hair, bulged at one cheek as he chewed on a plug of tobacco. He wore a grubby leather hip-length jacket that, either by design or surgery, had no sleeves, leaving the tattoos on his thick arms well displayed below his shirtsleeves. Cocksure and full of youthful arrogance, he could not resist the opportunity to demonstrate his prowess by vaulting onto the wall's crumbling top, from which height he then spat the glutinous contents of his mouth over an impressive arc in a show of general disdain.

Smyke watched the display with his lip curled in disgust, but he now turned his gaze back towards the house.

'Well, he's making us wait long enough!' he muttered, puffing himself up again after his earlier bruising. 'Summoned at this hour like lackeys!' he blustered, thrusting his pointed chin out resentfully. 'Sometimes I wonder why we need him.'

'Hah!' the young man scoffed, 'Face it, Smyke, without his money and his brig, we wouldn't have an operation at all! Anyway, there's not much for us to share these days, is there?' he added sarcastically.

Smyke's lip curled again, this time into a sneer.

The old man gave out a gravelly cough, brought up a gob of phlegm, and spat it out coarsely. 'Yeah! It's all right for you in that uniform!' he said, wiping his mouth with his sleeve. 'Its Bolton and me that takes most of the risk – especially since you don't keep 'em out of the way like you used to.' He cocked his head disdainfully. 'And there's goin' to have to be some changes in the way we do things, or I'm out – and without me to skipper the *Marguerite*, nobody gets anything!' he muttered darkly.

Smyke remained silent, his face a mask of contrived indifference as Bolton jumped in with some characteristic sarcasm.

'Oh, Mr Smyke won't suffer, Tregaskis; he hedges his bets,' he taunted. 'Still on the take down at the harbour, ain't yer Smyke? A tidy percentage by all accounts.'

Smyke shot the younger man a fierce glance. 'You watch your mouth, Bolton!' he hissed; but he was clearly in some discomfort at the charge.

As the senior tide-surveyor in Weymouth, Smyke was known by masters of arriving vessels for his penny-pinching approach in assessing their cargoes and reckoning the excise duty to pay. But he was diligent only to the point at which a sum could be negotiated for him to turn a blind eye to the portions of their cargoes that might evade taxation with a bit of collusion on his part. It was this selective vision that had provided him with a handsome bay-fronted house located on the Melcombe waterfront and a standard of living disproportionate to his rank. But not content with this, he was always on the lookout for opportunities to improve his income. His chance had come when he discovered that the prominent ship owner, Nicolas Pettigrew, ostensibly a local worthy, was also secretly the patron of the Chesil smuggling gang. The revelation came to Smyke by accident rather than by any cleverness on his part, but, spotting an easy shilling, he was quick to try a clumsy blackmail on the ship-owner to coerce his way in. He was pushing at a door deliberately left invitingly ajar for someone such as he. In return for a small percentage of the gang's profits, Smyke soon found himself supplying information on counter-smuggling activities - the movements of the riding officers, the revenue cutters, and the tidewaiters and so forth – and planting misinformation to draw his honest colleagues off the gang's trail.

At first, Smyke's contributions added greatly to the gang's success, but his usefulness had recently begun to decline as a result of changes in the structure of the Service. The huge losses of potential tax revenue resulting from so-called 'free trade', by now a national black-market of epidemic proportions, stirred a Government desperate to replenish its depleted war chest into enacting a number of emergency measures. Predictably, these hurriedly framed Acts were as quickly outmanoeuvred as they were passed, and there were officers within the Customs Service who, like Smyke himself, connived against the new laws for their own gain. Frustrated by all this apparent failure, the Customs' Board eventually decided to bring in a number of senior regional officers to implement the much-needed modernisation of the Service and rid it of corruption.

The subsequent restructuring in Dorset affected Smyke's position considerably. Where he had once been the officer in charge of the Weymouth area, he now found himself relegated to become merely the deputy to the new senior regional officer, Captain John Middleton RN (Retired), appointed to implement the changes for the whole of the Dorset coast. Smyke had felt the ensuing wind of change rip through his previously cosy life like a sudden squall. Not only had his value to Pettigrew's gang become doubtful now that he was no longer in charge, but his 'take' in the harbour was also drying up as Middleton's new, much stricter, import controls began to take effect. Worse even than this, however, was the increasing threat to his very existence through the possible exposure of his skulduggery. He had begun to fear that at any moment someone with a grudge, bargaining on a King's pardon, might now feel safe to report him without fear of reprisal. It was this fear that had been the instrument with which he had ruled in the seedy underworld of the harbour-front before Middleton's arrival, and he still tried to maintain this illusion despite the change of regime. But he could feel his power slipping through his fingers as each day passed, much as he tried to mask it. In the nightmares that had of late brought him bolt upright in a cold sweat in the middle of the night, he saw himself imprisoned, transported to the colonies - even hanging at the end of a rope. Involuntarily, he found himself inserting his fingers inside his collar to loosen it.

'Things getting a bit uncomfortable for yer Smyke?' the young man scoffed from his position on the wall, scarcely concealing his contempt for a despised official who had a foot in both camps but belonged properly to neither. 'If you'd done the bloody job you were paid for, none of us would be here tonight!'

Smyke's features twisted into an angry scowl.

Inside the house, in the dressing room adjoining the master bedroom, Nicolas Pettigrew stood before the oval mirror on his dresser and adjusted his wig. The candlelight gave his face a ruddy hue and its deep shadows lent more gravitas than his thirty-five years might otherwise have bestowed. He turned his head slowly from side to side, keeping his admiring eyes fixed firmly on his own reflection. He was pleased with his new wig. In silvery horsehair, it had three tight curls in rows on either side and, at the back, a short pigtail tied with a black-silk ribbon that overhung the satin collar of his coat. He thought it cut a dash. Leaning forward, he experimented with the shape of his eyebrows to make himself look stern, glaring fiercely at the reflection of himself. The candle flickered with his movement, and as the shadows moved around his eyes, the fleeting image of his father's face appeared before him, glaring back at him from the mirror in a look of mournful disapproval. The spectre might have been disquieting for some, but despite his genteel appearance and public station, Nicolas Pettigrew was not a man who occupied the moral heights, and paternal censure had rarely had the capacity to stir him.

It had thus been a matter more of pride than of shame that in the years since his father's death, the moribund shipping company that he had inherited had quadrupled its profitability through smuggling. But now he saw his empire threatened by the arrival of the astute and ambitious newcomer, Captain Middleton, who would not fall for the tricks Pettigrew had played on Smyke, a man whose greed had made him easy prey for grooming. No, Pettigrew had already decided what must be done - Middleton would have to be dealt with in some other way – and ruthlessly at that! It was simply a matter of his own survival, he realised, and he was pleasantly surprised that he had no qualms, especially since someone else would do his dirty work. But the solution he would now attempt to engineer must never on any account be attributable to himself, even by those in the gang whom he knew would be waiting impatiently outside. The thought of it brought a smile to his face as he gazed at himself admiringly in the mirror; he was confident that he could make it work - if he could no longer use Smyke as a shield, then he would use him as a sword.

It was time for the signal; he had kept them waiting long enough.

Pettigrew opened the door at the rear of the house holding a lighted candle and the three men entered without a word. They followed their host through a labyrinth of basement corridors on cold flag-stoned floors with only his candle to light their way. The scuffing of their footfalls and their muttered curses echoed in the narrow spaces as they stumbled along in near total darkness, Pettigrew's sinewy figure having blocked out most of the light from his candle. The group eventually reached a cavernous storeroom which was distempered white but which took on a yellow hue in the light of several oil lamps hanging from the two long beams that spanned the void. Inside, the air was musty and laden with the sweet earthy aromas of apples and loamy potatoes stored for the winter – laced heavily by the heady smell of liquor. Oak casks filled numerous arched recesses reaching nearly to the high vaulted ceiling, and in the centre of the room, a long scrubbed-pine table stood with a row of chairs along each side. A place for each of the visitors had been marked by the location of a pewter tankard, and in the centre of the table a large earthenware jug of wine sat between two thick candles burning with a steady flame from which thin columns of black smoke snaked lazily upwards.

Pettigrew sat himself at the head of the table with a flourish of his coat tails and waited silently while the others settled. Even in his mid-thirties, the signs of an opulent lifestyle already showed in his flushed cheeks; and his face seemed permanently set in a self-important expression, which was accentuated by his aquiline nose and petulant lips. In front of him, instead of the tankards provided for the others, he had given himself a glass of fine-cut crystal that sat alongside a bottle of his own selection. He poured himself a measure unhurriedly, indicating with a patronising wave of his hand that the others should do the same with the lesser wine he had provided for them.

Pettigrew opened the meeting in a curiously calm voice:

'Well gentlemen, another debacle. And we all know the reason why, I think.' He then turned to Smyke. 'Your contribution was distinctly unhelpful again, Smyke; and if we cannot now depend upon you to keep the Revenue off our backs, I fear that our operation has already become rather too vulnerable. Your confident assurances have twice now led us into disaster.' He paused, then let out a heavy sigh in a show of exasperation before casting his gaze towards the young Bolton who seemed anxious to speak. 'Tell me Bolton, how in heaven's name were you caught out so easily yet again? You quite clearly took too much for granted!'

Bolton poured out an acidic defence of his own role as shore-party leader on the calamitous night when Captain Middleton and his men had caught him unawares. He had been led into a trap, he asserted, and once the goods had been landed on the quay he was inevitably highly vulnerable. In his opinion, the group's method of operation had become far too dependent upon Smyke's diversions, and too big to bank on the mere chance of avoiding detection.

Even though Tregaskis could not have seen much from his escaping brigantine, he was quick with his sage nods of support for Bolton's views and his condemnation of Smyke for the failure.

Smyke shrank under the onslaught. His diversionary operation in Ringstead Bay had failed to provide the expected protection for Bolton and his men, and he had no explanation for Middleton's surprise attack. But what vexed him most as he sat resentfully enduring the criticism, however, was that Middleton had made him look a fool.

Bolton finished his diatribe abruptly, having evidently realised that he was repeating himself, and there was a brief and uncomfortable silence before Pettigrew spoke, throwing down the first of his challenges:

'Our association may, I fear, be coming to an end, Mr Smyke, unless, that is, you have any alternative proposals!' he said in a tone all the more threatening for its apparent lightness.

Smyke shifted in his chair and took a breath to speak but was cut off by Pettigrew as he continued self-assuredly:

'The issue before us this evening, gentlemen, is to consider the method of our operations in the light of the changed circumstances; to consider whether we should continue in some other way less vulnerable to customs' interference, or indeed whether we should continue at all.' Pettigrew glanced at each of the men questioningly but saw none of them willing to volunteer a view.

'I would suggest that we face a bleak choice,' he went on. 'If we cannot knock the Revenue men off their perch, in a manner of speaking, I do not believe that we have a satisfactory option but to close down. The success of our operation has been based on infrequent good-sized loads for maximum profit, with the minimum number of people involved to share it. A scaled-down operation would, for me at any rate, not be worth the candle.'

Tregaskis removed his tricorn hat and, placing it on the table, smoothed his ruffled grey hair into place with a hurried sweep of his hand. A loyal employee of Pettigrew's father for almost all his working life, he had progressed up the chain of command to captain the company's trading vessels. An honest and well-meaning man at heart, he had nevertheless been drawn into Pettigrew's smuggling when the young heir took over. At first his involvement had been almost accidental, but by degree he had been drawn further in, knowing full well that he was being manipulated but feeling powerless to extricate himself. While the going had been easy, he had overcome his aversion to the business and had taken his share of the profits like the others; but now that the risks of capture had become very real to him, he regretted his involvement and had begun to long for a quieter and safer life. If he had not felt so dependent on Pettigrew for his living, he would have gone off already to seek it.

'In my opinion, sir, it's too dangerous to bring the *Marguerite* in to land these big loads any more.' Tregaskis spoke slowly in a West Country drawl. 'As you say, we have become too vulnerable now that the customs are better organised, especially with their cutter about. I'd say, we should seriously consider closing it all down,' (he said this tentatively). 'The custom's attack the other night gave my crew quite a fright. We were only just offshore when the firing broke out - a few minutes earlier, and they'd have had us too. The men would rather go back to shipping legal cargo than finish up behind bars like some of Bolton's men. They're all family men, sir,' he added as if in explanation.

Pettigrew assessed his captain without expression for some seconds before replying. 'You may well be right, Tregaskis,' he said without conviction. 'But your vessel could no longer pay its way without the smuggling work - it would have to go, and you with it, I'm afraid. If I calculated how much she'd be worth and how much I'd save by laying off her crew, there'd be a strong argument for selling her.'

'Well, if that's the case, sir, and not wanting just yet to be out of employment,' Tregaskis responded quickly with a wrinkled smile, while shifting uneasily in his chair, 'there must be a safer way of doing it, surely? We could try holding off just outside the hovering distance and get Bolton to come out to us using his fishing friends to transport the loads in.' With this suggestion, Tregaskis glanced at his younger companion hoping for a favourable reaction, but getting no encouragement, continued quickly lest his argument should be interrupted. 'That way, we could stay out in clear water looking legitimate if we were spotted, and the boats could then disperse with their loads and be less vulnerable coming ashore in different places along the beach.' He paused nervously to scan the faces around the table hoping to see signs of agreement, but sensing a contrary mood, he hurried to a close. 'I admit that we would have to find a few more men to man the boats and move the loads,' he stuttered, 'but surely it could still be profitable?' He ended his proposition as an appeal.

Bolton shook his head vigorously. 'Safer for you perhaps, Tregaskis,' he said sharply. 'But I'll not get enough good men to face the open waters of the Bay so far out. Too many men have already been lost on Chesil coming ashore; you know as well as I that it's a perilous place for small boats if the weather turns.' He shook his head again. 'No, I think it's time we gave up your old tub altogether and switched to bringing the stuff into our old quiet landing places using faster sloops direct from the other side. That way we could out-run the customs if they came upon us.' He glanced at Tregaskis in condescension. 'Besides, if we did what you say, Tregaskis, we may never find you in the darkness, and signalling carries its own risks as you well know.'

Tregaskis had glanced at his employer apprehensively at his young friend's suggestion that the brig be abandoned, but he looked more pensive now as he took a swig from his tankard. Smyke still sulked, not offering any contribution at all.

Pettigrew took a sip from his glass in the pause that followed.

'Mr Tregaskis,' he said at last, 'you're right that it has now become too risky for us to bring the *Marguerite* into our usual landing stages; but Bolton is also right that it is too dangerous and too uncertain for the boats to come out to meet you. Neither would using sloops, fast or otherwise, to bring a large number of smaller consignments across the Channel be an answer for us. The higher costs and potential losses from capture and confiscation within a more diverse fleet would mean less profit for the organisation as a whole - and particularly for all of us around this table tonight.' He spoke authoritatively. 'And much of our organisation would need to be reconstructed to the point where it would become too complicated to control and therefore too hazardous, in my opinion.'

Pettigrew had already considered these alternatives. Crucially, a larger more diverse fleet would also mean dealing with a greater number of ships' masters thus increasing the risk to himself. At present, only a handful of men knew of his link to the Chesil network and he had them all in his pocket. This was the way he liked it, and he rather hoped that it might be allowed to continue just the way it was. But first, something needed to be done about Middleton and his irritating efficiency.

'No, I conclude that we must continue as we are or not continue at all. There is no middle way, I'm afraid,' he said emphatically. 'But if we are to continue, we would have to find a way to deal with the customs service, to divert them or put them out of action at least for long enough to give us some freedom. Even given a short respite from their attentions, we might pull in enough profit for all of us to retire, especially if we could get some really big loads through.'

Pettigrew was fishing for the response he wanted, and now he tried once more to entice it out.

'But since we seem no longer able to anticipate Customs' intentions,' he said looking impassively at Smyke, 'perhaps we have no choice but to wrap it all up? Another failure like last week would finish us financially anyway.' He let the question hang in the air.

Out of the silence, Tregaskis muttered under his breath: 'Better than getting caught, as we're bound to be sooner or later.' But the others seemed not so sure.

''Tis this new man Middleton who's the cause of our problems,' said Bolton after a further pause. 'Everything went wrong after he came in with his new ideas – he's ahead of us at every step.'

Pettigrew smiled inwardly; the conversation was now turning in the direction he had hoped, even without his prompting.

'True, Bolton, he has become too effective; indeed I sometimes wonder at his information.' Pettigrew levelled his eyes on Smyke enquiringly, and the others followed his gaze. But misinterpreting their glances, Smyke sensed accusation and his face flushed. He started to rise, pushing back his chair noisily, as if about to protest, but before he could speak, Pettigrew raised a placating hand.

'Sit down Smyke, no one's accusing you,' he said wearily, holding the man's eyes in sham appeasement.

Smyke sat down again with a grunt of acceptance, his expression one of hurt pride, still resentful but apparently mollified. The sudden tension in the room took some seconds to ease as each of the visitors sat uncomfortably waiting for someone else to speak. Tregaskis lifted his tankard to take another sup of wine, but seeing that it was empty, lowered it sheepishly daring not at such a moment to reach across the table for the jug to replenish it. Bolton gave him a withering look for his timidity and lifted his own tankard with a supercilious smirk on his face. A few more silent seconds passed, before Pettigrew eventually rose from his seat, picked up his glass, and strolled casually to the end of the room where he stood with his back to the others, apparently examining some of the barrels stacked there. The three seated men had watched him go but now looked back to catch each other's eyes questioningly. Unease descended upon the group again as each considered his own position, and this endured until finally Smyke cleared his throat as if to speak. On hearing this uttering, Pettigrew was already confident that Smyke had taken the bait: of the three men who sat at the table behind his back, it was the customs man who had the most to lose in every respect if Middleton continued to reign.

'We all know what needs to be done,' Smyke said darkly, 'and you can leave it to me. I'll deliver what you want, Pettigrew, but I'll expect to be rewarded for my trouble,' he growled.

Pettigrew turned. His face remained expressionless, but he nodded almost imperceptibly, holding Smyke's grim gaze steadily for several seconds before turning back to his barrels without speaking. The other men looked on with puzzled glances while Smyke remained silent, his jaw clammed shut. Pettigrew knew exactly what the customs' man would have in mind, and with his back still turned to the three men seated at the table, no one noticed the narrowing of his eyes or the slight twitch at the corner of his petulant lips.

Chapter Two

The daily briefing in the Customs House at Weymouth early the following morning was given by Captain Middleton in his customary clipped manner in the large office that he had commandeered from Smyke on taking over his new post. The room was spacious and enjoyed the benefit of a bay window with a south easterly aspect catching the morning sun, from which bright rays now streaked in to spotlight the captain seated at his desk. Assembled in the shady extremities of the room were the officers and men of the Weymouth and District customs service. The gathering numbered perhaps twenty in all, comprising all those not relieved of attendance by virtue of their patrol duties the previous night. To one side of the captain's desk, Smyke sat in a leather armchair, a privilege afforded to the senior tide-surveyor as a calculated sop for his demotion, whilst his colleagues stood, squatted or perched in various places wherever they could find space.

The captain's notices and instructions were by and large of a routine nature on this occasion, and thus, preoccupied by the previous night's meeting with Pettigrew, Smyke found his attention wandering. He sat sullenly watching the captain speaking without registering his words, irritated by the man's apparent ease in command. How easily, he lamented, had power slipped from his own hands, how quickly were allegiances transferring. His gaze drifted absently around the room taking in the changes the captain had made to the office that had once been so proudly his; trivial as the changes were, he still found himself peculiarly affronted by them. His fall had been swift after Middleton's arrival, and he still fumed at the humiliation of being relegated to a dingy little office at the back of the building instead. Worse, he had been buried beneath an ever-mounting pile of delegated paper work. And worse still, despite being Middleton's deputy, he was apparently no longer to be privy to his intentions, as clearly evidenced, at least in his mind, by the captain's supposedly secret operation a few nights before. He was about to sink into a further bout of melancholic brooding when the captain's attention was suddenly turned upon him.

'I see Mr Smyke has other things on his mind!'

The captain's ironic tones brought him sharply out of his reverie, and he found himself in the glare of amused glances from around the room.

Middleton continued his briefing without a pause, but his glances seemed never to return to Smyke throughout the remainder of the meeting, nor was Smyke's opinion sought on any matter. His face took on the hounded look of one rebuked as he sank further into his chair. But it was more than mere embarrassment that he felt; the captain's public ridicule was another blow to a damaged pride that turned smouldering resentment into fuming resolve. If he might have wavered in his undertaking to Pettigrew before that moment, he began thereafter to plot the course of his brave promise with bitter determination.

When a few days later word reached Smyke from an informant in Alderney of a smuggling operation being set up by the Portland gang to run a load of contraband into Church Ope Cove, he recognised an opportunity to act. The activities of the Portland gang were well known to Smyke: their hauls were always relatively small, but they were well planned and infuriatingly successful. In the days when he had been in charge of the Weymouth corps, Smyke had been on their tail several times, but it had never seemed quite possible to catch them in the act. The Portlanders were a wily group who had cleverly outmanoeuvred his clumsy forays into that craggy and dangerous terrain, making him the butt of humour in the taverns on the waterfront. He had brooded for some time on these ignominies wondering how he might settle the score, but now he saw a way of using Middleton to do the job for him while at the same time creating a trap to bring about the man's demise.

It was with a sense of gratifying irony during the following days that Smyke's embittered mind fashioned the details of a plan that was, boiled down to its essence, brutally simplistic. He would use the tip-off as bait to provoke his captain into mounting a counter-smuggling operation in the Portland cliffs. Then, certain that the captain would choose a high observation point from which to control the movement of his forces, Smyke would take the first opportunity to send the man to his death over the nearest precipice. It was almost too simple, but the Portland cliffs and quarries in that part of the Island were labyrinthine and treacherous, and lent themselves admirably to such a murderous act. Smyke rehearsed the scene over and over again in his mind: in the heat of the skirmish, with Middleton preoccupied in watching his careful plans executed, he would administer the coup de grâce - a mere push from behind at an opportune moment. And then so easy afterwards to claim that the man must have tripped and fallen accidentally in the darkness.

But the first and vital requirement for Smyke's plan to succeed was, of course, that Middleton should choose to lead the operation himself rather than delegate it to a junior, as he might well do if the scale of it were not thought to be sufficiently grand. This would therefore require the intelligence received from Alderney to be enhanced from its current rather modest proportions to become so tantalising that the captain in his vanity would insist upon seizing it for himself. And quite clearly, Smyke could not risk passing on the distorted information from his own lips, for in the aftermath of blame and recrimination inevitably following the captain's tragic death, he himself must not be implicated. Smyke therefore now needed to enlist two further players into his cast: first, a co-operative informant, and second, a suitable officer who would be trusted by the captain, yet was still a little too green behind the ears to realise that he was being set up.

From the small number of regular informants inhabiting the dingy taverns of the waterfront where most useful information circulated, there was one who could be relied upon to do Smyke's bidding without asking any questions. Identified by Smyke only as 'the Chandler' to protect his real identity, he had been used to pass information to selected tidewaiters and riding officers before as part of Smyke's deception to distract the Service from the activities of the Chesil gang. The Chandler thus benefited twofold from his shrewdly loyal association with Smyke since, in addition to being paid by those officers for the intelligence they received, he was also paid handsomely by Smyke for passing it. It was in his interests therefore to cooperate with Smyke's instructions on this occasion too, and he was briefed accordingly.

With this first player in the coming act primed and ready, only the choosing of the officer to receive the tip-off now remained, and for this second key role the obvious candidate was Andrew White. White was a young officer clearly well thought-of by the captain, and one of those officers already put in touch with the Chandler by Smyke in a relationship contrived to promote the required degree of trust. Through a number of accurate tip-offs from the Chandler, White had built a reputation for himself while unwittingly contributing to Smyke's diversionary tactics to shield Smyke's other paymaster. Indeed, such had the young officer's repute grown that Smyke had begun to think that the seeded information had better be switched to a different conduit lest the captain begin to think of White as a contender for his own position as second-in-command. Moreover, although Smyke did not understand why, the young officer's standing with the captain seemed recently to have been considerably enhanced by some unspecified contribution to the captain's latest success – the capture of Pettigrew's contraband! Perhaps sensing this favoured relationship, Smyke calculated that White would be ideal for the job he had in mind - and it was anyway about time that the young upstart was taken down a peg or two.

Unusually for a revenue officer, White was educated and clever, a personable young man of good but not wealthy family who had chosen a career of adventure rather than follow his father into the church. He was a tall and wiry individual who was made to look older than he was by his over-heavy eyebrows and the isolated strands of grey that had prematurely infiltrated his otherwise dark and closely cropped hair. As exemplified by his latest nocturnal exploit, he was regarded by his peers as a bit of a renegade, not always willing to toe the line and quite prepared to act independently without apparently fearing the consequences. Others emulating his rebellious lead had often found themselves in trouble with their superiors, but White's unconventional initiatives, as much by luck as good judgement, always seemed to have some noted outcome, thus deflecting criticism of his methods. This slight flaw in his character, however, in no way detracted from the impression quickly formed of him as mature and capable, and he commanded wide respect, especially since he appeared so exceptional in ferreting out intelligence. But like most young officers, he was still a little liable to place too much trust in his superiors.

It was Andrew White's routine at least once per week, other duties permitting, to meet his friend and junior colleague, Clifford Hayes, for a meal at the coaching inn on the beach road in the nearby town of Melcombe, a resort that was fast becoming quite fashionable as a watering place. This particular evening was one such opportunity in a week that had been so busy for both, that they had barely exchanged glances since their participation in the surprise attack on the smuggling gang a few nights before. When White arrived at the inn, Hayes was already seated at a table in the parlour, his chin cupped in his hands and apparently lost in thought, gazing into a crackling fire newly replenished with logs for the first of the evening's customers. White took off his coat and cap with an eager relish; there was a homely comfort and intimacy about the place that White enjoyed that was in such contrast to the threadbare garret in which he lodged. Hayes, in his dreaming, had not yet noticed White's entry and remained transfixed by the fire, his cherubic young face and his short blond hair aglow in the rosy hues of its flickering light. He was still a relatively raw recruit, enlisted under the new government scheme to encourage better educated young entrants into the service with improved pay and conditions, and, as one of the new training initiatives, Hayes had been allocated to White in the role of professional mentor. Diligent as he was, White had taken his duties seriously in tutoring the new recruit, and, over the several months during which their regular meetings had taken place, a friendship had developed between them.

'Sorry to be late, Clifford,' White said cheerfully as he arrived at the table, rousing his friend instantly from his reverie. 'I was passed a message from my informant suggesting a meeting later this evening, and I needed to return to my lodgings to change. Customs uniform, I fear, would not be suitable for the waterfront drinking hole to which he has summoned me!' he said mysteriously with a wink.

The pair ordered food and drink and fell into their customary exchange in which Hayes would raise the issues that troubled him, and White, in return, would offer suitable advice. Hayes had come from a military family, but, unable to secure a commission in his father's old regiment, he had elected to join the customs service instead, no doubt attracted by the new recruitment campaign. Although, at eighteen years old, Hayes was only a few years younger than his mentor, he was yet to achieve the self-assurance common in young men of such background. It may also be that Hayes' awe during early childhood of his largely absent and early-deceased father, combined with the maternally indulgent environment in which he was subsequently brought up as an only-child, had not equipped him well to withstand the generally coarse and rough demands of service life. In other occupations more sympathetic towards new entrants, his character might have had time to toughen; but the intermediate levels of the customs service was full of brutish thugs like Smyke who had won their positions of authority by intimidation and who gave no quarter to the weak.

'It seems that I can never get it quite right, Andrew,' Hayes complained bitterly over their meal, 'despite my most strenuous efforts! I cannot seem to make the books balance, and he castigates me openly for being a simpleton! How can I ever earn the respect of the men if I am treated to such open ridicule?'

Hayes was clearly distraught. It was unfortunate for him that he had been assigned as Smyke's assistant to keep the tally of the weights and volumes of imported cargoes and to check and countersign the calculations of the excise duty payable. This latter measure - to cross-check such calculations - had been brought in by Captain Middleton in an attempt to root out corruption in the force, but, since half measures rarely prevail against the connivance of the devious, it stood not the slightest chance of being effective.

'I will admit to you, Andrew, that I have reached the point where I will sign off anything he puts before me just to keep him off my back!' Hayes shook his head in exasperation. 'I just hope that I can soon be allocated to other work!'

'You must stand your ground, Clifford;' White countered robustly pouring his young friend another glass of wine, 'if you believe in your calculations, you must call Smyke's bluff. Don't let him ride roughshod over you, otherwise he'll have you where he wants you, like others in his band of cronies!' White paused in thought for a moment, then added evenly, 'Do you suspect him then?'

'It has crossed my mind that he sometimes tries to bamboozle me, but I cannot in all honesty accuse him. I'm not sure enough to bring doubt upon another officer, especially one so senior. I know I have to be stronger, Andrew, but despite my resolve, each disagreement with him makes me more unsure.'

The look of blank desolation that seemed to drain Hayes' boyish face of all colour troubled White deeply. It was not the first time that Hayes' difficulty in standing up for himself had been discussed between them, and White was gradually coming to believe that his friend did not have sufficient fortitude to earn his commission. He sighed uncertainly, pushed aside his unfinished meal, and reached across the table to pat Hayes' arm in a consoling gesture intended to rally the young man's spirits. His movement caused the candle in the centre of the table to flicker, throwing moving shadows across Hayes' face, accentuating the inner uncertainty that seemed to have gripped him; but White had no idea what to suggest to stiffen his friend's resolve. Then an idea struck him.

'Look, Clifford,' he said brightly in an attempt to lift Hayes' mood, 'I've told you of my intended errand to the waterfront later this evening - would you like to accompany me? You did well the other night on the beach and this would show you another side of front-line work – the rather seedier side I'm afraid; it would be good for your education!'

White smiled wryly; if Hayes could become as enthused as he was himself by the challenges of counter-smuggling operations, it might boost his confidence; on the other hand, an exposure to the grim underworld inhabited by his smuggling informant might put him off for good! In either event, he would have done his friend a service, he thought.

Hayes' eyes widened. 'Why yes, Andrew, I think I might enjoy that!' he said bravely, although he could not have had the faintest idea what he was letting himself in for.

'Right!' said White briskly, seizing the moment: 'Be off and change into your roughest seaman-like attire and meet me back at the office as soon as you can.'

'Should I come armed?' he asked, his eyes widening yet further. 'I could bring my father's pistol, if carrying it would be prudent?'

White smiled indulgently. 'What! That lovingly polished weapon that you showed me with such pride, Clifford? I think not!' he said emphatically, while inwardly shuddering at the thought of his young friend wielding such a handsome piece. 'Not unless you want to draw unwelcome attention to yourself!'

The waterfront around the small basin of deep water at the mouth of the River Wey was a crescent of humble cottages interspersed with boat sheds, chandlers, and a few inns, which with the benefit of sunshine made a lively and colourful scene. In darkness, however, with only sparse street illumination, and most respectable folk already tucked up for the night behind their shuttered windows, it had a desolate, almost threatening air that the chilling sea mists did nothing to dispel. The inhabitants of this dank night-time world were the footloose sailors and fishermen off visiting boats - and the vagabonds, the smugglers, and the thieves taking advantage of the night. A few of the seedier drinking houses dotted around the waterfront and along the narrow alleyways leading from the harbour, attracted the worst of such sorts. These were squalid drinking dens in which lonely men might lose themselves, diverted by the pleasures of alcohol and tobacco, and led a drunken dance by pickpockets and loose women for the money in their purses. They were mostly wood-framed hovels wedged between the newer stone and brick buildings that were taking their place as the former fell to ruin. By this process of replacement, the righteous burghers of Weymouth and Melcombe hoped eventually to rid their towns of such disreputable establishments and remove these evil temptations from their citizens' sight.

It was under the light of a lantern hanging from the porch of one of the more worn-out edifices that White and Hayes, now dressed in shabby seamen's clothes, waited hesitantly, their breath steaming in the cold night air, as they steeled themselves to enter. But just as White's hand reached for the latch, the door was thrown open with a resounding bang and a torrent of rowdy and drunken ruffians pushed past them into the street. In their wake, a smoky, booze-laden draught of foetid air followed in a rush, against which Hayes was unable to stop himself raising an effete hand to cover his nose in disgust. The shock of the abrupt assault on their senses had startled them both, and now they gazed with grim bemusement through the open door at the scene of drunken depravity that raged inside. Hayes pulled back, suddenly timorous, clutching at White's sleeve as he did so in an involuntary gesture of self-preservation.

'Good gracious, Andrew,' he called breathlessly, 'I begin to regret my bravado! If anyone recognises us, we'll be lucky to escape with our lives! Must we really enter?'

'I at least must enter Clifford,' White whispered confidently into his junior's ear, 'to meet my informant, who says he has some useful information for me.' He took a deep breath and pulled himself up to his full height. 'Look, I can't be seen to be dithering here - you may stay outside if you wish, but I must go in!' At this, White stepped forward through the doorway shaking off Hayes' hold and adopting the sullen air which his dishevelled clothes and grubby countenance were designed to reinforce. 'Come on man,' called White over his shoulder, 'look mean and surly to play the part, and catch no one's eye. Just follow my lead!'

Hayes hesitated agape, rooted for an instant to the spot where he stood, nervously glancing behind him into the threatening darkness of the misty waterfront, imagining what untold terrors might be lurking there beyond the dim sphere of yellow light that held him in the doorway. It did not take him long to decide what to do. Hurriedly, he followed his friend inside and was lucky to see White's tall figure already halfway across the crowded room, pushing his way through the crush of people and the haze of tobacco smoke. It was the panic of isolation rather than boldness that moved Hayes to follow, picking his way nervously through the jostling and unruly multitude that seemed to be placing themselves as obstacles in his path. Ignoring their inquisitive and aggressive glances, instead fixing his gaze firmly on the hazy form of his friend's disappearing back, he pressed on, fearing at any moment that he would be challenged. Nervously, he adopted a rigid grimace on his face that, in his terror, he contrived as a seemly disguise, yet but for the smoke in the dimly lit room, would have marked him out instantly as a fraud. When he arrived at the corner table at which White was already seated, Hayes sank onto the bench so closely alongside his friend that his cowed shoulders pressed against White's side like a frightened child looking for a parent's comforting arm, and completely oblivious of the other man at the end of the table who sat hidden on White's other side smoking a clay pipe with evident satisfaction.

White smiled wryly at his friend's stunned expression, recalling his own discomfort on his first occasion in such a den; but when he glanced again some moments later, Hayes' features had not moved and something in the young man's blank face alarmed him. White gripped the young man's arm sharply; and with a jolt, Hayes' focus returned as he turned his dazed eyes to look into White's enquiring face. As quickly as it had begun, Hayes' sudden absence, his sudden momentary loss of sensibility, had ended and the innocence of his expression seemed to indicate that he had not been at all conscious of the event. While White reproved himself for exposing his friend to what had clearly been a shocking ordeal, he was relieved at his friend's apparent return to normality. But his thoughts of Hayes were interrupted rudely by a cackle of malicious laughter from the shabbily dressed individual who sat alongside, although his utterances were barely audible over the dreadful din in the room. The man's mocking laughter faded abruptly:

'A *boy*,' the man taunted under his breath, his unshaven face thrown into shadow by his greasy tricorn hat. 'You brought a *boy* as your protector?' he derided roughly through a mouth festooned with blackened teeth.

White ignored the remark, glancing instead towards his friend to reassure himself that there had been no relapse. He motioned his young subaltern to help himself to some ale from the jug and pewter tankards that just then arrived at the table carried by the rough hands of an inquisitive landlord in anticipation of their requirements. The overbearing man hovered sullenly at the end of the table as White fished out some coins from his pocket and threw them onto the slop-wetted table. Picking the wet coins up with a disdainful sneer, the man wiped his hands on his grubby apron and disappeared once more into the smoke of the room without a word.

As casually as he could, White poured himself some ale and took a long draught from his tankard, scanning the room over the brim for signs of unusual interest. Then, assured that no one watched, he ventured:

'You sent a message, Mr Chandler,' his mouth still hidden behind his raised tankard, his manner stiffly formal, betraying both his own tension and his irritation at his informant's snide remarks. 'So, what do you have for me today?' he asked impatiently.

'Information you would sell your soul for,' whispered the informant slyly, flicking White a malicious but unseen glance.

White lowered his tankard and leant forward on his elbows, resting his brow upon his palms as if weary so that any onlooker would not have suspected what was taking place. The informant spoke in clipped rough tones that allowed no scope for question or repeat. White's disinterested pose, meanwhile, hid the sense of excitement that rose within him at what he heard. He would reflect upon the exchange in the years to come and realise eventually that he had been duped into playing the seminal role in a deadly game. But for the moment his blood was up and he was blind to caution. The monologue came to an abrupt end, and the noise of the room once more crowded back into White's consciousness. He glanced at his informant, wondering if there was more to come, but the Chandler sat in silence, puffing on his pipe and gazing absently into the room with a look of smug satisfaction on his face. White sat back and reflected briefly, then, under cover of the table, he passed a purse into the horny hand that waited there acquisitively. Without further glance or gesture, the Chandler then slid from the settle, got to his feet, and melted into the throng, while White sat for a while longer bottling his impatience to be off. Hayes turned to him expectantly but his taut features and nervous movements revealed an undiminished anxiety:

'Time to leave, Andrew?' Hayes asked hopefully.

'Yes, Clifford, I think it certainly is – I have some work to do before the morning!' White replied emphatically, motioning his friend to drink up.

Outside, the shock of the cold air on their faces seemed to bring Hayes suddenly back to normality, his flushed and boyish lineaments becoming animated as if released from some invisible constraint. He laughed out loud uncharacteristically.

'That was quite something!' he gushed, while grinning excessively. 'That was really quite something,' he repeated, his voice sounding delirious, effusive, as if he had consumed too much alcohol, yet no more than a sip or two of watery ale could have passed his lips.

'Well, my friend, it certainly seems to have been a new experience for you,' White replied with a puff of laughter, generously avoiding any note of ridicule. The buoyant mood persisted as the pair continued in the direction of the better part of town where their lodgings were located, eventually parting with a good-humoured farewell. Thereafter, White strolled on at a slower pace in a contemplative frame of mind as he sifted the information received; until, resolved, he was soon striding out again impatient to start drafting his report.

In his eagerness to make his mark with the captain, White had his summary report written and on Captain Middleton's desk by the middle of the following morning, and he now sat nervously in his superior's outer office awaiting a response. He did not have long to wait. There came the sound of quick and heavy footsteps resounding on the wooden floor of Middleton's inner sanctum, and the interconnecting door was thrown open to reveal the squat figure of the captain standing astride the open doorway.

'White! Get Smyke and come into my office straight away, if you please,' he ordered briskly from the doorway, disappearing just as quickly.

The captain preferred to sit when being addressed by those taller than himself, and this is how Smyke and White found him as they entered the office some moments later. The captain had removed his topcoat, and now sat in his waistcoat and shirtsleeves behind an ornate desk reading White's report. He waved a hand distractedly without looking up, indicating that the arriving pair should seat themselves. Behind him, through the wide bay window, a misty scene of fishing boats returning from their night's work drew White's eye as he settled himself in silence to await the captain's attention.

Smyke, meanwhile, let his gaze wander around the familiar room, noticing a large-scale maritime chart of the Dorset coastline newly hanging on the wall where it would benefit from the incoming light. He felt the familiar pang of bitterness as his eyes wandered around the coveted space of his former office, then brought his calculating gaze to rest upon the pensive form of the man who sat before him. How old was this usurper, this man who would be his undoing, Smyke wondered? Perhaps in his mid-fifties, he guessed; and, measuring the man's stature, he assessed him as definitely past his prime in any physical sense.

Middleton's lined face looked exhausted – probably, thought Smyke, from the expectations placed upon the man by a government department wanting quick results - expectations that seemed to have made the captain brusque and pompous in his manner. The dark brown wig that Middleton wore to hide his baldness made him look ridiculous; silver would have suited him far better. Yet Smyke also knew to his cost that it would be an error to underrate this man on the basis of appearance; what his superior lacked in stature was more than offset by intellect; and Smyke had learned to be wary in his company.

'Very interesting!' Middleton exclaimed, waving the report triumphantly. 'You've done well, White,' he said, smiling approvingly at the young officer who sat attentively upright before him. 'Have you read it Smyke?' His attitude towards Smyke was more off-hand.

'No sir,' Smyke replied disingenuously, for indirectly he had been its progenitor.

'Then you'd better take us through it again for Smyke's sake, White,' said Middleton.

White summarised his report for the two men with the fervour of the newly converted, relating the information received from his informant with enthusiasm. It was exactly as Smyke had intended, and inwardly the senior tide-surveyor could not have been more satisfied with the outcome of his manipulation. Outwardly, however, he was careful to adopt an air of pique as one upstaged by a junior, while adding just enough by way of gesture and comment to indicate some grudging support. And Middleton's reproving glances in return for such uncharitable reticence could not have been a clearer indication of his patronage of the young officer. The captain seemed also to take some pleasure at seeing Smyke outshone. It was a reaction that delighted Smyke, and as White's report drew to its conclusion, the senior tide-surveyor already knew that his plan would succeed.

'It looks like this will be an operation on quite a large scale, sir,' the young officer concluded. 'Apparently several vessels will be involved – all from the Channel Islands.'

Smyke could see by Middleton's quick eyes that his interest had been aroused by this, but his face remained sober in the manner in which old men have learned not to show too much too soon of their persuasion.

'Your source reliable?' the captain prompted brusquely. 'The Chandler, sir;' White responded in affirmation. 'He's not let me down before.'

Middleton sucked his teeth: 'Those cliffs around the Cove will make it difficult for us,' he said cautiously. 'What d'you think, Smyke?'

Smyke's reply was cagey, not wanting his endorsement to sound intemperate. 'I agree, sir; it would be impossible to surround the Cove completely,' he said in a pessimistic tone. 'And we'd need a lot of men to enclose it sufficiently to form an adequate trap, perhaps more than we've available.' He hesitated, feigning considerable doubt, but then admitted, as if reluctantly: 'But it may be possible to put the terrain to our advantage - if it were properly coordinated, sir. And it would be quite a coup if we could pull it off.'

'And perhaps if we deployed the cutter, sir,' White added enthusiastically. 'We might also nab a boat or two.'

Middleton nodded, seeming to be persuaded, and sat back in his chair pensively, swivelling it to gaze out of the bay window. The seconds ticked away, but eventually, interrupting the ensuing silence, White ventured to speak to his senior officer's turned back:

'I don't think that the Portland gang could mount such a large operation alone, sir, and so it's likely that other gangs are involved.'

Middleton did not respond to this but continued pondering for a while longer, his view still directed towards the scene outside, his elbows propped upon the arms of his chair, his fingers to his lips in a contemplative pose. When at last he turned back, he had a smug smile of satisfaction on his face, and Smyke knew immediately that his superior had taken the bait. If Smyke had judged Middleton's character correctly, the captain's response would be uncompromising in order to ensure success. Moreover, with such apparently high stakes, he would want to direct the operation personally, and this would mean that Smyke, as the captain's deputy, would be expected to accompany him as his adjutant.

'Right, both of you,' Middleton said briskly, coming to his feet. 'I want you to drop everything and work with me closely for the next few days to set this up!' He led the pair over to the wall chart and studied it closely. 'We'll tell no one of the location of the operation until deployment, and then, only those who need to know - I don't want this getting out through idle talk.' He waited for Smyke and White to nod their agreement before continuing:

'Smyke, you've tried to pin the Portland gang down before – you must have some idea as to who might be involved?'

Here, Smyke spoke the truth: 'The quarryman, George Easton runs the stone works around Wakeham and Church Ope Cove,' he said, running his finger over the area of the site on the chart. 'I've had my suspicions about him, but the islanders are a close-knit community, and I've never been able to get even a fragment of useable intelligence out of them - to have attempted a prosecution would have been out of the question.'

'Then this will be our chance,' said Middleton confidently.

Over subsequent days, Middleton developed a plan which suffered no compromise. Considering the reported scale of the contraband delivery, the response would need to be correspondingly large, and the activities of land and sea-borne forces co-ordinated carefully to achieve entrapment. It was a bold strategy, but not uncharacteristic of Middleton who had made his reputation on similar large-scale operations before. The plan took shape at a surprising pace, with Smyke attending to the majority of the logistical details, ably and enthusiastically assisted by Andrew White. One complication was that the force would need to be landed on Portland by sea under cover of darkness, since any approach in daylight, or across the causeway, would soon be spotted and the smugglers alerted. This aspect of the plan therefore required some special attention; moreover, the several units drawn from other forces along the coast needed to be billeted and readied nearby, and this would not be an easy task while also attempting to maintain the strictest secrecy. Both Smyke and White found it a taxing exercise with less than a week to get everything in its place, and it became essential to enlist a number of other officers, including Hayes, to help with the various organising tasks. Hayes, of course, was delighted to be relieved of his book-keeping duties and given an operational role, but White could not help but feel some disquiet to see his friend drawn in, especially when Smyke detailed Hayes to assist him as his runner on the night to convey any orders as may be required.

As for Smyke himself, although outwardly maintaining his customarily sullen demeanour, he was in fact inwardly ecstatic. Not only was the operation shaping up to give him exactly the opportunity he sought to deal with Middleton, but it would also leave the coast entirely clear for Pettigrew's gang to carry out its own operation unhindered in West Bay. This time there would be no scope for secondary operations since the whole force would be committed to this single task. In his mind's eye, he already revelled in Pettigrew's certain acclaim. It would be his vindication, restoring his reputation within the group: a double success for which he would expect a considerable reward in due course; and it was also a distinct pleasure to speculate on what opportunities might lie ahead for him within the customs service once Middleton was out of the way.

Chapter Three

The Isle of Portland

There is something about that combination of sunshine and seascape which floods the senses with pleasure and lifts the spirits to the skies, especially if it is a seascape as spectacular as the many which can be viewed from the cliffs around Portland. And for Jack Easton, perched on a craggy ledge above the East Wears, still breathing heavily from his steep climb, his spirits could not have been much higher. His sturdy figure might have been seen only moments before sprinting up the slope with relative ease, foot-sure and confident in his own domain. Squatting for a moment, he rested his broad back against a slab of stone that had been warmed by the sun, and turned his face towards the sea. In the opinion of the women of his acquaintance, it was a handsome face, well proportioned with broad-set dark-brown eyes set over a generous mouth and prominent jaw, which he would jut unconsciously when bent to a determined task. His brown hair, on this occasion whitened by stone dust and ruffled by his exertions, looked unruly, but its relative shortness and its curly resilience kept it from becoming wild. He wiped the beads of sweat from his forehead with his sleeve and let his eyes wander around that sphere of colourful contrasts that formed his view. Along the distant horizon to his left, across the wide expanse of Weymouth Bay, a line of small white clouds in an otherwise clear-blue sky marked the mainland, stretching eastwards from Durdle Door to St Aldhelm's Head. Filling his middle view, the sea was a patchwork of green and turquoise brushed by the gentle westerly breeze; and across it, the working sails of every shape and size moved about with ardent purpose. Immediately below him, stretching northwards perhaps two miles to the northern shore of the Island, sprawled the under-cliff, an undulating area of landslip and quarry spoil. Here, amidst a labyrinth of footpaths and sled tracks winding their way between scattered piles of rough-hewn stone stacked ready for shipment, autumn-tinted sycamore, stunted by the salt-laden air, struggled for existence amongst the brambles and blackthorn. Jack let his eyes pace out one of the familiar paths that ran through this rough and lumpy foreland towards a stubby stone pier that protruded bravely from the rocky shore. In relation to where he sat, the pier lay some two hundred feet below by vertical measure and half-a-mile to the northeast; he had stood on it just ten minutes or so before. On the pier, and looking from this distance like the bare poles of an abandoned Indian tepee, a derrick lay idle, its work for the day completed. Alongside the apparatus, a coastal vessel of some sixty tons burthen made ready for sail, its beamy hull sitting low in the water under the burden of a consignment of fine Portland stone that it would transport to London.

Standing about idly in small groups on the pier, a motley collection of men watched the ship's preparations for departure; a few sat astride the derrick's outstretched arm to give themselves an elevated view of the ship. These were Jack's men, his team of hardy quarrymen and masons, a tough and shabby-looking bunch inclined to be obstinate in their ways. He looked down on these distant figures with emotions ranging between pride and relief. They had been a difficult crew to handle in this his first project as foreman, to the extent that he had sometimes doubted his ability to pull them together as a team. While the younger ones had come round soon enough to his youthful style, some of the older hands had remained surly and uncooperative, being at first suspicious of Jack's credentials and thus wary of following his lead. But with a little skill on Jack's part, helped by a degree of luck in the lay of the stone, the heavy work had progressed with such surprising efficiency that the tensions between them had slowly melted away. It seemed at last as if the men were beginning to bond in the shared satisfaction in seeing a difficult job well done. Jack felt that its successful completion had established him as foreman in his own right rather than merely as his father's son, placed in that position by accident of birth.

The departing consignment also represented the quarry's first success of any significance in a difficult financial year. Already stretched to the limits of their credit, the men would now receive their due pay, and the firm would be able to fend off its creditors once again – at least for a time. Despite the high quality of their Whitebed stone and the excellence of their masonry, contracts had become increasingly difficult to win as the heydays of abundant and lucrative London projects drew to a close. And as a consequence, his father's once profitable operation had struggled to make ends meet in recent years. Jack exhaled with a long slow sigh of satisfaction; if the completion of the contract would not yet solve all their financial problems, at least the new income would earn them a respite, and he felt pleased with himself for the part he was playing in the firm's survival. Full of youthful optimism, he thought that perhaps this might be the turning point that the family had prayed for for so long.

Yet, Jack was amused to recall, it had been hard to persuade his father to let him get involved in quarry work in the beginning; it was his younger brother, Luke, who had been the one earmarked to take over the family firm. As far back as Jack could remember, his father had had quite different ambitions for his older son; the old man seemed to think that Jack should aspire to something better, given his relative success at school work. Perhaps his father foresaw the difficulties ahead and recognised that one son in the firm would be all that it could bear. But back then Jack could not understand why his father had seemed so adamant. With a quarry as his playground, however, Jack became besotted with the idea of becoming a mason. He had watched fascinated as these charismatic craftsmen had turned rough-hewn quarry stone into beautiful embossments and icons for the churches of London. It was as if stone dust had got into his blood, for through his impressionable young eyes Jack could see no other future. And taken by his boyish interest in their work, the masons had adopted him as their unofficial apprentice. From that time on, Jack would spend almost all of his free time in the quarry with a chisel and a mallet in his hands. Until eventually, worn down by Jack's constant pestering, his father had reluctantly given in and put him under the tutelage of the firm's master mason, a privilege afforded usually only to the best of students.

During the years that followed, Jack had excelled – he had a gift for it, the old master mason had said – indeed, some of Jack's work had even been displayed as examples of the work the quarry could offer. But as Jack had matured, he had not been content merely to be a skilful practitioner; he soon started to take an interest in business matters, assisting with estimates and business proposals, helping to win contracts - in those earlier, better days when there was still good business to be won. Thus his father had come eventually to accept Jack's future in the firm, giving him lately the greater responsibilities of foreman. And with this promotion, it now seemed that his father favoured Jack as his successor, while Luke appeared not to have any management ambitions at all.

Jack knew as well as anyone that business was more difficult now, but, spurred on by his recent success, he was convinced that he could bring life back to the old quarry and turn its moribund fortunes around. He dreamt of making new investment to modernise old-fashioned and inefficient ways, of building a new and exciting future for himself and the family. This dream was what sustained him and bolstered his spirits - this vision of success. He was flushed with a young man's unbounded optimism that one day soon his lucky break would come, that thereafter all would be happiness and contentment, and that there would then be no further need to gamble in the dangerous game of smuggling just to make ends meet.

Jack decided to wait and watch the vessel depart before continuing his journey home, wanting to see his consignment safely underway. The eastern shoreline of Portland, protected from the prevailing winds, offered good prospects for loading stone, but there were still dangers to trap an unwary master. The currents hereabouts were strong and in light winds a vessel might be swept helplessly into the swirling waters of the Race or back onto the jagged outcrops of rock that characterised the Portland coast. Timing and tide were therefore the essence of planning, and not all skippers employed in the stone shipment trade had mastered it.

He did not have long to wait until he saw the lines cast off. The heavily laden vessel was then pushed out by poles and pulled back simultaneously on her kedge, her crew straining at the windlass winding in the anchor line stretched tautly over her stern. For a long time, as she inched backwards into open water, her red-ochre sails hung lifelessly. But soon, as the first swirls of wind descended from the shielding cliffs, they stirred – lazily at first but with increasing intensity. Jack saw the crew run forward along the deck to hold out the foresail against the breeze to act as a weather vane, and watched fascinated as the ship's head turned. The sails now became agitated as the unhindered wind jostled the outstretched booms, which shook and swung eagerly from their masts like restless stallions impatient for the off. Even from where he sat, half a mile distant, Jack could hear the staccato percussion of the flapping sails whipping and cracking in the wind – on deck the din must have been deafening. Then, as the crew put their backs to haul in the sheets, the heavy canvas tightened as the wind was brought under harness and, with a final thundering clap, the sails snapped into a tight curve. With a sudden lurch of its tall mast the cutter picked up speed majestically and set its course for St Aldhelm's Head, clearly visible on the eastern horizon, its sheer cliffs shining brightly like a beacon in the sunshine.

For a while, Jack leant back upon his ledge to watch her go - she was a pretty sight - and, enjoying the warmth of the sun upon his face, he felt an almost overwhelming sense of contentment. And it was not only the vessel's dispatch that made his mood so buoyant, it was as much the news, relayed to him in the proper Portland manner through his father the night before, that Elizabeth was pregnant with his child. The news had come as a relief, for according to the unusual ways of Portland folk, it was not until Elizabeth's fertile state had been confirmed that the betrothal could be announced. Jack was at last confident that his marriage would be blessed, an all-important expectation in selecting a bride. If there were some small part of Jack that recognised the moral and pragmatic flaws in this ancient Portland custom, he did not allow it much room in his thinking for it seemed to his unquestioning mind a sensible precaution. A couple needed children to contribute to their endeavours and to look after them in their old age — it was surely as simple as that - and thus better for a woman to remain an independent spinster making her own way than to suffer the ignominy of wedded childlessness. The logic seemed so eminently reasonable, that he found himself perplexed by the contrary view — not realising that his urge to justify the practice revealed an inner unease. Such thoughts, however, were not going to concern him on this auspicious day and, feeling the warm glow of happy anticipation, he clasped his hands behind his head, closed his eyes and smiled into the sun.

It was the squawk of seagulls overhead that brought him out of his reverie; and opening his eyes, he squinted in the sunlight to spot the vessel now several miles out and making steadily across the bay; by its progress he realised that he must have dozed off. He lifted himself awkwardly up onto the ledge, his legs stiff from the period of inactivity and, bracing himself against the wall of the cliff as a precaution against falling from the precipitous ledge, he clambered to the top.

As Jack entered the broad drove that led down the hill into his home hamlet of Wakeham, he saw ahead of him, proceeding in the same direction as himself at a distance of some fifty yards, two familiar female figures walking arm in arm. Jack recognised them instantly as his own Elizabeth and her older sister Rose, and he increased his stride eagerly to close upon them.

Elizabeth and Rose Dale, daughters of Albert and Jane Dale of Fortune's Well, a hamlet lying under the hill on the north side of the Island, were so different in both character and appearance that they might not have been related at all. Elizabeth was fair-haired and blue-eyed with a complexion of pure pearl, whereas Rose had dark hair, dark eyes, and skin of a hue made ruddy by her greater love of the outdoors. Whereas

Rose, the older of the pair by several years, seemed more reserved and more demanding of the proper protocols from her suitors, Elizabeth was flirtatious, more conscious of her appearance, and more aware of its effect upon young men. Rose, as a rule, would wear her hair pulled back and tied simply in a bun, while Elizabeth would fashion hers into elaborate ringlets, fussing over herself endlessly in the mirror of her dressing table. Elizabeth was also more playful in her conversation with members of the opposite sex, her eyes dancing and flitting seductively as she talked, whereas Rose would be more reticent in her manner seeming at first rather reserved and straight-laced. Thus, while both sisters had enjoyed the attentions of young men on the island, it was the more coquettish Elizabeth who attracted the greatest interest, and while either might have drawn Jack's eye, it was she who had first engaged his attentions and she who had first captured his heart.

Jack, the elder son of George Easton, quarry owner and member of the Court Leat, the Island's council, was blessed with the sort of rugged good looks, confident assertiveness and engaging personality that is attractive to members of both genders. On first encountering Elizabeth, introduced in passing by a fellow quarryman onto whose arm she had then tightly clung, Jack was immediately smitten. Believing her already spoken for, however, he was inhibited at first from making any further advance. According to Elizabeth's subsequent recounting, her beau's attentions had strayed soon after, thus bringing their relationship to an end (although it should be added that Jack heard later that the former suitor had complained of being jilted for no apparent cause). Such are the protestations of former lovers in their contrariness, but it seemed to Jack that Elizabeth was quick thereafter to indicate her interest in him, permitting him to make a number of overtures without rejection. This had flattered and encouraged him, but it was a merry chase and a long time before Jack believed that he had won her. All that time Jack had been led on by her alluring eyes towards the fulfilment of her unspoken promise which, like an exotic butterfly in a summer garden, long evaded capture. And so it is with the heady brew of human attraction that, either in a reckless gamble or from sheer frustration, one of the parties eventually braves all to speak of love. It was Jack of course, taking his heart in his hands in the middle of the bustling weekly market where they had met quite by chance, who blurted out that he loved her and that he wanted them to wed. At that moment, nothing else existed for him in the world outside his head except for Elizabeth's pretty face, frozen in surprise. The moment lasted perhaps only a second or two, but for Jack it was an eternity as he waited for her response, and a moment that he would recall often.

'Jack!' she had exclaimed, shrinking at the public nature of his proclamation, her cheeks turning the same colour as the ripe French peaches displayed on the nearby stall, her eyes sparkling in a mixture of triumph and delight. Sweeping her arm airily at the bystanders whose curiosity had been aroused by the proposition, she had giggled: 'Since you have announced your feelings to the world, how could I possibly refuse you?'

Almost three months had passed since that day, and Jack smiled at the memory as he now closed upon the two sisters walking down the hill towards his Wakeham home for a celebratory Sunday tea with his mother. As the distance reduced further, he saw that they were engaged in an earnest conversation and was at first buoyed up by the conceit that it must be he who would be the topic. He eyed the two women fondly, finding himself bewitched by their feminine curves, so alluringly impressed through the folds of their long skirts as they walked with such light grace. But soon he came to within a distance where, although it was not possible to hear their words precisely, he could begin to determine the nature of their discourse by its tone - and he was taken aback by the apparent seriousness of it. He slowed, wondering whether he should intrude, but then, resolving that his presence could not help but lift their spirits, again increased his pace. He closed yet further, his presence still undetected, until he could begin to catch fragments of their conversation. But it was not quite of the nature he had expected. He was quite sure that he heard Rose say:

'...... a little late for such thoughts, Elizabeth?' delivered in what Jack took to be a gently disapproving tone.

His buoyant mood suddenly deflated, and instinctively he trod more lightly to remain unnoticed as he strained to catch other fragments of their discussion. Rose's voice was now sterner, admonishing in character, and although he could not quite connect her words to make them meaningful, a strangely disquieting mood descended upon him. There was then a silence of some seconds before Elizabeth's softer tones issued in reply; they sounded like the lame murmurings of a child in guilty admission of some mischief, but Jack could not make out her words at all.

While perplexed at the curious interchange between the two women, Jack knew he had come too close. He slowed, dropping back to a discrete distance, and then hailed them as if catching up. The women turned, taken by surprise to find Jack approaching so close at hand; then in an instant, their faces broke into fulsome smiles of greeting. But in that instant, Jack caught Rose's quick glance at her sister and the movement of her lips as she muttered something under her breath, and he could not help himself examining Elizabeth's face for the clue that might resolve the sudden pang of uncertainty he felt.

'Jack!' Elizabeth smiled tenderly, skilfully covering her moment of confusion. 'I've told Rosie of our news and she's delighted. She has agreed to be my bridesmaid,' she said breathlessly as she reached her slender arms up to his shoulders and raised herself upon tiptoes to kiss him lightly on his cheek.

Jack felt Rose take his arm. 'I'm so happy for you both,' she said, joining in the embrace and bringing her cheek up to brush against his with more than usual tenderness. Jack was so overwhelmed by such a display of feminine affection that, in the nature of one enraptured, he instantly forgot the moment of doubt that he had felt just seconds before. Wrapping his strong arms around their waists, he lifted them clearly off the ground, both shrieking with laughter and causing others in the street to turn and gape; and the threesome then linked arms and continued thus down the hill. For Jack, a man accustomed almost entirely to the rougher company and manners of men, it was intoxicating to be enveloped by the soft touch and gentle fragrances of his female companions, now pressed to him so closely that he could feel every enticing curve of their slender forms.

The betrothal was celebrated formally in customary fashion the following Saturday evening at a gathering of family and friends in the sisters' family home, perched on the steep sunset-facing slopes of the Island. From a total population measuring only a few hundreds, a sizeable proportion of the Island's population attended. The house was large by Portland standards, built of local stone like the majority of Portland dwellings, but, unlike them, it stood detached and prominent on the hillside bordering Verne Common. This befitted its owners, the industrious Albert Dale, who had become successful from the rearing of Portland sheep, and his thrifty wife, who owned and ran the ladies clothing shop and seamstress service in which the two sisters were employed as poorly-paid assistants. Albert Dale, a bluff, stocky, and matter-of-fact Yorkshire man, had migrated to Portland as an itinerant shepherd boy looking for work and found himself falling for a local lass, the now Mrs Jane Dale, a no-nonsense business-lady of limited generosity, imperious countenance, and steel will. There was no doubt on the Island that it was she who ruled the roost in the Dale home. Despite Albert being an outsider, a 'kimberlin' as Portlanders might call him behind his back, he was eventually absorbed into the landscape, having adopted the Island as his home and assimilated the ways and mannerisms of his neighbours. So effective had he been in this chameleon-like change of identity after twenty-five years on the Island, that a stranger might confuse him for a native, except, that is, when he had imbibed too much drink. On these occasions, which fortunately for his intolerant wife and doting daughters were rare, his cover had been known to slip and his origins revealed by the broadcast of his Yorkshire accent. This evening was to be one of those occasions.

By the time it came to the toasts (which were kept mercifully short), everyone, not least Jack's father-in-law-to-be, was in that happy state of fulsome inebriation which, while well advanced from sobriety, had not yet reached the untidy state of drunkenness.

'Ladies and Gentlemen,' Albert Dale called, grinning broadly with a full set of teeth. He spoke with only a slightly alcoholic slur in his proud if faltering voice from the shearing stool that served as his podium. 'Mrs Dale instructs me that I should say a few words,' he continued, his Yorkshire heredity now quite unmistakeable and his round face flushing bright red under an almost hairless head.

'And so 'ere I am, standing before you, our good friends and family,' he said, still beaming nervously and taking a deliberate breath to give himself a little time to collect his thoughts. He wobbled precariously on his stool, nearly falling from it, and earned himself a ripple of laughter by steadying himself with spreading arms.

'It seems that our Lizzie 'as finally settled upon the idea of getting herself wed, and we're gathered 'ere this evening to celebrate 'er betrothal to young Jack 'ere,' he said, glancing behind him to locate his future son-in-law who stood with his arm around Elizabeth's waist, suddenly looking abashed in the glare of attention. 'Now, we all know that this young man is strong and brave,' he said, trying to make a joke, and smirking in anticipation of his own humour, 'and that's exactly what he'll need to be, marrying our Lizzie!' There was muted amusement from some quarters of the room and looks of resigned tolerance from others at Dale's characteristic banality. 'No, she's a good lass,' he protested, ' she's turned a few heads in her time, but in turning Jack's, she's found a good man to love and cherish her - just what she needs to make her a contented woman. An' that's what all us men want for our women ain't it lads?' he added with a cheeky smile.

With her husband's speech rapidly straying from her script onto dangerous ground, Jane Dale could be seen tugging on his sleeve and muttering something crossly to him under her breath as he stooped obediently to listen. The speaker straightened, looked flustered, and wobbled again, raising a further ripple of laughter.

'Um, Mrs Dale tells me to get on with it,' he said, quickly. 'So let us simply raise our glasses to congratulate the couple on their betrothal and wish 'em a long and 'appy life together without too much quarrelling!'

A single call of 'Hear, hear,' was heard in response to this within the general murmur of approval arising from the gathering, while Albert Dale continued with a knowing wink:

'And, since Lizzie's already well on the way wi' it, let's also wish 'em lots o' little uns to keep 'em fed in their old age! Good luck to both of 'em, I say!'

He raised his glass in the direction of the couple and took a sip from it, initiating a chorus of similar gestures and a scattering of good-humoured if ribald comments from the male members of the assembly. Dale then descended from his stool with the steadying arm of his wife to help him and, mopping his face with a large white handkerchief, made a beeline towards the drinks-table in some haste.

Elizabeth managed to retain her composure throughout her father's short exposure, looking radiant in her new blue frock embroidered meticulously by her own hands. She seemed intoxicated by the attentions lavished upon her, while Jack, seen unusually in a fine shirt, silk waistcoat, and cravat, looked to be the happiest of men. The only incident of any discordance involved Luke Easton, Jack's increasingly wayward younger brother, who, letting gravity get the better of him after consuming too much of it, fell into the punch bowl. But this was nothing that a moment of scurrying with a bucket and cloth by the fastidious Mrs Dale, and a short exile in the cold night air for the disgraced miscreant could not put right.

Too soon, the celebrations came to an end. The jollity wound down as the house slowly emptied of its guests, the last of them dispersing cheerily uphill and down with lanterns alight, their merry chatter still echoing in the alleyways for a long time afterwards. Luke went off with a group of other young men going home over the hill towards the hamlets of Easton and Wakeham, and his voice could be heard above all others singing tunelessly at the top of his limited range.

Jack and his parents stayed on in the Dale's spacious drawing room to discuss the details of the wedding. Such events usually create interesting topics for discussion between the mothers of the betrothed, and this was no exception. It was a happy and largely harmonious intercourse reflecting the excited anticipation of the day, but Elizabeth, usually content to defer to her elders, found herself uncomfortably called to adjudicate between the two older ladies on a matter of disagreement.

'I think I really might prefer a pretty new dress for my wedding, mother,' she asserted petulantly, siding with Jack's mother, Eleanor, who had been attempting to argue on her new daughter-in-law's behalf. But Elizabeth's resistance withered instantly as she caught her mother's icy glare: 'But perhaps you're right,' she said, resignedly and rather timidly. 'Your wedding dress will look quite well on me, I'm sure.'

'Oh mother!' Rose admonished, coming to her sister's aid, 'I'm sure it looked just the thing in your day, but it is a bit passé. Elizabeth will have a new wedding dress, even if I must make it myself,' she asserted. 'Dearest mother,' she chided with her smiling eyes, 'you seem suddenly to have become even more parsimonious than father!'

Meanwhile, on the other side of the room, the two fathers conversed in more manly tones, exploring the business possibilities that the linking of their two families might bring. The two men were of like character - businessmen at heart - having both pulled themselves up from a poor beginning in life's great trial, and consequently always on the lookout for a good deal. However, ingenious as their speculation was in this respect, the combination of sheep farming and stone masonry did not immediately offer up any prospect for profit. On the other hand, by a nod and a wink, it seemed to be agreed between them that the Eastons might get mutton, and the Dales, fine wine or cognac for their respective tables in an exchange of favours.

Jack stood nearby listening in, but his attention had been drawn to Rose's gentle defiance across the room, and now he studied her more thoughtfully above his raised glass as he took a lingering sip of wine. Although a trivial issue on this occasion, this was not the first time he had seen her strength of will asserted, and he found himself increasingly admiring of it. Sometimes he wished Elizabeth would stand up for herself as robustly. Elizabeth's girlish ways had endeared her to him at first; but her lack of substance and resolve had begun to prey on his mind to the extent that he had recently confided his concerns to Rose in a moment of frustration, hoping to instigate some sisterly counselling. Her reaction then had surprised him, and now he recalled that conversation:

'That is her way, Jack,' she had replied, laughing. 'I'm surprised that you've not seen it before; she gets her way through her coy and pretty looks. She has her father wrapped around her little finger.' Rose had paused then, suddenly becoming more thoughtful, before looking at him quizzically with a mischievous smile. 'Did it work on you too, Jack?' she had taunted good-humouredly.

'I am sure that she loves me, as I love her,' he had insisted rather stiffly.

Rose had hesitated before replying. 'Dear Jack,' she had said at last, touching his arm tenderly, 'at present, she is in love merely with the idea of being married; and I say this only so that you'll understand how to treat her, because I love you both. She's still so young, but in her way I know she'll come to love you as you do her - just give her a little time to grow up.'

The unexpected directness of Rose's comments had rekindled the uncertainty he had felt at overhearing those fragments of ambiguous conversation in the Wakeham drove. At the time of their conversation, he had shrugged off her frank assessment as unmerited, but there had since been several instances where he had had cause to recall her words, and now, as he gazed at her across the room, they resonated again. Just then, almost as if sensing the inspection, Rose flicked her glance up to find Jack's eyes upon her, and for a brief instant their eyes locked. It was only an instant, but during that moment of time, her lips slid tentatively into a smile that he returned with his eyes as if communicating some conspiracy. In the space of a missed heartbeat, Jack recognised the alliance that had formed between them, and a curious feeling of loss hit him as if some prize had passed him by, initially unrecognised and now out of reach. As cover for his sudden discomfiture, he tore his glance away and rejoined the fathers in conversation. He would not risk another glance at her that evening, carefully avoiding contact with her and lavishing his attentions upon Elizabeth instead; but he was aware out of the corner of his averted eyes that Rose's glances returned to him from time to time.

When at last the hubbub began to flag and there seemed nothing more to discuss, Jack and his parents politely took their leave and started up the hill for home. Jack was the last to pass through the little wicket gate at the end of the short earthen path that led from the Dale's front door, and he turned to close it behind him. As its latch clicked shut, Jack felt a most disquieting sense of foreboding pass over him, as if the closing of the gate represented some act of finality. He paused to reflect upon it briefly, but let it pass – he could find nothing in his consciousness about which he should feel concern. Then, glancing at the house, he saw Elizabeth illuminated by lamplight standing at an upstairs window smiling, although she could only have been smiling at the reflection of herself in the glass panes against the darkness outside in which he stood. Rose stood close behind her sister, apparently unfastening the rear buttons of her sister's dress. The two seemed to be talking happily.

Realizing that he could not be seen, Jack allowed himself to gaze upon the picture of these two women in the window, framed like a lovely portrait; it was an image that settled him and filled him with a sense of completeness. Eventually, he turned away to hurry after his parents who had by now gone some yards ahead and were calling to him impatiently, but as he did so, the disquieting feeling returned, and he felt compelled to turn back to look again at the window. But now the curtains had been drawn and his view into the room thus cut off. He hesitated for a moment, fighting an almost irresistible urge to rush back and take Elizabeth in his arms to restate his love for her and erase the earlier fancies for which he now felt guilty. And there was a deeper unease, having no shape or form, which seemed to have crept into his mind and now lurked just out of understanding. After such an evening, this curious mood seemed quite irrational, and when his parents called again from further up the hill, he turned to follow, reasoning that it must have been the punch that had suddenly brought this melancholic mood upon him.

The following evening, in the back room of George Easton's cottage home in Wakeham, a meeting took place of an entirely more serious nature compared to the celebrations of the night before. Four stern-faced men sat around an old oak refectory table in the intimate glow of an elaborate candleholder brought in from the adjoining drawing room. Behind them, looming darkly on the plain distempered walls, their shadows hovered as if spying on the secret conversation taking place.

'Right, Gentlemen,' said George Easton, bringing some idle chatter around the table to an abrupt end. 'Let's get on with it! Captain Pritchett has a tide to catch!' Easton the elder sat at the head of the table, grey-haired, square-jawed, and as craggy by complexion as the quarries that he ruled, having risen by his wits from quarryman to businessman. Seated to his right, Abraham Pritchett, a woolly-bearded Scot wearing a grubby seafarer's cap, nodded.

'Aye,' he said briskly, 'we'll do it just as we did before, so this did'na need to take long.'

Jack, sitting opposite his father, shifted in his chair. 'Before we start, Father,' he interjected hesitantly, 'are we quite sure that we need to do this again? Respects to Cap'n Pritchett here, but surely now we've been paid for our last shipment we don't have to take these risks any more. The chances of getting caught must increase every time we make a run, and you said that our last one would be the end of it.'

'We're not quite out of the woods yet, Jack,' said his father resignedly, 'our reserves are still too low for comfort; at present, we'd run straight into cash problems again at the slightest hitch, with not enough in the pot to tide us over. Believe me, I don't like smuggling any more than you do, but if you don't want to have the bailiffs at the door next time a customer pays late, we have to keep going for a bit longer yet.'

'Losing your nerve, Jack?' cut in Luke from the fourth place at the table. 'I'm up for it, at any rate, father,' he said with a cock-sure adolescent smirk in the direction of his brother

'Jack's right to be cautious, Luke,' said his father frowning. 'You're still the new boy here, and mark my words it's not the game you seem to think it is. We do this cautiously and with no silly bravado on your part, Luke, remember that,' he said firmly, flashing a warning glance at his younger son. 'Now Gentlemen, if we are all ready, let's go over the details.'

George Easton ran the meeting like a general rehearsing a battle plan, calling each of his subalterns to account on the details of their different tasks as he moved briskly through his agenda. The format of the operation would be identical to that refined over the several previous occasions and so each participant's contribution was becoming part of a familiar routine: Jack would be lead coxswain of the boats navigating them to the rendezvous with Pritchett's brigantine *The Alice* off Portland Bill, and Luke would be put in charge of the ground party that would carry the load up the cliff path from the Cove and get it safely stashed away. The make-up of the consignment had already been agreed between George Easton and Pritchett on an earlier occasion and so this aspect of the planning did not need much discussion. This time, the consignment would comprise mainly brandy and tobacco, and Pritchett was pleased to confirm that arrangements for its assembly had already been made with his contacts in Alderney; indeed Easton's advance payment for the goods had already been passed to the supplier, as was the normal procedure. (It had been careless talk of this in a harbour-side tavern there, that had already set the operation upon its calamitous course, but the group could have no inkling yet of the deadly deception afoot. Thus are exemplary plans built on complacent assumptions prone to disaster; but blithely believing that their operation would be too small to attract official interest, the group pressed on through its agenda without the slightest pause for further thought on the possibility of this fatal flaw.)

Then came the time to discuss the details of the rendezvous, and at this point the captain rose from his chair to unroll a nautical chart on the table.

'Gentlemen,' he started, his soft Scottish brogue placing him in the lowlands by origin, 'we meet five days hence on the twenty-fourth at ten o'clock, two hours before midnight and second high water, one and a half nautical miles south west of Church Ope Cove.' He peered at the chart and stabbed a finger down. 'Here,' he said pointing at his mark, ' you can use the navigation lights here and here to triangulate.'

The two young Eastons now rose to scrutinise the position marked - Jack would plot the position later and work out the bearings from the lights to help him find it on the night – and after some quiet moments of study, all resumed their seats as Pritchett continued:

'I'll use the inshore passage under the Bill, inbound to the rendezvous, then head easterly for a while before turning south for home,' he said, looking at George, prompting a nod of acknowledgement from the latter. 'You can warn me at the Bill in the usual way if there is any sign of trouble,' Pritchett continued.

George Easton nodded his acknowledgement again; 'Two lamps on the ledge at White Hole will be the all-clear signal as usual - a fisherman trying for mackerel, as far as any outsider is concerned,' he quipped. 'If you don't see the lights, you must abort.'

'Right,' said Pritchett emphatically, then turned to address the younger Easton. 'Now Jack, timing will be critical for me, so you'll be there on time if you please, sir,' he said, raising a bushy eyebrow to emphasise the importance of his point. 'We must reckon on an hour or so to transfer the load to the boats, and you'll need to depart that position a good thirty minutes before midnight to have the back-eddy with you, otherwise you won't make it. The tide will turn against you and even your strong quarrymen won't be able to make headway against it.'

Jack nodded. 'At least it'll be neaps,' he said, 'that should make it less critical for us. Those boats will be heavy and slow on the return journey!'

This timed-rendezvous procedure was preferred because it did not require the brigantine to loiter close inshore waiting or a landing, an earlier smugglers' tactic now outlawed under the Government's new Hovering Act.

'As usual, no lights or signals from the boats,' chipped in George Easton, sternly. 'And take their pipes away from them, Jack, for God's sake: no one must be tempted to light up.'

Jack grimaced. 'You'll be the only man with a light, father; the usual signal from the church parapet if it's not safe to enter the Cove,' he confirmed.

The meeting continued thus in this vein until all details of the operation were covered, including back-up plans for subsequent nights should the weather or some other contingency cause the operation to be postponed. Other than the 'all clear' light at the Bill, there would be no safe way to communicate once *The Alice* had set off from Alderney.

The operation would require forty-two men to handle the consignment; seven in each of the six sturdy lerrets, the tough little Portland boats that were long of keel, broad of beam, and stable in a rough sea. In the small communities of Portland, forty-two men would represent a substantial proportion of the adult male population, and, considering the empty chairs they left behind at family supper tables and in the public houses, some subterfuges would be necessary to make their absence less conspicuous.

'I'll have my group ready,' Luke chipped in eager to make his contribution. 'Ten extra men ready to help carry the stuff off the beach, and some women at the top ready to hide it.'

It would be in this last phase of the operation, and in its later distribution to customers, that the womenfolk would play their vital part. Many would find secret hiding space in their homes; and when the goods were later delivered to customers on the mainland, it was almost guaranteed that no customs officer would demand that a lady lift her skirts. It was often a matter of much ribald speculation in the alehouses of the Island to reckon the tonnage of contraband taken off the Island secreted in these dark and mysterious places.

'Then are we agreed Gentlemen?' said George Easton at last. 'Are all the details covered?'

'Aye,' said the Scotsman briskly after a pause for thought, 'that's enough for me at any rate, and I've to be back to m'ship now - we sail back to Alderney on the evening tide.'

The business complete, they all thus rose to bid the captain farewell, following him towards the door.

'There's just one thing,' Pritchett said stopping in his tracks and turning back. 'Be careful how you go, George. The word down at the harbour is that this new man Middleton is canny. You've been safe 'til now, but times may be changing.'

With the departure of the Scotsman, the Eastons returned to their table and settled themselves around it to study the chart more closely, while Eleanor Easton, seeing the meeting over, chose the moment to carry in some refreshment for her men. Due to her chronic arthritis, Eleanor walked with a sort of upright fragility that lent a certain stiff dignity to her bearing, endowing her with an uncommon presence, so that when she entered a room, strangers' heads might turn to look at her with some deference. At home, however, as is regrettably the case in many domestic relationships of any length, such admiring acknowledgement was not as common as it perhaps should have been. Carrying the victuals with more than a little awkwardness due to her condition, she muttered irritably under her breath to see her men oblivious of her entry in their preoccupation with the chart. She cleared her throat pointedly to attract their attention and sighed with heavy irony:

'I expect you men will want something to drink now!'

The men looked up in surprise to find her approaching, and a chastened George rose swiftly to relieve her of her burden. There was a brief hiatus while the men fussed over her, taking her arm and holding her chair as she seated herself with evident relief, but then the conversation continued:

'This new Customs man can't touch us can he, father?' asked Luke in a tone that combined anxiety with incredulousness as he poured himself some wine from the newly delivered jug. Jack immediately took an interest in his question as did his mother, and both heads turned to the head of the table to hear George's reaction.

'No, I don't think that he'll be a problem for us, son,' his father said with such a reassuring air that to Jack it must have had a hollow ring, for he frowned. But, not noticing Jack's doubt, his father continued confidently:

'However good this new man is, Portland would be too difficult a nut to crack; why, it'ud take an army to trap us on our own ground - and no army could take one step on the Island without one hell of an alarm being raised! No, I think we're safe enough.'

But his wife was clearly not so sure. 'George, I've said my piece before about this smuggling of yours,' she said accusingly. 'You know I don't like you boys taking these risks; and the sooner you give it up the better, that's what I say, no matter how many of your numskull quarrymen might be keen to take part.' Mrs Easton had a way of looking at her husband that usually made him feel uncomfortable but he was not to be deflected on this occasion.

'Eleanor, I've given you my promise that we'll quit soon,' he said in a long-suffering tone. 'One or two more runs will see us clear financially and then, with luck, we should be able to give up the game completely. I don't like taking these risks either but, for the time being, it's a matter of sheer necessity!'

Eleanor Easton's expression suggested that her doubts were not in the least assuaged and she raised an eyebrow in the manner of one for whom the argument still has a distance to run. Then Jack took a breath as if he were about to add a comment of his own but seemed to think better of it and remained silent. Yet his glance at his father was curiously grave.

The days that remained before the scheduled rendezvous with Pritchett were hectic for Jack, for he had individually to communicate the detail and timing of the plan to every one of his forty-one boatmen, calling on each of them discretely. It would have risked too much, with respect to both accuracy and security, to have the word passed from mouth to mouth, and he would trust no one else with the task. Work at the quarry also continued to demand his full attention throughout that time, and the consequence of all this activity was that he had no further opportunity to call upon Elizabeth. Fretting at not seeing her for so long a period, he decided instead to send her a loving note, conveyed by the hand of a fellow quarryman living in Fortune's Well and passing her door on his way home. Having been uneasy about his involvement in smuggling, Jack had never spoken of it to his betrothed, all the while hoping that the activity would soon be behind him, thus never needing to be revealed. His note therefore avoided any mention of it, explaining his absence under the pretence of unexpected and necessary extra work at the quarry. He was therefore alarmed by the final paragraph of her reply a few days later, which read as follows:

By the way, I happened upon Luke this afternoon outside one of those inns near the fort in Castletown (I think he had been drinking for he was unusually talkative); he let slip what he (and you, as he had to reveal under my questioning) would be up to on Saturday night. I must say that at first I was surprised and a little shocked, but then I began to be rather intrigued and excited by the idea! I insisted that, as I am to be your wife, I should be able to come and watch and should not be kept from this adventure any longer. Luke was reluctant at first of course, but I eventually persuaded him, and later he called upon me to say that he had arranged for me secretly to observe your return from castle grounds. I am so thrilled that I shall be near you so that I may bring you luck and share some of your excitement!

I can hardly endure the long wait to see you again - we have so much to talk about.

Your affectionate and very own,
Elizabeth.
P.S. I will not tell my parents of this, for they would certainly not approve, but I have let Rose into the secret and she has insisted that she comes too!

Jack was horrified that Elizabeth (and indeed Rose) now knew what he, in his guilt, had kept hidden. His first instinct was to put a stop immediately to what he regarded as a crassly stupid idea and have words with his brother for revealing what should have been a closely guarded secret kept within the circle of those who took part. He would speak to Luke in due course, but what should he to do about Elizabeth now, he wondered. She now knew of his involvement in an illegal activity that had troubled him to the extent that he had not spoken of it.; but rather than condemning him as he had feared, she seemed to be excited, even admiring! As he reflected on this, he began to think that perhaps it would do no harm for her to be there on the night after all; indeed, it flattered his manly pride that she might be impressed to see him in a more adventurous light. In this way he was responding to the primeval urges deeply rooted in young men's characters to display their prowess to their mates, just as a peacock displays his plumage to his hen. His thoughts thus clouded by these vanities, it did not occur to him that Elizabeth and Rose would be in any danger, or that their lives would be changed forever by the events that were to come.

Chapter Four

Middleton's customs units, supplemented by a number of military platoons seconded from the nearby encamped regiment, were assembled secretly over a period of days within the walls of the Tudor bulwark on the Nothe, a fortified peninsular at the mouth of the River Wey constructed to deter a French attack. At the appointed hour, under cover of darkness, the combined force covertly embarked from the adjacent quay to be conveyed across the bay to King's Pier on the unpopulated north-eastern side of the Island. To avoid attracting attention to the assembly of the conveying fleet, the dozen small craft utilised for the transportation had been lent by a navy ship-of-the-line visiting Weymouth ostensibly on a routine visit. It was still early in the evening as the force disembarked at the pier, quietly dispersing according to the well-drilled plan, to make their way along the labyrinthine tracks of the under-cliff towards their predetermined positions around the Cove. On this dark, and as yet moonless evening, only the bare cliffs had looked down on their menacing advance, and no one lay resting on the ledges from which Jack Easton had so joyously gazed just two short weeks before.

By eight o'clock, Smyke, White, and Hayes, were already in position, and now stood attentively alongside their senior officer at the cliff-top vantage point overlooking Church Ope Cove. From here, Middleton would exercise command over the amassed forces, now wedged silently if uncomfortably into the craggy undulations a hundred feet below.

Meanwhile, in the top-hill villages of Portland, the smugglers' preparations for their night's work were well underway. It does not take much arithmetic to realise that even a modest operation such as the one described would have been obvious to an inquisitive observer without some obscuring subterfuge. Some of the men, well known to frequent the tables of the hostelries around the Island, had even gone so far as to dress their wives to resemble themselves sitting in their usual places for any constable who might peer in to see. But they need not have gone to so much trouble; the officer of the watch would not be making his usual rounds this evening, having received an unusual summons from the Weymouth Customs office to attend to other business elsewhere.

Jack Easton's forty-one boatmen had trodden their secret paths to the meeting point in darkness, cutting through the quarries and across the common land so as not to attract attention. A small clearing in the wooded valley below the cottages of Wakeham had been chosen as the rendezvous; and once all the men had assembled there, Jack led them down the path in the direction of the sea. His first objective was to gather the men in the graveyard of St Andrew's church, a short distance below, from which vantage point he would obtain a clear view of the Cove; here, they would meet his father waiting there on watch, before making their final descent to the boats. The men thus moved down the path in single-file; practised in the art of stealth, not a single word passed between them. The autumn winds and salty air of Portland had made short work of the summer canopy of foliage which otherwise would have enshrouded the descending line, and shafts of moonlight now penetrated the bare branches from a newly rising moon. Glancing up through the leafless arbour, Jack now noticed the patchwork of bright-edged stratus illuminated in the oblique light, drifting silently westwards; and between their pale shapes, he saw bright stars twinkling in a jet-black sky. He was relieved; this was a good omen of fair weather, and the relative stillness of the air suggested a smooth sea. In the quiet of this calm night, only the faint rustling of dry leaves alerted the patiently awaiting George Easton of the group's arrival; and as Jack entered the moonlit graveyard, he caught sight of his father sitting astride the boundary wall, peering up at him expectantly.

St Andrew's church stands precariously upon a broad ledge about half way down the descent from Wakeham under the ruins of an old castle not a hundred yards to the north. From the walled parapet bordering the graveyard on its seaward side there is an excellent view of the Cove and its approaches, and it would thus be from here that George Easton would maintain his lookout whilst the boats carried out their task.

Jack approached his father, leaving his men to settle themselves silently amongst the gravestones while he conferred. 'All quiet, pa?' he whispered.

'Aye, Jack, a little too quiet for my liking,' his father replied. 'Any sound you make could draw attention, so be careful of your footing on the way down - and watch closely for my signal on your return, I have an uneasy feeling about tonight.'

'You always feel uneasy, father, since you stopped leading the boats yourself!' Jack chided, wrapping his arm around his father's shoulders in a cheerful embrace. 'You've changed your tune - you seemed so confident at the meeting – if we have to do it at all, it seems a perfect night for it!'

The older Easton forced a smile and nodded tensely. Then, his manner suddenly becoming brusque, he took out his timepiece and held it up to let the moonlight play directly on its face; 'You'd better be on your way,' he said gruffly as he squinted at the position of its hand.

Except for the whispered lapping of the surf on the stony beach directly below, George Easton could hear no sound as the men slid their lerrets into the sea; and he watched the little craft pull away, bobbing in the gentle swell as the oarsmen found their rhythm. One by one, the six silhouettes crossed the moon's silvery reflections in close line-astern and disappeared into the darkness to the south; in each boat, six oarsmen strained at their oars in unison, and, standing in the stern of the lead boat, Jack set the course and pace as coxswain. As he watched them pass out of sight, George fell into a quiet introspection of mixed emotions. On the one hand, he was proud to see his capable son leading his men out to sea, whilst on the other, and made more poignant by this very sight, he lamented the fading of his own powers. But while he might have envied his son's youth and strength, his appetite for such work had also waned. Perhaps it was just as well, he mused, that a new generation had taken over. While they would carry all the burden and the risk, however, he must now sit and fret ashore, more anxious for his son's safety than he had ever been for himself. His confident words after the meeting with Pritchett seemed now to ring a little hollow. He recalled Eleanor's misgivings and knew that they were not entirely misplaced; he shared her darkest fears even though he would never have admitted it. And he had meant what he had said - just a few more runs and that would be an end to it. It was in this lonely and melancholic state that he let his gaze wander up into the moon's ambiguously laughing face - just as passing cloud encroached; and he was plunged into almost total darkness.

Not more than one-hundred and fifty yards from George Easton's lookout point, standing patiently on the cliff top overlooking the Cove, four Customs' officers had watched the boats depart. A chilling breeze had since blown up from the east, so that they now wrapped their heavy coats about themselves more tightly. The breeze had quickened the passing of the cloud and made the moonlight intermittent. A recent period of darkness had cloaked the officers' view, but now the moon had re-emerged so that details in the Cove could once more clearly be picked out. The scene down there was still; but against the stark whiteness of the moonlit beach, gaps in the line of craft from which the six boats had departed were as conspicuous as missing teeth. To each side of the opening, craggy arms of rock jutted darkly into a sea that now shimmered in the moonlight. And stretching north and south beyond these rocky outcrops, the water's edge was strewn with jagged stony debris, making the Cove an isolated haven on a hazardous shoreline. To the right of the waiting group lay the southern extent of the Easton quarry, an untidy litter of rough-hewn blocks amongst scattered spoil – the prospect, a bleak landscape in the pale light. Beyond this rough ground stood Rufus Castle, a Saxon ruin whose broken walls towered like an ancient bastion on guard. And behind it, at a lower level than where the party stood and therefore hidden from their sight, lay the old St Andrew's Church, amongst whose leaning gravestones a solitary George Easton waited anxiously for his boats. He was entirely unaware of the brooding might lurking so close at hand which had so stealthily crept upon him in the darkness; but then neither were the officers aware of him.

Navigating by reference to the flickering coal-fires of the two lights located near the Bill to provide a warning transit for the Shambles Bank, Jack and his boats reached the assigned location after a steady row assisted by the last hour of the ebbing tide. The estimation of his position had been helped by the intermittent moonlight that, from time to time, had bathed the distant rocky shoreline in a steely-grey light, allowing him to pick out the details of some distinctive caves. Arriving at slack water, the boats would be able to hold their position with little effort, and so Jack gave the order to raft up in a loose cluster to await the rendezvous; in the darkness, he would not want them to drift apart. Grateful for the respite from their labours, the men leant on their oars and fell into quiet conversation as the boats circled and bobbed on the inky blackness of a glassy sea. Just then, a cloud passed across the moon throwing the gaggle of boats into utter darkness with nothing to distinguish sea from sky, the stars and their reflections both equally bright. Some of the younger men, hanging over the side for amusement, marvelled at the eerie phosphorescent specks that darted from below like comets. To Jack, still standing alert for the arrival of the *Alice*, it seemed suddenly as if the boats were not boats at all but some unearthly caravan of vessels drifting in a black void amongst the infinity of stars surrounding him like a sphere. Conversation faltered then petered out as the men lapsed into an introspective silence, perhaps feeling the same terrifying vulnerability in the vastness of the enveloping cosmos. Jack knew this feeling and allowed himself to sink into its embrace; it was almost spiritual, a recognition of his tiny place in space and time, a sublime and profound feeling of humility at the immensity of the firmament. Quietly yet unabashed and without conscious thought, his own voice sounded in his ears uttering a few lines of a half-remembered prayer:

> *'Guard us, Lord, who brave uncertain seas;*
> *If we be lost, then help us find our way,*
> *And stiffen our resolve if we take fright,*
> *And bring us through the dangers of this night.'*

He was somewhat taken aback when, after the brief moment of total stillness that followed his oratory, a few of the men closest to him added a quiet, *'A-men'*, as he had not meant his thoughts to be broadcast. And to cover his embarrassment, he added quickly with a louder and laughing voice: 'And may the good Lord deliver us all safely to our wives and sweethearts after this night's work be done!'

Which prompted the inevitable and mirthful chorus: 'And let them not find out about each other!'

'And Amen to that too!' chuckled some of the others with feeling.

The mood lightened with the moonlight reappearing, and before long some episodes of muted sniggering and laughter broke out, drifting across the quiet air between the boats like the gentle swell which bore them. Jack smiled inwardly, guessing that the mirthful sounds had been triggered by hoary tales of the deep, crafted with such malicious pleasure by old lags, designed to scare the first-timers out of their wits. In Jack's boat, his own apprentice, Ben Proctor, sat listening with wide-eyed astonishment to a wizened old-timer who muttered some mischief into his ear. The boy shifted nervously, peering over the side with apparent apprehension before recoiling from it in fright as if some horror lurked there. But a bony prod in the youngster's ribs and the old man's wheezing laughter gave the game away. Realising immediately that he had been duped, the boy's retaliation was swift; a playful struggle then broke out between the two as the boy sprung upon his aged compatriot in mock attack, beating the retreating old man into aping submission in a good-humoured wrestle which set the boat rocking wildly.

'Steady now, boys,' Jack asserted firmly, 'I'm in no mood for a swim tonight!'

With some residual fractiousness, the squabbling pair settled back into their places under the restraining hands of those who shared Jack's desire to avoid a soaking.

'By the look of it, lads' Jack chuckled, 'young Ben here has swallowed the bait - hook, line, and sinker - on his first night out!' There was a further ripple of amusement as the embarrassed Ben made another playful lunge at his neighbour, and the boat rocked precariously again. 'All right, all right!' called Jack with good-humoured authority as he steadied himself, 'let's leave at that shall we? We'll drink to your initiation later, Ben!'

'Aye, aye, coxswain!' returned the boy, sliding back into his place in affected obedience, a broad smile creasing his eager upturned face.

It was not long afterwards that the dark shape of the "*Alice*" slid upon them borne upon a gentle breeze, her arrival announced only by the muffled sounds of running halyards and furling sails, mixing with the soft slip-slap of the sea against her graceful prow.

'Ah, Mr Easton,' boomed the Scottish voice of Pritchett, who stood on the sprit looking down like a wild and bearded Neptune from his chariot. 'Not a bad piece of navigation, sir, my compliments to you!'

'And to you, captain, for finding us! It's a fine night to be out,' Jack called jovially across the gap closing between them, but then his tone turned at once more businesslike. 'As soon as you're ready, sir, we should transfer the consignment without delay; we shall have a long slog back if we miss the tide.'

The boats were swiftly and deftly manoeuvred to bring three boats along each side of the *Alice's* hull, in which position the transfer of the consignment commenced using the ship's davits. It was a slick, well-rehearsed operation, which proceeded without mishap and with hardly a word spoken. Into each boat were lowered fifteen to twenty kegs and casks of various sizes, carefully distributed under the thwarts to keep the vessels on an even keel, a process that took a little time since some manhandling was required to achieve a safe trim. It was not until eleven o'clock, therefore, that the convoy started back towards the Cove, and even with the helpful tide expected, it would take more than an hour's strenuous effort to reach it. Moreover, the heavily laden boats were now the devil's own job to row.

Smyke was the first to spot the distant black silhouettes as the boats entered the shimmering moonlit path that lay to the southeast. Squinting in the brightness, he was at first unsure that his eyes had seen correctly and he chose to hold his tongue. The thickening cloud was obscuring the moonlight for longer periods now, and at that moment, a further spell of darkness hid the shapes from his view. When the moon's reflections once more reappeared, he could make out the boats clearly. This time there was no doubt in his mind. He quietly clutched his superior's arm to draw his attention to what he had seen.

'Well done, Smyke!' Middleton whispered, leading the group closer to the cliff edge to get a better view, 'but we shall wait until they're on the beach before we spring our trap; they'll have lookouts posted for sure, and an alarm signal at this stage would ruin the operation. Anyway, there're more of them to come yet.'

Seeing the captain move so close to the precipice, Smyke's pulse began to race; despite his deadly scheming, he was almost taken by surprise by the opportunity that might suddenly present itself. Steeling himself, he manoeuvred closer for the fatal push, disguising his movement as positioning to get a better view of the approaching boats. The captain's fall must appear an accident - careless footing too near to the edge. But Hayes and White remained too close around the captain for him make his move unseen. Heart pounding, he lurked in the half-light waiting for a chance to close upon his target. His companions were so engrossed in their observations, that a chance may come at any moment. Then suddenly an opening came. His limbs tensed as he prepared to pounce. But just then Hayes threw a casual glance behind and the moment was lost. Smyke caught the subaltern's eye and nodded sagely as if expressing approval at the progress of events. Hayes looked away. Smyke repositioned and manoeuvred again, coming within an instant of striking on several occasions soon after. But on each occasion that he moved closer to the captain, either White or Hayes looked back or got in the way at the last moment. Infuriatingly, the juniors seemed glued to their superior's side. Smyke dithered. It seemed that he would have to send them all over the cliff to achieve his objective, and this contingency passed through his mind - even though he knew that he would have a hard time convincing others that it was a mere accident that had sent them all to their deaths. But eventually, he gave up, clenching his jaw in frustration, realising that he would have to bide his time a little longer for a better opportunity to come.

The boats drew closer. The officers now counted the six of them strung out in a line, crawling up the coast from the south, their progress seeming ponderously slow. Hayes speculated absently into the darkness that they must have been down near the Bill for their rendezvous, while Middleton and White scanned the sea expectantly for signs of the larger vessels that they had been led to believe would be involved.

'Their other craft must be close behind – or perhaps they plan to approach from a different direction?' Middleton ventured hopefully. 'Anyway, our Cutter should soon be approaching, and then we shall have them all in the bag!' he said with resolute confidence, grinning triumphantly. 'What say you, Smyke?'

Smyke returned an enigmatic smile that cracked his tense features, but gave no answer other than to incline his head in feigned deference to his superior's assessment.

It was just after midnight when Jack's boat reached the mouth of the Cove, and he called his exhausted oarsmen to rest easy while he waited for the other boats to catch up and assemble alongside. The landing phase was always the most dangerous, and he knew he must temper the men's inclination to rush headlong for the shore in their eagerness to get the night over with. A freshening breeze had raised the surf to a slightly higher pitch since their departure, and he could now hear it breaking ahead. Jack well appreciated the dangers of beaching in strong surf; a moment's inattention could put a boat beam-on to the waves, flipping it over and spilling everything into the sea. Thankfully, the surf seemed light tonight and they should be spared this difficult task, but they would be at their most vulnerable to entrapment in the enclosing promontories of the bay, and he thus resolved to direct the boats' approach carefully to minimise their risk.

'Keep your eyes peeled now,' Jack called softly to the other boats as they gathered around him. 'And watch for any signal from the church.'

With the heavy loads aboard, it was not easy for the oarsmen to manoeuvre their awkward craft into position, and, to Jack, it seemed to take an age before they had got themselves into line. The dark and threatening outlines of the rocky cliffs now towered above them like a fist poised to strike, a deeper shade of blackness in the gloom that suddenly descended as the moon was once more obscured by passing cloud. With the reassuring absence of any signal from his father, Jack reckoned that the coast was clear for his approach, but he would wait for the cloud to pass to be sure.

It was Jack's plan to take his boat in ahead of the rest so that he could warn the others off should he encounter any problem, a precaution adopted to safeguard his men as well as their valuable consignments. If alerted thus, the others had been instructed to head immediately for the alternative landing points further up the coast. But Jack was confident that he would reach the beach unmolested, given the Revenue's lack of interest in the past. And it was therefore in a relatively sanguine state of mind that he commenced his run in - just as the moonlight reappeared.

Countless hidden eyes had watched the boats assemble from various positions along the Cove's craggy perimeter, and these now looked down with heightened interest as the first boat headed in. At the centre of the crescent, from behind the walls of the old castle where Luke had left them with other waiting womenfolk, Elizabeth and Rose craned on tiptoes to look down. To the former, in her girlish innocence, it was a moment of thrilling anticipation, while the latter felt distinct unease. And to George Easton, standing on his parapet scanning the terrain below, there was no sign of anything untoward. In the moonlight, the scene was as pale and as still as death, except for the rolling surf's soft and rhythmical caresses that had begun to lull him into a state of weary complacency. If only he could have seen beyond the castle where Middleton and his companions now watched so attentively, he might even now have averted the catastrophic train of events that was to follow.

A young officer of the Dorsetshire Regiment had impatiently watched the boats' slow progress from the under cliff, and when he saw them at last positioning for their approach, he had alerted his platoon to be ready. Aroused from his restless slumber by the officer's warning, a sixteen year-old recruit could not resist the temptation to take a look at the scene below, poking up his head in curiosity over the boulder behind which he had uncomfortably lain. Unfortunately, in repositioning himself from his cramped hiding place, he lost his footing and slipped, causing the boulder to become dislodged and fall onto the rocks below, shattering noisily into fragments from its eventual impact. By this time, the first of the boats was already approaching the beach, and the alarmed young army officer looked up sharply to determine the effect of the minor avalanche, muttering expletives under his breath. At first, it seemed as if the rock fall had gone unnoticed against the noise of the surf and he was reassured. But then, to his horror, he saw the boat stop suddenly in its wake, and he watched transfixed and perplexed as it turned itself around to head out from the Cove. At that moment, his eye was caught by a light high above him being swung furiously from the parapet of the old church, and he realised that the alarm had been raised. Mortified, he now swung his gaze to see the other boats manoeuvring to make their escape; it had the makings of a disaster; and that *his* platoon might be the sole cause of such a shambles piled an ignominy of failure on his young shoulders. Feeling panic rising in his breast as he stared wide-eyed at the commotion, he was at first paralysed into inaction. However, schooled as an officer to use his gumption and not dither, he thought it best to act decisively and thus he gave the order for his men to rise up and rush the beach, hoping that a few well-aimed shots might well force the boats ashore. With this act, the young man compounded his platoon's initial bad luck, tearing apart Middleton's disciplined chain of command, and obliterating any chance of restitution that a period of inaction might otherwise have brought. The gaff, so to speak, was blown, and once his men had risen from their foxholes and commenced their noisy charge towards the water's edge, there was no going back.

With the rush of the surf in his ears, Jack had not heard the rock-fall, but he soon saw his father's warning lantern swinging at the lookout point, and with alarm he shouted for his crews to turn their boats away. At first, seeing no activity on the shore, he wondered if the signal might have been a false alarm which would shortly be rescinded, giving him a chance to try again and thus save themselves a long row. But, even as his mind wavered, he saw a score of dark silhouettes running towards the water's edge from the foot of the cliff, and there was no longer any doubt in his mind that his boats were under attack. Suddenly all hell broke loose as a deafening volley of gunfire resounded seemingly from all directions at once, the retorts rebounding loudly from the surrounding cliffs. Musket shot zipped and whined through the air, hissing like water sprinkled on a hot iron as the lethal projectiles plunged into the sea around them. 'Put your back into it lads!' Jack shouted. But in their panic to pull hard, someone on the starboard side pulled his oar out of his oarlock, and there followed a moment of frenzied chaos as oars clashed and clattered and the boat slewed almost to a stop.

'Stop all! Get that oar remounted quickly man!' Jack shouted above the persisting barrage, struggling to bring the crippled boat back onto course; meanwhile the starboard oarsmen bent themselves to sort out the entanglement and remount the stray oar.

'Steady now! Oars at the ready!' Jack called, seeing them one by one bringing their blades back into alignment, their anxious faces now turning back to him, anticipating the order to row. Amongst them, he caught the frightened eyes of young Ben Proctor who stared back at him so imploringly as if clinging to his last hope. 'Ready on my command, stroke?' Jack called, struggling to keep his voice calm, yet his position standing so prominently at the stern was the most vulnerable of all. 'Now pull! – pull! - pull!' he shouted in swift and steady rhythm setting a fast pace that he knew they could maintain only for a short time. The heavy boat accelerated slowly in the wake of the other boats now some fifty yards ahead. Jack could see their oarsmen throwing up plumes of spray in their frantic retreat; they looked already to be out of firing range, but shots still rang out from the shore in loud and frightening volleys, hissing and whining around his own craft alarmingly. He expected to be hit at any moment.

Then suddenly the shooting stopped, and he thought he too must have pulled clear; but then, from seaward, Jack heard the unmistakable sound of flapping sails, and turned in apprehension to see the dark form of a cutter moving in from starboard to cut off their escape. Now he realised why the firing had ceased so abruptly; the cutter would take over the pursuit - and find them an easy prey weighed down so heavily with their load! It occurred to Jack that he should jettison the consignment, but it was already too late for that - harried by such close pursuit, he could not spare the time. It was now every boat for itself as the six crews clawed frantically northwards heading towards the shallow water into which they knew the cutter would not dare to follow. But Jack's boat, the last in the line, had the most difficult task, and his escape route was rapidly being closed off as the cutter made to block him. He shouted at his oarsmen to pull with every ounce of strength; they gave him everything they had, their faces meanwhile contorted in agonies of exertion. Yard by yard, the other boats began to pull clear as the cutter lost the wind and slowed, and Jack's might also have slipped the noose had not the cutter launched its two pinnaces to come between it and the open sea. For all their trying, Jack's men could never outrow those sleek craft with their fresh crews; there was now nothing for it but to head towards the rocks. If Jack could reach the shore before his pursuers, he and his crew might yet make their escape - providing the soldiers ashore did not anticipate their intentions too soon. But the moonlight was no friend on this unhappy night, and the young officer on the beach was in no doubt about Jack's objective, quickly dispatching his men along the shoreline to head off Jack's desperate bid for freedom. Jack watched the soldiers clambering over the rocks towards him with dismay; they moved with surprising speed despite the obstacles in their path. It was now a race against time to beat them to his intended landing spot. The pinnaces too were moving in fast behind, flanking him on either side. And in the panic to escape, Jack's boat was still moving at high speed as it hit the rocks.

High above the scene, Middleton watched open-mouthed as the renegade platoon rushed the beach, and stared on in utter disbelief as the resulting chaos ensued. His carefully laid plans now seemed in total tatters unless the arriving cutter could force the boats ashore where his men could still entrap them.

'I'll break that young officer's neck when I get hold of him!' he seethed. 'The imbecile has wrecked the entire operation! And where, by the way, are the smugglers' other vessels, Smyke?' Middleton's facial contours became creased in consternation as he cast his gaze around. He took a breath and held it, clamping his lips tightly shut, in an obvious effort to cool his anger. Then, bringing his voice back under control, he added in a moment of determined optimism: 'perhaps they're far enough behind not to have been alerted by all this damned noise! We may well round them all up yet!' With this, the lineaments of his face formed into a curious leer that lay somewhere between exasperation and wishful thinking.

Smyke nodded an encouragement, yet he alone knew that his captain's hopes would never be fulfilled; there would only be one major smuggling vessel in this night's operation, and she had slipped away long ago.

Middleton resumed his observation of the cutter's approach as its sleek hull now closed upon the scurrying boats - easy targets in the signal foam of their thrashing oars - and for a time, their capture seemed assured. But then the closing vessel seemed to slow, clearly losing the wind in the shadow of the cliffs, and the boats began infuriatingly to pull ahead. Suddenly, the race seemed lost, and Middleton's heart sank..

'They're going to get away!' he shouted with incredulity. 'Good God, what a shambles! Can I depend on no one tonight?'

But when he saw the cutter launch its pinnaces, his hopes were raised again, immediately recognising the ploy to cut off the trailing boat from the other five, who by now were fast disappearing into the darkness. The tactic appeared at once effective, for the target boat was seen abruptly to veer towards the shore with the pinnaces in hot pursuit. At this point, however, both boat and its pursuer were lost from Middleton's view behind a rocky bluff.

Middleton reacted fast. 'Smyke!' he said gruffly, 'Send the order quickly for the men to spread themselves along the cliffs to round up the bla'guards when they come ashore. They'll all have to land sooner or later - make sure that our men are waiting for them!'

Smyke nodded and made to turn away (White and Hayes had meanwhile moved a little distance along the cliff edge to maintain a view of the scene below), but Middleton added an afterthought:

'And there may be ground parties still secreted at the head of the Cove – have the church and the castle checked - I want anyone hiding there taken too if they haven't had the sense to scarper. Then have the whole area swept for stragglers!'

'Aye, sir,' Smyke answered and set off at once for his two juniors, whom, reaching, he led further down the path while he spoke in urgent tones. Many platoon leaders (those more disciplined than the unruly cohort that had broken ranks) still patiently awaited instructions despite the general mayhem that now reigned. The orders thus relayed, the subalterns were duly dispatched upon their way in some haste. Smyke watched them disappear into the gloom before turning back, recognising that in their going his opportunity had come. Somewhere in the darkness ahead, his captain now stood alone.

From his position standing at the helm, Jack was thrown violently from the boat as it crashed into the rocks at speed, hitting his head heavily on a large stone block and momentarily losing consciousness. The oarsmen, having something firmer to hang on to in the collision, fared somewhat better, untangling themselves from the resulting melee and scrambling ashore as quickly as their limbs would carry them. The customs men moving along the shoreline had by this time closed the gap in their attempt to intercept, but their progress was slow across the craggy and slimy boulders that littered their route. Meanwhile, the two pinnaces hovered menacingly to seaward, their crews apparently unwilling to risk being pressed onto the rocks in the swell, and evidently also reluctant to open fire in such poor light with soldiers in such close pursuit. It was at this point that the cloud again obscured the moonlight to give the escaping cohort a chance to break out of the tightening noose. Jack came to his senses to find himself half-immersed in a rocky pool, and opening his eyes to see lanterns fast approaching, he thought the game was up. But with no moon, the soldiers evidently did not see him and passed by; Jack heard them cursing volubly as they tripped and stumbled amongst the rocks. Seizing the opportunity for an escape behind them, he leapt up and started for the cliff face; he knew every inch of these rocky shores from his childhood adventures there, and, heart pounding, he clambered up those familiar ledges in full flight. It was a mad and reckless race in the semi-darkness, but he made it to the top undetected and threw himself prostrate onto the soft grass of the cliff edge, exhausted.

Smyke returned along the cliff path with cat-like tread, cloaked by the moonless gloom that had recently descended, and saw that his superior had moved back from the precipice to prop himself - somewhat dejectedly, Smyke thought - upon on a nearby block of stone. This was not quite as Smyke had imagined the moment when he would send the senior officer crashing to his death. In his scheming, his victim had always stood on the cliff edge where it would not have taken more than a shove to dislodge him. It was to have been a simple act so easily assessed later as an accident in the darkness; an act that would not require him to come face to face. Seeing that his approach had not yet been noticed, he stopped short and pondered for a while upon his options. Smyke was a large and powerful man, and he was in no doubt that he could overpower Middleton and throw him over the edge. But this would become a violent struggle for which he had not, and was not now (in the stillness of his cool inspection), mentally prepared. He needed the blood to be up for such brutal violence; and moreover, the man would surely scream his head off as he fought, bringing others swiftly to his aid. Smyke thus shrank from the prospect, thinking himself more prudent than timid; yet faced with the stark reality of bringing a man to his death more aggressively than by a simple push, he found that he simply could not do it. Instead, he stood silently watching his victim like a mantis in a quandary, while his hands toyed absently with the two flintlock pistols lodged in his belt. He had already primed and charged his weapons and he knew that it would be almost impossible to miss at this short range. His face tightened as he pictured himself drawing them, aiming, and firing, but he recognised immediately that such recklessness would surely put the hangman's noose around his neck, for the finger of accusation could only fall upon himself. Smyke thus stood hesitating in the semi-darkness undecided, the object of his deliberations still unaware of his presence. He watched in silence as the captain brought a weary hand to his brow then pull a flask from his pocket and raise it to his mouth. But before the flask reached the captain's lips, he stopped, suddenly seeming to sense a presence, and turned with a visible start to find Smyke nearby, standing calmly in the darkness. A look of guarded alarm passed briefly across his face as Smyke, caught in the inquisitive gaze, adopted a purposeful air and moved forward as if his approach had not been interrupted. Apparently unsuspecting, Middleton relaxed his guard and offered up the flask to his returning adjutant in a comradely gesture of reconciliation, his face wrinkled with a show of wry resignation. His grandiose operation had degenerated into chaos and he was patently embarrassed by it. But Smyke felt no sympathy; he took the flask yet could not meet the captain's eye, feeling only cold indifference for the man.

'Come on Smyke,' the senior officer said in a tone which could have been encouraging or mocking, as if he had interpreted Smyke's sullen manner as disappointment, 'it's not *that* bad. They'll think twice before they try it again - and we might yet catch a few!'

Smyke nodded, mimicking his superior's resigned spirit with undetected irony, and took a draft from the flask, wiping his lips with the back of his hand while steadfastly averting the other's eyes. He grimaced as the fiery liquid scorched his throat while struggling to rally himself out of his inaction, then raised the flask again and took a longer draft. He mused grimly that the night's work had never been destined to be an outstanding success for Middleton, given that the whole operation had been a set-up from the start, but the chaotic turn of events had made the situation more confused than he had ever envisaged and this had unsettled him.

But just then, Hayes returned, running up the path from the direction of the Cove, panting heavily, and Middleton turned anxiously towards him as the young officer approached. Hayes spoke in fragmented sentences broken by his laboured breathing as he conveyed the disappointing news that only two of the shore party had so far been apprehended - two unlikely and bewildered women found hiding inside the walls of the old castle. Moreover, while the pursuit of the boatmen continued, as the distant sporadic gunfire seemed to testify, none had as yet actually been caught – it seemed that the rocky foreshore and intermittent darkness were frustrating the chase.

Smyke's thoughts went into a spin as it began to dawn on him that the opportunity for his deadly deed was slipping away. On an impulse, he decided he must act – it must be now or never, he realised, for the chance may not come again. Whether it was the alcohol or the sight of Middleton's turned back that spurred his action, Smyke would never try to analyse, but grabbing a lump of stone from the ground, he swung it wildly at the captain's head. Smyke's attack caught Hayes' eye immediately, but the young officer had no time to react even as Smyke's murderous purpose became evident. His startled glance, however, was enough to warn his captain. Instinctively, Middleton turned and raised his arm to fend off the blow; and so, instead of delivering the lethal stroke intended, Smyke's wild swing was thrown wide of its mark, and the heavy stone came down on Middleton's right shoulder, shattering his clavicle with an audible crack. Gasping in agony, the captain fell into a faint, his legs buckling under him. Hayes' instinct, standing so close at hand, was to reach out and grab his superior to arrest his fall, but Middleton's weight was too much for him and both went down awkwardly at Smyke's feet. Enraged, Smyke pulled the boy up bodily, and threw him aside.

'Stay out of this you young fool, or you'll go the same way!' he growled through gritted teeth; his mad eyes flashing in the moonlight.

Had Hayes been less timid, less appalled at Smyke's monstrous act of violence, he might have pulled the pistol from his belt and shot Smyke there and then. Instead, cowering under the attacker's dark and threatening form, Hayes was overwhelmed with fear and lay paralysed, his white face frozen in horror, his eyes and mouth extended as if in a silent, terrified scream. Smyke had judged the young officer's character well in discounting his further involvement.

While Smyke was thus diverted, Middleton regained his senses, staggered to his feet and tried to make a run for it; but bent over in pain and clutching his injured arm, he had not moved more than two stumbling paces before Smyke turned back. Snatching up the stone again, Smyke grabbed Middleton from behind and swung the heavy lump at his head with force. This time, the right side of the captain's skull took the impact square on, and the blow knocked him sideways, reeling yet closer to the cliff edge where he fell to the ground in a crumpled heap. Smyke thought that this would see an end to it, but unbelievably, Middleton struggled up again, raising himself up doggedly on one knee.

'In God's name Smyke, are you out of your mind?' the captain spluttered through swollen lips, blood glistening on his battered face in the moonlight. 'Hayes! For heaven's sake,' he pleaded, 'get this mad man off me.'

But there was no stopping Smyke now; in a few quick strides, he was once more beside his half-kneeling victim, looming over him in the semi-darkness like some deathly spectre pitilessly preparing for the coup de grâce. A contemptuous leer split Smyke's ugly features as he weighed the stone contemplatively in his hand and then discarded it carelessly. Middleton must have realised then that he was lost, for his expression became desolate as he gazed hopelessly at the recumbent Hayes who still seemed transfixed in fright. With slow deliberation, Smyke grabbed Middleton roughly by the shoulders, spun him round, and threw him yet closer to the precipice with the strength of one possessed. The hoarse scream which might have brought others to his aid, died in Middleton's throat as he fell unconscious to the ground.

Not far away along the cliff edge, Jack lay listening anxiously to the sporadic gunfire continuing below. He prayed silently that his men would not be hit or captured. Then with a sudden pang of alarm, he remembered Elizabeth and Rose. They would have been watching from above the Cove, and he realised that they too would be in danger unless Luke had managed to get them away. He pictured them hiding, abandoned and vulnerable, unschooled and not knowing what to do. With these disquieting impressions in his mind, he resolved immediately that he must get to them, and started to get up. But then out of the darkness, he heard voices near at hand, and he stiffened in a paroxysm of terror that stilled his breathing and almost stilled his heart. Fearing discovery was upon him, he held himself motionless, fighting every instinct to flee, hoping that his inert form would not attract attention. He buried his head in his arms to hide his pale skin from the revealing moonlight, and his nostrils were filled with the smell of damp earth. There was a brief period of silence and then the voices resumed, this time strident and angry, and then there were sounds of a scuffle. Some one seemed to be pleading, as if begging for mercy, although Jack could not make out the words clearly. Realising then that it was not he who was the focus of attention, he risked some movement, slowly turning his head in the direction of the commotion. At first, his straining eyes saw only vague dark shapes in the dim light – it seemed as if they were writhing like some macabre dance of phantoms; but then, in an interlude of moonlight, the shadowy figures were given form. He stared uncomprehendingly at first; not twenty yards away, a man knelt cowed with another towering over him threateningly, while a third lay nearby, apparently unable to move. Jack raised himself to his knees wondering what to do – this was the time to make a run for it, he thought – but something made him hesitate. Then he saw the kneeling man spun round viciously by his tormentor and thrown bodily towards the cliff edge; and suddenly, the attacker's murderous purpose became clear as a strangled scream died abruptly on the night air. Whether Jack's response arose out of common humanity or from a belief that he might be rescuing one of his own men, Jack would never try to resolve, but without thinking, he leapt up and ran towards the group as fast as his stiffened legs would carry him.

Smyke became aware of the sound of heavy footfalls behind him only an instant before Jack's running body hit him heavily from behind at speed. In the impact, the wind was ripped from his lungs as he was knocked headlong, falling across the prostrate body of his wounded victim with an agonised gasp. For a few seconds, Smyke lay motionless in a daze, wondering at his fate, winded, face down, and staring directly into Middleton's swollen and bloody face. In a moment of curious detachment, he found himself noticing his victim's bald pate, streaked with blood and grime, shining grotesquely in the moon's light. Then his victim's eyes opened and stared back at him in impotent terror through sockets darkened in shadow and blood, and rank odours of sweat and fear filled Smyke's nostrils. Transfixed by that ghoulish sight, Smyke hesitated a second too long, for he next felt himself pulled up roughly by the shoulders, and turned to face his attacker who, seemingly in slow-motion, was gathering himself to lunge a clenched fist directly at his jaw. In those instants which intervened before the blow struck home, two reactions flashed through Smyke's perverted mind in quick succession: First, there was astonishment not to have been set upon by officers come to his senior's aid, and second, there was relief that his attacker appeared to be a single unarmed civilian. He realised thereby that he was not yet entirely undone; but in that instant of revelation, his assailant's fist crashed heavily into his jaw and blackness engulfed him as he felt his legs give way.

It could only have been minutes later that he began to regain his wits as the sound of voices raised in animated discussion nearby infiltrated his consciousness. For a moment, he remained quite still, listening for any sign that he might be observed. Then he slowly lifted his head to scan the scene around him. The moonlight shone again, but he could see from the quick passage of the scudding clouds that the period of relative brightness would be short-lived. Alongside him to his right, only inches from the cliff edge where he had fallen in the last assault, Middleton lay groaning and, some yards away in the other direction, he could see Hayes and the interloper stiffly facing each other. At first, he thought that they were merely engaged in some discussion, but then he realised that Hayes was holding a pistol in his outstretched hand.

'The boy's stupid,' he thought with cynical relief; 'he seems to have roused himself from his fright only to attack the first living thing he sees! The poor sod can't tell his arse from his elbow.' And Smyke recognised immediately that he might now get his chance to finish what he had started.

'Don't be a fool! he heard the stranger plead, 'It is not I who you should arrest, but that man there. You saw what he did - I only tried to stop him.'

Hayes appeared to waver and let his pistol arm drop, but then raised it again sharply as the stranger took a step towards him.

'Stay where you are or...or I shall shoot!' Hayes shouted nervously, waving the weapon in the other's direction while fumbling in his tunic with his other hand.

Smyke guessed that Hayes was reaching for his whistle and realised therefore that he must act quickly to save his skin, for others would be upon the scene in minutes once the alarm was raised. The plan that formed in his now desperate mind was as devious as it was clever, and he reacted swiftly. Without a moment's hesitation, he raised himself to his knees, put his hands underneath Middleton's prostrate body, and rolled him silently over the ledge. The captain uttered not a single sound as he fell, and only Smyke heard the muted thud as the limp and wounded body hit the anvil head of the flat rock fifty feet below; the platform broke the poor man's fall and terminated his life in an instant. Smyke now turned his attention to the others and was gratified to see that they still stood facing each other in a stand off, apparently unaware of his action, while Hayes continued to fumble for his whistle. Passing cloud then once more threw the scene into semi-darkness and a strange and unexpected silence descended that endured for several seconds before being abruptly shattered by a piercing whistle blast. Smyke always carried two pistols in his belt for good measure, and now he quickly drew one of these and cocked it, moving stealthily in the darkness towards the standing pair, coming up quietly some yards to one side of the stranger's back. He raised his pistol and took aim, but at that moment the moonlight once more asserted itself, and from the startled look of bewilderment which came into in Hayes' young face, Smyke realised that his approach had been noticed.

'Mr Smyke! What are you doing …..?' Hayes cried incredulously; but his cry was cut short. There was a blinding flash and a deafening report that echoed like a canon shot against the higher cliffs rising steeply behind them. A man fell dead; but it was not the civilian who slumped to the ground mortally wounded, it was the young officer whose life had expired so unexpectedly with a pistol ball lodged in his heart.

As the reverberations of the shot subsided, the sounds of other whistles were heard not far away, and Smyke knew then that there was not much time for him to complete his plan. Having fallen to the ground at the shock of the explosion, the stranger now struggled to his feet and turned to face him evidently somewhat dazed. Smyke already had his second pistol in his hand, and, with no time to lose, he cocked it and fired it directly at the stranger's head. Another blinding flash and loud report echoed from the cliffs and the stranger fell where he had stood. Now, with only moments before his alerted colleagues were upon him, Smyke carefully placed one of his own smoking pistols alongside his junior's dead body, picking up the young officer's unspent pistol from the ground where it had fallen. His second spent weapon, he now threw to fall adjacent to his other victim, then quickly flung himself into a recumbent state some paces off, where he would be found as if recovering from some ghastly assault.

Smyke had been clever; he would be able convincingly to assert that it was the stranger (assumed to be one of the escaping smugglers) who had stumbled upon the three Revenue officers standing at the cliff top. In the desperate struggle that had ensued, Middleton had been cruelly pushed over the edge to his death, and Smyke himself badly beaten and left lying on the ground as evidenced by his bruises. He would also report that

Hayes had been shot with one of Smyke's own pistols grabbed from his belt by the stranger, and that Hayes had bravely returned fire even as he lay dying - a courageous final act which had left both men dead. The sound of the two shots and the position of the spent pistols lying alongside the two bodies would surely leave no doubt as to his explanation of the tragedy (which he would assert he had watched in horror as he lay recovering from his own beating).

Smyke had indeed been clever, and no one would ever have suspected the truth of the matter except for two things:

Firstly, the weapon which now sat in Smyke's belt was not his own. In itself, this might not have mattered but for the fact that Hayes' pistol was a private weapon, not one of the normal service weapons issued by the armoury and carried by the other officers that night. While not conspicuously different, it differed in the detail of its brass butt-cap, which was slightly more ornate, and it was, of course, absent of the crowned *GR* stamped upon the flat-locks of service weapons. Smyke could not have spotted this detail in the darkness and would not notice it for some time. Neither would Andrew White, the one officer who might otherwise have recognised the weapon, having immediately become distracted and distraught at finding his friend Hayes lying dead as he arrived.

But the second error that Smyke had made would be of far more serious consequence although it would take some time for its full effect to be felt. It would not be until later that evening when he became aware of it and he would react violently in an attempt to put it right; but by then he would be restricted in his freedom to act.

Chapter Five

Jack regained consciousness with piercing pains shooting between his temples like hot needles. In such discomfort, it was instinctive to lift his hand to explore his head for damage, and his fingers stumbled clumsily upon a rough dressing, sending an explosion of bright sparks across the insides of his eyes. He winced in pain, but then more carefully resumed his exploration to trace the route of bandages wrapped around his head. For a time, he struggled to remember what had caused the injury, lying quite still in the darkness as he trawled his aching brain for clues. Then piece-by-piece, disjointed fragments of the previous night's events fell into place like the heavy levers of an old lock, until eventually all the images of his last conscious moments coalesced into a continuous sequence. The images were so vivid that they kept recurring in his mind until they became a terrifying blur: the desperate fight on the cliff top, the gunning down in cold blood of the frightened young officer, the barrel of a pistol then turned upon himself, the crack and splutter of the flintlock, a flash of brilliant white light, and then, at the end, an instant of stinging pain as darkness had closed in. Clearly, the shot had been meant to kill him and he had been lucky to escape with a mere flesh wound. Half an inch of aiming error had saved his life. He opened his eyes in a cold sweat but could see no light; he felt confused and forsaken in the black and silent void in which he now found himself. Then, moving his right hand tentatively about him to get his bearings, he established that he lay upon a bed of crude construction against a stone wall which was wet to his touch. He tried to move his body but found himself shackled at both ankles. As he bent to yank against the retraining chains, he felt the flesh and sinews of his whole body detonate in pain as if every part of him had been subjected to a violent beating. He lay back, exhausted.

'My God, I am in purgatory!' he thought, grimly, 'and am I blinded too?' he cried out miserably into the echoing darkness.

The shock at finding himself in such a desolate situation moved him beyond comprehension, and for a time he sank into a deep trough of hopelessness that had no form and no sensation save for an icy grip that made him utterly impotent.

For how long he lay there so forlornly, Jack later found it hard to estimate, for he must have fallen in and out of consciousness several times; but when he finally came to his senses, he became aware of a single shaft of sunlight piercing the damp void like an arrow. The light emanated from a chink in the wooden shutters blocking up a barred opening in the wall above his head. He tried to raise himself to explore it but was forced back by the protest of his limbs, and his ribs ached as if he'd fallen heavily. He tried to lift himself again several times and failed, falling back each time onto his back, his face contorting in the agony of his efforts. But eventually, he overcame his pains and raised himself onto his haunches. The heavy shackles grated painfully on the raw flesh of his ankles as he lifted himself to his feet on the wooden frame of his bunk; but eventually he was able to bring his eyes up to the chink. Through it, he saw a segment of a harbour scene with several small boats sitting at odd angles in glistening puddles of shallow water, and he recognised it immediately to be the harbour of the Mere. He realised then that he was imprisoned in Portland Castle whose squat and menacing form lay adjacent to the small fishing harbour on the Island's north shore. Jack slumped back onto his bed, bewildered; the cold damp air smelled of mould and stagnant water and suddenly he felt very cold. In the faint diffusion now permeating his dungeon, he gloomily surveyed its mildewed walls and flagstones. It was a cavernous space with a curved outside wall with recesses extending indistinctly into the gloom. Beyond the foot of his bed, a rust-streaked iron door ran with condensation, and above him, a vaulted ceiling elevated itself into a darkness that concealed its details from his view. His gaze had wandered aimlessly at first but then he felt it drawn as if by some compelling power to where the sun's narrow beam had now moved, its focus inching around the wall inexorably with the earth's rotation.

What he saw illuminated in that small circle of light sent an involuntary shudder running up his spine like some scurrying creature, and he felt the hairs on the back of his neck stand on end. Directly in its centre, there appeared a bruised and bloody head. In Jack's dazed state it took some seconds fully to comprehend the object in his view, but as the details resolved themselves, he saw that the head was connected to the crouching figure of a man who sat shivering on his bunk with his arms wrapped around his knees. Jack saw immediately that he had been badly beaten: his tattered clothes hung from his bent form in shreds, his head and shoulders were blackened with congealed blood, and the raw flesh around his bruised face glistened in the reflected light. The face was so swollen that at first Jack did not recognise it, but then in a terrifying flash of realisation, he saw that it was Ben Procter, the young first-timer from his own crew.

'Ben!' Jack gasped incredulously, stunned to see the boy in such a state.

His first instinct was to leap from his bed to go to the young man's aid but as his feet hit the ground the chains snapped taut, yanking his legs from under him and sending him headlong onto the unyielding stone of the floor. His hands stung agonizingly as they took the impact and he yelled out in pain. He reached out desperately, struggling to span the remaining distance to his friend while the shackles cut deeply into his flesh. But even at full length he was still a yard short, and for a while he lay there, eventually propping himself up on his elbows, as the boy continued to gaze blankly into the shaft of light, like a frightened animal caught in a lantern's glare.

'Oh Jesus! Ben, what have they done to you?' Jack called breathlessly. He saw his friend's eyes shift in the dark slits between his blackened eyelids, but there was no reply. 'Ben!' he called again but with the same response. 'Listen to me, Ben,' he cried, now in a more urgent tone. 'We both have to get through this! Don't give up on me; we need to be strong. Come on boy, speak to me!' he called imploringly.

At last, Ben stirred, and a look of recognition entered his eyes. He lifted his head off the cradle of his knees and smiled pathetically.

'Jack,' he breathed, with a catch in his throat. 'Oh, Jack!' He licked his swollen lips and perked up, suddenly seeming anxious to explain himself almost as if it were an apology.

'I tripped...' he spluttered. 'I tripped as we ran for it across the rocks, ...my leg got trapped between the boulders...and...and they were on me before I could get myself free.'

Ben's stricken face creased in wretchedness and his voice faltered while he struggled to breathe; he seemed desperate to continue but his strength was clearly failing fast. Seeing him so weak, Jack began to be concerned for his young friend's life; he wanted to embrace his friend, to comfort him, to help him to hang on, but he could not get any closer, and lay impotently just out of reach. The boy rallied himself, speaking again in a fragile and slurred voice:

'The others... got away,' he said, his breathing very laboured. 'No one... was brought down here with me at any rate. They...they threw me in this cell and beat me. They wanted names, Jack, but they got nothing out of me,...I promise you that.' He uttered this defiantly through gritted teeth. 'Then I saw you dragged in and thrown to the floor. I.... I thought you dead at first,' he said convulsing into a coughing fit that brought a goblet of some dark liquid to his lips that he spat onto the floor.

There was a pause while Ben brought his breathing under control. 'My interrogator followed you in... Smyke, the others called him - he was the roughest of them all... I think my ribs got broken from his kicking. He sent the other officers away, then slammed the door and laid into you like a madman, all the time raving...calling you a murderer. I swear he was trying to put an end to you there and then. But then the others came back in and he stopped. They dragged you onto your bunk and chained you up, and they've not been back since. You'd already be a corpse but for them, Jack.'

It was at this point in his young friend's fractured report that Jack got his first inkling of what might lie in store for him, and his heart missed a beat in a sudden pang of dread. He remembered the name Smyke being shouted by the young officer shot at point blank range; it seemed clear now that Smyke had intended Jack slain so as to leave no witnesses to this cold-blooded murder. That he had survived had surely been a lucky accident, but now this madman must want to finish the job to save his own skin. 'But what drove him to such brutality in the first place?' he wondered.

He cast his mind back further and remembered the shadowy attack he had watched in horror as he lay on the cliff top before his reckless dash to the rescue. He now knew the identity of the aggressor; 'but who was the victim, and what has become of him?' he wondered. Whoever it had been, it seemed likely that he must have perished too. Jack's mind thus raced, trying to comprehend what might have lain behind Smyke's murderous rampage, but he could not fathom it at all. His prospects suddenly seemed as bleak and as cold as the stone floor upon which he still lay and, at last feeling the chill penetrating to his bones, he lifted himself up and dragged himself painfully back to his bunk where he slumped exhausted. But then a sudden thought hit him and he sat up again sharply:

'The ground party, Ben, did they all get clear?' he called urgently, as thoughts of his family and the two sisters cascaded into his mind as if suddenly released from the restraint of his earlier preoccupations.

'I... I think so, Jack, but...' The youngster hesitated for some moments, his breathing catching in his throat as if obstructed, '...but I

think I heard women's voices when I was first brought in; most likely...
some other poor sorts locked up here like us to rot.' His voice had
become very weak as he spoke these last words, faltering then fading
completely at the end, as his head sagged then sank onto his knees. But
his report of women's voices brought a further painful turn to Jack's
apprehension, and his sense of dread increased with the awful
presentiment that Elizabeth and Rose might even now be suffering just as
he.

'Ben!' he called desperately. 'I must tell you what I know... what
happened at the cliff top, so that if I am not believed, or ...or if I do not
make it out of here, then our people will hear the true story. You'll only
be charged with smuggling and so must soon be freed, and then perhaps
the truth will prevail - at least at home...'

But there came no response from the shivering figure crouching on
the bunk opposite. Jack called to his young friend again, but there came
no reply; he called a third time, louder and more desperately now, but still
there came no answer. Frantic to reach him, Jack jumped from his bunk
again and yanked and tugged at his chains like a man possessed, but to no
avail; the chains were anchored so firmly in the wall that they could not
be shifted. He screamed for help; his voice booming in the cavernous
emptiness of the room; but if anyone outside heard his cries, they did not
choose to answer. Eventually, Jack sank back onto his bunk exhausted,
sweating, cursing in exasperation, and for some time he sat watching the
figure crouching on the other bed knowing in his heart that his young
friend was dying.

The shaft of light moved on as the earth spun on its axis and
eventually it faded and died, with darkness once more returning to the
cell. Jack tried a few more times to rouse his friend calling into the black
void, but got nothing in reply. And in the nightmare of his situation, his
tormented mind was suddenly gripped with the possible consequences of
what he had been told, made worse now by his worries for Elizabeth and
Rose. But while he was concerned for them, he feared for himself more.
Smyke would want him dead, that was very clear, but the alternative was
already obvious too: if he survived this abandonment, he would be set up
to take the rap. Sentences for smuggling had never been harsh, more
likely to be a fine than imprisonment, but for murder he would hang.

It was not until he became aware that the shaft of light had reappeared
that he realised that he must have slept and that a further night must now

have passed. His first thought was of Ben and he called out instinctively into the gloom. The focus of the light had not yet reached his friend and so Jack could not see him clearly; he was only visible as a shadowy crouching form sitting silently and motionless in the semi-darkness. But when at last the shaft alighted upon Ben's face, any lingering hope that Jack had harboured was cruelly extinguished, for there was no vestige of life remaining; and underneath his young friend's bruises, a pallid translucence had seeped into his skin.

'Ben!' Jack cried out distraught, but he knew at once that he would never again hear his friend's boyish voice.

'Ben, my young, *dear* friend...' he spoke sadly into the empty, echoing space and was immediately overcome with a terrible grief that brought his shaking hands to grip his weeping face in abject despair. How long he wept in memory of Ben's cheerful innocence and good nature, he could not reckon, but eventually he became aware of a pain in his bladder and he stood up to relieve himself against the wall. As he urinated, his empty stomach churned sickeningly, the ghastly image of Ben's battered body frozen into rigormortis hovering before him wherever he looked. Suddenly he felt nauseous and faint and was seized as if by a cold hand, his body becoming wracked in violent convulsions as he retched repeatedly. But there was nothing but acrid slime in his stomach to come up.

Jack would watch the shaft of light traverse his cell twice more before he heard another sound. Each time he would watch the light pass across his dead friend's face – and each time he would cry out as he looked upon its features. And by the fourth day, Jack himself was failing fast and falling into delirium.

The shrill scrape of rusty bolts sliding in the iron door penetrated Jack's fading consciousness as he lay inertly on his bunk. He had a dim awareness of what followed, but at first it felt more like another ghastly hallucination to his tortured and demented mind.

The door was thrown back with such force that it hit the wall with a resounding crash, and Smyke came in accompanied by two customs' officers as big and ponderous as himself. The three men took a cursory look at the curled-up corpse on the other bed, poking it as if to confirm that no life remained; then Smyke broke away and came across to examine Jack. It occurred to him later that Smyke had probably hoped to find him dead too. Jack felt, rather than saw Smyke's dark form through gummed-up eyelids barely prised apart with such failing effort. A sense of fearful vulnerability swept over him at his tormentor's overbearing presence; and in the dim light, his black cape and beaked cap gave him the semblance of a carrion crow eying dead meat. The others joined him. They conversed in dull tones. But to Jack's fractured senses, their words echoed incomprehensibly like distant voices in a tunnel. He struggled to sit up and clear his head but did not have the strength and so fell back again exhausted.

'He's alive!' someone said, in surprise. There was a short pause, then Smyke threw a glance across the cell to Ben's lifeless figure on the other bunk. 'Get that body out of here.' He spoke in a curiously matter-of-fact tone. 'Take it to the morgue, wash it down, and straighten it out; the constables must not find him here nor in that state. Then bring this man something to clean himself up, and some food and water to revive him – we can't leave him any longer and he mustn't appear too neglected if he's to go before the magistrate,' he said. 'And clean this place up – it stinks of piss and shit!'

Turning on his heel, Smyke left the cell leaving his two men to struggle out awkwardly with Ben's stiffened corpse. To Jack, watching blearily from his bunk, it seemed surreal. After some minutes left alone and feeling oddly at peace, Jack was conscious that someone had re-entered the cell. He turned his head and saw one of the men carrying a bucket, a jug, and a wedge of bread and other morsels of food on a plate, all of which he placed indifferently on the floor beside Jack's bed. Then, without warning, Jack was startled out of his reverie by a cold wet cloth thrust into his face and rubbed around violently. A stab of pain shot through his head as the man's rough hands made contact with his wound, and he heard himself groan.

'Wash yourself and eat!' said the officer dispassionately, picking up the bucket and heaving its contents vigorously at the wall which Jack had used as his latrine. It was cursory hygiene, for not all the excrement found its way into the cell's central drain, and so the grumbling man had to fetch a second bucket to sluice the remnants away. As the officer busied himself in such bad temper, Jack sat up, holding the wet cloth to his face trying to revive himself.

'Tell me, man, what am I supposed to have done to be held in such inhuman conditions?' Jack pleaded through the cloth. But the officer merely looked at him with a sneer on his face.

'You'll find out soon enough,' he taunted as he departed with his bucket, slamming the heavy door behind him. And once again, Jack found himself in gloomy silence, almost as if the events of the past few minutes had never occurred. After a moment of morbid reflection, Jack responded to the urgent signals from his stomach, and he reached down eagerly, his fingers at last finding the plate and the jug left for him. Within an instant, he had heaved his aching legs over the side of the bunk, picked up the plate and jug from the floor and had set about devouring their contents. He ate and drank like an animal, tearing at the bread and hunks of cold meat with his teeth and gulping down the water ravenously until his belly at last felt full. Then, with a loud belch into the echoing void, he fell back on his bunk, sated, and soon fell into a uneasy doze.

He awoke again to the sound of bolts sliding in the door, and opened his eyes to see Smyke entering, this time accompanied by two different officers whose uniforms identified them as constables rather than Customs officers.

'It's most irregular to have kept him so long, you know,' one of the constables complained haughtily. 'He should've been handed over to us as soon as you arrested him. He looks in a pretty poor state too; what in God's name have you done with him?'

'A Customs matter, officer,' Smyke replied shortly, clearly irritated at the questioning. 'It was vital to keep him isolated while we interrogated him. He murdered two Customs men, for pity's sake! If we'd let you put him inside one of your overcrowded gaols, we'd never have got anything useful out of him about his smuggling network. Anyway, he's all yours now, so be satisfied with that! You can take him straight to the gallows as far as I'm concerned.'

This was a plausible response. But the truth of the matter was that Smyke had had no better idea of how to deal with the surviving Jack other than to hold him in isolation in the hope that he would die from his pistol wound and his beating, hastened by the cold and damp of the cell. Or perhaps he thought he might get another chance to silence the only living witness to his crimes. But since neither eventuality had come to pass, and with such a hue and cry from an outraged population to bring the killer of Middleton and Hayes to justice, he could wait no longer. He would thus have to employ other methods to save himself from the noose.

The constable did not look entirely convinced at Smyke's bluff, but shrugged resignedly as he leant to place iron armlets on Jack's wrists.

From the tone of the constable's disapproval, however, Jack sensed an opportunity to level accusations of his own, hoping that Smyke might betray himself with a guilty reaction in the presence of officers of the law. He thus tried to rally himself to speak out and struggled weakly against the hands that handled him so roughly. But in his lame state he was quickly restrained, and his thoughts were so disjointed after so much isolation that when he tried to articulate his words, it came out as a mad rant.

'He's a cunning one,' Smyke retorted mockingly. 'He spins this cock and bull story about me, yet he all but killed me too. I thank God still to be alive!'

And unfortunately for Jack, the constables seemed completely in agreement with this.

Thus the die was cast for Jack Easton, but it was not until the following day, as he waited for his committal hearing in the basement cells below the magistrate's courtroom in Melcombe, that he was to learn who else would join him as co-defendants.

The cells in Melcombe had the single advantage over those in Portland Castle of being reasonably illuminated, although it is true that the light was of the dismal, rather than of the bright and cheerful kind, coming as it did down a barred delivery chute directly from the level of the busy street outside. The light thus flickered constantly with passing pedestrians, horses, and carriages, whose feet, hooves, and rims respectively clattered noisily on the cobbled pavement above. The architect of this historic building, formally a guildhall but now drafted into civic use, had neglected to allow adequately for drainage in the basement, not anticipating the use to which it might eventually be put. Consequently, when rainwater found its way in through the opening or by seepage through the subterranean walls, it pooled in stagnant rivulets between the stones. In the centre of this space, and thus straddling the sodden area, there were four cells, constructed like cages from iron bars such that each was joined to the other on two sides. In one of the cells, perched on a wooden bench to save his feet from the damp, sat Jack alone and apprehensive. He had been in that state for some hours without any communication from his gaolers, when there came the sound of a key turning in a lock. He heard the hinges scrape as the door was pulled open, but, by then, he was past caring who might enter and so did not look up. But then he heard a gasp and his name called out, and this caught his attention immediately.

'Jack… Jack, is that you?'

It was the voice of Elizabeth, but spoken with such frail timorousness that it shocked him. Jack looked up startled, afraid of what he might see. It was worse than he had feared; the dishevelled figures of Elizabeth and Rose stood forlornly at the open door with the guard hovering behind them. Elizabeth stared back at him aghast, her pale blue eyes reddened from lack of sleep, her fair hair matted by her own sweat. At the sight of him, she clutched her grimy face and broke down into a fit of unrestrained sobbing. Jack's heart went out to her. His first instinct was to take her in his arms, to comfort her like a hurt child, but, of course, the bars prevented him, and he shook the cage angrily at his impotence.

'Elizabeth! Oh God, what have they done to you?' he called helplessly.

Meanwhile, Rose comforted her sister, her arm wrapped around Elizabeth's waist in support; her dark features looked more composed, but clearly she had suffered too; and their sullen expressions and crumpled clothes betrayed the discomfort that both must have endured. The two women were pushed into the adjacent cell by the constable who seemed to take pleasure in slamming its door closed and jangling his keys provocatively as he found the lock. For Jack, whose fears for Elizabeth and Rose had wishfully, until this moment, been displaced by hope as the days of his confinement had passed, it was a crushing disappointment. He clutched the bars separating their adjacent cells, contrite and ashamed:

'I'm so sorry that you've been caught up in this,' he murmured, mortified that two such innocents had become entangled in the dirty game in which he and his family had played the leading part.

'You should never have been there that night - it was insane of Luke to involve you, and I should never have permitted it,' he said in bitter self-reproach.

Elizabeth looked at him pathetically and again broke into tears, burying her head in Rose's bosom.

Rose spoke for them both, her dark eyes levelling directly at his: 'There's more to this than we know, Jack, you can't blame Luke or yourself,' she said calmly over Elizabeth's sobbing head. 'Some evil was abroad that night, and we've been engulfed by its consequences, I'm sure of that.'

The constable sniffed indifferently and shuffled towards the door, muttering carelessly: 'You'll all be called this morning.'

The three prisoners waited until the constable had closed the door behind him and then embraced each other as best they could by reaching through the bars.

'Jack, you're to be charged with the deaths of the two men on the cliffs,' Elizabeth exclaimed tearfully. 'The newspapers are making so much fuss about it. They say that you will certainly hang.'

She seemed terrified as her eyes searched his as if imploring him to refute the statement, but then she was distracted by the dirty dressings around his head, and her hand went up instinctively to touch it.

'What have they done to you?'

In bitter tones, Jack told the two women of the cliff top events of that fateful night; of his cruel abandonment in the dark cell of the castle; and of Ben's horrible and lonely death with not a single hand, not even his own, raised to help him.

'That man Smyke will pay for this,' he said at last with quiet determination. 'Whatever evil scheme he had in his perverted mind that night, he has set me up to die for it. But what of *you*? I hoped and prayed that you'd get clear; I can hardly bear to see you in this state!'

The sisters told him of their capture, speaking in turn, each adding some detail to the story as it occurred to them until the whole picture became clear. They had watched Jack's boats approach in the moonlight while all had appeared calm, then looked on in horror as armed men had rushed the shore and the shooting had broken out. With Luke elsewhere and being unsure what best to do, they had perhaps dallied too long, and when they had come eventually to try to escape, they had found their route already crawling with Revenue men. For a time, they had successfully hidden in the ruins of Rufus Castle hoping to remain undiscovered while all hell broke loose around them. Unluckily they were eventually found and apprehended.

'We have been so cruelly treated, Jack,' said Elizabeth clearly still in a state of heightened distress. 'And there is one officer above all, this same man Smyke as you describe, who seemed even to take pleasure in it; while at the same time he taunted us that you would hang for the murder of his colleagues,' she added almost coming to tears. 'Whatever the truth of it, it seems his version has already been heralded as fact in the newspapers.'

At this, Elizabeth broke down into a further bout of bitter weeping, comforted by her sister, while Jack looked on helplessly. Rose met his concerned glance above her sister's bowed and sobbing head.

'May Heaven preserve us all, Jack,' she said evenly.

The hearing before the magistrate was brief for it had already been determined that the case would be committed to the Dorchester assizes because of the seriousness of the charges. With their hands shackled and with a constable at both ends of the line, Jack, Elizabeth and Rose were brought up a narrow staircase into the dock from the basement cells below. The room was rectangular in shape, lofty to its ornately decorated ceiling, and clad with depressingly dark oak panelling to three-quarters of its height. A long table stood in the centre of the room, and it was towards one end of this that the threesome was now ushered. At the opposite end of the room, half concealed behind a high bench, a sombrely dressed magistrate sat imperiously in an elaborately carved chair fashioned to resemble a modest throne. He sat head bowed, apparently engrossed in some papers, while the clerk stood before him addressing him confidentially. The three prisoners thus stood unacknowledged and bewildered under the hostile gaze of the disdainful faces in the public galleries on either side of the room. Not even afforded the simple dignity of shaving for the five days of his imprisonment Jack was a wretched sight; his clothes and bandages were filthy and his face pale and haggard with deprivation. The two sisters looked little better; their clothes creased and dirty, their faces smudged with grime, their hair dishevelled and unkempt. This is how the representatives of the newspapers would paint them in their evening editorials. In the eyes of the reporters, the three were already guilty of the most terrible of crimes.

Jack tried hard to gather his wits, searching vainly for a friendly face amongst the onlookers, but saw only leers or haughty condescension instead. He failed to see his father and Albert Dale sitting glumly silent amongst the restless crowd.

Then, in front of him, at the opposite end of the table, he recognised the smug face of Smyke and, forgetting his restraint, he lunged forward, throwing the constables off balance as a rush of spontaneous anger welled up within him. He shouted angrily:

'That man there is the one who should be standing here today!'

But the constables were quick to restrain him as all eyes in the court stared in self-righteous and affronted condemnation.

'Mr Easton, you will restrain yourself!' the magistrate called from his lofty seat, then shifted his glance towards the now standing Smyke. 'Mr Smyke, it is you who bring the charges I believe? Kindly relate them to the accused,' he ordered.

Smyke cleared his throat self-importantly.

'Your Worship, I bring several charges against the man facing you. Charges of the most serious nature against officers of the Crown: those of killing, assault, and smuggling. And against the two women: I bring the charge of aiding and abetting in those felonies.'

'And will you produce sufficient evidence of these crimes, Mr Smyke?'

'Your Worship, I myself was a witness; indeed, I was assaulted in the affray and suffered badly from it. And I will produce other officers who took part in the operation who will testify as to the parts played by the accused. I can also produce evidence of the contraband recovered.' Smyke looked grim - he was now in his stride and continued fluently:

'I believe that you will already know, Your Worship, that a senior officer was pushed to his death that night and that a brave young man was killed in his duty trying to apprehend the male criminal standing before you. Both officers tragically leave stricken families behind them as a result of his murderous attack.'

If the magistrate was moved by Smyke's accusations, he did not show it, and only the scratching of his feathered-quill on parchment broke the period of silence that followed. Jack shook his head in disbelief, a sense of helplessness rising in him like panic; and Rose and Elizabeth were stunned into uncharacteristic speechlessness by the accusations as they stared at the accuser wide-eyed and mouths agape. The magistrate looked up gravely, swinging his gaze between the three standing defendants.

'John Easton, Rose and Elizabeth Dale, there is clearly a case for you to answer and the charges are indeed most serious; you shall therefore all be sent for trial before a judge.'

A buzz of comment ran along the public seating.

'Order!' demanded the magistrate.

'A date for next quarter sessions, Clerk, if you please.'

'Two weeks from today, Your Worship, on the seventeenth in Dorchester,' came the reply.

'Then you will all go to trial at the next quarter sessions in Dorchester on the seventeenth,' the magistrate continued. 'Until then, because of the seriousness of the charges against you, you will be remanded into custody. Do you understand?'

Jack was enraged. 'All I understand is that I am innocent of killing those men, and these ladies had nothing to do whatever with any crime that night,' he spat vehemently.

'Then you will have the chance to prove it at your trial, Mr Easton,' replied the magistrate coolly. 'Constables! Take them down if you please.'

Chapter Six

Fourteen days remanded in custody would have been punishment enough, but it was merely the beginning of the suffering that was to follow for Jack and the two sisters. It is difficult to exaggerate the conditions of unspeakable filth and deprivation in which prisoners were kept in that terrible place, and the new inmates were but three of many unfortunate and unhappy souls who learned to fight for their survival there. And in that desperate struggle, against starvation, against disease, against the inexorable loss of sanity that such conditions made almost inevitable, the battle for honour and decency had already been lost. It was clear that the rule of the strong already prevailed amongst that sad cohort as Jack and the two sisters arrived; and Jack was quick to see that the burden of protecting his companions would fall to him alone, for they would not survive without him. The gaolers too were a law unto themselves; their income callously extracted from their inmates to whom little but the merest sustenance was available without charge. And those who could not pay or barter stole from those who could, or withered from malnutrition. The lucky ones got to stick their hands out through the begging grate to receive the paltry scraps handed down from kindly passers by; but it could never be enough. Typhus stalked amongst the lice and fleas that found the squalor such a happy breeding ground, and many souls would perish in its deadly embrace. Some who had the stomach for it, earned favours from the guards by carrying out the bodies of those who had succumbed; but not all those who they carried so zealously away had quite given up the ghost, and a lonely death awaited them in the cold company of those piled up ready for the paupers' hole. But if those still clinging to life in the squalor of the gaol were sufferers, then most were also victims in life's lottery even before they had arrived, forced by starvation into desperate acts in order to survive, living like the detritus in the gutters in which they foraged in order to eke out their sorry lives. Like some Breugel scene, it was a squirming underworld of ugly depravity in which man, woman, and child alike might lose the last vestiges of humanity in the daily struggle to exist; and to the three young Portlanders, on whose bright island nothing of the like could be imagined, it was a hell on earth.

There being neither the right nor the availability of legal assistance, counsel for the unhappy threesome came only from their fathers who managed to call upon them only once during the fortnight after an extortionate payment, pressed grudgingly into the grasping and grimy hand of the head warder. To the disconsolate inmates who received them, bleak images of that one hurried conversation with their fathers, made inconsolable and distraught in their helplessness, would return to haunt them in future nightmares: loving hands reaching out; the desperate embraces through cold iron bars; whispered consolation and messages of love; and packages passed furtively, while acquisitive and hungry eyes looked on.

And for a tearful George Easton, it was also absolution that he unconsciously sought from his son; for the seed of guilt was growing within him that he was to blame for their predicament. Still in a state of shock, he had not yet heard the inner voice that would accuse him later; for it cannot be denied that had he been more vigilant, he might have forestalled the tragic consequences which were now unfolding. Whatever other skulduggery had been afoot that night, with more attention he might have prevented the catastrophe that threatened such frighteningly uncertain consequences. He wanted so desperately to hold his son in his arms and feel the reassurance that Jack did not blame him, but, in the circumstances, he was able to do neither.

'I shan't contest the charges of smuggling, father,' Jack said earnestly, trying to lift his father's evidently low spirits. 'It would be foolish to do so, and I hope that my honesty will add credence to my plea on the capital charges. I shall simply tell the truth of what happened and trust in the Lord that the jury will believe me.'

George Easton nodded grimly and tried to sound reassuring: 'It'll be one man's word against another's, Jack. The jury should not convict without corroboration, and if you tell it as you saw it - Smyke will surely be seen for the killer that he is.' But with no witnesses to counter Smyke's accusations, both men knew that justice could be a fickle mistress, and neither son nor father felt himself able to look the other in the eye.

Then Elizabeth and Rose, tearful from their adjacent conversations with their father moved closer while Albert Dale himself hovered in the shadow of George Easton's shoulder, a handkerchief clutched to his nose. He seemed in a worse state than his daughters as he looked upon them through reddened eyes unable to tear his uncomprehending gaze away.

'And what have we done to deserve such awful treatment, Mr Easton?' pleaded Elizabeth, barely holding on to her composure while Rose stood stoically by her side.

'There is some terrible game afoot, Elizabeth my dear,' Easton replied softly, reaching through the bars to hold her hand. 'I fear that you dear ladies have been tarred by the murders committed that evening, even though you were merely onlookers. You must try to keep your spirits up; and never fear,' he said bravely, 'we'll see you soon again in the bosom of your loving family.' He tried to sound confident, but sadly, subsequent events would prove him wrong.

During the torment of the following days and nights in that squalid hole, the three captives suffered so terribly that little respite came from the oblivion of sleep. All three unhappy souls sank yet deeper into abject despondency, trapped within a degrading and debilitating process from which they began to fear they would never escape; a process which would allow the truth to be perverted, even turned upon its head. Yet from that one bittersweet paternal visit, they were at least sustained with just enough physical and spiritual replenishment to see them through their ordeal.

At last, the day of the trial arrived, for which the notification was sprung upon them without warning or chance for preparation even as their rudimentary morning ablutions were attended to. The downcast threesome were hastily roped together with others from that terrible pit who would also face trial on this day of judgement and brought into a courtroom administered by a visiting judge from the capital. In the normal manner of such events, this would be a parade of miscreants to which judge and jury would dispense justice with amazing speed such that all would in turn be tried, judged, sentenced, and dispatched to their fates by lunchtime. Jack led the procession into the long dock, his jaw locked in tight-lipped defiance. New bandages now covered his wound, and his father's clean top-coat, exchanged for his own, had restored a little of his damaged self-respect. Elizabeth looked terrified, her doleful eyes darting here and there, glancing around the courtroom like a frightened spaniel, while Rose held herself stiffly upright, her face fixed in an impassive and unrevealing mask. The five others who entered behind them, a rag-bag of ruffians and sundry felons, seemed more resigned; they had evidently been in court before. The procession halted when all had entered the dock and, as the gate was closed behind them, they turned and sat obediently at the stern instruction of the constables who watched vigilantly, batons in hand. Concerned for Elizabeth's mental state, Jack turned to find her eyes welling with tears and her lips quivering in fright; he reached out for her hand, but his manacles were chained to the belt around his waist, and so he could not make the distance. Instead, he held her eyes in earnest intensity, attempting to steady her, while at the same time struggling to quell his own unease that even now turned in his stomach and caused his flesh to tremble.

Below him, in the well of the court, a few clerks in wigs and gowns conferred calmly, their dusty books piled untidily around them; to them this was just another working day. To their left, the twelve men of the jury sat elevated neatly in two rows of six, their well-cut clothes and tidy perukes identifying them as gentry or the well-to-do of the town, their aloof countenances, masks of propriety. Jack studied these prim faces as they studied his across the separating space; and he wondered whether there were any amongst them who had not already made up their minds.

The public seating occupied the entirety of a steeply raked mezzanine floor, formed in the shape of a horseshoe that arced around the room on three sides. In the front row of the centre section of this construction, having a clear view of the dock and its occupants, the four Easton and Dale parents and Jack's brother, Luke, sat together in subdued and apprehensive silence. Jack glanced up and saw that they returned his glance, but he could do no more than nod weakly in their direction, expressionless in his anxiety. Jack noticed too, but did not recognise, a young Revenue officer in uniform sitting quietly nearby whose head and shoulders rose markedly above those of his neighbours making him rather prominent in the front row. In the rows behind, leaving not one single seat unfilled in the whole of the public gallery, a colourful assortment of townsfolk variously stared, jostled, and chatted in cheerful anticipation of an entertaining day - a discordant din on a sober occasion where at least one man in the room would be fighting for his life.

At length, a door to one side of the elevated bench at the head of the room opened and a clerk called 'All rise' in a piercing voice. The chatter stilled abruptly as the imposing scarlet-clad and bewigged figure of the judge swept in and, acknowledging his clerk with a curt nod, promptly took his seat. There was some evident uncertainty amongst the crowd as to whether to follow his example, resulting at first in some untidy restlessness in the public seats, but this quickly settled into an expectant hush as the clerk introduced the first of the cases to be heard. With the calling of the first charge, it became clear that it was the intention of the court to dispense with the matters appertaining to the five other miscreants before proceeding to those of the more notorious threesome. And in their turn, all five of these bit-players in the prelude to the awaited drama pleaded their innocence to an assortment of offences ranging between a bungled highway robbery to the stealing of a chicken. They were a cocky and wily bunch of rogues whose earnest denials might have convinced the untutored as to their honesty, but would not sway the jurymen who had most likely heard it all before. All were found guilty on the uncorroborated evidence of those who had brought the charges, and the five delinquents were thus dispatched in turn to suffer public punishment by flogging, pillory, or the stocks. And all this was accomplished in the space of less than forty minutes, while Jack and the two sisters watched, troubled that the sword of justice had not shown itself especially willing to dally on the finer points of law. Then, after a brief adjournment to allow the ageing judge to relieve the pressure on his bladder, it was their turn to face Smyke, acting both as prosecutor and chief witness, and portrayed in the popular press as the wounded hero and champion of all honest folk of England.

This was a trial in which truth would not prevail against the frenzy of public outrage that followed the death of two of His Majesty's customs officers; and also a trial at which the judge lost control of the courtroom on more than one occasion while the mob bayed for Jack's blood at every one of Smyke's perverse accusations. Jack's account was simply and honestly put, but his earnest words were shouted down by the crowd and ridiculed by Smyke; and importantly, there was no evidence to support it. Unfortunately for Jack, prejudice against him had already so seriously taken hold, that without legal counsel to present his case more eloquently, his own nervous articulation could not possibly sway those already predisposed to think otherwise. His protests at Smyke's outrageous lies seemed lost like cries for help in the face of a storm until, worn down by the effort of making himself heard, he gave up trying, placing his fate instead in the hands of the Lord and wanting only to preserve the little dignity he had left. Smyke, on the other hand, told his untruths with easy assurance: he had seen everything clearly even as he lay badly beaten on the ground. First, he had watched Easton wrestle Middleton over the cliff to his death, and then he had watched him shoot Hayes with one of Smyke's own pistols wrenched from his belt. Smyke's touching and seductive portrayal of Hayes' courageous retaliation was pure theatre, which drew a murmur of admiration from the court. Without the young officer's bravery, Smyke asserted, the murderer might never have been caught, and it would thus be disrespectful to this brave and loyal officer's memory to believe Easton's preposterous story. Furthermore, that the smuggling episode was uncontested was surely indictment enough of Easton's character. A confessed criminal, after all, could not possibly be trusted to tell the truth. Smyke's evidence had the advantage too of being supported by the officers who were first to arrive on the scene: they had testified as to the positions of Hayes' and Easton's bodies and the two spent weapons at their sides. If the jury had not already been convinced of Jack's guilt before, then this powerful (if circumstantial and, as we know, contrived) evidence could not but influence them towards Smyke's version of events. 'Surely, members of the jury,' he concluded earnestly, 'there can now be no remaining doubt of his guilt in your minds?'

After thus disposing with his arguments on the primary case, Smyke now turned his attention to the two young women sitting at Jack's side who had listened to the earlier malediction with mounting alarm. Their inconsequential part in the affair was unmercifully exaggerated, causing both sisters to shrink in horror at the sordid images painted of themselves as Jack's smuggling collaborators scheming to profit handsomely from their night's dirty work. They refuted it of course, tearfully indeed, but the evident scepticism on the faces of the jury showed their protests had fallen on deaf ears; Smyke's poisonous invective had turned the trial into a rout. And when Albert Dale stood to speak on their behalf, his brave words were received with equal derision, just as George Easton's entreaties for his son had been scoffed at earlier - as nothing more than a father's natural defence of his wayward children. Thus the trial was brought to its close with the great majority of those present clearly under the impression that the case against the defendants had been convincingly made.

In the jury room, however, it emerged that not all the members of the jury had been convinced of Jack's guilt, at least not beyond reasonable doubt. Jack's apparent sincerity and consistency under cross-examination by the judge had impressed two of their number enough for them to resist a guilty verdict on the capital charges. Murder carried an automatic death penalty, but without unanimity it would be difficult for the judge to send him to the gallows; and fortunately for Jack, these stalwarts were not persuaded to change their mind, even in the course of a heated debate that had, unusually for such cases, lasted over an hour. Eventually, a resigned foreman threw in the towel and reluctantly led the jury back into the courtroom to return the majority vote.

'And how were your votes cast?' demanded the judge evenly.

'Two - not guilty, ten - guilty, your honour,' came the slightly peeved reply.

At this, Jack visibly slumped where he sat; from the earlier mood of the court, he had become increasingly resigned that Smyke's competent oratory might swing the jury completely against him, but now, with the split vote he could at least hope that he would not hang. His family and prospective in-laws in the gallery looked uncertain as a wave of noisy protest erupted from the public seats around them, causing them to shrink in apparent dismay.

'Hang him!' shouted someone from behind. 'Drawn and quartered!' yelled another from the side through cupped hands. Smyke also joined vigorously in the objections, shaking his papers violently; but during the enduring uproar, Jack noticed that the uniformed customs officer seen earlier sitting near his parents in the gallery, remained inscrutably still. At length, the judge regained order in the court, his rotund face quite reddened from his repeated calling as he struggled to be heard above the din.

'Members of the jury,' he commanded, once the last murmur had eventually been silenced, 'have you reached a verdict on the third charge of the assault on Mr Smyke himself?'

The foreman stood again.

'Yes, your Honour,' he said   'We find the accused guilty on that charge - unanimously. And on the fourth charge of smuggling to which all three defendants have offered no evidence, we find nothing at all in their favour to mitigate the sentence which your Honour may feel it his duty to make.' This latter statement was beyond the remit of the hapless man, but he had seemed eager to offer it, possibly believing that some gesture was required to mollify the crowd's displeasure at his jury's equivocation on the capital charges. There was some muted applause at this, but it quickly died as the judge stood to announce that he would now retire to consider his sentence.

The judge was neither an unkind man nor was he unwise but, newly appointed to the King's bench, he had a natural desire to avoid controversy especially in a case that had attained such a degree of notoriety that his ruling would undoubtedly be brought to the critical notice of his peers. So great, indeed, was the interest in the trial, for example, that the Dorchester News, normally a weekly news-sheet, had already advertised that they would publish a special 'Trial' edition that evening; and other reports would certainly reach the legal press. He therefore followed a more than usually structured approach in considering the severity of his sentences; and in marshalling his feelings on the matter his reasoning was approximately thus:

Firstly, he had felt sympathetic to the jury's difficulty on the capital charges, for he had not been entirely convinced himself of Easton's guilt: something about Smyke had irked him, and the man's testimony was rather too pat and too theatrical for his liking. Moreover, the two character witnesses, Albert Dale and George Easton, both reputable men of reasonable standing, albeit the parents of the accused, had spoken passionately on Jack's behalf, and this had given him some cause to doubt that Easton would have behaved in the way described. Indeed, in his summing up, he had directed the jury to be careful in their deliberations, since they would be weighing one man's word against another's with only circumstantial corroboration of the facts on Smyke's side. On the other hand, ten of the jurymen had been convinced; and even as judge, he had neither sufficient certainty himself nor adequate grounds to override their judgement, a course that would have been seen as extraordinarily cavalier. In view of the prejudicial publicity, he could ask for a re-trial in the hope of reaching a less equivocal finding; but this would risk a different jury finding Easton unanimously guilty, making it difficult to avoid Easton's execution, a disposal he instinctively wanted to avoid. Without unanimity, he could at least sentence in some other way. If he were too lenient, however, he would certainly be criticised by the population in its clamour for exemplar punishment in such cases. The consequent probability that his reputation (and therefore his career) might be damaged if he were not sufficiently robust also occurred to him, as did the prospect of a riot in the courtroom if he did not please the crowd. And so he found himself torn between his own sympathies leaning towards acquittal, and the jury's majority verdict and public sentiment that seemed to demand execution. This was a dilemma indeed, and one on which he pondered for some time. In the end, his political instincts held sway, but this was one of those occasions in his life on which in due course he would come privately to regret that he had not been more resolute in following the inner voices which spoke to him too quietly at the time.

The judge returned in sombre mood to make his pronouncement to a stilled and expectant courtroom.

'Mr Easton, would you stand,' he ordered eventually, having seated himself and arranged his papers, and he waited as Jack struggled to his feet to the accompaniment of the rattling of his chains. 'You stand convicted on two charges of murder perpetrated against officers of the Crown while in the course of their public duty. These crimes are punishable by execution,' here the judge paused for effect, ' but, as you have heard, the jury's verdict was not unanimous, and I will therefore spare you from the hangman's noose.'

There was an audible groan of dismay from the public gallery; but both he and Jack remained impassive, their glances locked in pregnant anticipation while waiting for the silence to be resumed and communicating feelings to each other which can better be imagined than described. Elizabeth reached up to squeeze Jack's trembling hand as the judge continued:

'On the charge of assault, you have also been found guilty, and you have admitted to the charge of smuggling which aggravates these more serious convictions. On the combination of these offences, my sentence must reflect the grave nature of the crimes carried out, and I am therefore sentencing you to be transported to the American colonies in penal servitude for a period of fourteen years.'

Jack rocked back on his heels as his brow crumpled in a frown; he had not realized that this must be the inevitable outcome of the judge's earlier pronouncement, and his mind reeled in confusion at the potential consequences for his life. He hardly heard the judge as he continued:

'Furthermore, Mr Easton, - smuggling seems to enjoy a sort of popular ambivalence which is difficult to understand given the damage it does to the nation's economy and indeed to its security at a time when any dealings across the Channel, not least those of an illegal nature, give succour to an enemy and undermines our defence.' This was the official line from the capital being trotted out here by an individual whose closest friends in London would know to be a hypocrite (at least as far as his regular consumption of contraband French brandy was concerned).

'Others must see that such activities will not be tolerated, and therefore you, Easton, must be made an example.' He said this adopting an admonishing tone, then paused for effect while hoping that his imminent pronouncement would be seen to be sufficiently harsh to quell the continuing unrest he detected in his larger audience.

'I am therefore going to add to your sentence the condition that you never again be permitted to return to this country. In other words, Mr Easton, you are to be exiled for life.'

Jack's face paled visibly.

'And furthermore, Mr Easton, I must warn you that if you are discovered attempting to set foot upon these shores again, you will be hanged forthwith without further trial.' The judge paused, feeling some satisfaction as a chorus of muted approval rippled through the public gallery; it seemed, for the moment, as if he had found a satisfactory compromise; indeed, to some, banishment to the colonies would represent a fate worse even than death. 'Constable, take him down if you please.'

Jack was led down the steps in a daze, blind to the horrified faces of his family and deaf to any sound save that of his own heartbeat. There then followed a short hiatus in the proceedings during which papers in the courtroom were shuffled importantly before it was the turn of Elizabeth and Rose to stand before the judge; and they did so in trepidation, still in a state of shock after hearing Jack's fate determined.

'Caroline Rose Dale and Dorothy Elizabeth Dale,' the Judge began, 'you have offered no satisfactory evidence to refute the charge of aiding and abetting a smuggling operation in which two officers tragically lost their lives, and therefore for the same reasons, you too will be transported to the American Colonies in servitude.' The judge's last words were delivered in such an indifferent tone that he might have been telling his clerk that it was time for lunch, which may be what he had in mind in view of the hour. 'However, in view of your lesser role,' he continued with a little more compassion, 'you will serve there for only four years after which you may return to these shores - that is assuming that you perform your duties satisfactorily and that your return is at your own expense and risk.'

Elizabeth's knees buckled as she fainted, but Rose caught her and guided her to the floor, crying out angrily as she went down on her knees: 'You don't know what you do! Your minds have been bent by that man's clever words!' She shot a vehement glare at Smyke who watched dispassionately from across the room with a supercilious sneer upon his face. Her bitter words were all but drowned out by the unsympathetic uproar that had arisen in the public benches, but there was no ambiguity in the fierceness of her accusation for any who could see her face. The constables rushed into the dock to pull the pair to their feet and hustle them roughly down the stairs to join Jack waiting miserably in the cells below. Amidst the din and the commotion, the five relatives sat in sombre silence staring uncomprehendingly at the scene. But a few in the room, the judge and Andrew White amongst them, took note of Rose's defiance, and their thoughtful faces showed that they had been struck by the directness of her charge; and for just a moment they wondered how close to the mark her words had come. For the time being, their pangs of unease would quickly pass, but for the unhappy threesome locked once more in the gloomy isolation of the basement cell, nothing would ever be the same again.

Chapter Seven

The funerals of the two dead officers were conducted jointly at All Saint's church in the nearby village of Wyke in which both families of the deceased had lived. The church stood on an elevated site so that its tall and castellated tower rose above the roofs of all the village houses; and on top of the tower, the flag of St George hung limply at half-mast in recognition of the sad occasion. From the sloping churchyard adjacent to the church, glimpses of Weymouth Bay could be gained across the rooftops, and, through the headstones and the leaning trees, the outline of Portland was visible as a dark smudge in the misty distance. It was a grey day under a leaden sky, which befitted the sombre mood, but although the ground underfoot was soggy from earlier downpours, it was at present not raining. It seemed that officers of the customs service from the entire south coast must be there, for they outnumbered the grieving families and friends, and dominated the scene; and their dress uniforms glistened with medals and shiny leather belts polished especially for the occasion.

At the burial ceremony that followed a moving service at which a civic dignitary spoke solemnly of duty and sacrifice, a volley of pistol shots would be fired over the graves. It was thought that this would be a fitting tribute to the departed souls, and consequently six officers from the Weymouth office had been chosen to form a firing party. As the now most senior officer in Weymouth, and in recognition of his part in bringing the perpetrator of the crimes to justice, Senior Tide Surveyor Smyke had been put in charge. Amongst the party was Andrew White, Hayes' closest service friend and unofficial mentor; by his glum demeanour, he was the one most visibly affected by his friend's death.

The mournful gathering crowded around the two adjacent graves as the vicar recited the customary prayers after which the families paid their last tearful respects to their loved ones by throwing flowers onto the lowered coffins. A woman's sobbing broke the doleful silence as others shuffled forward to do the same. Some distance behind the assembly, the firing party had already formed up into a military line, and at a signalling glance from the vicar, the waiting Smyke called his men to attention in a quiet voice. Taking this as his prompt, a trumpeter, seconded for the duty from the nearby regiment, lifted his instrument to his lips and played the Last Post in such pure and unfaltering tones that few remained unmoved by its mournful cadences. At last, as the melancholic echoes of the tune's final bar died away, Smyke called the order for his men to cock and raise their weapons. There was a brief interruption in the flow of the drill whilst one of the officers fumbled with his firing mechanism, but soon all were ready to fire their blank charges into the sky. On Smyke's command, the party pulled their triggers in unison, and six flintlocks sprung closed, sending explosions down the line in a ragged and spluttering volley. In the still air, the acrid smoke of gunpowder hung about the men for a while as Smyke called them quietly through the drill for the final presentation of arms.

It was as the firing party was being dismissed to join the throng of other officers, that Andrew White first noticed that the weapon lodged in Smyke's belt was different to those issued to the other officers; its brass butt cap was more highly polished and it seemed a little more ornate. The sight of the weapon evoked an instant curiosity; it reminded him of the weapon which his dead friend Hayes had owned, a weapon handed down to Hayes by his military father. He edged closer trying to make out the decorative feature on the stock; he would recognise that beyond question if it were the same weapon, having studied and admired it in the past at his friend's invitation. But Smyke seemed at once aware of White's interest and brought up his hand as if to cover the weapon from view. He made the move look nonchalant, but White was sure he saw alarm flit across Smyke's face before he quickly turned away. White followed as Smyke melted into the gathering, taking glimpses of the weapon as he circled his subject discretely. Was it mere coincidence, he wondered, that as he did so, he found Smyke's eyes meeting his on more than one occasion? And did he imagine Smyke's anxious glances?

Later, while reflecting on the inconclusive episode, White felt the first stirrings of suspicion in his breast. He had heard Jack Easton's conflicting story from the public gallery at the trial and had been moved by Rose Dale's accusation, but at the time, it seemed inconceivable, preposterous even, that Smyke could have committed so heinous a crime. After all, what possible motive could there have been for him to kill two fellow officers? And would he then have been so reckless as to wear Hayes' pistol at the funeral service, a weapon that must have been stolen on the night even as his friend lay dying or dead? No, surely not, he thought, it was indeed a preposterous notion; he must have been mistaken about the weapon in Smyke's belt; and surely he must have imagined the man's shifty behaviour? Most certainly! But it would be a matter of recurring curiosity to White that he would never again see the weapon in Smyke's belt; and he would also begin to wonder if he might have been duped. The faulty intelligence of the Portland operation had, in retrospect, fallen almost too conveniently into his hands; and although he could not think of any motive, he had been made to look a fool in the eyes of his colleagues with his hopelessly overblown report. Without this fateful document, prepared so eagerly in his impatience to impress, both his friend and his senior officer might still be alive today, and his own promising reputation not stained.

It was coincidental that on the same day as the official funeral for Middleton and Hayes, a less formal funeral service for Benjamin Proctor took place at St Andrew's Church at Wakeham. As has already been described, this Norman edifice stood on a precipice at the foot of the lush valley that descended from the village to the Cove through an opening in the cliffs. Some said it was this opening that had given the Cove its name of 'Church Ope', while others thought it might rather be 'Hope' from what it offered seamen seeking refuge from the sea. But it was not hope that was the pervading sentiment at the gathering on this occasion; the assembly's mood was more one of desolation, guilt, and accusation. The mildewed walls and cobwebbed dilapidation of the ancient church further reinforced this forlorn disposition, which not even the spectacular seascape viewed from its cliff-edge parapets could dispel.

The gathering on this mournful day was not so different in composition to that which had taken place in much happier circumstances not long before at the home of the Dales in Fortune's Well to celebrate the betrothal of Elizabeth and Jack. But the three young people now incarcerated in Dorchester prison would not be attending today and their absence cast a deep shadow on the already gloomy proceedings, worse for some even than the dreadful sorrow which all felt at the loss of young Ben. After a sombre service, the coffin was conveyed with due solemnity by six quarrymen from Jack Easton's gang in which the deceased youngster was a popular apprentice, and lowered gently into its grave. The grieving parents and relatives had led the mournful procession and now stood in tearful introspection at the graveside. Amongst the supporting crowd of fellow mourners gathered around them were the four ashen-faced parents of Jack and the two sisters who took no special place, but who shared the painful poignancy of the moment almost as if they were burying their own. After the priest had muttered his final words of prayer, an awful silence descended which endured for some minutes during which only an occasional sob or sigh could be heard. Most bowed their heads not able to risk another's glance; some at the graveside gazed sorrowfully at Ben's coffin now resting alone in the cold earth, while others stared wistfully across the parapet and down into the Cove where the ambush had taken place. Of all those gathered there, even including the tough and burly quarrymen on whose broad shoulders the coffin had been borne, not many would be clear eyed. At length, the silence was broken by the sound of earth landing on the coffin as Ben's parents said a last and tearful farewell to their young son, whose yet unexplained death they still could not fully comprehend.

For some time after, as others filed past the graveside in similar and respectful duty, there seemed a reluctance to disperse from the graveyard. Instead the mourners gathered in small groups and stood about morosely. One of these groups comprised George and Eleanor Easton, and Albert and Mrs Dale who had followed the former couple in paying their condolences to the grieving family just moments earlier. They stood together rather awkwardly in a curious and embarrassed silence for a while, and then, without even a murmur of excuse, George absented himself and walked to the parapet from which, some moments later, he could be seen gazing thoughtfully out to sea. Eleanor had watched him go but was not at first inclined to follow; yet now she glanced across to him suddenly in concern. Like her own shattered spirits, his had been floored by the prospect of losing a favourite son to the other side of the globe, but now something deeper appeared to preoccupy her husband which had drawn him yet further into himself. Ill at ease in her present company, she made to excuse herself to join him, but in the instant of her departure her eyes met those of her companions and saw in their stiff countenances an expression that, though subtle, conveyed an accusation of betrayal. It is extraordinary how much can be communicated in the slightest cast of an eye, the merest tightness of the lineaments, or the least change in the angle at which the head is held; and in that instant, Eleanor comprehended a shocking notion to which she had been oblivious before. Her husband and her sons would be blamed for the tragedy that had befallen this close community; her men had led them into the disaster that had left a young man dead and had taken two lovely daughters from the bosom of their homes with such frightening uncertainties ahead.

Unsure of whether to be affronted or ashamed, she lamely took her leave of the Dales to join her husband at the parapet on which the two of them sat for a while in a strange isolation of their own making. When Luke had in due course reached the head of the solemn queue of condolence and had taken his turn at casting earth into the grave, he sought his parents out and stood alongside them in a sort of silent communion, not quite knowing what to say. George was the first to break the uneasy silence:

'What could have possessed you, Luke, to take those girls to the castle,' he said hoarsely. 'They should never have been anywhere near - it was an unthinking and vain thing to do, boy!'

'When I heard the firing I tried to get back, father,' said Luke petulantly, bridling at the accusation, 'but I found my way cut off. The Revenue were all over the place; there was no chance for me to get back to them. I tried father, honestly I tried!'

'Well, you try to explain that to the Dale's, boy! You'd better hope that those girls get through all this, or you'll have to answer for it. As it is, our name is blackened on the island - there are some who already regard Smyke's accusations as the truth of it, and as ten of the jurymen found Jack guilty, I cannot blame them!'

And as for the Dales - if their suffering at this moment could not be as acute as that of the Proctors, it came very close indeed. The imminent dispatch of their own precious children to those distant and unknown shores of America, seemed almost as final as death itself. So tentative was their hope of their offspring's survival, so afraid of the terrors that might befall them, that the sum of their fearful uncertainties would mount up over the coming years to make the Proctors' intense but inevitably diminishing grief seem almost a blessing.

At length, the gathering in the churchyard dispersed as the mourners made their way back up the wooded path towards the village in small and silent groups, their dark and sorrowful forms rustling the fallen leaves in the descending gloom of dusk. The Eastons were the last to leave, receiving in all that time not a single word of condolence for the fate of Jack as if some taboo had enshrouded his name; but as they started up the hill, two of the men walking a little way ahead fell back. As the Eastons approached the pair now waiting in the shadows off the path, George slowed to let Eleanor and Luke move ahead.

'You go on, I'll catch up,' he said evenly under his breath.

George recognised the men as his own; men who had been lucky to slip the noose on that fateful night, both of them in Jack's crew who, with Ben, had scrambled ashore when Jack's boat had hit the rocks. In the dim light, they seemed to brood and had a conspiratorial air about them, as if smouldering for some redress.

'We're with you George, no matter what is being said - we know Jack is innocent.'

George heard the words and nodded, but his grainy face betrayed no emotion.

'The constable tol' us that Ben fell in the undercliff as he tried to escape,' continued one of the men, 'and that it was his injuries from this that killed him. But I saw him taken, George, an' I'm pretty sure he never tried nothing - as far as I saw, he went with them like a lamb.'

'And why were we not given his body until four days after?' broke in the other accusingly. 'You should ha' seen his bruises when we got him back, George - I reckon he was beat to death.'

George already knew this from Jack, as he also knew that it was Smyke who was responsible for Ben's death and for the other killings that night, but there was much wild and malicious speculation on the Island. In his sensational and gloating report of the convictions, the editor of the special Dorchester newssheet published on the evening of the trial had unfairly omitted Jack's testimony, but George, debilitated by his guilt, had neither the energy nor the insight immediately to refute the one-sided indictment. Smyke's untruths were thus now well rooted, and it seemed to George that it was already too late for the trajectory of Smyke's lies to be reversed; indeed, his belated protestations had sounded lame even in his own ears, and received suspiciously by his listeners; clearly his account had been too much too late to be believed. A bitter feeling of betrayal - that his own island folk had been so quick to condemn – now burned within him like cholic in his belly and he no longer had the heart to try to persuade them otherwise. 'Let them think what they like and be damned,' he thought angrily. But his spirit had taken a terrible blow.

The loyalty of the two friends who now stood so expectantly before him was touching. Undoubtedly they hoped for a fiery response from their former leader and they seemed ready for a fight, but they would be disappointed. George might well have risen to their call and rallied them, to lead them off on some mission of revenge, but he knew that such an act would be futile and reckless. His assessment was undoubtedly correct, but it was not only this wisdom that stopped him: his resilience had been shattered by a sense of shame that it was he who was responsible for the disaster, and his confidence and courage for such adventures had simply drained away. As organiser and lookout for the operation, he blamed himself for the calamity, as he knew others would be blaming him in the quiet of their parlours. He had resolved never to lead again; he would never again presume to direct young men to risk their lives for the sake of a cheap tot of brandy for others to enjoy, whatever the profit. His failure that night had lost him his beloved son, his successor and his prodigy, and with him, the young man whose death they had mourned today and the two dear daughters of the family his was to have joined by marriage. He had already caught the accusing glances from their grieving parents, initially so outwardly polite and sympathetic to his own loss, and their faces could not hide their reproach. Defeated and demoralised, leaving his two friends with only a doleful look in which he conveyed the most abject and pitiful remorse, George turned and walked away without a word.

Chapter Eight

It was by good fortune that *The Rotterdam* was due to call at Weymouth during the following week on its way to Annapolis, capital of Maryland, one of the thirteen British colonies in America. Had this not been so, Jack and the two sisters might have been forced to suffer the squalor of their filthy and over-crowded prison several months longer while awaiting the resumption of transatlantic crossings in the Spring. Jack had meanwhile become gravely concerned about Elizabeth's deteriorating condition; she seemed to suffer terribly - as much from anxiety and fear as from any fever - and that the former state could precipitate the latter, Jack felt quite certain, especially with Elizabeth now over three months gone. Yet there seemed nothing that he or Rose could do to revive Elizabeth's failing spirits, much as they had tried. Although she had pluckily rallied several times in the days since the trial, no sooner had she risen from her melancholy, the very effort of doing so seemed to put her right back into it. It was as if she had awoken each time from a terrible dream, only to have her hopes dashed again by the grim realities surrounding her. She now lay sleeping peacefully on some tattered rags and straw that served as her bed on the cold stone floor, her head nestling in her sister's lap. Rose, her eyelids drooping in weariness, stared fondly at her sister's features and distractedly caressed her brow. Jack, leaning on a blackened water barrel nearby, looked on thoughtfully. Dearly as he loved her simple gentleness, he needed Elizabeth to be strong, for his own reserves were already low. Rose's stoicism, on the other hand, had impressed him greatly, but Jack feared for them both; their female forms seemed so fragile and vulnerable that he wondered how they could survive the rigours that he knew would lie in store.

He poured himself a mug of water from the barrel and took a swig. Grimacing at its bitter taste, he spat it out in disgust as his attention was drawn to an older couple nearby. Like Rose with Elizabeth, the man cradled his wife's head in his lap; and Jack watched piteously as, with withered and shaking hands, the old man absently removed strands of hair from the woman's pale and still face; she was clearly already dead. Jack could not bear to look at the man's stricken countenance and tore his eyes away, glancing around his prison in sudden and terrified despair; 'how many of these poor devils will survive?' he wondered. In the close confines of this dark dungeon, over thirty men and women fought for air; a morass of tangled humanity lolled and sprawled around him, having let go both dignity and self-respect. All that remained for any of them now was survival; nothing else mattered. Pitiful, ragged unfortunates - thieves, vagabonds, a few abandoned women brought so low as to sell themselves for bread – common people he might have despised had he encountered them in the streets only weeks before. Yet now he had begun to see them in a different light; sharing their suffering, he could not help but feel that they, like him, might rightly bear a grudge against those who had cast them into this bear pit. If his fellow inmates had not been born into these dreadful margins of existence, then powerful and indifferent forces had most certainly driven them into it. And if there were no longer enough honest work for the nation's people, then how else was one expected to survive if not by wit and petty thievery? These were the discarded vassals of a callous ruling class pursuing wealth and power by any means and blind to their suffering.

Jack had felt a growing compassion for these wretched helpless people as they, like he himself, awaited an uncertain and uncomfortable fate. He had watched the embers of resentment and anger first flair and then fade in their eyes, and in the place of that dying fire, he had watched the dull cast of resignation set in. And in their pallid and drawn faces, he had seen the glaze of fatalism drain away the very essence of their lives. If he had not yet succumbed to it, then he already felt its tentacles reaching out stealthily to ensnare him too. His resistance had been subdued by cold and hunger, and with no word from the outside since the trial, his spirits had reached their lowest ebb. It was as if his former world had ceased to exist and all the values and props on which his life had been built, removed. He would eventually come to see this moment as a turning point; it felt as if the counters of his past had been reset to nought; and he knew that he must accept whatever God and fortune would offer him and force himself to grapple with a new beginning, whatever that might be.

He looked again upon the pitiful shapes of Elizabeth and Rose still huddled together in their shared despair, and came to a quiet resolution: for their sake and for his, he would no longer dwell upon a life to which he might never return, the life he could and should have had. Instead he would call upon all the guile, and all the strength and resolve that he possessed to protect them and preserve them until they could be returned to the bosom of their family at the end of their terms. And as for himself, he must make America the land of his future now; and until a new life had been built when he again might become his own master, he must put aside all thoughts of revenge and retribution. The sisters' and his own survival must be his primary goal, and he must secure it whatever trials might lie before him.

On the day before their ship was due to sail, Jack, Elizabeth and Rose were taken with others in their miserable cohort by open cart to the outskirts of Weymouth and then led shackled in a line through the back alleyways of the town - the drivers had apparently not been paid to take them all the way. It was a bright late-October day on which the last residue of summer sunshine and the cold winds of approaching winter mixed in confusion. Bright cumulus charged like bold white stallions across slits of sky formed by the dark and teetering upper storeys overhanging the labyrinthine route. The gutters stank of putrefying waste with all manner of filth left there to rot in puddles of grey liquid that would not drain away. The stampeding clouds threw these squalid passages into a quick alternation of dark and light. In the brightest spells, shafts of sunlight penetrated these dingy caverns to make the greasy lanes a path of glistening slime; but then the hastening cloud would once more throw the alleyways into almost total darkness in which the shuffling line of downcast figures became almost blinded by the contrast.

There were perhaps twenty convicts in all, guarded by half as many red-coated guards from the local regiment who seemed more worried by the mud on their boots than the state of their miserable charges. The male prisoners led the line, with the women following behind, a few of them with bewildered children clinging to their skirts. The two Dale sisters were amongst this second group, walking side by side, both staring fixedly ahead to hide their shame from the glances of passers-by. Elizabeth was clearly struggling to be strong, yet her lips trembled and tears streaked her grimy face. If they thought themselves harshly treated, they would do well to reflect on the fate of others from the prison who had not joined them in their journey and would make a different sort of outing soon enough - by night, piled up on hand-carts, to an unlamented burial in the paupers' grave.

Word of the dismal procession had evidently passed quickly through the back streets, for at every corner a sea of common faces met them to leer and taunt. Some of the prisoners walked on in oblivion, but those still with wits about them found it almost unendurable to be treated so hurtfully as the objects of such abuse. And it was not only hard words that were hurled; a variety of missiles were landed on their wretched targets too, and Jack was one such unfortunate. Hit from behind by something heavy that seemed to split apart on impact, he shuddered as the clammy coldness oozed down the middle of his back and, lurching in revulsion from the stench that simultaneously erupted, he stumbled on the slippery cobbles underneath his feet. 'Am I so hated?' he wondered in despair. 'And what makes the common masses so despicable when they gather as spectators in such self-righteousness to turn on those whose lives have been so blighted?' Their behaviour seemed mindless and ignorant, and had he not feared for his life, he might have pitied them.

Mercifully, it started to rain, and the taunting crowd thinned rapidly as the straggling line reached the more exposed area of the quayside where there was no shelter from nearby buildings. The few tormentors who still followed now were mostly children, but even they lost interest as the shower became a downpour and they bolted for cover, shrieking with laughter as they ran, without a thought in their hollow heads for the miserable souls who had no choice but to trudge on. Then suddenly, Jack felt hands grabbing at him from the side. Instinctively, he ducked, recoiling in anticipation of the blow he felt sure must follow; but instead, he heard his mother's voice and felt her face pressed to his in a fierce embrace; she wrapped her arms around his neck and hugged him so tightly that he stumbled.

' Be strong, my son,' she whispered hoarsely, her voice tremulous. 'We'll wait for you, however long it takes, Jack. Pray God you'll someday return to us.'

Jack felt the warmth of his mother's lips upon his wet cheek and heard her sobbing breath roar in his ear; and then he saw his father push in to embrace him too, his unshaven face tortured with anguish; he was too overcome to speak. Jack could not free his arms to return his parents clinging grip, he could only lean his head towards them, pressing it to theirs, forehead to forehead, as the rivulets of cold rain mingled with their tears.

'Mother! Father!' Jack sobbed, suddenly overcome. He strained to free himself from his ropes, gritting his teeth with the effort, desperate to be rid of the restraint so that he could return their embraces, to hold them in his arms one last time. But at that moment the guards closed in upon them and tore his parents away, throwing them sprawling onto the cobbles of the quay. Jack was enraged at the guards' brutality, and he kicked out angrily; but they responded quickly and leapt upon him, and the rope's tenacious grip allowed him no possibility of escape. He was quickly overpowered; but still struggling against the soldiers' hold as he was forced bodily to move on, he craned his neck to look back, and between the startled faces of those following behind, he caught glimpses of his brother rushing to his parents' aid. The line became ragged for a moment as his wild struggling yanked the taut ropes connecting him to his compatriots - until more guards arrived with their beating sticks and lashed out to regain control. At this, the other captives fell into a sort of cowering obedience, ducking and wincing at the blows brought down upon them, but Jack, defiantly turned once more and shouted back:

'Mother! Father! Luke! Do not forget me!'

He saw them look up, but then a stick came down sharply across his face and a searing pain brought the salty taste of blood into his mouth; he swore at the guards, but he knew that his last words to his family had been spoken. Few others saw the prisoners take their final steps on English soil, but in the distraction caused by Jack's struggling, Elizabeth and Rose had snatched a few last tearful moments with their parents relatively undisturbed.

The Rotterdam was a frequent caller at Weymouth. Primarily a cargo ship employed to bring tobacco from Virginia and Maryland to Europe via Cowes, the local port of entry, she enhanced her profit by delivering settlers to the New World on her outbound journeys. The settlers she conveyed, however, would not be those who could afford better - as a cargo ship, she was not equipped for the manners and expectations of the well-to-do. Those who would occupy her gloomy and cramped decks were forced more by circumstance than choice to endure such discomfort: those who fled persecutions of one sort or another, for whom the odyssey offered life in a more tolerant land; or those whose dreams enticed them to escape the feudal serfdom of a peasant life. A few of these might raise the fare and thus arrive in the new land free to make their way as they pleased in trade or business. But the great majority of the travellers on this ship had perforce contracted themselves to be sold into the service of colonial landowners in exchange for their conveyance. This was gladly done as a way of escaping what they wished to leave behind, but the years of virtual slavery that would follow would make it a high price to pay; and many would pay a yet higher price in their bid for freedom. Nevertheless, the lure was compelling and many would risk it, for once their indentures were served, they would become freemen in a land of new opportunity, many even qualifying for a headright of fifty acres – an infinitely better prospect than they left behind.

Space aboard *The Rotterdam* would also be allocated to another group – the ragged poor and miserably dispossessed, cleared off the land and out of the parish poorhouses and put aboard without redress; people who might otherwise perish in destitution on the city streets. For them, there might at least be a chance of salvation as indentured servants, and their transportation would remove a troublesome underclass from the sight of polite society and save the inconveniences of their upkeep. Grouped with them for similar reasons were the convicts, the underclass, those whose often petty crimes did not warrant a more terminal disposal. Aboard the ship, they would be reviled and shunned by their god-fearing and reluctant companions.

The transportation of this mixed cohort was a pleasingly efficient undertaking for a mother country seeking to provide labour for its new lands while at the same time ridding itself of a costly burden. At a time when hanging was increasingly abhorred by the righteous, and when prisons were little more than grim holding houses for debtors or for those awaiting trial, it was a convenient confluence of reason, opportunity, and demand.

The Rotterdam had arrived at Weymouth with its lower deck already three-quarters full, the ship's owners having been contracted to convey a mixed consignment to Annapolis following a tendering process in which a borough committee had selected them as the lowest bidder. While the contract price was uneconomic in itself, the owners nevertheless expected to make a profit on the sale of the ship's human cargo to eager buyers waiting at the destination. There was thus an incentive for them to sail at maximum capacity and at minimum cost - commensurate with preserving the greatest weight of human flesh in a condition that would fetch a good price. This was a finely balanced equation in which the judgement of the ship's master had sometimes proved faulty.

In the forward parts of the ship, there were a dozen or so travellers who would pay their own way; they would enjoy the privilege of dining at the captain's table and the freedom underway to walk the upper deck when the weather permitted it. But the majority of the voyagers on this trip were taken from the streets and workhouses of London; a hundred or so men, women, and children of work age crammed uncomfortably into the cargo deck with perhaps ten square feet apiece. These unhappy souls would be forced to remain below in their cramped quarters throughout the voyage; those who had paid for their voyage would, after all, not want their promenade invaded by the unrefined habits and rank odours of the lower orders!

Then finally, there were the prisoners: twenty convicts from the capital's Newgate prison, whose souls had been sold to the shipper by a sheriff eager to be rid of them at any price, and a dozen more who had been put aboard en route from Surrey and Kent. The crew treated all transports with suspicion, but the convicts were distinguished from the others by being shackled and separated by a temporary bulkhead erected at the rear of the cargo deck. It would not be until safely at sea that the soldiers who accompanied them would release them from their irons if not from their confinement.

The ship now lay alongside the Weymouth quay awaiting her consignment of additional convicts while taking on supplies. There was relief, if not much levity, amongst the cohort already locked below decks from the temporary pleasure of peace in a sheltered port; and most now sat crouched or huddled under blankets in their cramped and cluttered spaces in private solace after fourteen days of rough seas. Conditions were, if anything, worse than those of the places from which they had come – their clothing and bedding were damp and dirty, and the humid air, infiltrated with pungent vapours drawn from the bilges, stank of urine, vomit, and sweat. The hatches would remain closed and guarded whilst in port to deter escape, but in reality, few would have the strength or the stomach to try. It was a miserable existence with only the basic necessities provided by a disinterested crew in a ship well past its prime.

It was into this unhappy and unhealthy scene that the new batch of unwilling travellers, including Jack, Elizabeth and Rose, was reluctantly led. Few watched them as they approached the ship now sitting at deceptive ease alongside the quay, with the square sails of her tall masts furled and her seamen casually smoking their pipes on the foredeck. But from the bay window of the captain's office in the Customs House immediately adjacent, the newly promoted Captain Smyke could be seen looking down, his dark and pointed features bent oddly by the uneven glass of the windowpane. He would have been wise to take more cautious note of Jack Easton's belligerently defiant demeanour as he was led up the gangway to the main deck. Instead, he smiled with smug satisfaction to see Easton pushed aboard so roughly that he fell onto the deck. Smyke watched with amusement as Easton straightened himself, but was unable to look away quickly enough to avoid catching Jack's eye as the Portlander turned to look up at the window almost as if drawn by some presentiment of Smyke's contemptuous gaze. In that instant, Smyke saw recognition flit across Easton's face and instinctively stepped back into the shadows of the room to hide himself from further inspection; but he could not fail to see the look of raw malice that was now directed at him from the deck of the ship below.

It was at that moment that Andrew White entered Smyke's office to find his superior retreating backwards from the bay window clearly in a state of some anxiety.

'Is everything alright, sir,' White asked, curious as to his captain's odd behaviour.

'Of course, of course,' Smyke replied brusquely. 'The convicts have just been taken aboard and they make so much noise that it disturbs my work,' he added crossly, attempting to cover his fluster. 'Easton is with them,' he said dismissively, 'good riddance to him is what I say – I hope they feed him to the fish!'

White stepped over to the window and looked down to see Easton standing tethered on the ship's deck in the pouring rain with other convicts jostling around him, all apparently awaiting further direction from the guards. They were by and large a filthy rag-tag of surly vagabonds, but Easton stood out from the majority by his defiant bearing. White was surprised to see that this upright man now returned his gaze, and while he watched he saw Easton raise his tethered arms to point a finger seemingly at him directly, mouthing some words which he could not make out through the glass, save that they were angrily shouted.

'I think he still protests his innocence,' White said over his shoulder with delicate but contrived lightness. But he got no more in reply than an irritable grunt from his captain whom he now observed to be busily moving some papers from one side to the other of his desk without apparent reason. His superior's curious behaviour, while unremarkable taken in isolation, added a further bead to the thread of small but noted anomalies in relation to the Easton case which would lie unquestioned in White's memory for some years. But there would come a time, when eventually prompted to recall the events of the past few weeks, that these memories would connect in his mind to form into a substantial conviction. Until then, he had more than enough to think about in recovering his reputation and career.

Chapter Nine

Faced with the barrier of the northern European landmass, the warm surface waters of the Gulf Stream divide to flow both north and south. The northerly branch is drawn up between Iceland and the British Isles to replace the cold polar water flowing southwards off the ice shelf at depth; the southerly branch sweeps down past the coast of Portugal and North Africa before taking up a westerly course west of the Sahara. Here, the flow merges with a branch of the equatorial current flowing northwest. At first, this stream moves parallel to the northern coast of South America, then, flowing between the Caribbean islands, it sweeps into and around the gulf bounded by the Vice-Royalities of New Granada and New Spain and the French territories around New Orleans. Emerging from the gulf between the Spanish provinces of Cuba and Florida, the stream then turns northwards to flow up the Eastern seaboard to the British territories of North America and thence eastwards again back towards Europe. All these currents together form a continuous conveyor of massive proportions; a giant cyclone circulating inexorably around the North Atlantic; a thermal engine driven by the sun and given direction by the Earth's rotation. The currents are as well known to global navigators of European sailing ships as the swirls and eddies of tidal waters are known to coastal fishermen.

Crossing the Atlantic from England, therefore, would call initially for a southerly outbound route aiming well to the East of Madeira, and not turning westerly until south of the latitude of the Canaries. A ship might then be carried the whole way across the Ocean by the current, assisted by the prevailing south easterly trade winds at that latitude. En route for the British-American colonies, the vessel would turn north westerly abeam Bermuda and head either to the ports on the eastern seaboard or into the Chesapeake. This would be a journey of some four thousand sea miles if a steady course could be maintained but much more if forced to tack against an unfavourable wind. The average time of crossing the Atlantic following this route would be about ten weeks, but as little as six or seven weeks could be achieved on the swiftest of voyages.

It was a well-worn path for *The Rotterdam;* she had sailed it countless times before like many others employed in her trade, to satisfy a seemingly insatiable demand on both sides of the Atlantic for labour on one side and tobacco on the other. Speed was therefore of the essence, with few concessions being made for comfort; and providing the ship and its crew could take the strain, full canvas would be held on until the very imminence of catastrophe.

On this crossing, *The Rotterdam* had made exceptionally good time, driven at breakneck speed since passing the Canaries by cyclonic gales that pushed her ever westward on huge and wind-whipped seas. The scampering vessel had already passed sixty degrees of longitude, three degrees south of Bermuda, and her weather-beaten captain, motivated by his likely profit, would soon turn her north-easterly for the final run into the Chesapeake. But below decks it had been an interminable nightmare. On Jack's deck, it was a miserable scene of dank and dismal chaos; a jumble of aching exhausted bodies pummelled incessantly by the violent motions of the ship. Lanterns, long extinguished through want of oil, swung wildly from their pivots, as shafts of insipid yellow light pierced the slatted hatches and danced about to form an interlacing lattice in the gloomy salt-laden air. And if the crossing had been fast, it had also been at a cost. Of the hundred and fifty souls penned below decks that had set off from Weymouth six weeks before, ten had already perished, their wasted corpses pushed with scant regard to ceremony into the raging sea. And many more lay huddled in their damp blankets groaning in fevered sickness, or in the quieter stages of a dissipating death. Some of the afflicted were fortunate in having loved-ones attend them, but most lay miserably alone. All suffered from dehydration and lack of good food. In better conditions, three hot stews of salt beef or mutton would have been served each week, but the crew had not ventured down to light the stove since the onset of rough weather. For the seamen, it had been the most prolonged run of bad weather ever experienced in these latitudes; for those on the cargo deck, it had been unrelenting purgatory.

With no help from the crew, these pitiful souls had been abandoned to fend for themselves as best they could, making do with dried salt-beef and worm-infested biscuits from the barrels of supplies provided. And since the water had by now become tainted with brackish infiltration from the bilges, it was wine or cider that had had become the liquid refreshment of preference; indeed these were the only safe liquids to drink. Some had been quick to seek the consoling embrace of intoxication, and many of the snoring lumps lying around the lower deck had already consumed enough to slip into that blissful state of stupor that took away all pain. But for others, the brew had made things considerably worse, and they now lay wretchedly in their own vomit, wishing they were dead. And all the while, the maddening wind howled and shrieked through the straining spars, thrumming the taut rigging like some giant bow, sending a deep and disturbing pulsation through the carcass of the ship that resounded in the depths of their despair. If someone had opened up a hatch, there were many who would have plunged through it gladly to seek oblivion in the raging sea.

As a seaman himself, Jack was one of the lucky ones who, despite the dizzying motion of the ship, were still able to move about the convicts' deck without succumbing to sickness himself. Thus, along with the few others having that coveted constitution, he had been able to give some small administrations to the sick and the frail. Rose, meanwhile, had committed herself selflessly to caring for her ailing sister whose condition had deteriorated further during the voyage to become a serious cause for concern. She now sat wearily propping herself against a bulwark cradling the resting Elizabeth in her lap while watching Jack on the other side of the deck kneeling beside a recumbent form. The ship lurched violently and another torrent of seawater spurted through the planks above her head. Elizabeth stirred at the jolt. Groaning, she rolled over in Rose's lap and retched a stream of watery yellow liquid onto the deck. Jack heard Rose's alarmed call, and turned to see her beckoning to him urgently. He started across the cluttered deck immediately to reach her, picking his way with utmost care through the maze of huddled shapes that lay in between. The ship lurched again as if hit from the side by some giant hand and Jack fell to his knees, cowering at the deafening crash of some heavy item falling onto the deck above. A fine mist of seawater filled the dingy space and dripped in icy rivulets onto his back. He waited for the violent motion to subside, then picked himself up and continued awkwardly towards the two sisters on all fours. Reaching them, he crouched by their side to listen to Rose's entreaty:

'She is very sick, Jack. Can you not find fresh water - and dry blankets to keep her warm?' she pleaded.

Jack shrugged helplessly. 'Those are our most desperate needs for everyone here, Rose,' he said. 'We've tried to raise help from the crew, but no one answers our call. I don't know what more we can do.'

Rose nodded resignedly; she had seen how untiringly Jack and his compatriots had worked to bring small comforts to the many who suffered in this interminable storm; but she felt her sister's life draining away and knew that unless help could be obtained quickly, she might lose her forever.

At the sound of Jack's voice, Elizabeth's eyes opened to look up dimly into his face; she ventured a frail smile, but this vanished as a ripple of pain creased her forehead. Jack shifted his position to bring his face closer to hers and gently took hold of her hand; it felt cold and limp, but after a moment he felt a fragile returning squeeze from her fingers. He delicately removed some hair that had become stuck in the clammy sweat glistening upon her pale brow, and he moved the palm of his hand down to rest warmly upon the coolness of her cheek. He felt her head press towards him and saw her eyelids flutter softly as she smiled again; and then, in a tender caress, she reached up weakly to touch his face, letting her fingers move up his bearded jaw. Her gaze searched his anxious face and came eventually to fix upon his eyes with such penetrating intensity that he felt as if she had reached inside his very being to touch his heart. For a moment, the pair gazed at each other unmoving in that gentle loving embrace – he, anxious for her state; she, with an enigmatic calm verging on serenity. The moment passed too soon. Her smile faded; her hand dropped to her side; and she slowly closed her eyes even as her gaze still clung to his. The tears, brimming until now in her eyes and squeezed out by their closing, now descended each cheek in slow procession. Jack felt the warm wetness reach his hand, and with his thumb, he wiped it away, brought it to his lips, and kissed it. He raised his gaze to Rose in silent query, but found the image of her face hazy as his own welling tears clouded his sight. Rose returned his gaze, reaching up gently to touch his cheek in a shared moment of consolation; she held his eyes for a moment, her face strangely calm, then bent her head to examine her sister's face. At length, she looked up again; 'She's sleeping,' she said quietly.

'What will become of her, Rose?' Jack asked solemnly, already fearing the worst.

Rose shook her head; 'She's taken nothing for two days now and her face is so pale. I fear that we shall lose her Jack if we cannot warm her and build her up.'

'I'm sure that she must be in the grip of typhus, Rose,' Jack whispered. 'Others have already succumbed – it's the infection from scratching these wretched bites - it gets into the blood. And there's no surgeon aboard to bleed her. She needs warm dry blankets - and clean water or she will go the way of the others.'

Jack sounded exhausted and demoralised. He glanced once more at Elizabeth's sleeping face, and then lifted his eyes, shaking his head in despair. 'I don't think I can save her, Rose,' he said quietly bowing his head. It seemed an admission of defeat, but then, as if driven by some last surge of resolve, he looked up again, his face set with renewed determination. 'I'll try again to get some help from the crew – I'll attract their attention if I have to break through the hatch!' he said firmly. 'Cuddle her, Rose - use your body heat to revive her if you can; we must be within days of sighting the coast - if she can hold out until then, we may save her yet.'

Jack leaped up and made his way aft, this time with a vigour born of desperation, and clambered up the companionway to the hatch above. It remained firmly fastened and could not be shaken open despite the frantic yanking and pulling to which he subjected it. He hammered upon the grating until his hands bled from the blows, and he screamed through the slats with all the voice that he could muster. But it was to no avail; his hammering and screaming were as faint whispers against the thunder of the storm. Eventually, realising his efforts to be futile, he descended, now resolved to break his way onto the deck.

'Ned!' he called to his sturdy friend who now hovered at the foot of the companionway, attracted by the clamour of his attempt to break out.

'Help me get this open! I'll get fresh water and dry blankets if it's the last thing I do. I can't just let her die!' Jack shouted in a determined voice, while scanning the deck for something that could be used as a lever. His tall companion nodded.

'Aye, Jack!' he said emphatically, his eyes following his friend's glances in the search. And spotting a handrail loosened by wear, he stepped over to the bulkhead and wrenched it off, putting the full weight of his broad shoulders into the task. Ned Holder, a lumbering giant of a man with whom Jack had teamed up to care for the sick, was an unlikely candidate for the caring role when judged by his conviction for robbery, but his strength had made short work of the handrail fixings and he soon rejoined Jack with the new tool in his hands. The hatch was fastened from the outside with a belaying pin, but by pushing the handrail through the slats at an angle, Jack was able to dislodge it.

The two men now slid back the hatch enough to allow Jack tentatively to poke his head through the gap created. Immediately, the thunderous roar of the sea and the demented shrieking of wind in the rigging assailed his senses as if he had been caught up in a maelstrom; his first instinct was to retreat back into the shelter below, but he steeled himself to press on as he surveyed the dismaying scene before him. The deck was awash with foam and cluttered with fallen debris and damaged equipment torn from its housings in the continuing storm. Rain lashed down in torrents from a mottled sky of low and scudding nimbostratus that seemed to brush the mast-tops as it whistled past. Shards of insipid yellow light radiating from the distant horizon glinted in the spars and rigging giving them a ghastly hue that evoked impending doom. The ship seemed somehow charged with electric potential that made the hairs on the back of his neck stand on end. He glanced nervously astern and his blood ran cold; towering precipices of black water were marshalling behind him, threatening at any moment to overwhelm the ship. *The Rotterdam* was being tossed and tipped alarmingly as each wave roared under her hull, throwing the horizons into sickening confusion; Jack was appalled and terrified at how puny the craft looked in such a monstrous sea; it seemed impossible that the ship had survived the fury being unleashed upon it.

Huddled for shelter in the lee of the windward guardrail, several men in black capes and sou'westers crouched amongst a tangle of fallen ropes and canvas; Jack guessed they were the deck-crew standing by for action aloft. 'God help them too!' he thought as he glanced up into the spars, surprised to see so much sail still set. But the ship ploughed on gamely through the thundering surf, bucking and rolling with each tumbling wave. He tried to call the sailors' attention, but his voice was lost in the howling wind. He raised himself on the step, cupping his hands to his mouth, and shouted again, but still could not make himself heard. At last, he pulled himself clear of the hatch and started over towards them, scrambling on all fours to stay out of the wind. The ship lurched and shuddered as another mountain of water crashed against the straining hull and the deck was suddenly awash as cold foam from a breaking wave spewed over the windward rail. A tumbling mass of salty water rushed headlong to engulf him, spinning him helplessly down the leaning deck onto the leeward rail. The impact ripped the wind from his lungs, and for a moment he thought that he would be swept overboard as the torrent clawed at him with malevolent force; but luckily, he found himself instead pinned against the overhang where even the huge pressure of the water could not tear him loose. Half-blinded and choked by the flush of stinging brine, he rose to his knees as the ship righted, and he started again to crawl towards the men still crouching at the opposite rail. Jack recognised the peril he was in, for at any moment he could be swallowed up by another deluge, but for Elizabeth's sake he felt compelled to struggle on. He realised now why the lower decks had been left unattended; no one could move safely in such conditions. He knew that he must act quickly or perish. Glancing over to the hatch, he saw Ned urgently beckoning him back; but impelled by his mission, he pushed himself on, while icy needles of rain stung his flesh. Jack crawled closer to the group, using the fallen ropes and equipment to provide purchase, but the men had not yet seen him; their heads were down against the deluge. He called to them repeatedly so as not to startle them by his approach, and at last one of them looked up. At first, the man seemed quite taken aback but, calling to the others to hold on to him, he reached out to pull Jack into the shelter of the guard-rail.

Jack wedged himself in gratefully.

'We're desperate for help below!' Jack needed to shout almost directly into his helper's ear to make himself heard. 'We need water and dry blankets! Can you help us?' The muscles of his cheeks seemed to have become paralysed by the cold so that it was a real effort to articulate each word.

The man looked at him helplessly, glancing at his fellows as if for confirmation, then shook his head. 'The whole ship is battened down against the storm,' he shouted back, cupping his hand to his mouth. 'Everyone on board suffers just as you all do. Even your guards took to their bunks days ago. What can we do but endure it.' He shrugged helplessly, looking at the skies.

The man pointed aft towards the quarterdeck on which two helmsmen clad in heavy-weather oilskins stared intensely at the compass housing as they wrestled with the ship's wheel. Behind them, bracing himself against the mast, another man stood alone scanning the seas ahead in fierce concentration.

'The captain drives the ship hard to make his profit,' the sailor shouted. 'But she's a good ship and she'll take it. Our best hope is that he gets her into shelter quickly. We're all in God's hands until then. The weather must pass eventually, and it'll not take long at this rate before we sight land.'

'Surely something more can be done for the sick and dying below?' Jack pleaded; but the man simply shrugged and shook his head. Impatient and desperate for some other answer to his pleas, Jack turned his attention again to the captain on the quarterdeck, but he found himself instead the object of the seafarer's scrutiny. The two men held each other's eyes briefly in passive recognition of each other's state; one, the master of destiny, the other its slave. It was at this moment of comprehension that the cold feeling of abandonment seeped into Jack's heart just as the icy rain and spray had already chilled his flesh. Jack knew then that God had turned His back on him; he felt stripped of all hope, impotent and alone, and realised that Elizabeth was lost.

One of the men grasped his shoulder.

'You must get back under cover,' the man yelled, reaching up to lift a small leather bucket from its stowage under the rail.

'Here,' he shouted. 'At least take some advantage of the rain.'

Jack started to protest, but the sailor simply shrugged and shook his head. In his heart, Jack knew that the man was right - there was no hope of salvation here; despite his valiant efforts, he would return with no more than a pail of rainwater, and he had exhausted himself in acquiring it.

When he reached the hatchway, he found himself so numb with cold that he was hardly able to lift his limbs. Ned had vanished below having closed the hatch, and with monumental effort, Jack pushed it open again and clambered over the housing. The ship lurched again as he did so and he lost his grip on the wet wood, tumbling down the companionway to land in a heap at its base, the pail spilling its precious contents onto the deck. It took a while for his eyes to accustom themselves again to the dim light below, but the rank air was warm by comparison with his exposure outside, and for a moment he took comfort from it while he caught his breath. Slowly, the veil of darkness lifted as his sight adapted, and looking across to where Elizabeth lay, he saw that Ned now knelt with Rose at Elizabeth's side. By their demeanour, he knew instantly that something was wrong, and he felt the cold hand of dread grip his heart.

'No!' A stifled cry caught in his throat 'She must hold on!' he shouted.

Pulling himself up quickly, he scrambled across the deck, clinging to the last vestiges of hope and careless of the huddled bodies that lay in his path; he could not - he would not admit the thought which both his instincts and his companions' downcast faces told him. He arrived at their side still shivering from his soaking and fell to his knees; Ned reached up to place a comforting hand on his shoulder.

'I tried to call you, Jack,' he said quietly.

The message in his tone was unmistakable, but Jack would hear nothing of it; he searched his friend's eyes for some sign of hope - there was nothing but sadness there. Almost reluctantly, as if by doing so he was letting go, Jack drew his eyes away, fearful of what he must now see for himself. Elizabeth's face was ashen; all life had drained from it; her eyes were closed, her expression, one of complete tranquillity and peace. Jack picked up her hand just as he had only minutes before, but this time there was no answering movement in her fingers, no flicker of her eyelids, no crease across her brow. He put his hand to her cheek, but felt no returning pressure as he had felt before. He bent down, bringing his cheek to hers, and whispered into her ear in sad and final acceptance of her passing:

'Good bye my dearest....' But his utterance was strangled as he choked, unable to stop himself from weeping. He cradled her limp body in his arms and held it in a long and tight embrace, his own body shaking silently as convulsions of grief and anger wracked his frame.

Rose, meanwhile, her face pale and expressionless, stared blankly into the squalid gloom that surrounded them. Absently, she brought her arms up to enfold the pair in her lap, and rocked them gently as a mother consoling a weeping child.

'May God protect you in Heaven, my sister - better than He has on this earth,' she whispered into the air.

By cruel irony, the storm subsided the day following Elizabeth's death, and guards and crew once more descended to the convict deck to inspect the devastation there; and those still capable of it, were quickly put to work to sort out the shambles and clean up the mess. Elizabeth Dale and her unborn baby were not the only casualties of that fearful tempest; twelve other souls on board had passed on, and several more lay near the death that would very soon consume them. Their bodies would be collected by the guards and thrown like so much detritus into the sea, leaving a grisly trail of flotsam bobbing for a time in the ship's wake. Jack and Rose watched all this sickened, exhausted and dazed - and in utter disbelief of the sheer horror of it all.

Chapter Ten

The Rotterdam's destination, Annapolis, was the capital of Maryland, one of the thirteen semi-autonomous colonies of British North America. These thirteen colonies, stretching from Maine in the north to Georgia in the south, occupied a relatively narrow strip of land on the Eastern seaboard of a vast continent in which several competing colonial forces manoeuvred both to outdo each other to exploit or displace the indigenous population in their quest for new possessions. To the north and west, stretching from the St Lawrence to Louisiana, the French with their aboriginal allies saw the encroachment of British colonial settlement as a major threat to their own interests, and this had already brought the two great powers into conflict. Recent diplomacy (culminating in the Treaty of Utrecht in 1713), had seen France ceding Nova Scotia to Britain and withdrawing claims to Newfoundland and the Hudson Bay, but this would only make them more vehement in defending their territories in the south. Further west, stretching from the central southern interior to the Pacific coast, and along the Gulf of Mexico to Florida, Spanish conquistadors still looked for gold and conversions to their catholic faith. Surrounded thus, the British colonists may well have felt hemmed in. And settlers moving ever westward in their search for land on which to found their homesteads, would soon spark a bloody French and Indian reaction.

At dawn on the tenth day following the storm's abatement, the Rotterdam slipped quietly past the anchorages off the Virginian settlement of Norfolk and entered the Chesapeake, a broad inland waterway that to its most northerly extent at the mouth of the Susquahanna River, measured something in excess of one-hundred-and-fifty nautical miles. The captain had made good use of his time since the passing of the storm, and the ship had once more been restored to order and made ready to receive clients awaiting her arrival. So as not to draw particular attention to the two classes of lower-deck traveller, the temporary bulkhead that had previously divided them had been removed; convicts might fetch a lower price in the bargaining if too much was made of the distinction. And like stock prepared for market, a bit of cleaning up, good feeding and fresh air had masked a multitude of blemishes. Thus, when the buyers came on board, they would find a selection of decent specimens from which to take their pick.

Maryland in January is bitterly cold, and on the windless dawn of *The Rotterdam's* arrival in Annapolis the skies were almost cloudless to the top of the haze layer that lay upon the earth like a worn blanket. A few swirls of cirrus suspended high up in the dark-blue stratosphere flared bright crimson from a sun still hidden below the horizon, streaking a glassy sea with blood-red reflections like careless brush-strokes. Becalmed in the early hours on light and variable airs, the vessel's boats had been launched to tow her the last few miles into port; she now moved with stately grace under their power. A fiery sun at last appeared, and soon tendrils of moisture curled up from the still water to form a thin mantle of mist that yielded to her passing and closed again behind her in gently enveloping swirls. Up on the masthead platform, the lookouts stood in the clear air, calling out their observations to the blinded helmsman on the quarterdeck below. To larboard, a line of tall evergreens marked the nearing shore, serving as a guide to lead them in. At last the harbour entry mark was reached and the ship drawn around the headland into the broad mouth of the river. And there, seen rising above the mist from their lofty perch as if nestling upon a raft of cloud, lay the city of Annapolis emblazoned in the morning sun.

For those waiting on the harbour front for the vessel's arrival, heralded an hour or so before by a messenger on horseback from the Bay shore lookout post, only the ship's sails, hanging lifeless in the flat-calm air, were visible as she came into view. It made an impressive sight to see the craft shed her misty shroud as she glided in, the blood-orange sun silhouetting her dark majestic lines and setting her sails aglow. Ashore, caught in the new morning's bright radiance, the tall roofs that capped the colourful facades along the quay sparkled with frost that steamed gently, shaking off the cold of the winter dawn. As the ship slid finally towards its allotted berth, dark shadows of her tall masts moved silently along the waterfront like stealthy phantoms creeping in to steal the precious light. Then men appeared on the waterfront as if from nowhere as she glided by, to catch the mooring warps. And suddenly the peace of the early morning was shattered by their coarse instructions as the vessel's motion was checked and she was at last made fast. *The Rotterdam* had arrived.

On the quay, a small number of onlookers, perhaps ten or twelve in all, watched impatiently as the ship's gangway was run ashore. The group seemed made up mainly of well-dressed men wrapped in long overcoats against the cold; some stamped their feet and swung their arms about themselves; and puffs of steamy exhalation evaporated above their heads as they passed the time in expectant conversation. As if at some unseen signal, there was a movement of this gathering towards the ship as a gangway was run ashore. The ship's purser then appeared on deck. With his seaman's cap perched on the back of his head and wearing a long dark coat buttoned all the way up to his neck, the officer descended to the quay clutching some papers in his hand:

'A fine morning to be sure, gentlemen,' he called to the assembly in a jaunty Irish brogue. 'By the look of yuh, I expect you'll be having an interest in what we have aboard?'

'It depends what state they're in after the hammering you give 'em on the way across, Purser!' shouted one wag. 'And whether there's any good-lookers amongst 'em!' shouted another.

A ripple of laughter erupted, which was brought to an end abruptly as a tall man, dressed in a heavy brown overcoat and wide-brimmed leather hat, called in an educated voice from the back of the group: 'Well, tell us what you've got for us, purser. Let's get on with it, and be about our business - I'll want a good twenty of your best and get on my way on the next tide.'

At this, there was a bit of a commotion as others spoke up, competing for the attention of the officer; many had travelled for several days to secure servants and tradesmen at the port and they would not want to go home empty-handed. The mixture of accents and intonations amongst them revealed that not all were of English stock; one or two were clearly of Saxon or Scandinavian extraction, but all had mastered English in their way. The beleaguered purser struggled to regain order, but as the commotion subsided, some of the buyers noticed that another gangway had been run ashore further forward, and that the paying passengers were now disembarking. A few broke away and moved quickly towards the assembling group – the landowners would offer paid work there and then for the prized skills that they sought. The majority, however, remained with the purser - they wanted bonded general workers, labourers for their plantations and domestics for their homes who would not be able to quit on some whim and move on. Hard-working servants, indentured at the right price would earn them the highest profits, and these were therefore in the strongest demand.

'There'll be enough for all, gentlemen, I assure you!' the purser called above the din. 'We have near one hundred and thirty good servants aboard, all eager and willing to do your bidding.'

The chatter subsided, and his voice then took on the tones of one speaking a well-rehearsed script, outlining the conditions of sale:

'I hold their indentures, signed and sealed, binding them to serve those to whom they are assigned. Some have a craft or a skill, gentlemen - there are carpenters, brick-layers, and blacksmiths amongst them - others will make good labourers or domestics; and I will take your bids as we move amongst them so that you can judge their fitness and character for yourselves. My acknowledgement of the highest bid will form the contract between us, which I shall note in my papers, and your word will be your bond. Payment will, of course, be required in sterling or the equivalent in poundage of tobacco.' Here, he paused briefly for effect. 'And I will want to see the colour of your money, or your promissory note duly authenticated by an actuary, before your new vassals leave the ship!' he added with a mischievous smirk, winning him a ripple of good-natured laughter. Thus encouraged, he ploughed on with the same breezy delivery:

'You'll be familiar with the rules on children and youngsters, gentlemen - children of work age sold with a parent will add three pounds to your invoice, and I will accept the best bid for any sold separately. You get any babes in arms with my compliments!' he added to another buzz of laughter.

The crowd was now in good humour at the prospect of a good choice, and impatient to get aboard to take their pick of the best.

'Finally, gentlemen!' the purser raised his voice to regain his audience's attention. 'We have a few convicts aboard, but they are not of the rough kind, and you can expect good service from them if you treat them fairly. You'll get up to fourteen years out of them for the same price as four to six years from the others. Furthermore, as they are here on penal servitude there will be no obligation on your part to offer them headright land or other emoluments on completion of their sentence.'

The buyers were then led aboard and assembled on the deck; and here they were divided into smaller groups and put under the supervision of the purser's assistants before being taken below.

On the cargo deck, all the litter and mess of the voyage had been cleared away and the hatches opened to let in the daylight and the sea air to brighten the otherwise dismal scene - and flush away the rank odours.

All those now waiting there were fearful of what might lie ahead and many sat about in small groups looking apprehensive. Families clung to each other, praying that they would stay together in their indentures, but there was no guarantee that this would be so; indentures would be sold to the highest bidder, and thus for some, there would be some heart-rending separation in store. A few might even trade away their offspring to leave the ship free and unencumbered. And others might be forced to do the same if a high enough price could not be raised on their own heads, as might apply, for example, if a parent were judged too puny or too old for hard work. And perversely, the spouses of those who had perished on the voyage with more than half the distance completed could be sold for a double term of indenture to recompense the ship owners for lost income. To a compassionate observer, such treatment would seem heartless, but it was the blatant norm in these times that impoverishment, or gullibility, or just plain bad luck, might damn a fellow into such slavery and deny him the most basic of human rights. There was thus some fear and trepidation amongst those who now sat and waited for their fate to be decided by the men who now moved arrogantly around their sanctuary. Crewmen guarded all the hatches and companionways, and red uniforms wandered amongst the convict cohort; the guards seemed at ease, but their quick eyes showed them to be alert for any sign of trouble.

By the time the buyers' groups reached the after deck where the convicts sat waiting in sullen silence, their number had dwindled to a handful, as many had already departed having completed their intended business. Some still haggled with assistants over those who had been slow to sell, now being bartered away for yet longer periods of indenture to pay off their debt to the ship. Elsewhere, women could be heard sobbing, men pleading, and little children wailing at the prospect of impending separation; for them to be torn from one another in such heartless commerce was the business of a cattle market.

But Jack's heart had become hardened by his own experiences, and he remained unmoved at such desolate sights and sounds. Since Elizabeth's death, he had become withdrawn, his mind hovering between angry retribution and reckless self-destruction. He felt as empty as the hollow ache in the pit of his stomach. The barbarous acts that he now observed would not stir him. He cared nothing for them, or for himself or what became of him. He had abandoned all hope and had thus resigned himself to whatever fate might lie in store. And neither Rose nor his new friend Ned could rouse him from his despair.

'Stand up!' growled one of the guards sharply as a buyer approached accompanied by an assistant carrying a clipboard under his arm. The buyer was the tall man earlier described: an imposing individual, still wearing his long dark-brown overcoat but now carrying his hat in his hands. His hair, pressed in at the sides and slicked down from the hat's wearing, was blond and long and held back in a short pigtail. He stooped as he passed under the deck beams and Jack and his two companions clambered awkwardly and reluctantly to their feet. The buyer had fair and open features, a neat moustache, and engaging blue eyes that now scrutinised the three prisoners standing sullenly before him as their details were described. He pursed his lips dismissively; the three prisoners were in a poor state - ragged, unkempt, and downcast - and he seemed inclined to move on; indeed he made as if to do so, but the assistant spoke up quickly to divert him.

'These men are strong, sir, despite their appearance, and they would clean up well. They have taken the voyage rather badly, I fear.' He moved closer to his customer and whispered something privately into his ear.

'Oh, I see,' the buyer replied in an understanding tone; and then to the three standing, he said compassionately: 'I am told that you have suffered a loss. I am very sorry to hear it - the crossing can be cruel indeed.'

He made to move on nevertheless, but then hesitated. Whether out of kindness or from revived interest, he turned to face Jack directly as if something about him had attracted his curiosity. But Jack did not lift his gaze from the deck.

'I address you, sir!' The man spoke assertively with an impatient wave of his hat, but Jack did not respond, except to clamp his jaw. The assistant, no doubt irritated by Jack's impudence, poked him in the chest crossly with his board. 'Pay attention, man,' he said curtly. 'This gentleman will speak to you.'

Slowly, Jack lifted his head to meet the buyer's gaze; his reddened eyes seemed sunken deep into their sockets. There was no expression whatsoever in his face, and his long tangled hair and unkempt beard gave him a fearful countenance; yet the buyer did not seem put off.

'The purser's assistant here says you work in stone,' the buyer suggested evenly. But it took another prod from the assistant before Jack replied.

'I am a quarryman and a stone mason,' said Jack quietly in a flat and expressionless voice.

'Are you indeed?' The buyer seemed strangely interested. 'And where from?'

'Portland. I quarried Portland stone and carved it.' The sudden memory of a former life that now seemed all but lost to him brought a catch to his throat, and there was a long pause as Jack sank once more into a sullen introspection. But then Rose spoke up. Perhaps she had sensed the kindliness of this buyer by his manner and had recognised a chance for them all that might be better than she had seen negotiated elsewhere on the deck.

'He is a master mason, sir, well known in Portland for his carving skills. He worked in his father's quarry as foreman - a good man, sir, well respected and loved by his men. Don't be put off by his appearance or his manner, sir,' she said softly. 'He has lost his betrothed and his unborn child on this terrible voyage.'

'And what of his crimes?' the man asked of the assistant.

Consulting his list, the assistant replied. 'I have…' He stopped dead in his tracks as he read along the line of his notes. 'I have murder, sir, and smuggling,' he stammered, his voice trailing off to nothing.

'Indeed?' returned the tall man lifting his eyebrows in surprise. 'And what have you to say on this?' he asked of Jack without rancour. Again, Jack was slow to respond, and again Rose spoke up for him.

'He tried to save a man's life, sir. And instead, found himself wrongly accused of murder by a corrupt officer who was himself the perpetrator!' Rose spoke earnestly. 'And some of the jury must have understood this, for he was not hanged on those charges. But the court could not bring itself to disbelieve the testimony of a government official, and this man is thus the victim of a gross miscarriage!'

'And the smuggling?' the man asked.

'I cannot refute that, sir. It is almost a way of life with many who live by the sea.'

The buyer considered for a moment, then, turning to the assistant, he seemed to make up his mind.

'I believe I will take this man; he has skills that may become useful to me in due course. How many years must he serve?'

'Fourteen, sir.'

'And his price?'

'Thirty pounds sterling, sir'

'So much for a felon? I think twenty will do.'

'Then shall we agree on twenty-five?' suggested the assistant, hopefully.

The buyer eyed the object of the bargaining critically. 'Twenty is my offer,' he said firmly. The assistant considered for a moment then nodded. 'Then twenty it is,' he said.

'And you will take that in tobacco?' asked the buyer.

'Aye, sir, that we will,' said the assistant looking pleased with himself. And he was right to be; at that price, the margin would be over ten pounds taking costs into account, and the Sheriff's payment for transporting the prisoner would add another five or six. The assistant must have thought it quite a profitable transaction.

'And will you take the others, sir?' he ventured.

'No, I think not. I have now completed the purchases I had intended.'

The assistant made as if to speak, but then seemed to think better of it, possibly not wanting to push his luck; the sale of Jack Easton, on paper a risky prospect, for such a good price must have seemed fortunate indeed. Besides, the other two - a strong man and an attractive woman - should be easily enough disposed of in due course. The two men thus turned to walk on, but as they did so, Jack seemed suddenly to draw himself up to his full height.

'Wait!' he called, taking the departing pair by surprise by his confident tone. The two men stopped and turned back.

'Sir, I find myself now bound to you by unfortunate circumstances to use my skills and labour at your behest.' Jack raised his head and looked the buyer straight in the eye as he continued: 'You seem to me to be an understanding man, so understand this. This woman and this man go where I go, and without them your payment for my services will be wasted, for I shall not work.'

'Then you will be whipped until you do!' said the assistant seeing his good sale threatened by the attitude of this belligerent upstart. He caught the attention of a nearby guard and summoned him crossly.

'Whipping me will see no work from me,' said Jack calmly in the manner of one believing that he had nothing to lose. 'I would rather die than be torn from my friends.'

At this moment, he would indeed rather have been whipped to death than be separated from Rose, who now represented everything that he held dear from his former life; and the prospect of losing Ned, now his only friend and companion in the uncertain times ahead, was suddenly unthinkable.

A red-coated guard arrived at the assistant's side puffed-up and ready to take rough action.

'Stay back!' ordered the buyer, seeing the fierce glare of defiance in Jack's eyes. The two men stood face to face for some seconds with neither yielding their glance. The assistant shook his head despondently; he must have thought his sale already lost; but then the buyer smiled and turned towards him. 'Perhaps I can find room for the other two,' he offered. ' My plantation is big enough and there will certainly be work for them, but I will pay ten pounds each and not a penny more.'

For an instant, the assistant hesitated, perhaps wondering whether to push the price higher; but if so, he quickly changed his mind and accepted the offer gracefully.

'And your name, sir?'

'de Burgh, Sir Michael de Burgh,' the tall man replied.

Chapter Eleven

The New Hope estate was founded in Southern Maryland by Sir Roland de Burgh in 1661 on land originally part of the patented territories granted under charter to the first Lord Baltimore some thirty years before, and made available by his Lordship's heirs on good terms. No doubt, the transfer of title was greatly aided by the interest of King Charles II whose patronage of Sir Roland recognised the support that he had rendered to the King's father during the civil war, and also for the help later given to himself in assisting his subsequent escape.

The younger Charles was nineteen years old and living in France when his father was executed following the defeat of English Royalist forces in the civil wars. The Royalists of Scotland at once summoned the young heir to be their King, and in 1650 he landed in that country, was crowned at Scone, and, with ten thousand Scots, marched into England set upon reclaiming his father's throne. This was an inglorious venture for the would-be King, he being soundly defeated and his army put to rout by Cromwell at Worcester. For six weeks, Charles wandered about the country, a fugitive with a price of one thousand pounds upon his head, famously hiding in an oak tree and disguised as a servant. But many, including the likes of Sir Roland, sympathised with his plight and gave him aid, and with their help, the young fugitive eventually made his escape to France. For the ten years of Charles' exile, Commonwealth men ruled the British Isles. It was an unforgiving regime, and Sir Roland's well-known Royalist loyalties quickly led to his expulsion from the Parliament in which he was previously a distinguished and incorruptible member. This was punishment enough, but when his secret support of Catholic rebels was discovered, he was sentenced to execution and all the lands and title that he possessed were immediately confiscated. But in the nick of time, Charles was recalled to the throne in 1659, and those who had been most loyal to him during his exile were rehabilitated and recompensed.

By then, however, the staunchly catholic Sir Roland had made powerful enemies, and he no longer desired to remain in a country so apparently hostile to him and his beliefs. Thus, despite the King's manifest wish to see him brought back to influence within the new Parliament, Sir Roland chose instead to emigrate to the New World and build a new life for himself in Maryland where he already had connections. Indeed, many catholic families had already fled there escaping persecution. Clearly, Sir Roland hoped to establish his new home in a land where, under the protection of an Act passed by the new Maryland Assembly, religious tolerance was more likely to be maintained. With the King's patronage, Sir Roland acquired one thousand acres of largely uncultivated land on the Eastern shores of the Potomac River in St Mary's county.

In the seventy or so years since the family's arrival in Maryland, a profitable estate had since been created. Out of what was once entirely woodland, save for a few rough clearings left behind by acquiescent Yaocomaco Indians, several hundred acres of good planting land had been created. In addition, a further one hundred acres had been made suitable for grazing livestock, and two large fenced enclosures erected to accommodate residential and farm buildings. In the smallest of these enclosures, surrounded by well-tended domestic gardens, stood the residence of Sir Michael de Burgh, grandson of the late Sir Roland, son of the recently deceased Sir William, and inheritor of all their titles. The residence was modest by the standards of those on other large estates but adequate for him and his new wife, there being as yet no children to accommodate. The house was built chalet-style with gabled windows in the roof and a veranda that ran the full length of the house. It was of clapboard construction – riven oak cladding on an original post-in-ground frame - but it had substantial brick chimneys at either end, and large rectangular windows on the ground floor having fine views of the river to the front. In the other enclave, surrounded by a wattle fence to keep the chickens in and the wolves out, were several rows of rustic wooden huts with thatched roofs built to accommodate the slaves and servants kept by the estate to farm it. Both the black slave cohort imported from the Ivory Coast and the white indentured servants brought in from England lived in these huts. While colour, language, and culture may have distinguished the two groups, their owner treated them more or less the same; indeed, sharing the same hard work and primitive living conditions, there grew a sort of bond between them despite their differences.

Two years had now passed since Jack Easton, Ned Holder and Rose Dale had arrived at the de Burgh estate with nineteen others procured off *The Rotterdam* in Annapolis on that cold January day in 1751. Their passage to New Hope had taken a further two full days by coastal cutter, the journey first southwards down the Chesapeake, offloading some of the cohort at the Mattapani estate near Cedar Point at the mouth of the Patuxent River, and then up into the Potomac. By comparison with their Atlantic crossing, the voyage had been tolerable; and to be given decent food and dry clothing was indeed a luxury. But the mood amongst the mixed group had been gloomy nevertheless, subdued as it was either through grieving for lost loved ones or troubled by the uncertainties that lay ahead. Jack recalled little of that voyage. So preoccupied was he with thoughts of Elizabeth that he could not be roused from his despondency.

In the tidewater areas of Southern Maryland, numerous broad and navigable tidal rivers penetrate the peninsular, especially along the Potomac, and the creeks that feed these rivers were favourite places for settlement. The New Hope estate had been built on a broad spit of wooded land that lay between the Potomac and one of these tributaries, and it was thus possible to bring quite large coastal vessels right into its heart along a sheltered creek. It was by this route that the unhappy cohort had arrived during the late afternoon of the second day of their journey, just as dusk was falling. Jack would always remember walking up the lantern-lit path from the landing stage with mixed emotions. While he would never come to terms with the state of servitude that his arrival represented, there had been some small comfort in the welcoming greetings extended to them by the existing residents of the compound into which they were delivered. It could have been much worse. And looking back, Jack would come reluctantly to admit that it was these modest yet unacknowledged gestures from his new compatriots that made him feel at once that the worst was behind him.

The early months on the estate had been a hard apprenticeship for all the new arrivals, their compliance ensured through threat of punishment or deprivation of comforts. Rose had immediately been put to work as a domestic servant in the residence, and Jack and Ned allocated to work in the plantation. As a housemaid, Rose attended to the needs of the de Burghs, her duties requiring her to be up before dawn to light the fires and then assist the cook in preparing the couple's breakfast. She spent the day cleaning and attending to the kitchen garden and domestic animals, and quickly had to learn the necessary skills of milking, churning, weaving, and cutting a chicken's throat. In the evenings she might be given a few hours' mending or darning before being dismissed to her bed, a simple horse-hair biscuit stored under the stairs during the day and unrolled on the scullery floor for her to sleep on at night.

At least Rose had the relative comfort of sleeping on a wooden floor. Jack and Ned were not so lucky. Living in a hut that they shared with two other new arrivals, their beds sat on an earthen floor that was cold and damp in the winter despite the straw matting which served as insulation; and in the summer, it crawled with insects that crept under their blankets and ravaged them at night. They worked all the hours of daylight that God sent, six days a week, fifty two weeks a year - save for the odd privilege day earned from time to time by special favour of the overseers; and this was usually when the weather was not good enough for the work in hand and thus not much good either for anything else - except sleep. They tilled the soil, they dug ditches, and they felled timber and cut it into planks or fencing posts, or chopped it for the fire. But much of their time was spent in tending tobacco throughout the various stages of its growing cycle: separating the seedlings and planting out, hoeing out the weeds, nipping out the buds and fighting the annual running battle with the hornworms that would decimate the crop if you turned your back for five minutes! And then in due course, when the tobacco was fully-grown, there was the unpleasant business of the harvest when everyone on the estate turned out to cut the rank and clammy plant and bring it in to the sheds to cure. This was Sir Michael's cash crop, the means by which he prospered and by which the workers earned their bare subsistence, and thus it was the focus of everyone's interest. Few would be trusted to grade it since the price it would fetch would depend upon its quality, and Sir Michael himself would supervise its ageing and fermentation until it was ready for packing. But it would be Jack and Ned and others like them who would have the heavy task of rolling the hogsheads down to the quay and loading them into the barges to be taken up river to the bonded warehouses at Charlestown.

All this activity was supervised by trusted overseers who had the power to make life miserable for any who did not toe the line. But it was certainly not the cruel regime that reputedly existed elsewhere in the southern colonies, and the bound workers of New Hope counted themselves lucky in this respect. Indeed, as a man not deaf to the controversies of slavery, Sir Michael saw himself as something of a father figure and was kindly disposed towards his servants. Perhaps he also recognised that their resentment would never win him good work and thus he sought their good opinion.

Outside the long working day, Jack and Ned also had their own domestic duties to attend to. No one cooked for them, no one kept house or fixed the roof, and no one washed or darned for them. Nothing got done unless they did it for themselves or exchanged services or favours with their neighbours. It was an all-consuming tedium that all but eliminated the opportunity for the soul-searching that Jack in particular might otherwise have been prone to. And it was a healing distraction from the prolonged grieving that had caused him to retreat into himself.

And so it was that these two years had passed before either Jack or Rose began to take stock of their situation and start thinking of their future, while in that time they had hardly communicated, so entirely separate had their lives become. Even when by chance at Sunday service they had encountered one another, neither seemed to have very much to say; and neither had Ned seen either of them smile, despite his occasional attempts to ease the awkwardness that seemed to have developed between them. Sometimes, in his bleaker moments when lying awake at night unable to sleep, Jack's tormented mind would turn to thinking of escape and of the elaborate and terrible revenge he might one day visit upon Smyke. But he had felt himself unable to act until Rose reached the end of her four-year term. It would not be until she returned home, he reasoned, that he would be free to make his move. Perhaps he also recognised that escape would be never be easy, for there would be nowhere safe to hide; and travel would be dangerous with a price upon his head. It was well known too that punishment for absconding was severe: besides a likely flogging by the overseers and the withdrawal of scarce privileges, a man's term could be increased by one week for each day at large, one month for each week, and one year for each month. Jack had therefore decided to bide his time.

It was on a warm Sunday morning in the May of 1753 that things began to change.

Thanks to the enlightened attitudes of the young Sir Michael, none of the servants or slaves was required to work on Sundays - except of course for some of the domestics who took it in turns to be on duty in the residence. And it was a tradition at New Hope that everyone on the estate, regardless of faith or understanding of language, should attend church at least once during the day. On most Sundays, a peripatetic priest would take the morning service. But today, due to some emergency elsewhere within his extended parish, he was unable to attend, and so Sir Michael would lead the service as lay reader. The church was small and had only thirty seats for the fifty or so residents who would normally be mustered, and so many of the men would always find themselves standing at the back. Like all the buildings on the estate, the church was wood-framed and clad in overlapping board, but to give it some distinction as a house of prayer, it had been painted white and had a pinnacle perched upon its roof to house the bell. Glowing brightly in the morning sunshine, the little church stood on a low grassy knoll overlooking the sandy shores of the Potomac that, at this point, was six miles wide. On clear days, its elevation gave the church a good view of the Virginian coastline lying low and dark on the opposite horizon across the broad expanse of bright water. A path, worn down to bare earth by the passing of many feet, meandered through scattered trees towards the church door, and along the path, in slow and ragged procession, walked figures in twos and threes dressed in the sober clothing provided by Sir Michael for such occasions. Dappled sunlight warmed their backs as the little bell called urgently from the tower.

The service proceeded, as it often did on the occasions when Sir Michael led it, in a somewhat disjointed manner. Without the musical accompaniment usually provided by the priest's assistant on his accordion, few could cope with the tunes even if they knew the words. Lady de Burgh's afternoon Sunday school for the Christian tutoring of the black slaves had not yet been as effective as had been hoped, and for those not yet familiar with Christian liturgy, the service was always a bewildering experience. A few stalwart voices rang out bravely above the mumblings of the rest, whose shifting glances studiously avoided Lady de Burgh's critical attention as she mouthed each hymn at them with exaggerated diction. But because attending church was the preferred alternative to working in the fields, most at least put on some show of taking part; and the overseers present were a reminder to all that there was little choice but to comply.

Mercifully, the service was over quickly on this occasion. Having born enough discordance before getting halfway through the hymn list, Sir Michael brought the service to a premature end and led the way out with his flustered lady wife clinging to his arm. It was customary for Sir Michael and Lady de Burgh to await the passing of the congregation in the porch so as to see and be seen by each of their servants and slaves as they departed. Whether this was a kindly gesture by Sir Michael or the assertion of his authority, Jack could not determine, but when he eventually arrived at the porch, Sir Michael acknowledged him more civilly than usual.

'A word with you, Easton, if you please,' he whispered into Jack's ear as he passed, 'would you wait for me outside?'

Jack shrugged sullenly and stood aside while the rest of the congregation passed by, feeling slightly awkward to have been singled out. Eventually, after the last of the servants' respects had been paid, Sir Michael detached himself and led Jack by the elbow towards the shore. He was unusually polite.

'You said that you were a stonemason, Easton? Would you like to use your skills for me in that capacity?'

Jack was surprised and taken aback. Sir Michael had not referred to Jack's stone-working skills since their first meeting on *The Rotterdam* over two years before, and he had not thought of its mention since.

'You ask it as if I had some choice?' he mused insolently, at which Sir Michael looked a little ruffled.

'Come, come, man!' he retorted. 'You know that when it comes to creative work, one needs to have one's heart in it - it cannot be demanded – or turned on and off like a faucet! I ask it, I will not try to compel you!'

Jack softened. 'What exactly had you in mind?'

'I would like it to be my legacy to create a mansion of some distinction at New Hope. I plan to extend my current residence and have in mind some ornamental carving here and there, perhaps a stone hearth and mantelpiece for each of the two main fireplaces as a start. What do you think?' He hesitated. 'There would be some privileges in it for you,' he added, his face taking on a hopeful expression.

'I have carved Portland stone, but am not familiar with other stone. Is the local stone good enough for carving? I have not seen much evidence of it.' Jack's tone was sceptical.

'The whole of Southern Maryland appears to sit on sand and gravel, but I have acquired some stone from further up river in Virginia. I am told that the type is occasionally used up there for ornamental work but there are few who can work it with any skill. Would you look at it?'

Jack nodded without enthusiasm. In truth, his interest had been aroused although he would not want to be seen to be too eager; Sir Michael had mentioned privileges - perhaps Jack might extract more by playing hard to get? He sensed that his luck might be on the turn.

'Come with me to the quay then; my first consignment of stone has just been unloaded there.'

The two men walked back past the church along a wooded path and descended into a shallow valley overhung with ash and maple trees not yet in leaf. Under their empty branches, bluebells and wild garlic were scattered in flowering profusion, a bright carpet of blue and white like a reflection of the sky. At the bottom of the path, the woods opened into a tranquil creek that Jack knew well, although not from this side - the path along which he had been led on this occasion was normally out of bounds to servants and slaves. On the other side of the water, he could see the commercial quay sitting empty and lit up in a shaft of sunshine that penetrated the trees. Whenever he'd been permitted to visit the quay before, it had bustled with activity in which he had laboured hard; he feared to reckon the number of hogsheads that he had seen rolled down the track to reach it. From there he had often looked on wistfully as the tobacco had been dispatched up the Potomac to Charlestown where he knew that cargo ships would be waiting to take it on to England; and it was therefore impossible to look upon the quay without thinking of home.

On this side of the creek, opposite the quay, a rickety pier stuck out awkwardly across a bank of mud. A sturdy broad-beamed sailing boat about thirty-five feet in length sat alongside it, and, closer in, two smaller fishing boats lay drawn up on the shingled beach. 'It's no wonder that servants and slaves are not normally allowed here,' he thought; 'it would be far too tempting to see such a ready means of escape so close at hand!'

Sir Michael saw Jack's interest in the boats.

'Are you a sailing man?' he asked.

'Aye, sir. But I doubt I'd make it back to England in one of those!'

Sir Michael laughed. Patently, it had not occurred to him that Jack would ever contemplate escape.

At the foot of the pier, a number of large stone blocks had been stacked, and it was towards these that the pair now strode.

'What do you think?' asked Sir Michael, patting the blocks proudly, his tone hopeful.

Jack bent down to examine the stone closely and, scratching the surface of one of the blocks with his fingernail, he rubbed the minute particles loosened by the abrasion between his fingers. He recognised it as an oolitic limestone not dissimilar from his own Portland base-bed stone in texture, but having a slightly browner hue. The grain was fine and even-textured, and there were no fissures or imperfections that would interfere. Jack thought that it would probably carve well enough.

'I'll need some tools,' he said, not wanting to sound too compliant.

'I took the precaution of bringing this,' Sir Michael said producing a small stone chisel from his pocket. 'There are more tools back at the house - I had them shipped over from England.'

Jack took the chisel and scraped it across the surface of the block - the chisel moved easily, leaving a smooth edge to his cut. He dragged his finger along the groove and examined the dust and fragments loosened by the instrument. It was a fine powder, not too gritty, and there were no larger shell fragments embedded in the stone to get in the way of any detailed work that might be required. He felt a pang of nostalgic delight to feel the balance of a chisel in his hand after so long, and to feel the warmth and texture of the stone on his hands. Memories of his father, his brother, and his quarry comrades flooded into his mind. Held back from entering Jack's conscious thoughts since the beginning of his exile in a determined defence against self-pity, the images of their faces seemed to crowd in as if a dam had suddenly been breached. Their faces were startlingly vivid, almost as if they stood before him. And then, his mother and Elizabeth appeared as if from the stone itself; they seemed to be calling him although he heard no sound. But even in the certain knowledge that they were phantoms of his imagination, he would not resist them. Instead he let the fond images play before his eyes and soak into his consciousness like an infusion - he had kept them out too long.

'Well?' prompted Sir Michael impatiently, evidently puzzled by the length of his deliberations.

Sir Michael's sharp word brought Jack out of his daydreaming with a jolt and the images melted away, leaving only the background of the tranquil creek where they had floated before his eyes. Yet was it also only in his imagination that in their stead, the pretty melody of a song thrush seemed suddenly to fill the air with lilting cadences of which he had been completely unaware before?

'It may be workable with the right tools,' he said clearing his throat.

As Jack set off for the fields with Ned the following day, a servant girl from the house intercepted him.

'You're not to go to the fields today, Mr Easton, you are wanted at the house.' The girl could not have been more than fourteen years old, yet she was precociously assertive. 'It's the master - he wants to see you right away.'

As Jack approached the residence, he could see Sir Michael on the veranda, dressed in breeches, riding boots, and a white open-necked shirt of loose cut. He stood at the wooden balustrade, gripping it like a sea captain on a quarterdeck, looking down on a bend in the river that came quite close to the house. His home was not a building of any architectural note, but its brick chimneys, located one at either end of its rectangular floor plan, lent it a more imposing appearance than its size might otherwise suggest, and the large glazed windows gave it an elegant air. Looking down the river to his left, Jack could see the entrance to the creek which led to the landing stage where he and Sir Michael had talked the day before, and to the right, perhaps half-a-mile distant, a wooded spit of land marked the river's outflow into the Potomac. Beyond the spit, a few small whitecaps indicated a moderate wind over the open water, but here in the shelter of the trees, the wood smoke from the chimneys climbed almost vertically for thirty feet before being swept into vortices. The location for the house had been well selected.

'Ah, Easton,' Sir Michael called, spotting Jack's approach, 'come straight up.'

Jack did as he was bid and climbed the wooden steps onto the veranda where Sir Michael led him to a slatted table on which a row of tools had been laid out. Here, with what Jack thought resembled the demeanour of a nervous schoolboy awaiting the judgement of his efforts by a master, he motioned Jack to examine the collection. Jack scrutinised each tool in turn - there were about ten chisels and punches of varying shape and size and a selection of wedges, hammers, and mallets; all looked to be of new manufacture and of good quality.

'Advice was obtained on their selection,' Sir Michael said anxiously.

'So I see,' Jack replied impressed, 'but these alone will not last long. They can be sharpened of course, but I may need a few replacements eventually as they wear.'

'Yes, I did anticipate that.' He pointed to a small chest that lay to one side of the table. 'You'll find sufficient spares and other tools in there.'

Jack nodded. 'Then perhaps you'll show me what you have in mind.'

Sir Michael led Jack into the house where the smell of beeswax and floral fragrances assailed Jack's starved senses, instantly evoking memories of his parents' home in Portland. But Jack's home in Portland was nothing like this. Despite its modest exterior, the house was airy and light inside and sumptuously furnished with fine European furniture and oriental rugs. In the hall, a tall grandfather clock ticked quietly against the wall, and in the centre of the room an oval Queen Anne pedestal table stood decorated with spring flowers and several small trinkets of silver. At the end of the hall, an ornately carved staircase wound out of sight to the first floor, and on both sides, several highly polished double-doors led off. Immediately to his left, a spacious living room, and to the right, a large dining room could be seen through wide openings. The walls of both rooms were clad in pale polished wood from floor to ceiling and were decorated with a variety of oil and watercolour paintings of country and maritime scenes. Sir Michael led Jack into the living room towards a redbrick hearth and chimneystack that dominated the far end of the large room in which a number of comfortable chairs and occasional tables had been arranged.

'These bricks were obtained by my grandfather from the ships which used them as ballast. There is another similar chimney at the other end – you can see it opposite,' he said, pointing the length of the house across the hall into the dining room. 'And I have in mind using the stone to improve them both in similar fashion,' he hesitated. 'But, of course, I will accept your advice on this. Perhaps a stone hearth here and a fascia and mantle here,' he said indicating the proportions intended.

'And this is my family crest,' he said moving over to one of the paintings on the wall in which the disembodied head and shoulders of a wistful old man hovered over the family coat of arms.

'That was my grandfather,' Sir Michael explained noticing Jack's glance. 'He was made Baronet by King Charles - Charles the First of course - in happier times before the rout by that barbarian, Cromwell. My grandfather chose the devices of his bearings to reflect both his own and my grandmother's ancestry. The roundel here above the chevron on the shield, and here in miniature inserted into the Baronet's crown, represents my great-grandfather's ancestry; he was descended from a line of warrior knights going back to the Crusades,' Sir Michael said proudly. 'I believe that he added these wavy lines after moving to New Hope. They are supposed to represent the ocean that separates us from his homeland. The rose and fleur-de-lis here on the sinister side reflects my grandmother's line. She was descended from Huguenot Protestants who fled France late last century, escaping Catholic persecution.' At this, he paused to smile whimsically. 'Ironic isn't it, that a Huguenot progeny, should convert to Catholicism to marry my grandfather, and then find herself fleeing Protestant persecution in England - she was a Fleurie hence the rose and fleur-de-lis devices,' Sir Michael offered this last information as an aside. 'And doubly ironic that my father was to become disaffected with Catholicism and bring my siblings and me up as Anglicans! It does rather make a nonsense of it all, doesn't it?'

To Jack it felt awkward to be spoken to in this almost familiar manner by a man normally so distant and aloof. They talked, if not as equals, then at least as if he had been recognised as having some worth.

Jack examined the coat of arms closely, taking some time to consider how he might set about the task of carving it. It was an elaborate design with swirls and banners enveloping a lion rampant proudly offering the shield on which the family devices were displayed. It would take some carving but, although he had never tackled anything quite so intricate before, the artisan within him relished the opportunity to develop his skills. Perhaps he also saw advantage in getting closer to the man who in every sense controlled his future. In this respect, his instincts would eventually prove correct.

'Will you do it?' Sir Michael asked at length.

Jack considered for a moment longer, then smiled at his master.

'Yes, I would like to give it a try,' he said at last, 'but I shall need a workshop of some sort.'

'Of course. I have in mind one of those huts,' Sir Michael said pointing through one of the windows to a cluster of out-houses nearby.

'And I shall need an assistant.'

'You may choose who you like,' Sir Michael replied.

'And there is one more thing, Sir Michael.' Jack wondered whether he might be pressing his luck too far, but decided nevertheless to try one last request. 'I would like to send word home to my family who even now will not know where I am or even whether I am alive or dead. Your house servant, Rose, who you will remember was my travelling companion on *The Rotterdam* will certainly wish to do the same. We also have the painful and belated duty to inform her parents of the tragic loss of their second daughter, Elizabeth, during the crossing. It will be devastating news and a difficult task to perform, but a necessary one all the same. I want your help to get these letters back to England.'

'Ah, yes,' Sir Michael nodded gravely. 'You may give the letters to me when you are ready and I will ensure that they reach your homes with all speed. I travel to Charlestown several times a year to see the shipping agent there, and I am sure he will find a trustworthy captain to get your letters on their way.'

'Thank you,' said Jack in a business-like tone, not yet ready to reveal his gratitude to a still-resented master despite a dawning realisation that he was warming to the man. 'Then I will do my best for you.'

There was a brief contemplative silence before Sir Michael continued, his face now set with a curious cast of humour around his eyes: 'I well remember the day of your arrival,' he said, '- and your obdurate defiance! It was what impressed me about you – and I have a feeling now that our paths were somehow destined to cross. I believe that we will be of service to each other in the future for, mark my words, Easton, I see difficult times ahead in this new colony of ours, and good men to trust with its defence are hard to find.'

Jack nodded with due gravity, assuming an expression that he thought appropriate to such weighty sentiments - while inwardly wondering at Sir Michael's meaning.

Chapter Twelve

Looking back on it in years to come, Jack would see his first commission by Sir Michael as a turning point on his long path to rehabilitation and restitution, but he did not recognise it as such at the time.

'Ned,' he said cheerfully as he burst into the hut after returning from his meeting with Sir Michael, 'how'd you like to be an assistant mason? I think we might be spared from the fields for a while!'

It was the first time Ned had heard any tone of lightness in his friend's voice since he had known him. Ever since their earliest times together on *The Rotterdam*, Jack had been morose; and the death of Elizabeth had thrown him into a deeper gloom which had persisted, making him poor company. By contrast, when he thought about it at all, Ned reckoned himself content. Certainly he had had to work harder than he had ever worked in his life, but the regularity of his work, the dependability of his shelter, and most important of all, the reliability of his sustenance, had given him a feeling of security that he had never before enjoyed.

As a young man, Ned had followed his father into pig and sheep husbandry on common land in Berkshire. It was a life of bare subsistence, but it was all that he had ever known. He had never married; the harshness of his working life had given him little opportunity to meet young women in the locality, and when he did make overtures they seemed put off by his poor prospects - if not his odours. And so he had lived with his parents in a rented cottage until the common land on which they grazed their beasts was enclosed thus denying them their living. With nowhere to put their stock, the family had been forced to sell up and move to meagre if not squalid lodgings in the nearby town of Newbury while seeking other work. Sadly, the upheaval had proved too much for his mother who had died soon afterwards – followed quickly into eternity by a distraught and penniless father. Within the space of a season therefore, Ned had found himself orphaned, made homeless, and cast into an uncompromising world alone. For a time, he had wandered from farm to farm as an itinerant shepherd taking work wherever he could find it. The peace and open spaces of the countryside suited his temperament, but the work was intermittent, and in lean times he had drifted into the towns in search of work of any sort to tide him over. And when there was no work to be found and starvation threatened, the good souls who dispensed charity to the poor had helped him until he could find work again. This had been the pattern of Ned Holding's life until he had fallen in with bad company.

Ned was a burly man with big hands and a wild mien formed in his years of rough living, and this and his almost total absence of guile had made him an attractive accomplice for the unscrupulous. Over six feet tall, he would have looked threatening in an alleyway at night, and he was thus just the right man to block the way of passers-by while his two wily partners rifled their frightened victims' pockets. Eventually the night watchmen had sprung a trap and caught him in the act - it had taken three of them to hold him − while his disloyal fellows, fleeter by foot than he, had got away scot-free. And so Ned had taken the rap for their robberies and was consequently sentenced to hang. However, for reasons explained earlier, transportation was commonly offered as an alternative and, happily for Ned, this offer was made in his case. Perhaps the judge saw in Ned some redeeming quality that warranted a second chance? It would be fair to say that Ned was not generally known for his quick thinking, but it did not take him long to decide what he would do.

Since then, he had often reflected on his subsequent good fortune in finding a friend in Jack. It had been Jack who had spoken out for him on *The Rotterdam* and by so doing had brought him to New Hope, and now it was Jack again who would lead him in a new and more interesting direction, relieving him of the hard labour in the fields. And moreover, he was delighted to see Jack's sudden change of mood.

One of the old outbuildings not fifty yards from the main house was allocated to Jack and Ned to serve as a workshop. However, the pull of gravity, and the battering of winter winds over the building's long existence had warped its uprights so that it now leant at a precarious angle under the weight of its rickety roof. The first tasks of their new employment, therefore, were to restore sufficient stability to the edifice to save it from collapse, and to patch up the walls and roof to protect its inhabitants from the wind and rain which passed through the structure almost unimpeded. If these essential objectives were quickly achieved, it cannot be said that the result of the improvements was pleasing on the eye. While its roofline remained roughly horizontal, its elevations were distinctly rhomboidal, and its cladding and roof-tiles a hotchpotch of angles, shapes, and textures which lent it a derelict if not intoxicated air. It was perhaps just as well that the workshop was hidden from the view of the house by a cluster of bushes and small trees. Eventually, the workshop was declared ready for use, and a dozen men were enlisted from the plantation to haul the stone up from the creek and deposit it outside the door. At last, everything was in place for the work to begin.

Jack's first job was to take measurements of the fireplace, and then come up with a number of possible designs for Sir Michael's approval. The landowner proved quite hard to please and thus it took several amendments to Jack's drawings before he was content to allow him to proceed. The chosen scheme included a broad arched fireplace with a large keystone at its apex on which the coat of arms would be carved. About one foot above the arch, a stone shelf would span the construction, and this would sit on two stone brackets carved to resemble clusters of wild roses. At each side of the arched opening, a plain wall of stone would extend laterally by about one foot and be finished with a simple fluted return that would connect with the pattern on the hearth. To facilitate construction, Jack then divided the design into blocks of various sizes to be carved individually and then assembled like jigsaw pieces to form the whole in-situ. No mortar would be used except to provide a backing key to bed the stone onto the bricks of the existing chimney, and so the fireplace would be held together entirely using geometrically-cut joints and friction.

Over the following months, Jack devoted himself to his art; sometimes immediately satisfied with his work, more often so exasperated with the result that he threw long-worked pieces away in disgust to start all over again. But slowly, block-by-block, the fireplace took shape in his workshop. And all the time, Ned worked as the dutiful assistant, helping his friend by splitting the stone, fetching and lifting more from the diminishing pile outside, and cutting and smoothing the blocks. For both, it became so completely absorbing that they often lost track of the time of day, working well beyond the hours that they had previously worked in the fields.

Their work drew frequent visits by Sir Michael himself, curious, as well as impatient, to see how the work was progressing. 'I see that you work long hours – I am impressed!' he said jovially on one occasion. 'I shall have food sent over from the house - I would not want you to wilt from lack of nourishment!' Clearly he was pleased with what he had seen.

And it was probably no coincidence that he nominated Rose from his household to be the one to keep the pair supplied. Her slender form would now be seen making the short journey from the house to the hut carrying a covered tray at the beginning and end of each day. For Jack especially, the more frequent contact with Rose was at first an uneasy pleasure; their previously separate living and working arrangements had given them little contact. In truth, neither had gone out of their way to seek the other's company, both coping with their grief at Elizabeth's loss and their separation from loved ones at home by burying themselves in the routines of their work. If Jack had seemed gloomy to Ned, then he had seemed sullen and withdrawn to Rose, and her earlier sympathy for him had long evaporated in her resentment that he seemed to care little for her own feelings of sorrow and loss. Moreover, the memory of their flirtatious glances at that long ago betrothal celebration had become a matter of recurring remorse which had driven a wedge of awkwardness between them; if their apparently mutual attraction had excited her then, she had buried it in guilt since; it now seemed such a betrayal of her dead sister's memory that she had sometimes wondered if God had been punishing her for it. And it had been no excuse either that Elizabeth had shown her feelings for Jack to be uncertain even in betrothal. While her sister's misgivings had vexed Rose at the time, and she had lectured her sister on constancy, she realised that she had been thinking more of Jack than of her sister and was ashamed that her loyalty had been so divided. Such do the regrets brought on by the loss of a dear one become tortured, especially for one so hopelessly indecisive and also so clearly in need of sisterly love. Rose had not shaken off the notion that she had let her sister down, and thus she had needed and had sought the penitence of solitude.

Jack, on the other hand, had come to feel that Rose blamed him for everything that had transpired and was shunning his company; and this feeling had by now become entrenched in his mind to create a void of misunderstanding between them that neither seemed inclined to put right. Thus it was that when Rose made her first visits to the hut, little more than awkward glances passed between them, and this uneasiness had persisted for some time as the stonework continued. But by degree and aided by the interventions of Ned whose simple sensitivity seemed tuned to alleviating their discomfort, Jack learnt again to be easier in Rose's company, and she apparently in his.

After four months, the work on the first fireplace was finished and the structure lovingly installed to the great pleasure and pride of the de Burghs who immediately set the duo to work on a similar fireplace for the dining room. And after this was finished, yet more commissions followed from neighbouring landowners who had admired Jack's work on their visits to New Hope. This was a matter of great satisfaction to Sir Michael who began to derive a useful income from the fees he charged for his servant's work. And to Jack, this exploitation of his skills did not seem an unreasonable exchange for the further privileges which he and Ned were afforded - they were, after all, still convicts, and few of their fellows could aspire to such favourable treatment by their masters. Perhaps more important for Jack than anything else, was that he could work again with his beloved stone, using his skills and artistry rather than the brute strength of his labour in the fields. The work had proved both cleansing and uplifting, and it had given him back his self-respect.

Because of his success, they were soon allocated more comfortable living accommodation and awarded the status and privileges of foremen, allowing them some freedom to travel in the immediate locality; and Rose, who had until now merely delivered food to their workshop, was allotted time to keep house for the two men. While still somewhat basic and little more than a converted store-shed, their new quarters were quickly made to feel cosy under Rose's resourceful administrations. Thus, as the end of their fourth year at New Hope approached, life for the threesome had taken a distinct turn for the better. And as Jack reflected upon his improving fortunes with each passing day, he felt the weight lifting from his shoulders and the narrow-sight of gloomy introspection broaden into a brighter and more optimistic view. In it, he saw a future in which he might once more regain control of his life and was buoyed up by it. It was with this new outlook that Jack entered a period of relative calm in his enforced stay at New Hope, the keen edge of his bitterness blunted by these small victories over adversity. For a time, his thoughts of home would also be displaced by the fulfilment that he now drew from his work, and his resolve to settle the score with Smyke was temporarily forgotten.

The first day of the new year of 1755 dawned frosty and clear after weeks of gloomy overcast, and Ned was already away with a party of men to drag some new stone up from the quay in the belief that the sled would move more easily on the frozen ground before the sun had a chance to soften it. Inside the workshop, warmed by the heat of a blackened wood-stove which puffed and creaked as if it were exhausted, Jack worked with great concentration on his latest design. Through the window, a horizontal sun beamed in to illuminate his current piece of work that basked in the light and shone like a golden icon in the smoky haze that filled the room. The door latch lifted with a loud clack, and Rose backed in awkwardly carrying her morning tray. Turning to kick the door shut behind her, she immediately seemed to be thrown into a mild fluster at finding herself and Jack alone.

'Oh!' she said a little breathlessly, 'is Ned not here? I have brought you your breakfast.'

'Put it down near the stove, Rose, he'll be back soon, he's down at the quay,' Jack mumbled, still bent over his work, preoccupied with some item of detail.

'It's good of you to bring it over for us, thank you,' he added, smiling, and holding her eyes with his for just a moment too long, so that it suddenly became a little awkward between them. She dropped her eyes as he turned his away, neither therefore noticing the slight flush coming into the other's cheeks. He cleared his throat and returned to his work, quickly losing himself again in concentration. But it was not more than a few minutes later that he put down his chisel and straightened His eyes still locked upon his piece, he put his hands to his sides and arched his spine luxuriously, then took a few steps back to gain a more distant perspective, his head tilting from side to side in critical assessment. Then, as if taken by surprise, he realised that Rose was still in the room:

'Oh Rose, I'm sorry, I thought you'd...' he said diffidently, his voice tailing off as he saw her smiling.

'I love watching you work Jack, you look so content,' she replied warmly, and walked around the bench to stand next to him in order to inspect his new carving from his angle. It was a fine piece of work to be sure; a chamfered keystone on which had been carved a fleur-de-lis motif.

'It's very good, Jack,' she said in genuine admiration, impulsively wrapping her arm through his, and letting it remain there for some moments as she leant forward to examine the detail more closely as if to balance herself. At last she let go and straightened while still remaining close by his side, not seeming to be in a hurry to move away.

Jack had become instantly alive to her nearness in the warm intimacy of the room, and her touch had tingled with an almost electric pleasure from which he still trembled. The sensation had taken him quite by surprise; it had been so long since he had felt a woman's tenderness. Desire surged urgently through his veins. He could feel her presence tangibly, almost as if her whole body was still pressed against his side. A rush of heightened sensitivity skittered across his flesh like a shiver and the hairs on the back of his neck seemed to stand on end. His breathing shortened and his heart began to pound at such a pace that he could hear his pulse throbbing in his ears. He caught her scent – musty fragrances of the herbs and soaps of the scullery never smelled so sweet! Jack could barely stop himself from reaching out and pulling her to him. He turned towards her and their eyes met. Her lips parted in an enigmatic smile, her upturned face, demure, her soft brown eyes, inviting. He felt himself drawn towards her as if by some magnetic force and sighed as if giving up the struggle to resist, almost letting himself yield to its power. Almost. But his limbs would not move; something had paralysed him as if he had been stung while his thoughts simmered in a heady cauldron of guilt and desire. He struggled inwardly, torn in two by the conflicting feelings, but then his ardour cooled. The penetrating logic of his mind had once more imposed itself, bursting the bubble of his heightened emotions like the point of a knife. It was the sister of his betrothed who stood before him: how could he betray Elizabeth's memory, how could he let himself give in? He interrogated her eyes, wondering if his inner turmoil had been exposed, but she dropped her gaze and abruptly turned away.

'Sit for a while, Rose,' Jack called quickly, clearing his throat to steady his voice. 'We could share a little of this cider?' He lifted the jug from the tray that she had brought in and offered it up. 'I'm sure that Ned would not begrudge you a sip from his cup.'

There was a trace of nervousness in her expression as she turned back, but she signalled her consent with a smile and accepted the cup offered with warm grace. Jack opened the doors of the stove to reveal the blazing fire within, and the two sat themselves in front of it, the blast of radiant heat lighting up their faces as they sipped in silence, both staring with thoughtful intensity into the flames. Jack was sure that he had given himself away, and felt embarrassed by it, but he ventured some conversation:

'Your time must nearly be up, Rose. What will you do?' he asked, trying to keep his voice neutral.

'I'm not yet sure, Jack,' she replied carefully after a moment's thought. 'My heart draws me back to England, to my parents, to all that I knew and grew up with. But when I think of returning without..,' she hesitated, '..without my sister, my mind recoils from the thought.'

'Your parents will know of Elizabeth's death if our letters have found their way home, Rose, and your return will be a great consolation to them. I think that you must obey your heart.'

'Must I, Jack?' She looked at him curiously, levelling her dark beguiling eyes on his. 'And what will become of you?' she asked softly.

For a moment, Jack paused, unsure of what to say. He returned Rose's gaze, examining her face in the glow of the fire; her eyes sparkled with the reflection of the flames, and he noticed now how prettily her lashes curled, how lovely was the sheen of her long dark hair. Her face had lost the drawn grey hues of earlier times and now looked bonny and full of life once more.

'You should not think of me, Rose – you must think of yourself. I am exiled - I have become reconciled to making a new life for myself here.' He spoke lightly, bravely even, but in his heart he knew that her going would leave a yawning gap in his life, just at a time when he was coming to terms with his loss. Yet he could not know what she herself felt. He looked into her eyes, searching for some indication of her underlying feelings but found himself unsure of her intent; her gaze was so alluring, so expectant, yet he was as incapable of interpreting its signals as he was of unravelling his own jumble of thoughts. Their shared experiences bound them together so that it seemed inconceivable that they could part, but no words had passed between them that spoke of anything greater than friendship. At heart, he still felt himself inhibited by the spectre of a disapproving Elizabeth – unsure if it would be an affront to her memory for him to press his suit, afraid that Rose would lose respect for him if he tried. Moreover, he would remain a convict slave for many more years to come while she would soon be free, and he could not ask her to make the sacrifice of binding herself to someone so imprisoned in poverty. In this confusion, Jack came to reason that he must not beg her to stay. 'To do so,' he thought, 'might bring her womanly sympathies into play and precipitate a decision that she might regret.'

Rose searched his eyes for meaning, just as he had searched hers, immediately recognising the same uncertainties and fears, the same longings and doubts that she herself had felt. She had spent most of her four-year term daydreaming of her eventual return, with mounting and joyful anticipation as the years had passed. But her eagerness for the long-awaited date to arrive seemed recently to have waned. She knew why, of course. It was the renewal of her friendship with Jack that had cast everything in a new light, and now she was not at all sure what she felt. The odd estrangement between them in the early years had all but excluded him from her thinking so that it had never occurred to her that she would face a difficult choice when the time came to leave. Until recent months, there had been no question in her mind - she would return to England and be glad to put all this behind her. But she studied him now, as she had studied him often over the recent months since Sir Michael had thrown them back together, and she knew that he stirred her heart again just as he had before. His looks, his gentle toughness, his buoyant character - all this endeared him to her, as did the brilliance of his work and the kindness and affection he had shown towards her. Her intuition whispered that they could love one another; she could see it in his eyes, and her heart gave a little flutter of delight at the thought. But, like Jack, in different ways she too was torn; the idea of choosing to remain instead of returning to England, of thus choosing a life of continuing servitude with Jack bound for ten more years, frightened her out of her wits. She was therefore quite certain that for his sake, she must not encourage him until she had made up her mind, not realising that her beguiling smiles and her tender embrace of his arm had already begun to do just that.

'Perhaps you are right, Jack,' she said letting the moment pass. And with that, an opportunity was lost that both would quickly regret. Yet there would be several similar inconsequential occasions over the coming weeks when one or the other would come close, but not quite close enough, to bring themselves to make the declaration that hovered uncertainly in both their hearts.

It was not until two months later that things were brought to a head in a rather unexpected way. It was now Spring, the season of hope and promise after a prolonged and miserable winter, and four years since the threesome's arrival at New Hope. Sir Michael had developed a habit of visiting the workshop at the beginning of each week, and today, being the day after the Sabbath, he would visit as usual. He had taken a great interest in Jack's work, especially since it continued to provide good income for the estate; but on this occasion it was more than pecuniary interest that was on his mind. As Sir Michael entered, Jack and Ned were standing at the workbench covered in stone dust readying a hefty block for carving, this time a boss for the church altarpiece on which a simple cross would be carved. Oddly, Sir Michael hovered at the door holding it open while beckoning to someone unseen outside who apparently needed some encouragement to enter. Jack craned his neck curious to discover who would be keeping his master waiting, and was surprised to see Rose hesitating outside the door. But caught by Jack's puzzled glance, she became flustered, at first retreating from view before reappearing, her face flushed by the three men's bemused scrutiny. Eventually she came in without a word and stood uncertainly by the window while Jack and Ned exchanged glances, baffled by her strange behaviour. Jack wondered what in God's name could be afoot, but he found it yet more puzzling when all three of them were invited to sit with him, drawing together the odd collection of chairs and stools that littered the workshop. Sir Michael was an enlightened master, humane and considerate to his servants and slaves, but to sit in his presence, except in church, was indeed uncomfortably odd.

'I have recently been speaking with Rose on the subject of the completion of her period of indenture,' Sir Michael said getting down to business in his usual forthright manner. 'And this has also given me cause to think about *your* futures too,' he said squarely meeting the two men's bewildered eyes. 'I have brought Rose with me to discuss the matter because I rather suspect that she will have an interest in the outcome of what I have to say.' Sir Michael's lips twitched with the glimmer of a smile as he flicked a subtle glance at Rose who, in turn, quickly averted her eyes, seeming to find something on the floor which drew her interest.

Sir Michael continued: 'I have come increasingly to harbour some uneasiness as to your status here, Easton, as I have got to know you better and as you have proved yourself so helpful to my estate. I know full well that I am entitled to ask what I like of you while you remain indentured, but I seek to make things more satisfactory for you.' He paused uncertainly, then added by way of further explanation: 'I see you as a good man, Easton, and I want to induce you to remain here as a freeman on whose loyalty I can count for support. I want good men around me whom I can trust, rather than embittered servants who might feel unjustly done by. At the same time, I am conscious that your criminal record will be a permanent impediment to your status here, and I believe that it is my Christian duty to help redeem you. That is as far as others are concerned,' he added quickly, 'for I know that you protest your innocence.' Jack took a sidelong glance at Ned, hoping for a sign of understanding as to where Sir Michael's rhetoric was leading, but got none. Ned's expression was more than usually blank. After an instant of reflection, Sir Michael went on: 'To be frank, Easton, I believe that we can be helpful to each other and, to come at last to the point, I have a proposition which I hope you will find attractive.'

This made Jack sit up; having helped his father manage the quarry business in Portland, the word 'proposition' had always captured his interest quickly.

'My proposal is this:' Sir Michael went on, 'in exchange for your continuing to provide services to me on a basis agreeable to us both, say, for the next seven years, I will free you from your indentures with immediate effect. And, furthermore, I will make available to you fifty acres of good land and the wherewithal to build a homestead on it for a nominal quitrent.' He raised an eyebrow, pausing briefly to gauge Jack's reaction. 'You may farm the land for your own living, and I will give you a field horse and whatever else you need, within reason, to help you set yourself up. After that of course, you must pay for whatever you purchase in the normal way, or by further service to me or through the sale or exchange of whatever marketable commodity you produce. In addition, I would expect you, as I would expect all my tenants, to serve under me in the defence of our lands and freedoms if it falls upon me to form a militia.'

At this, Jack's eyebrows wrinkled perceptibly and he took a breath as if to speak, but Sir Michael raised his hand; he was not yet finished. He now turned to address Ned who looked perplexed in his struggle to keep up with the pace of the discourse.

'As far as you are concerned, Holder, if this offer is accepted by Easton, I am prepared to sign your indentures over to him, so that it will be up to him how he discharges you.'

Jack shifted uneasily in his chair, uncomfortable at Sir Michael's last remark but chose to let it pass.

'And what after the seven years are up?' Jack asked evenly.

'Assuming you keep to your side of the contract during that period, then the land will become yours, and I shall have no further call upon you, save, I hope, for your continuing good neighbourliness,' Sir Michael replied.

Jack nodded, satisfied, but then returned to the earlier point that had troubled him. 'You mention militia service, Sir Michael?' Jack spoke slowly choosing his words carefully. 'To be clear with you, I would serve only to counter hostility against us, I would not follow a commander bent on any reckless pursuit or on any unjust or dishonest mission.'

'Of course, man, of course,' Sir Michael replied earnestly. 'As a freeman, you would be free to follow your conscience, but I hope that, like any honourable man, you would rise to your responsibilities. This condition is merely a precaution and unlikely to become an issue; at present there are no threats which need concern us.'

Jack sat back in his chair and gazed through the window, his face inscrutable as he collected his thoughts, while Rose and Ned glanced at each other expectantly, awaiting his reaction. Sir Michael quietly excused himself. 'I'll leave you to think it over,' he said kindly as he left, and for a good half-minute after the door-latch had fallen, it would have been possible to hear a pin drop as Jack continued his thoughtful gazing. Eventually, his face wrinkled and broke slowly into a smile; then, without warning, he leapt up with a great whoop of glee, slapping his thigh in excitement, a broad grin creasing his face almost from ear to ear. Ned leapt up too, enveloping his friend in a bear hug as he yelled his congratulations, and the pair danced a little jig around the workshop in demented excitement, laughing hilariously as they stumbled and tripped on their way.

Rose beamed, delighted to see Jack in such gleeful spirits, her heart full of joy for the freedoms which both she and now Jack had regained. Yet Sir Michael's proposals had not come as a surprise - she had been told of his thinking the previous evening when unusually she had been invited to sit with the couple for a serious discussion about her future. And the news had thrown her into an immediate tizzy, for her womanly intuition told her at once that a restraint holding back Jack's amorous advances would now be removed; she wondered if Sir Michael had already guessed that this might be the case as his reason for letting her into his confidence. As she had walked with him towards the workshop that morning, she had suddenly been overcome with uncertainty about the decision that might soon be thrust upon her. In accepting Jack's proposal, should it come, she would be sealing her fate, locking herself in to a life of peasantry in a country still short of the amenities that she had become used to at home; and she was not sure if she was up to it. Even at the door of the workshop, she had drawn back, her heart racing with excitement and apprehension at the same time. But now, seeing Jack so happy at the prospect of the new life before him, she had made up her mind. She gazed affectionately upon the two men now speculating happily about their new freedoms, and she laughed with them out loud. There was no longer any doubt in her mind - they had become her family now. It was as if she was seeing Jack again for the first time, just as she had a lifetime ago in Portland when his attachment to her sister had put him out of bounds.

Jack had been bowled over by Sir Michael's proposition, and his mind still reeled as he rambled on excitedly to Ned about the future. Out of the corner of his eye, he had become aware that Rose was watching him and had begun to exchange fond glances with her as he talked, seeing his own happiness reflected in her face as she had shared his laughter. Something in her eyes told him that things had changed from her perspective too, and he wondered if he might risk a proposition of his own - certainly the major obstacle to the sharing of their lives had now been removed. And in the heady intoxication of his excitement, he began to see at last what to others had been patently obvious for some time - that they were made for each other – and he resolved that he would put an end to his self-doubting reticence.

The buoyant mood in the workshop ran its course until, noticing the glances passing between his two companions, Ned took the hint and excused himself. After the amusement of his playfully obsequious leave-taking had died, Jack and Rose were left facing each other in an awkward silence, their glances first turning from coyness to an expectant estimation of each other and then finally into knowing smiles. Jack knew then that Rose would stay, that she had made her choice. Just as she knew that he had made his. And they moved towards each with joy in their hearts to embrace. It was a desperate embrace, fierce and clinging, charged with the force and tang of past denial. But when they kissed, their kisses were not hungry or salacious, but tender and caressing; the kind of kisses shared between lovers who are already friends. Yet it was the sublime feeling of peace that each would remember best of that moment; a shared sense of arrival after a rough passage, an invigorating feeling of renewal, a sense of putting behind them all the horrors of the past.

And for a while they would indeed be happy and content, building a new life together on the land that Sir Michael would make available to them in accordance with his offer. But unfortunately their difficulties were not yet entirely behind them.

Chapter Thirteen

October 1757

Two relatively happy and fulfilling years passed for Jack and Rose as man and wife, during which time their energies were so entirely absorbed in building a life for themselves on their new land that they had time to think of almost nothing else. It was a time of renewal and healing for both in their joint endeavour as they learned to live as a married couple, and as each gradually let go of the past and became accustomed to thinking of a new and more optimistic future.

The fifty-acre plot allocated to them by Sir Michael was situated on a broad spur of elevated ground wedged between the Potomac and a winding but navigable creek at the southern extremity of the New Hope estate. It was good land, blessed with fresh water, fertile soil, and timber in abundance – in fact, it had every commodity necessary to build up a small farm and a decent living for its hard-working inhabitants. During the period, Jack and Ned had also kept up with the contracted quota of stonework for Sir Michael's estate as well as developing a useful income carving for some of the wealthier landowners in the area. In this, Jack had found it profitable to extend his carving to hardwood to which he had found his skills adequately transferable; there seemed to be a call for such work in the finer residences of St Mary's County as others had come to hear of him. It was as yet a modest supplementary income, but one that had provided some of the little comforts that had furnished and equipped their new home. It was the farm itself, however, that would provide the essential staples of living and, assisted by some men loaned by Sir Michael at the start of his tenancy, it had been Jack's first task to get some land cleared and planted. By their first Thanksgiving, they had been able to put in store sufficient victuals to see them through their first winter without too much borrowing, and by the end of their second summer at New Hope Farm, the lives of its inhabitants were at last beginning to feel secure. It would thus seem unjust and cruel after so much had been accomplished that the past should still be capable of reaching out to unsettle the couple's hard-won stability. But that is indeed how it would feel to Rose on the day on which Jack decided that he must return to England.

There are few things which could have stirred Jack to such a precipitous decision after so many years had passed since his uncomfortable departure from England now almost seven years before, especially since his life with Rose had taken such an unexpected turn for the better. In other circumstances, it might have been possible to allow the bitterness of the past to fade - to forget his pledge of revenge against Smyke whose evil deeds had caused him so much sorrow and loss. But the news he had received in a letter from his mother had re-ignited a quiescent fury to the point of incandescence - it was the news that his father had taken his own life. And it did not make it any easier to know that the news was already more than a year old, the letter having taken so long to be conveyed by the hands of well meaning but dilatory travellers.

On the day of his decision, Jack had been working the top field since dawn, struggling behind his mare to steer his home-built plough through the acre or so of ground baked hard by a long hot summer. His tanned and sweat-streaked face was contorted with strain as he pulled the weary beast to a halt and leant his weight heavily upon the handles of his apparatus to rest. Pulling out a flask of apple-press from his jacket pocket, he gulped it down thirstily then let his gaze wander as he caught his breath. It was one of those blissful days in late October where the sun had traced its shortening path across a cloudless sky to bring the Autumn colours into spectacular relief. From his elevated position, he could see a schooner in the distance drifting down the Potomac on the ebb, its sails glowing amber in the late afternoon sun. Through the thinning trees, the ship seemed suspended in their branches like a gleaming bauble. And below him, perhaps a hundred yards from where he now rested, nestled into the head of a little wooded creek, lay the heart of his new farmstead, a cluster of wooden buildings lit up brightly in the golden light. Jack gazed at it with pride, fondly remembering the kindness of the New Hope servants and slaves who had turned out to help build it. It was a wedding gift more valuable than any that could have been contemplated - the gift of their labour, for they had nothing else to give. Smoke curled upwards from the chimney of his cottage sitting prominently in the centre of the cluster, and seeing it made him think of Rose who would by now have gone inside to prepare the evening meal. The picture of her in his mind brought back the memory of his mother's letter, and his heart sank again as he contemplated telling her what he had resolved to do.

Jack was exhausted, but he wanted the field finished today for there would be much else to do before he could depart on the dangerous journey that he was now determined to make. With grim satisfaction, he surveyed his work. Where this morning had stood the straggly remnants of the tobacco harvest, freshly-turned soil now lay ready for planting the winter wheat; he would give the field a break from tobacco next year to help it recover. He urged his old mare once more into action and started down the gently sloping ground, his plough swinging erratically as its blunted point bucked and swerved in the rough and stumpy earth. Arriving at the tree line, he pulled the mare once more to a halt. The stoic beast shook her mane and snorted as Jack wrestled her and his apparatus into position for the final pass across the field. His manoeuvring at last completed, he rested again, pushing his hat to the back of his head, and drew a weary arm across his forehead to clear the sweat from his brow.

Leaning back upon the handles of the plough, he let himself be taken by the angry and bitter thoughts that had kept him from his sleep since reading of his father's sad demise. Jack had tried desperately to erase the picture of it from his mind, yet he could not stop himself imagining the desperate and lonely agonies that must have driven this tough and brave man to throw himself from the cliffs.

On his first reading of the letter, Jack had felt strangely numbed, unable to locate his feelings for a father he had not seen for so long; his foremost thoughts were for his mother whose distraught tones cried out through an unsteady prose fractured by her distress. But then, the memories of his father had penetrated the shroud that his mind had long drawn over that episode in his life, and once again, he had felt the sharp pain of the long-ago moment of his last embrace, snatched as he had been led along the quay. Jack's troubled dreams had returned immediately, and in them he had seen his father before him almost as if he had been real. The image of him had been so vivid that Jack had felt the tight grip of his father's arms; had sensed the tall man's unshaven stubble rasp upon his cheek; and he had seen the haunted look in his father's eyes - it was a look of despair.

His mother's written words had seemed almost spoken aloud, borne to him by the wind; they had torn at his heart like the sobbing voice of a lost child. She had written that his father had never recovered from Jack's exile, that he had blamed himself severely for it, burdening himself yet further with the death of young Ben who he believed would have lived but for his failure. And when Jack's news of Elizabeth's death had reached him, he had driven himself into yet deeper despondency seeming to take upon his own shoulders the burdens of grief and recrimination both of her parents and of Jack himself at the loss of a daughter and a wife and the unborn child that she had carried. The sorrow and dishonour that he had heaped upon himself, his mother wrote, had finally brought him down; he had become inconsolable so that nothing seemed able to drag him back from the brink. Elizabeth's death had been the final straw that had brought this proud man to abject despair, and in one unhappy and reckless act, he had ended his suffering for ever.

Inwardly, Jack had raged as he pictured the pitiful decline of a beloved father brought so low; and this by the same calamitous misfortune that had so nearly brought himself to his knees. Smyke had been the cause of his father's death just as surely as if the shot he had aimed at Jack on that fateful night had instead buried itself deeply in his father's breast. The painful memories of that terrible time, rekindled by the belated letter, had brought Jack to a reappraisal of his present state, and suddenly all that had been achieved since seemed hollow. At first, he had retreated into self-pity, enfeebled by the odds against redress, but this had been quickly consumed by a fierce anger that had welled up within him. Bridling at his own impotence, Jack pictured Smyke as he had last seen him, standing smugly at the window overlooking the Quay as he had been led shackled onto the ship at Weymouth, his face warped by the mists of bitter memory, gloating through the distorting glass. Jack hated the man as he had never hated before; it coursed through his veins like a galvanising current. If Smyke had stood before him then, he would have been punched senseless in a purgative frenzy of savage revenge. There were some things, he realised, that after all could not be left undone; despite all reason, despite pious restraint, despite the risks involved – he must make Smyke suffer just as he had suffered. That he could still feel such raw and unrestrained animosity after so much time both surprised and frightened him.

Over the last few days, he had had time to reflect. He was calmer now, but he had reached his decision; whatever the risk and whatever the cost, he must go back to England to bring Smyke to account.

Jack yanked the reins and whistled shrilly.

'Get along now,' he shouted through gritted teeth.

The sky was already dark as Jack entered the kitchen of the little wooden house to find Rose preparing the evening meal. The amber glow of lamplight reflected off the bare-wood walls, and the cosy warmth and homely smells of hot corn bread contrasted starkly with the damp musty air that he had left behind him in the stable. Rose was kneeling by the fire with her back to the room administering to a cooking-pot that was suspended on chains over the red embers. Even part-masked by the fullness of her clothes, her comely figure caught his attention straight away, and he moved over to her and ran the back of his hand affectionately down her neck as she worked.

'Ned and Sebi not in yet?' he asked lightly.

'Ned was in the barn earlier checking the tobacco,' she replied reaching up to take his hand and bring it to her cheek. 'Then I believe he went off to feed the chickens and the hogs - he'll be back soon enough, with supper cooking! And Sebi's been in the garden most of the afternoon; he brought some squash and sweet corn in - look!' she said brightly letting him go, pointing her spoon towards the table. She looked up at Jack and smiled, her pretty face shining with perspiration as it glowed in the reflection of the fire. Some strands of her long black hair dangled fetchingly over her forehead drawing his eyes to hers, but her expression changed as she seemed to sense Jack's troubled mood. Raising herself from the hearth, she rubbed her hands clean on her apron, and wrapped her arms gently around him. He returned the embrace, and they held each other for a while. At length, she pulled herself back, still holding his waist, and examined him squarely; Jack knew that he must present a doleful picture.

'You've been thinking of your father,' she said softly. It was a statement rather than a question, but her eyes spoke her concern. Jack pulled her to him and kissed her gently on the lips.

'I'm sorry I've been so down-hearted, Rose, but I have settled it in my mind now.' He searched her eyes, wondering if the time was right to tell her of his plan, trying to gauge what her reaction might be. He thought back fondly to the day when she had made her decision to stay with him and not return to England, remembering their first embrace. For both of them, it had been a salvation and re-birth; a delivery from the lonely isolation in which they had both sought solace after Elizabeth's death. The wedding had taken place in the little church on the shores of the Potomac, in front of the stone altarpiece that he had been carving on the day that Rose had said she would be his. On the front of the piece, a relief of the cross had been carved, but on the reverse, hidden from normal view, he had carved a miniature rosette in honour of her name; theirs was the first wedding following its installation. Jack smiled at the memory, and seeing the joy reflected in his face, Rose smiled back, bringing her hand up to caress his cheek.

'I'm glad,' she said softly, reaching up to kiss him. Then, in an abrupt change of mood, she laughed. 'Now go and get yourself cleaned up – you're disgustingly filthy!'

Just as she spoke, Sebi pushed open the door and backed unsteadily into the room carrying a pile of logs in his arms that left only the top of his tightly curled grey hair visible as he passed.

'Comin' through! Comin' through!' he called as a warning.

Jack moved over to steady him and relieve him of some of the load, and between them they transported the logs to the hearth where they stacked them carefully in a pile.

When Sebi had first arrived at the Easton homestead two years before, he had done so as a slave, having been retired early from New Hope and transferred to Jack's ownership as a further gesture of good will on Sir Michael's part. But Jack had indicated to Sebi instead that he would work not as a slave but as one whose labour would earn him rights and benefits equal to those he enjoyed himself (the same offer he had made to Ned), running the new farm on a sort of co-operative basis. In taking this initiative, Jack had won Sebi's loyalty immediately. For the first time in his life, Sebi was treated as equal to a white man, finding himself in a mixed community whose fates were shared. In return, Sebi's conscientious and cheerful contribution had proved instrumental in bringing the little farm quickly to a happy state of self-sufficiency. Indeed, Ned often quipped that under Sebi's black skin, he must have green fingers, for within months of his arrival he was already bringing in produce from his newly created kitchen garden. There always seemed to be a glint in his eye as if he was amused by some perpetual comedy that went on secretly inside his head, yet the reason for this happy disposition was mystifying. He had been taken from the Ivory Coast as a twelve-year old and had spent his entire adult life in slave labour, not all of it under the relatively benign regime of New Hope. As if that hadn't been enough, his woman (for he had never been permitted to call her 'wife') had died of river fever in her thirties; and only two years later, a careering hogshead on the rolling-road had mowed down the youngest of his children. Yet nothing seemed to get him down.

'Yeah, Mr Jack, you go an' get yoursel' cleaned up like Miss Rose says!' Sebi said grinning. 'There's a strange smell aroun' here and it ain't me!' he said waving his hand in front of his face.

There was then a sudden sound of heavy footsteps on the veranda outside which seemed to make the whole house shake, and the door was thrown open as Ned's large presence entered and immediately dominated the suddenly crowded room, his face reddened and his hair dishevelled by the exertions of the day.

'Mmmm! Smells good!' Ned said, revealing the first of his priorities at once, for his large frame needed some feeding. 'What's cooking?' he asked enthusiastically.

'Old Molly's finally gone in the pot.' Rose sighed feigning sadness, glancing over her shoulder with a wry grimace. 'Stopped laying, so...,' she added, leaving the inevitable conclusion hanging in the air. With a few giant but stealthy strides, Ned crossed the room to crane over Rose's hunched back as she busied herself once more in front of the fire.

'So we know what to do with you when you stops cookin'!' he said directly into her ear, grinning from ear to ear.

Rose shrieked, and swung around at him in mock attack, an iron ladle raised menacingly in her hand. Ned cowered in feigned surrender, his arms raised over his head as he retreated back across the room laughing, throwing a conspiratorial wink at the others at the same time. Sebi grinned back enjoying the banter, but Jack had hardly noticed the horseplay - his mind had been elsewhere.

As had become customary during their time at the farmstead, the meal passed discussing the day's work and planning for the days ahead. But Jack's preoccupation since the arrival of his mother's letter had changed the mood in the house, and tonight his brooding seemed even more distracted. Rose, of course, had read the letter, but while she shared her husband's sadness, she could never share his grief. She glanced at him, wondering how she might bring him out of his despondency, and was disconcerted to catch him already looking at her curiously. For a moment, she searched her husband's enigmatic gaze not understanding its meaning, but then some instinct of foreboding hit her, and slowly an icy feeling of apprehension crept across her heart as she began to fear what his earlier remarks might have meant.

At the end of the evening meal, it was the routine for everyone to share in the clearing up, and normally a time for ribbing and happy laughter brought on by the relaxing effects of Sebi's cider. But tonight Jack seemed to have retreated into himself again, and conversation had become strained. Ned had made some brave attempts at conversation in his simple way, but they seemed trite in the heavy atmosphere; the normal happy spontaneity seemed to be unattainable. Glancing over her shoulder from the washing-up tub, Rose caught the bewildered glances which were passing between the two men behind Jack's back as he stood absently collecting items from the table. She caught their attention, and a subtle flick of her head was all that was required to indicate that they should leave early tonight; and Jack was so lost in his thoughts that he neither heard their lame excuses nor even noticed their quiet departure. Suddenly, he and his wife were alone.

Rose then took her husband by the arm and leant her head upon his shoulder.

'Come and sit down,' she said gently, coaxing him into the chair and reaching for the cider jug. And he sat compliantly as she poured a measure of the golden liquid into his beaker before seating herself beside him.

'The news of your father seems to have hit you hard, my love,' she said softly, prompting him to talk.

'Rose, I'm sorry for my brooding, but it is not only my father's death which has been on my mind.' He spoke falteringly. 'My stomach turns when I think what he must have been going through even as we moved here, but the news of his passing has also brought back the memories of that terrible time.' He shook his head despairingly. 'That night we were captured, the squalor of the gaol, young Ben dying there in front of my eyes, that terrifying crossing, poor Elizabeth's horrible death...all those awful, awful things that happened to us. I cannot seem to get the nightmare out of my head.' Jack's face was strained, and a troubled look came into his eyes as he turned towards her. 'Don't you see?'

'Jack, you should not torment yourself so. I thought that we had put all that behind us. Think of what we have made for ourselves here...' Rose answered, trying desperately to divert her husband from his destructive train of thought; but Jack interrupted:

'I know we have rebuilt something of our former lives, Rose, and we must thank God dearly for it, but it cannot ever be the home we could have had...a home with our families around us...a proper place in our own community... a history not tainted with the shame of my conviction. In the eyes of our neighbours here, we are still convicts - we will always be regarded with curiosity, if not suspicion…we can never hold our heads up here despite our success.' Jack's bitterness tumbled from his lips in a torrent, pent up for a long time but now released at last - fragments of thought, recrimination, and guilt, strung together like dull black beads.

'And my family back in Portland ….it seems as if I have closed a door on them. If I had been there, father would still be alive today - and my mother not on the point of ruin, for the quarry has apparently fallen upon hard times.'

He pressed his hands to his face and brought them down over his lips in a gesture of despair. Rose pulled her chair closer to her husband and wrapped her arm around him, gently massaging his shoulder with her hand. She leant her head against his and tried to console him. Her words were softly spoken.

'You say this as if it were all your fault, my dear. You cannot be to blame. How could you have done anything to change any of the terrible things that have happened? Do not be so hard on yourself. Instead, think of our new life, and our new baby…'

Jack softened at this mention of their child, and its mention stopped him in his tracks just as he seemed set to continue his self-reproach. For a moment he was quiet.

'Yes, my dearest Rose, you and our new baby are everything to me, now and in our future together which, God willing, will be long and happy.' He paused, again apparently in thoughtful introspection. 'But I cannot reconcile our future without considering the past. The thought of Smyke, still free, his crimes unanswered… How can I live in any honour with this unresolved? He is the one who has brought all this upon us. I had thought that I could put it all behind me, but my father's death has shown me that I cannot. I know that I can never bring back those poor souls whom we have lost, but I must try to bring Smyke to justice. Even if I fail, I will at least know that I have tried, and not spent my life impotently skulking here in exile.'

Rose now began to shake her head, suddenly appreciating where her husband's words were leading.

'No, Jack! You cannot be thinking of going back!' she said, incredulously, her earlier fears now confirmed in stark substance. 'There is nothing you can do. You are exiled. If you go back, you too will hang - and our child brought into this cruel world without a father!'

She stood quickly, scraping her chair backwards, and moved behind him, throwing both arms tightly around his shoulders in a fierce embrace.

In the silence that followed, the stillness of the room was broken only by the flickering shadows cast by the flame of the oil-lamp that hung suspended from the ceiling. Jack stood and turned to face his wife bringing his hand up to caress her cheek; but she shrugged off his embrace, pulling back from him, shaking her head, tears brimming in her eyes.

'No, Jack, no! You cannot go!' She turned from him to hide her tears, but Jack grabbed her by her shoulders and spun her round to face him.

'Listen to me Rose!' He shook her firmly, protesting, urging her to understand, his face intense. 'D'you think that I *want* to leave you? I feel that I *must* for the sake of our future, that it is my duty! It would be so easy to shrink from the undertaking, but I cannot allow this terrible injustice to blight our name for ever. Can you not see that? I know that I can put this right, but what is even more important for me is that I try. I still have friends who can help in Portland, and I promise you that I shall not put at risk all that we have built up together here. Trust me, and with God's justice I will not fail you; and if I go soon, I can be back before our baby is born.'

Jack's words were fine indeed, and as he spoke them, the articulation seemed a worthy justification of his plan and said in honourable language that he hoped might sway his wife if not to endorse it then at least to acquiesce. And in the main he felt that they were true, yet he would not dare to utter the deeper motive for his goal, for he knew that Rose would never condone a mission of pure revenge.

Chapter Fourteen

The soft patter of raindrops on the shingled roof intruded upon Jack's consciousness and brought him out of his slumber after a fitful night. He opened his eyes and for a while lay quite still, idly watching the shadows harden in the room as dawn's soft fingers probed the cracks in the shutters. Rose lay beside him still asleep, her breathing slow and even. She seemed able to sleep whatever troubles prevailed, yet he had tossed and turned throughout the night, flipping into and out of consciousness as he reflected on their argument the previous evening. Cross words had been spoken in its heat, but they had been hasty volleys fired between instinctive positions defending individual points of view, and in the end both parties had realised it in declaring the temporary truce that had led them exhausted to bed. The discussion would undoubtedly resume, and he dreaded it. He knew that she could not prevent him going, but he would rather have her support than fight her resistance, and the thought of leaving her smouldering with resentment was deeply troubling.

Undeterred, Jack's mind began again to work on the details of his plans, and his pulse quickened as these thoughts raced through his head, turning his initial excitement into anxiety as he counted the difficulties he would face. He found himself fighting an almost irresistible urge to leap from his bed to tackle them, but he recognised that there were some matters that would need attending to before he could begin. He clasped his hands behind his head and gazed into the dark void of the pitched roof above him as he forced his mind to readdress the issues that concerned him. There was no doubt in his mind now that Rose would cope in his absence - she had proved herself to be just as resourceful as he; indeed, were it not for her pregnant state, he suspected that she might have argued to come with him. With Ned and Sebi on the farm, and with others at New Hope to lend a hand, there would be enough labour to keep abreast of essential work. During the winter months, little heavy labour would anyway be required – the sowing of the winter wheat, perhaps some fencing or a few repairs - and with the tobacco already curing, all that remained to be done once it was ready, would be to pack it and take it to the quay. His stonework quota for the Estate was also completed for the year and so Sir Michael would have no call upon him for a while, and as far as subsistence was concerned, Sebi's kitchen garden had already put more than enough in store for the winter ahead. And for purchases of seed or staples, their credit was good, and a reserve of coinage and notes had been built up from payments for his carving work - he would take a little of the latter to cover his travelling expenses, he thought. It had been a good year; on his few acres of tobacco, he could reckon on a yield of six hogsheads, clearing five pounds sterling each, assuming it all cured well enough to pass inspection. His timing, he reasoned with eminent self-satisfaction, could not have been better.

Jack was therefore confident that he could go. 'And the sooner I can get away the better; the creeks will freeze over if I leave it any later,' he thought. Besides, he had set himself the target of being back before the baby was born in early June; and reckoning on eight weeks for the journey each way, he would have perhaps only two months in England before needing to return. Whether that would be enough to accomplish all he intended, he could only guess at, but any delay now would contract the time available. And this may be the only chance he would ever get.

Rose stirred and rolled towards him, bringing the softness and warmth of her body to rest gently against his. Jack looked expectantly into her face hoping that she would wake, but her eyes remained closed and the steady rhythm of her breathing continued uninterrupted. He felt a desperate need to talk to her, to hear her words of counsel; it was unlikely that she would have changed her hostility to his plans, but he had previously sought her advice on all matters of importance and would have valued it now. Disappointed, he sank back into his thoughts. There were still too many unknowns for him to grasp the true scale of his undertaking, and the uncertainties had loomed larger as the days had passed. Now, he tried again to grapple with the most difficult problem of all – how it would be possible to prove his innocence after so much time had elapsed. 'The answer must lie within the customs service itself,' he reasoned. 'Surely the organisation cannot be entirely corrupt! Somehow, I shall have to find someone within it who will help me expose Smyke for what he is.' But even assuming that those who might help him could be identified, he could not simply approach them without risking his own freedom - indeed his life would be at risk the moment he was recognised.

The first needles of sunlight through the shutters' cracks glistened like crystal necklaces hanging in a line, projecting a pattern of interfering circles on the opposite wall like raindrops on a pond. Jack gazed at the pattern, marvelling at it for a while as the focus of his mind faltered, flitting from one thought to another in hopeless disarray.

'I shall put my trust in God to guide me and let things unfold as they will,' he resolved at last. It was a simple faith that right would prevail - easier to rely upon than reason - but some inner sense told him that he would succeed.

Yet Jack was under no illusions about the difficulties he faced. Rose was frightened by his plan and had tried to argue him out of it late into the night. Her disquiet had tempered his bullishness, but he could not seem to shake the conviction from his mind that it was the right thing to do. Moreover, it seemed to him that by not rallying to this inner call, he would somehow have failed himself as a man. Principles were important, and that he should go was becoming as firm a conviction to him as faith to the devout, and he was growing ever more resistant to the challenge of any who might doubt him. This was just as well.

Later in the morning during a break in their work, Jack decided to tell Ned and Sebi of his intentions in the hope that he might get some comradely support and understanding. On the contrary, Sebi was astonished that Jack should take such a chance.

'You won't evah get out of that country alive,' he said rolling his eyes and shifting his weight uneasily from one lanky leg to the other. 'And anyway, what you think you doin' leaving Miss Rose all alone with a baby comin' on? You must be mad, Mr Jack!'

Ned was less forthright.

'I can't believe that you'd put yoursel' through that crossin' again, Jack. An' at this time of year!' he said incredulously. 'Why not ponder on it a for a while, and then, if you find yoursel' still set upon it, go in the Spring when the weather will be better. Anyway, you'll be lucky to find a ship before then.'

Thus Jack did not get the unequivocal endorsement he had anticipated from his peers. But this did not surprise him; how could he expect them to understand what drove him when he had not revealed the true depth of his thoughts? How could anyone understand his motives, unless their bitterness could be focussed, as his was now, on the single and hated form of one individual whose evil light needed to be extinguished for the sake of all the good which it had corrupted? With such thoughts, Jack's mission was turning inexorably into an obsessive crusade, but this was what it would need to become, considering the obstacles that would lie in his path.

The journey to the trading settlement at the head of a nearby tributary, took Jack two hours by boat the following morning, but it was the only place he could expect to find out information on sailings to England without alerting Sir Michael as to his intentions. He also intended to procure some essential items of hardware for his voyage, although he had decided not to mention this to Rose, not wanting to alarm her. Since gaining his freedom, he had always enjoyed calling in at the Ordinary at the settlement for refreshment and to catch up with the news. It was little more than a wooden shack perched on the riverbank with a rickety pier sticking out from it on stilts, but it was the closest thing to an English alehouse that could be found in this part of Maryland. Sir Michael had put it out of bounds for his servants, fearing that they would fall to drinking and gambling and thus neglect their work. But Jack was freed from such restrictions now, and it had become a special pleasure on his trips for provisions, to take a drink and smoke a pipe in its cosy ambience; indeed the former prohibition lent it a deliciously illicit quality in his mind. Along with the scuttlebutt and gossip that was its daily currency, it was also routine to find notices about shipping arrivals and departures displayed there for the benefit of traders and travellers. As Jack sat at his table listening out for news of such movements from his fellow patrons, his eye was drawn through the smoke-laden air to a bulletin posted upon the opposite wall. On it was printed news of a shipment of African slaves, imminently expected to arrive at the port of Dumper, Virginia, on the British merchantman, 'Rebecca'. In itself, this information would not have been particularly useful, but something made him read on nevertheless.

"...After discharging its Cargo in Dumper, Va., the Vessel will sail to the Port of Charlestown, Md. with a consignment of fine European Furniture and Iron Goods which will be sold by Auction. A Cargo of Tobacco will then be loaded for transportation to Cowes, Isle of Wight, England. Enquiries regarding the availability of Space for the shipment of Goods on this reliable and sea-worthy Vessel should be directed to the Shipping Agent, Thomas Harding Esq, Charlestown."

As he read the middle sentence of this passage, Jack's pulse quickened, and he read it through again to make sure that he had understood it. 'It could hardly be more convenient,' he thought. 'I could sail to Charlestown inside two days. And from there, with luck, I could be in England in six weeks or so!' His thinking was blind to any concern about the likely discomfort of a winter crossing; he was so dazzled by the prospect that from Cowes he could reach Weymouth by packet-boat within a day, that it would not have deflected him anyway.

The innkeeper had known Jack to be rather dour, keeping himself to himself whenever he had visited the Ordinary previously, and so he must have been astonished to see Jack suddenly become so excited. Downing the remnants of his ale in a single gulp, Jack slammed his mug down on the table and wiped his smiling lips with the back of his sleeve. 'Another, if you please landlord! And have one for yourself!' Suddenly, the pieces of his plan were slotting into place, and as they did, so the dangers and difficulties seemed to diminish; but in the back of his mind there was yet the niggling matter of travelling papers to attend to. Normally the approval of the Governor (or someone with his authority) would be required for travelling abroad, and this would certainly not be forthcoming for an exile. It was an irritating detail that he would have to resolve in due course, but he would have enough money in his pocket, and he suspected that there would be ways around the bureaucracy if he were prepared to pay. Jack was anyway not one to be put off by particulars such as this; his thinking seemed to have an unconscious ability to side-step inconvenient obstacles – and in his current frame of mind especially, he was irredeemably optimistic. Thus, galvanised by the sudden realisation that his departure would be sooner than he had thought, he was at once excited and alarmed by its imminence.

Jack was rather later leaving the Ordinary than he had planned, and so his collection of seed and other supplies from the general store had to be accomplished in haste to ensure that he would have sufficient time for the other important task he had set himself - the purchase of a pair of travelling pistols and a supply of powder and shot. Jack was intent on taking his time over this, since he would need some instruction and practice before he returned home.

It was therefore already dusk as Jack arrived back at the farm to find Rose and the others already in the kitchen in anticipation of their evening meal. On his entry, he immediately felt an awkwardness descend upon the group that suggested that the topic of conversation before his arrival had been himself. It also seemed very odd that during the meal no one brought up the subject of his declared intentions. Instead, every topic except the one he regarded as the single most important issue of the moment seemed suddenly to demand such prolonged discussion that no gaps were left. Every time he drew breath to venture some interjection, someone would leap in to cut him off. It was surreal, but something in the nervous manner of the others, suggested that some pre-arranged agenda was being followed and he felt unwilling to challenge it. It was not until after the meal had been cleared away that Rose took over the conversation.

'Jack,' she began uneasily, glancing at the others, 'you won't be surprised that we've been talking about your intention to return to England, since it obviously affects us all.'

Jack pursed his lips, mildly irritated that he was to be challenged again, especially now that his spirit was fired with the desire to be on his way.

'To come to the point straight away, Jack,' she continued, 'we feel that you should ask yourself whether it really *is* so important to go back after so much time has passed since your father's death, especially now that we have built a new life for ourselves here?' She paused and flicked her eyes nervously at Ned and Sebi, getting their nods of support in return.

'It must be over a year since your mother wrote her letter, and everything will have changed since then. Luke will have looked after her well - you must know that - and her grief will surely have passed by now. So, what good can your going back bring?' Rose hesitated, gathering the strands of her argument together, her face flushed and earnest. 'The journey itself would pose risks enough, Jack. Do you not remember that terrible, terrible crossing we had to endure? Do you really want to subject yourself to that again?' She paused, leaving the question hanging in the air. 'And then there seems to me to be so little chance of finding justice in England now that you are already convicted and after so much time has passed, that the great risk of your capture can't possibly be justified. Jack, I beg you to reconsider!'

Rose had made her plea and now fell silent while her eyes continued to look imploringly at her husband. Jack reached across the table to take his wife's hand and he squeezed it gently; her plea had pulled at his heart, and for a moment his resolve wavered. In some ways, it would be a relief to acquiesce, to allow himself to be dissuaded; and he knew how she must feel. She was afraid of losing him and would be desperate to divert him from this quest; she had lost her sister and had given up her chance of returning to her family, choosing instead to stay in Maryland with him; and now he was planning to leave her, bent upon some reckless adventure from which he may never return.

'Rose, in your heart, I think you know why I have to go,' he replied gently. 'If I cannot find justice, then at least I shall have tried to do my duty to my mother, to you, and to our unborn child. For the first time in this new country of ours, I find myself free to act - to do what my heart tells me is right. Would I not be taking the coward's way out if I did not respond to this call? What can be more important than to clear our name?'

There followed an uneasy silence, broken eventually as Sebi cleared his throat. Unusually, his face had taken on a serious complexion; as the oldest in the homestead, he undoubtedly saw himself as patriarch.

'Maybe it's not my place, Miss Rose, but you asked us to stay, so I guess you wan' to hear what we have to say.' Sebi spoke the English of the plantations, mixed with the musical cadences of a mother tongue long forgotten. He took a breath and exhaled slowly, looking across at Jack to catch his eye.

'I believe I knows you well enough Mister Jack havin' bin with y'all these past two years, an' so maybe what I got to say will help.' He took another slow breath. 'Mister Jack, Miss Rose told us your story, and if it's how she says, I know any man would want his revenge, but I am with Rose on this. It all seems like a million miles away and in a different time, an' I think you gotta ask yourself if it really is so important to go back jus' to settle a score. Especially when you got so much to lose. Rose is right, things will have moved on since that letter was wrote, and your ma cannot want you to return with a price on your head. If she's lost her husban', she don' want to lose a son too!'

Rose nodded gravely, apparently pleased to have Sebi follow her line. But Sebi continued, this time with more equivocation in his voice.

'But there is another side to it, Mister Jack, and I put this as an older man as well as your frien' – an' you have to be the one to weigh it, for only you can.' He paused to consider his words. 'You also have to ask yoursel' whether you can come to terms with leaving this undone; for if you cannot, your regrets will take hol' of you like a poison in your soul.' Sebi glanced towards Rose who looked back at him curiously, her eyebrows wrinkling as Sebi answered her unspoken question. 'Miss Rose, that would be a poison which would lose you the man you know; I've seen what this can do to a man when it becomes a thing of honour - it would tie him up in knots.' Then to Jack: 'Mister Jack, if you don' go, you mus' be easy in your mind about it, and be able to put it behind you fo'ever. Ask yourself whether you can do that. Your answer lies there.'

Sebi's advice was coded and balanced, and while not obviously an unreserved endorsement, it nevertheless seemed to Jack to be a gentle prod for Rose that his decision would be as much a matter of the heart as of the mind.

Jack looked at Ned who shifted uncomfortably in his chair.

'Jack, don't look at me, it's for you to decide,' he said raising his hands in a gesture of denial. 'I think I understand what's driving you, but it's for you and Rose to talk this out, and you won't be helped by me. Who am I anyway to give advice?' He paused and then added, 'but if you do decide to go, you know that things can run along here until you get back – it's all the same to me.' He looked sheepishly at Rose. 'Sorry Rose,' he said with a slight shrug of the shoulders, as if some promise had been broken.

For a moment, Rose sat silently in her chair. Her head remained upright, but her eyelids had lowered. She bit her lip, and bowed her head as if looking into her lap, and then, without a word she stood and walked quietly out of the room. The men sat in silence for a long time not daring to speak or catch each other's eyes. At last, it was Ned who spoke.

'How will you get there?' he asked.

As the sun set on the eve of his departure, Jack walked alone up the shallow slope in front of the house to a spot which commanded a good view of his homestead and the creek beyond. He and Rose often came there together to sit on a chestnut bench he had placed under the trees for shade, and nearby on a grassy knoll they had erected a small headstone as a monument to Elizabeth's memory. Under the stone, the couple had buried the few mementoes of Elizabeth's life that they had brought off the ship as keepsakes - a necklace, her shawl - a lock of her long fair hair cut off so tenderly before her body was taken away and cast into the sea. The burying of these things was meant to mark the end of their mourning and the beginning to their new lives, and on the headstone, Jack had carved the inscription:

> *"In loving memory of*
> *Elizabeth Dale*
> *1725 - 1750*
> *Lost at sea but never from our hearts. "*

In the rays of the setting sun, its vermilion face stood in solitary splendour, surrounded by the fallen leaves that covered the little knoll like a patchwork quilt made of every autumn hue. He lowered himself to sit on the bench, and sat for a long time, allowing tender thoughts of Elizabeth to drift through his mind like the gentle breeze that stirred the fallen leaves around him. And in these soft rustlings, her voice seemed to whisper his name as he brought the image of her pretty face into his mind's eye. Elizabeth's death and the loss of his unborn child had traumatised him to his core and his grieving had been a long and lonely journey – but that he could now think about her without weeping showed just how far he had come. The pretty image could not be held for long, and it faded before his eyes to be replaced by his last memory of her - a melancholic picture of the frail and dying figure cradled in her sister's lap. And, suddenly becoming bitter, he vowed silently that she would be avenged.

After some minutes of quiet reflection, he got up and made his way back to the cottage still hoping to put things right with Rose who had petulantly remained behind, still angry with him for his pig-headedness. He so desperately wanted her approval, and the lack of it unsettled him. But the picture in his mind of a triumphant return stiffened his resolve, and he was sure that she would come to know that he was right.

On the morning of departure, Jack awoke to the familiar and comforting sounds of Rose moving about the kitchen. He slid his hand over to her side of their bed to feel the shallow indentation in the mattress where moments before she had lain beside him. It was still warm to his touch, and it evoked tender and intimate memories of their past love-making. The differences between them in recent days, however, had cooled their ardour and neither had been in the frame of mind for sexual frolics. He now regretted losing the opportunity to seduce her out of her discordant mood; it might have been a happier memory to take with him on his journey, and he wondered wistfully when he might lie with her again. Reluctantly, he clambered out of bed into the cold air of the room and wiped the condensation from the windowpane to peer outside. A sullen cloudy overcast hung heavily in the sky from which wisps of grey vapour drizzled into the treetops and drained all colour from the view. He feared that this would not be an auspicious start to his journey.

He and Rose ate breakfast together, sitting at the table in the kitchen, but neither had much appetite and what little conversation took place skirted the real issues that still separated their two minds.

'I've made up some food for you both to take with you – enough for a few days at least,' she said coolly. 'Once you're on board your ship, I suppose they'll feed you.' There was not much enthusiasm in her voice. 'I'm glad that Ned will be with you as far as Charlestown; I shall feel a little easier in my mind when he returns to tell me that you've found a berth on a safe ship.'

'Yes, he'll be good company for me,' Jack acknowledged. 'I've not been that far up river before. You'll need him to bring back the boat in any case, as I can't be sure to where I'll return. Once my business in England is complete, I intend to take the first available ship back to Maryland, to whichever port she sails. More vessels sail to Baltimore than up the Potomac these days, so its as likely to be there.'

Rose nodded and allowed a moment or two to pass in silence. Then she sighed, as if steeling herself for another argument. 'You know my feelings on this matter, Jack,' she said, tensely. 'I know that my opposition vexes you and that it is supposedly a wife's duty to support her husband, but I won't hold my tongue. I won't condone this adventure of yours; what is done is done in my book, and yet you are prepared to abandon me and everything here for what you call justice and honour!' Rose hissed these last words vehemently, her watery eyes glaring with exasperation at her own impotence. 'I think that something baser drives you and I will not admire it!' she cried adamantly with a catch in her voice.

'Rose, my dearest,' Jack appealed to her, his expression, contrite. 'Please let us not quarrel at my departure. My mind is made up. I want your blessing, but with it or without it, I will go; and I will prove to you.....'

'Those words again!' Rose interjected angrily. 'You make them sound so noble yet they threaten everything we have! If you must go, then go and get it over with; but don't expect me to cry at your...at your...' she stopped, suddenly falling into a fit of sobbing, dropping her head as she fumbled in her skirts for her handkerchief. At this, Jack rose from his chair and moved around the table to kneel alongside her, wrapping his arms around her. He held her for a while then slowly coaxed her face to his and kissed her, tasting the salty wetness of her tears upon his lips.

'It breaks my heart to see you so upset, my love, and for all the world, I wouldn't go if I could see any other way,' he entreated. 'You know that I love you dearly and that I shall hurry back to you just as soon as I can – just count off the days as they go by, I promise you that I'll return before six months have passed.'

Jack was now on the verge of breaking down himself, and seeming to recognise this, Rose straightened, pulling herself abruptly back from her plunge into self-pity. She dabbed her reddened eyes with the corner of her handkerchief, drew herself up and placed her arms around Jack's shoulders in what seemed to be a gesture of resignation; and for a while the pair remained motionless in that consoling embrace. At length, sensing that the time for his departure was near, Jack stood up and pulled Rose gently to her feet. Hands clasped, they held each other's eyes in a lingering but desolate gaze from which neither drew comfort, each searching in vain for a signal of submission. Eventually, with a bewildered shake of her head, Rose sagged and rummaged crossly in her apron. 'This is for my parents,' she sniffed, taking out a letter tied with a red ribbon. 'You can bring me back theirs in return. And will you please send word to me of your safe arrival in England?'

'I'll try Rose, but I'll probably beat it back!' he said, trying to make light of it. 'Trust me, I'll be back with you before our baby is born.'

'And pray God that our baby does not grow up as stupid and pig-headed as his father!' she said flatly, her unsmiling face clearly struggling to retain its composure. 'I'll pray for you both.'

Their glances were uncomfortable; hers was laced with accusation and resentment, his with guilty obstinacy, but neither wanted to part in acrimony and so each made an effort to present the face they would want to be remembered by. There seemed no words adequate to mark such a parting and so none were attempted. Instead, he kissed her lightly, almost apologetically, and she returned the gesture by smiling lamely and squeezing his shoulders with her hands. And this is as far as they got because at that moment, Ned's knock at the door brought their difficult farewell abruptly to an end.

Chapter Fifteen

To make best use of the river currents, Jack planned to use the last of the ebb down the creek to reach the Potomac as the tide turned. They would then have about six hours of flood tide up river to help them towards their destination some forty miles northwest. Just an hour after leaving Rose at the house, with the discomfort and sadness of his leave-taking still heavy in his heart, Jack stood impatiently on the gravel beach waiting alongside his boat while Ned paid his last respects to nature behind a tree nearby. Dressed up warmly in their oilskins and beaver hats, they looked like frontiersmen about to set off into the wilderness, but it was typical of Jack's planning to be prepared for the worst, and conditions on the Potomac could be treacherous at this time of year.

In the cold moist air, Jack's breath steamed as he ran a critical eye over his loaded craft, mentally ticking off his inventory one last time. Everything was in its place and secured. Listlessly, he picked up a pebble and threw it into the still water and watched the ripples move slowly downstream; 'Just as well,' he thought, for there was not a breath of wind to stir the damp canvas of the sail, now hanging lifelessly from its gaff. In the distance, the faint sound of cartwheels rumbling on the rutted track marked Sebi's return to the farm, having delivered the pair earlier; he had left with only a grunt of farewell, simply eyeing Jack with a wrinkled smile and flicking his hat with a dismissive gesture. Jack guessed that it had been Sebi's way of avoiding an emotional parting, which would have done no good for either of them; but it had left him feeling suddenly very alone. As the sound of the wheels diminished, stillness settled on the scene, broken only by the hollow shrieks of a nearby pair of coots. 'The quiet before the storm,' Jack thought with not a little apprehension.

At long last, and apparently oblivious of Jack's impatience, Ned emerged from the trees, tying up his oilskin trousers as he sauntered towards the boat without the slightest concession to haste.

'Better be off now, Ned,' Jack said, bottling his impatience. 'We've a long row before we get any wind, by the look of it.'

'Come on then, Jack, put your back into it!' Ned replied cheerily, spitting on his hands.

The boat was small, only nineteen feet long, but it had a wide beam with high freeboard to give it good stability and righting; Jack had bought it from an oyster-man in Leonardtown two years before, for fishing. It had been sturdily built from overlapping elm planks in clinker construction, and Jack had since added a small cuddy in the forepeak for weather protection. The latter improvisation justified itself immediately - as the two men slid the boat into the water, a light sea mist rolled in and within minutes everything unsheltered was covered in a film of moisture. Pushing the boat off the gravel, the two men climbed aboard and took up their positions side by side on the thwart; and bringing their untidy strokes quickly into unison, they rowed themselves out into the deeper water. With the favourable current, the craft made good speed and Jack soon saw the landing stage fade into the mist behind them. Its disappearance seemed somehow symbolic, disquietingly final like a door closing, and suddenly he was afraid that he might never see it again. He glanced at Ned rowing alongside him with such unquestioning loyalty and he smiled inwardly; it was a great comfort to have his friend with him.

It took forty minutes of steady rowing to reach the mouth of the creek, and they shipped their oars to rest, allowing the boat to drift for a while on the current. There was still no wind, but from the swirling eddies in the water, Jack could see that the tidal stream in the Potomac had already turned just as he had calculated. At this point, the Potomac was over six miles wide, and in the persisting mist, the distant Virginian shore was shrouded from view. It seemed as if the little craft were headed for the open sea; not even their first turning point, an island only three miles to the west, was visible ahead. To Jack, it suddenly began to feel a bit intimidating.

'Well, Ned? Are we up to this?' Jack asked, only half joking. The little creek looked safe and inviting by comparison, and they were leaving its comforting security behind. But there was no hint of apprehension in Ned's voice as he answered.

'Well, we can't turn back now, Jack, can we! We haven't even started on our supplies!' he said with a wry smile. But just at that moment, the sound of distant shouting caught their ears, and they sat up quickly and looked about. Ned was first to spot the figure on the beach on the south side of the creek's entrance, and he pointed. It was Rose - running across the sand towards the waterline, clutching her skirts with one hand and waving with the other. Her bonnet fell off as she ran, but she didn't seem to care; her long dark hair trailed behind her like a mane. Behind her, on a bluff, between the trees lining the beach, Sebi stood beside his wagon. He was waving too. They were only about a hundred or so yards away but the current was now drawing the boat further out and the distance between them was opening. Jack's heart leapt to see his wife, and he was instantly overjoyed that she had come to see him off. He stood up and waved his arms wildly, rocking the boat alarmingly as he shouted her name. Then he saw that she was shouting too and cupped his hands to his ears, straining to hear her words over the distance. At first, he could not quite make them out, but then suddenly they became clear.

'I love you, Jack!' she cried. 'God guide you and bring you back safely! Forgive me....' But her words faded again on the air.

'I love you, Rose, I love you!' he shouted back, and he could see that Rose had heard him for she blew him a kiss with a swing of her arm. He did the same in an exaggerated gesture, and they waved to each other again. But then the sail began to flutter into life as the current bore them out of the land's lee and, almost losing his balance, he sat himself on the thwart as the boat began to heel. Within moments the sail filled, pulling the craft forward in an unhindered south easterly breeze, and the passing water began immediately to ripple audibly underneath her prow. Ned had grabbed the tiller and was steering her onto their planned course out into the river, and Jack now moved forward to adjust the main sheet and use his weight to bring the craft back onto an even keel. But he continued waving to the diminishing figure on the beach until well after she was lost from his view in the mist. And Ned caught him glancing astern several times thereafter, smiling to see the light of contentment in his friend's face. 'She loves you, Jack,' he said.

This second parting had been more painful for Jack than the first of the day, but his heart was full of joy. To have heard her words of love and to have shouted his in return would eradicate the earlier bitter scene from both their minds. She had given him permission to go! And the sense of guilt that had dogged him had suddenly been lifted from his shoulders. Now he was fired with a renewed determination to succeed.

By early afternoon, the fair wind and gentle tide had carried them nearly twenty-five miles up river, and bright sunlight had begun to perforate the mist. The sun's belated appearance, however, was a mixed blessing. Its warming rays relieved the frigid dampness stiffening the bones of the two sedentary men, but they also stirred the moist air into turbid fog banks that clung tenaciously to the river. This patchy fog was probably only a few feet thick, but it covered the little craft like a shroud, smothering its crew and obscuring their horizontal sight to a range of fifty yards at best. With only the compass to guide them, they were navigating blind, with no land, no feature of any kind to help orientate their minds, while the swirls and shifting shadows in the vapour played with their confused senses, creating all manner of fleeting impressions. 'Is that dark patch land to larboard?' Jack wondered, in a moment of uncertainty; and what strange shape was it that he glimpsed at the limits of his view? These phantoms faded before he could determine whether they were objects or shadows, disappearing into the folds of mist as quickly as they had appeared.

In their dulled state, it took some time for an unexpected sound to penetrate their consciousness above the soporific music of water against the hull. It was an odd sound, muted and faint at first but growing louder and sharper by the minute, until eventually it became recognisable as the slow and steady beat of a bass drum. Sound bounds and rebounds readily across open water, and in the limited visibility, they could not be sure from which direction it emanated. The beat faded and then returned, then faded and returned again, and each time the sound returned, it grew louder. Still it was impossible to tell from which direction the beat came. And then another sound became discernible through the mist: the doleful sound of voices singing a slow lament, a sonorous dirge that resonated with loss. The two men glanced at each other and then around about them in dismay as the singing grew steadily louder, seeming to come from every direction at once. But still nothing could be seen. Then suddenly at the edge of his view, Ned caught a movement that drew his attention immediately astern, and the consternation quickly vanished from his face as he pointed, speechless, his jaw dropping in disbelief. Alarmed at his friend's frightened gesture, Jack followed his gaze, and he too froze at what he saw.

Above the breaking mist in a patch of pale blue sky, seemingly suspended and lit up in the bright sunlight, a row of human forms bore down upon them as if riding some ethereal contraption. At first the sight was incomprehensible, and both men continued to stare wide-eyed from the fragile craft that lay directly in the spectre's path. But then, in a flash of recognition, Jack bellowed a warning to his friend as he threw the tiller hard over to turn their boat rapidly aside. Ned was dumbfounded, wondering what on earth his friend was up to as he lost his balance and fell onto the tread boards in a sprawl of arms and legs. But when he raised his dazed head above the gunwale, he immediately realised the peril they were in. Fifty yards behind them, the huge bulk of a ship's hull sprung from the mist like a beast charging from its cover and bore down on them at speed. The thundering roar of its bow wave grew ever louder as Jack's puny sail clawed at the wind, straining desperately to pull them clear of the monster's path. But there was not enough time. The little boat was lifted bodily as the massive wall of water hit it hard, spinning it dizzyingly like a straw in the wind, burying its bow into the water and bringing the gaff down in a tangled heap. Miraculously, the boat was not swamped; its cuddy had stopped it from nosing under and its freeboard had buoyed it up. But the collision was not over yet. The ship's long hull roared by, bumping and scraping the tiny craft violently as the water's suction held it in its deadly grip. Both men clung desperately to the thwarts, watching aghast and helpless as they found themselves drawn inexorably towards the ship's tumbling wake. The breaking wave of boiling water hit them like a sledge, pitching and rolling the boat so violently that it looked inevitable that it would capsize. Both men let out a terrified scream as a torrent of swirling Potomac swept over the submerging gunwale threatening to swallow the boat in one great gulp. As their vessel tipped, both men instinctively scrambled upwards to the opposite beam, retreating from the water as it gushed in. It was this instinct that saved them from immediate disaster - their countering weight checked the boat's further rotation. But for several seconds more, the craft's fate seemed to hang in the balance as the two men dangled over the upended beam, wondering which way she would fall, and startled to be looking at the dagger-board now well clear of the water. Then, slowly at first but with accelerating momentum, the precipitous angle subsided and the boat fell onto an even keel, with both men tumbling back into the hull amidst a tangle of sails and rigging.

They lay there for a moment, breathless and dazed, watching the heavy vessel disappear into the mist as it ploughed on unperturbed. Emblazoned upon its stern were the names '*Rebecca*' and '*Bristol*'. And on the deck, clusters of half-naked black men were clearly visible. It was from these poor wretches, Jack realised, that the doleful voices had come as they had sung their sad laments to the accompanying rhythm of a drum. And up along the topsail yards, a dozen or more crew teetered on their footropes readying to furl the sails, but not one man looked behind to see the tiny boat and its two drenched occupants floundering in their wake. What had been thick fog to Jack and Ned at surface level, would have been no more than mottled wisps from the lofty decks of this tall ship charging up the Potomac under full sail. And, as for Jack and Ned, their good progress had been abruptly halted in an instant. There seemed nothing for it now but to row the boat to the nearest shore.

It took Jack the best part of two hours to repair the gaff and other damage while Ned collected wood and set up camp in the shelter of a promontory. With a little coaxing, a fire was soon lit and built up into a substantial pyre around which a latticework of sticks and twigs was erected on which to drape their sodden clothes. Fortunately, not everything had received a soaking and Jack's most valuable possessions, including his two pistols and powder, had remained completely dry in the tightly wrapped oiled-canvas bag in which he had placed them against just such a contingency. The sunshine eventually broke through later to provide a little comfort for the pair, but darkness was soon upon them, and the blazing fire became a welcome prop for their fragile spirits, still shaken by the shock of the afternoon's near-catastrophe. It seemed ironic to Jack that his mission had so nearly been scuppered by the very ship on which he hoped to find a passage; but at least he now knew that she had arrived!

The following morning, dawn broke fresh and clear, and the men awoke restored and in good heart to a breakfast of oat cakes and dried fruit thoughtfully provided by Rose in her parting gift of refreshments. In contrast to the day before, the visibility was excellent, there being no trace remaining of the mist as the sun's blood-red orb appeared above the trees behind the camp. Across the blue-grey water, six miles distant, the shallow sandstone cliffs of the Virginian shoreline could be seen shining brightly in reflected sunshine. The air was cold, but the breeze was again favourable from the southeast; and very soon the sails were flapping as the two men threw the last of their things aboard, pushed the boat into the water, and leapt in.

The distance ahead now measured only about twenty miles all told, and with little attention needed on navigation in the good visibility, it seemed to Jack a timely opportunity to brief Ned on certain safeguards that would be necessary from the very moment of their arrival.

'I shall need to hide my identity once I am in port, Ned,' he said. 'And you'll have play along, I'm afraid. I can't take the risk of my name reaching the ears of the English authorities from my fellow travellers or crew. There are rewards for information of returning exiles and so we won't be able to trust anyone. That's why it was so important that no one at New Hope got wind of my departure.'

Ned nodded, amused. 'That should add a bit of mystery to our stay,' he said with a puff of laughter. 'What are we going to call you then? Smith?'

Jack looked a bit embarrassed. 'I'd thought of Stone, actually,' he offered tentatively. 'It's a common enough name, close enough to Easton for me to avoid error, I hope; and anyway, I rather like it.'

Ned smiled. 'Rather appropriate, I'd say,' he said. 'I think I could get used to it.'

'It's also important that, as far as anyone else is concerned, my reason for travel is solely to visit my grieving mother in Portland following the death of my father - that might get me a bit of sympathy and prevent too many questions being asked. And you mustn't mention anything of my other motives,' Jack said emphatically.

'All right, Mr Stone, I shall be especially careful not to let the cat out of the bag!' Ned said, giving his friend a mock salute. 'But won't you need papers to prove who you are?' he said frowning.

'We're going to have to get round that somehow, Ned. I'm carrying a bit of money and hope that I can sort something out with a back-hander or two if necessary.'

Ned feigned astonishment. 'And I thought you were an honest man!'

By early afternoon, they had reached the entrance to the Tobacco River, and Jack turned his boat to follow it the last five miles to Charlestown at its head. High up on the crest to starboard, an imposing manor house looked down, the first sizeable building he had seen along the route; this was the landmark he had been told to look out for: - Saint Thomas' Manor standing like a sentinel on guard at the river entrance. The sails flapped lethargically as the wind died in the lee of the high ground, and the two men resignedly pulled out their oars to row. Some small fishing boats passed them heading in the opposite direction, and here and there larger boats swung at anchor. Some of their crews eyed them curiously as they passed; their unfriendly inspection made Jack suddenly apprehensive - until now, his journey had been known only by people he could trust; from now on, strangers would become involved.

The Tobacco River was comparatively wide at this point, perhaps a quarter of a mile at the entrance, and its slow movement and dark coloration showed it to be deep. But its width narrowed quickly as they moved further in to no more than one hundred yards. On both sides, the ground rose into woodlands of red maple and tall pine, but there were large areas between them where the trees had been felled and replaced with tobacco plantations coming right down to the water's edge. The tobacco plants had already been cropped and the fields left in an untidy state, looking parched and dusty in the afternoon sunshine. Here and there, numerous landing stages jutted out into the navigable stream across wide muddy banks, and behind them open-fronted barns stood brim-full of yellowing tobacco leaves hanging to cure. Alongside the landings, flat-bottomed lighters lay empty, marooned by the receding tide; and on the glistening mud, scores of little white birds scurried hither and thither probing for food. But there were few people about, and the river had an unexpected air of tranquillity for one reputedly so busy; clearly, with the winter almost upon them, business was coming to a close.

It was already dusk when the lights of Charlestown at last became visible at the head of the river, and from Jack and Ned's low perspective, the buildings on the waterfront were silhouetted darkly by the purple of the twilight sky. Lamplight glimmered in their windows and sinewy reflections snaked across the still water to show them the way in. As they neared the harbour, adjacent to warehouses on the southern edge of the town, a small coastal craft was spotted lying alongside a quay, its hull resting askew on the mud, its mast leaning at a precarious angle. Behind it, Jack could see a narrow channel leading to a small dock; he lifted the dagger-board and steered the boat in.

Chapter Sixteen

Charlestown was a thriving community renamed from Chandler's Hope thirty years before when it became the seat for Charles County, Maryland. It was also the naval port of entry for the county, and had become its economic and cultural hub. The pride of the town was its new church, re-built in brick only a few years before, which sat like an offer of redemption between the gaol and the courthouse and directly opposite the Centennial Hotel, a well-known drinking refuge for visitors. The well-to-do - the plantation owners, administrators, officials and the like - had their residences on the edge of the town, well away from the hustle and bustle that might have disturbed their peace. They lived in a row of imposing two-story brick and timber-built residences built on the high ground to the east of the town that commanded pleasing views of the river valley below. In the centre of the town, around the public square and along the street going out towards the school, several trading stores, a smithy, and a barber were located amongst the town-houses and cottages of the ordinary folk. And, as a port of some importance, the town offered the usual facilities and services for mariners: warehouses, chandlers, a shipwright offering repairs, a rope-maker, and of course, a scattering of inns and ordinaries. It was indeed a metropolis by the standards of the day and an important way station on the post-road from Philadelphia to Williamsburg - the Potomac being crossed by ferry further along the route.

It was not surprising, therefore, that when Jack and Ned entered the Centennial Hotel, they found it simply buzzing with people. And with a consignment of European goods from England imminently expected on the vessel *Rebecca*, traders from miles around - and not a few chancers - had flooded into the town. Indeed, on checking in, the new arrivals were very lucky to find accommodation available at all. They therefore did not quibble when they found their quarters not much bigger than a box room in which pulling off their sailing garb required acts of considerable contortion within the pressing confines of the walls and the low ceiling boards. Eventually, dressed in clean but somewhat crumpled clothes, they descended to the lobby, desperate to satisfy their, by now, voracious appetites.

The hotel's saloon was gloomily lit by ornate but badly tarnished oil-lamps hanging from the beams, and several wax-encrusted candle-sconces on the walls. The room pulsated with conversation; and every table was so brim full of chattering patrons that at first it seemed unlikely that the two newcomers would find a place to sit. A few heads had turned in idle curiosity to examine Jack and Ned as they had entered - indifferent faces made hazy by the tobacco smoke - but they had lost interest now. Feeling ill at ease at the crush and chatter of the crowd, Jack was at first inclined to retreat, but then Ned spotted an empty table in the far corner of the room and led the way towards it using his imposing size to clear a path. It was a relatively large room, and to reach their objective it was necessary to negotiate a route between the crowded tables that lay in their path like the construct of a maze. At one table, a group played a game of Snake, rattling the die with animated banter fuelled by the forfeitures of drink; at another, a game of cards was being played with quiet but intense concentration; and at yet another, there was earnest talk of fighting with the French and Indians further west. At this table, several men stood listening attentively behind those seated, and, curious to hear the news, Jack and Ned dallied at the perimeter of this group.

The discussion was fast becoming a heated exchange, but an interjection from one of the participants in quiet and measured language instantly gained the attention of the others. He was a bespectacled gentleman with quick and intelligent eyes, dressed well but soberly in a black dress-coat and black silk neck-band wrapped over a pure white shirt; Jack imagined he might be an official of some sort passing through the town; clearly his words commanded his audience's respect.

'After Bradock's inglorious defeat at Fort Dusquesne, the French and their Indian allies have clearly been emboldened by their victory,' he asserted in an calm but authoritative voice, 'hence the Shawnee and Delaware attacks on Pennsylvania and the Iroquois turning against New York. The French use their Indian friends' resentment of our westward intrusions to their own ends. They would no doubt be delighted to see us removed from all the lands that we now possess.'

'And Bradock's tactics were hopelessly inept,' contended a man dressed in a hide-skin coat. 'The Indians crept upon them as they would do a herd of Buffalo while the British marched in military lines across open ground. They were picked off from the cover of the surrounding trees and slaughtered as they scattered; you might as well send a cow in pursuit of a hare as an English Red Coat loaded up as they are! If they'd listened to us it would have been different.'

'That's as may be,' replied the official-looking man evenly, 'but we colonists were tardy, penny-pinching, and disingenuous in our support of them, and hopefully we will both learn from our mistakes following that misadventure. The British regulars protect the mother country's interests certainly, but, for the present, they also protect ours. We should remember that.'

'If they don't get our cooperation, then that's because they're so pig-headed and treat us as second rate,' interjected another.

'Perhaps we deserve their contempt. It is sometimes difficult to tell - there are always two sides to any argument,' reasoned the official. 'And I am certain that we are currently incapable of doing the job better for ourselves. The fact of the matter, gentlemen, is that our militias are not yet well enough equipped or trained, nor are our colonial governments working together in providing adequately for our own defence. Our part-time troops are farmers' sons and runaway servants looking for booty and adventure, and our Governors and Assemblies often act like petulant and quarrelsome children. Until we can come together in a united and committed manner, we will depend upon the motherland to help us.' At this, a murmur of peppery affront erupted around the table, against which the official raised his voice and his hand to silence them.

'Yes, I see your pride is hurt, but Mr Pitt is now in charge,' he countered evenly, 'and his proposals should help to calm the irritations that exist between us. Now at last we have someone who takes a proper interest in our affairs. Let us hope that we can soon find a way of working together to defend our mutual interests, gentlemen, otherwise I fear that more settlers will lose their scalps. Or else we shall all be brought by French devotion back under the rule of Rome!' At this assertion, his audience reflected silently with some nodding their heads gravely.

Then someone standing near Jack spoke up: 'The word in Philadelphia is that a counter-attack is likely next year with Pitt's forces already on their way. Could be upwards of twenty-five thousand British troops I hear, with the same number of provincials promised from Massachusetts, Connecticut, and New York. No doubt they have the Hudson and the St. Lawrence in their minds. That'll make those French bastards' eyes water!'

'I'll believe that when I see it,' said another derisively, provoking a few contemptuous smirks amongst his companions, 'the British couldn't make the party last time! Anyway,' he continued, 'who amongst us would join a militia to be treated like shit by British regulars?'

'As I said gentlemen,' interjected the official quickly to stem the tide of derision beginning to swell, 'I do not believe that we currently have any choice. But at least, the British will be picking up the bill for their troops this time and our officers will now rank equally with theirs. And with British firepower and discipline and our better knowledge of Indian tactics and the terrain, I hope we shall now see a turn in the tide.'

At the mention of militias, Jack remembered his contract with Sir Michael to join his New Hope brigade should there be a need to form one; and suddenly his ready acceptance of Sir Michael's terms began to feel a trifle hasty. Sir Michael's confidence that no threat existed now seemed somewhat misplaced, perhaps even contrived, for surely he must have known about the situation that he had just heard described. Jack cleared his throat. 'And what is Maryland's position in all this?' he asked.

The official looked up quickly and focussed on Jack's face, screwing up his eyes; Jack must have been hard to see in the gloom outside the table's circle of candlelight. Others at the table followed his gaze making Jack shrink inside at the attention.

'A good question;' the man replied, 'our lower house seems to have its head in the sand, and our proprietary government apparently sees no advantage for itself in making any contribution at all! I would call that complacency wouldn't you? And the Virginian and Pennsylvanian assemblies are not much better; Washington calls them our 'chimney corner politicians'; they seem outwardly so tenacious of liberty yet they put all manner of technicalities in the way to avoid financial or moral commitment. And yet I would suggest that we have as much to lose from French attacks on our borders as do New England and New York. It is as well that our northern brothers are prepared to put their hands in their pockets, but we should take care that Maryland and Virginia do not become a soft underbelly - an easy romp for a French advance by which they might encircle and isolate the north. Think then of the Spanish in Florida, and of the Carolinas isolated and vulnerable to the south, and you will begin to see that we approach a turning point of historical proportions, Gentlemen.'

The mood at the table was now contemplative, while elsewhere in other segments of the room, the loud chatter and alcohol-enhanced laughter continued unabated.

'And the news from England?' Jack raised his voice against the background din.

'Warring with the French again!' another of those seated called back in an ironic tone, 'preparing for an invasion from across the Channel no doubt! I hear that their friends the Prussians are to be billeted on the south coast now, and can anyone wonder? - the British Army are all abroad! And if they're not careful, those Froggies will sneak in through the back door to get off with their women whilst they're away!' he exclaimed slapping the table in mirth; but none of his companions joined in.

'Aye, they're fighting the French on both sides of the Atlantic,' chipped in a wise old head in a Scottish accent, taking out his pipe, 'and an Army in India too - the British are stretched, too stretched in my opinion. I'll wager that any boy who can wield a stick will find himself conscripted. Is it any surprise they want to raise our taxes?'

There was some shaking of heads and mutterings of displeasure at this, and Jack decided to take the opportunity of the distraction to move on. If he felt any disquiet at what he had heard, then it was quickly put aside for he had other things to attend to in the pursuit of his objectives; and at present the fighting was still a long way off.

The open fire blazing in the hearth adjacent to their table was at first welcome, but it soon had them stripping off to their shirtsleeves in the blast of radiant heat. The innkeeper, a large thick-necked man wearing a dirty leather apron, was standing at one of the other tables joining in some ribaldry. He flicked an indifferent glance at the new arrivals with the air of someone who saw a lot of travellers and liked to make them wait. Eventually, he broke off his conversation and made his way towards the fire, dallying here and there with others of his acquaintance along his circuitous route. He reached into the flames and lit a splint, conveying it to the table of the waiting pair to light the candle slumped in the centre of their table. Hiding their impatience, Jack and Ned quickly ordered food and drink - mutton stew, a jug of ale, and some bread. Its coming seemed to take an age, but when the inn-keeper eventually returned, Jack ventured a casual question, anxious not to lose a useful opportunity.

'I hope to find a place aboard the *Rebecca* when she docks,' he asked. 'Who do I need to speak to in the town to arrange a passage?'

The innkeeper shrugged his shoulders and looked around the room.

'There are some men here from the advance party,' he said, 'but I can't see 'em right now. They come in yesterday to get things organised for the loading; any of them'll help you. You'll have to ask around.'

Jack scanned the smoke-filled room but, not wishing his position to become conspicuous so early after his arrival, he decided not to pursue the matter further at that time; besides, he had a most enormous appetite, and his meal now lay enticingly before him.

At an adjacent table, a group of men played cards while several others stood behind them looking on with absorbed interest. One of those standing closest to Jack's table had overheard his earlier exchange with the innkeeper and, unnoticed by Jack, he turned to examine the pair who were already consuming their meal with obvious pleasure. Later, as Jack and Ned sat drinking in quiet conversation, the man approached. He was a well-dressed and well-groomed individual with an air of confidence about him that Jack associated instinctively with authority.

'The innkeeper tells me that you are looking for a berth on the *Rebecca*?' the man opened disingenuously in an educated and slightly patronising voice. 'My name is Hayward, I am a shipping agent here, I may be able to help you,' he said gesturing politely to the empty chair; 'perhaps I may join you?'

Although a little taken aback by the man's forthright approach, Jack took him at face value, and recognising that he would need assistance to achieve his objectives, he invited the man to sit down, inquisitive as to what might come of it. After a few guarded preliminaries, the conversation turned to the visitors' reasons for travel, and despite Ned's warning glances, Jack nevertheless allowed himself to be drawn out, if carefully and only to the degree that he had intended.

'I should be able to arrange a passage for you, Mr Stone,' Hayward said eventually, suddenly becoming more business-like. 'The *Rebecca* does not usually carry passengers, but in your circumstances, I think that they will make a concession. Let me have a look at your papers will you, and we'll see what can be done.'

Again, Jack was taken aback at the directness of the enquiry, being thrust so suddenly into a deception that he had had no time to rehearse. He replied quickly that he had not had time to organise the required permissions in his haste to reach his mother without delay, and that he had hoped to make arrangements in the town. At this, the man looked doubtful.

'Then that could present difficulties for you,' he replied sucking his teeth, 'for I do not believe that it will be possible to obtain papers within the short time available.'

Jack's face could not help but reveal his disappointment; it had all begun to feel too easy and he had suspected that there might be a catch.

'However,' the man added after a thoughtful pause, 'there may still be a way that I can help you, even if it costs a little extra for the favour that I shall need to call in,' he said with a meaningful smile. 'I have an acquaintance at the shipping office whom I feel reasonably sure will be able to place your name on the manifest - with a little persuasion, if you know what I mean. Perhaps you will permit me to make a few discrete enquiries?'

Jack did not wish to appear as if he expected to pay a lot for the favour and so he hesitated; he was not schooled in the manner of such negotiations. But the offer seemed genuine enough even if it were unlikely to be motivated entirely on altruistic grounds. And being a man with a secret, unwilling to place himself in the hands of officialdom where awkward questions might be asked, he felt inclined to go along with his new friend's proposition; after all, he reasoned to himself, what other options did he have?

'Well yes, that would be helpful,' he said at last. 'And I am grateful for your help.'

'Right then,' the man said taking out his timepiece and examining it as if considering a schedule of some sort, 'meet me tomorrow evening at six o'clock in front of the shipping office by the quay; I should have been able to speak to him by then. And bring enough money to pay both for your ticket and my friend's fee; ten pounds or so should be enough, but bring a little more with you to be sure.'

This did not seem unreasonable to Jack; indeed, to have the complication of such arrangements taken out of his hands was somewhat of a relief, and he had not expected to spend much less for a transatlantic fare, especially in view of his status. Nevertheless the sum would account for nearly all he had thought reasonable to bring with him, not wanting to leave the homestead short of cash.

'D'you think that we should trust him?' ventured Ned quietly as the man left.

'Its worth a try Ned; but we'll need to be on our guard.'

The following evening at the appointed hour, Jack and Ned waited as arranged in front of the shipping office in the dim pool of light emanating from the oil lamp that illuminated its front door. If Jack had any reservations about the imminent transaction in which he was to participate, he had suppressed them, preferring not to think unkindly of Hayward who had struck him as a decent sort. But, nervous of the general dangers of an unfamiliar street at night, he had taken the precaution of giving half his money to Ned for safekeeping and, additionally, he had come armed with both his pistols already primed and charged.

The shipping office was a single-story wooden extension added to the north-end of the courthouse. While they waited patiently outside its open door, Jack and Ned watched the activity inside with idle interest. A throng of chattering landsmen, evidently tobacco farmers registering their loads for shipment, jostled impatiently for the attentions of a number of hard-pressed and flustered clerks. The latter, uniformed in black aprons and cuffs over white shirts, darted hither and thither behind a long serving counter in their attempts to keep up with the demands upon them. Gradually, the busy throng diminished as business proceeded, and eventually the office fell quiet. It was by now well beyond the arranged time for the meeting, and Jack was on the verge of giving up when Hayward emerged from the darkness of the adjacent alleyway, which Jack assumed must lead to the office's rear entrance. Acknowledging the pair's presence with an exultant wave of papers, Hayward beckoned the pair to follow him back into the alleyway. Pleased that the plan seemed to have succeeded, Jack followed without a second thought, but the frown on Ned's brow betrayed his immediate sense of unease. With Jack already in full stride, Ned grabbed his companion's sleeve, but Jack shrugged it off, reassuring his friend with a confident glance.

Entering the alleyway, the two men were temporarily blinded by the sudden lack of light, and they halted, unsure of their footing, whilst their eyes adjusted to the darkness. Jack knew instantly that he had led Ned into a trap, and it was at that moment that they were set upon from both sides at once. It felt as if several men were involved, for the force of the onslaught knocked the wind from Jack's lungs. Immediately overcome by their overpowering strength, Jack found himself pinned hard against a wall while greedy hands rifled through his pockets. But then his mind began to clear and, managing to free one of his arms, he lashed out wildly with a clenched fist. Miraculously, his thrust made contact with the jaw of one of his assailants who was knocked sprawling backwards by the blow into the supporting post of the stairway opposite, knocking him senseless. Then Jack lunged forwards using the wall behind him as a prop, throwing his second assailant off-balance, and kicked out hard into the man's surprised and stumbling form. Jack felt his boot make contact with the fellow's ribs, and heard his groan as he doubled over clutching his chest. Then, shifting his weight, Jack swung his boot directly upwards into the man's crotch, forcing a shrill and agonised gasp through his victim's clenched jaws. Finally, in a coup de grâce, Jack rammed his fist upwards into the man's chin with such power that he heard the splintering of broken teeth. But, even as Jack nursed his aching knuckles, another attacker was upon him from behind and a further struggle ensued.

Meanwhile, furious at being duped, Ned was more than a match for the two assailants who set upon him. Using his height and weight, he threw the first off-balance with a sudden lurch, then kicked out sideways, hitting the man's head hard with edge of his heel and sending him reeling. Taking the other assailant by surprise with the force of this manoeuvre, Ned then struck back sharply with his left elbow, staving in the man's windpipe and sending a strangled shriek into the night air. Then, twisting rapidly, he took a grip of his victim's neck and with his right fist, thrust a punch directly into his abdomen. The man doubled over in agony clutching his stomach; but as his head fell forward, it met Ned's upcoming knee, breaking his nose with a loud crack and causing blood to stream down the man's face in full flood.

The rage with which Jack and Ned fought had surprised their attackers, and it was some time before they began to regain the upper hand by sheer force of numbers. Recognising that they could not win against such odds, Jack pulled one of his pistols from his coat; but he was unable to cock it before he was set upon again, this time in a frontal attack. The weapon in Jack's hand added a hard and heavy impetus to the blow he landed on his adversary's forehead, knocking him to the ground, his head gashed by the barrel's foresight. For a moment, Jack stood unmolested, breathing heavily in the semi-darkness; but then, seeing Ned almost overwhelmed on the other side of the alleyway, he cocked his pistol, raised it and fired into the air. There was a spark as the flintlock struck, a spluttering flash of flame, and a loud explosion that was magnified several fold in the confines of the narrow alleyway. As the reverberations from the report died away leaving a ringing silence in his ears, Jack shouted to the mob to get back while pulling out his other pistol and swinging his aim between them. The rumpus came to an immediate end, but as the robbers pulled back into the shadows, one of them lunged for Ned from behind, bringing a knife to his throat.

'Drop your weapon or your friend dies!' he screamed.

It was Hayward! The 'gentleman' who Jack had so naively trusted, but this time there was no civility in his well-spoken voice, only a sneering tone. Jack winced at his own stupidity at being taken in by the man's cunning – 'how could I have been so gullible!' he wondered. The two men faced each other in an impasse for several seconds as Jack calculated the chances of making his second shot count. But he could not risk it. His pistol pointed steadily at the partially hidden head of his friend's tormentor, but its accuracy could not be guaranteed. Ned stared back, eyes wide, his jaws clenched, as the knife pressed into his throat.

'Drop your gun!' Hayward repeated angrily. Jack flicked his eyes about, assessing the odds. Five other men now stood around him in various states of readiness; two were clearly up for more and ready to pounce given half a chance. Another with a bloody face was catching his breath, bent over with his hands on his knees – he might fight again if the call came. The fourth and fifth were probably out of it completely; one nursed a broken nose, the other a dislocated jaw. Jack realised that the odds against him were stacked too high; and with a knife to his friend's throat, he knew he was beaten. Slowly, he lowered his weapon, un-cocked the action and dropped it and its spent companion to the ground.

'Take what you want,' he said, defeated, 'just let my friend go!'

Still holding the knife to Ned's throat, Hayward then rifled through his captive's pockets, finally pulling out a purse in triumph. Jack offered no resistance either, and his purse was taken in similar fashion. Then, with both men at knifepoint, it was the turn of the attackers to get their own back with some punches of their own.

Fortunately, however, Jack's shot had been heard and the sheriff and his constable were soon on the scene, arriving at the far end of the alleyway. Suddenly the tables had turned again and Jack felt the restraint upon him loosen as his captors took flight. Summoning the last of his energy, he leapt at one of the fleeing assailants as he ran, hurling himself recklessly into the air to grab the man's shoulders from behind. Their combined momentum sent them both stumbling to the ground, with Jack's full weight coming down hard on top as they both fell headlong.

He heard the man's ribs crack with the impact, and lay winded for a few seconds listening to his groans; 'This one won't get away!' he thought grimly, feeling satisfied with himself. But it was Hayward that he wanted; and lifting himself up quickly, he scanned the dim scene, wanting to settle the score. On the other side of the alleyway, Ned held one of the assailants in an arm lock, and further down the passage, the sheriff and his constable were struggling with two of the others; in the darkness, it was difficult to see if Hayward was amongst them. Then the shouting and scuffling subsided as more watchmen arrived upon the scene, and the fight was brought to an end.

'Their victims don't usually resist,' a dismayed sheriff said, surveying the bloody aftermath of the battle. 'You boys don't mess around do you?' And Jack was left wondering where he'd learnt to fight - he'd never seen himself as a violent man.

But two members of the gang, including Hayward, had escaped, and with them had gone Jack's money. It seemed a small consolation that his pistols had not gone with them too, for without money he would find it difficult to continue, weapons or not. The pair thus returned to the hotel dishevelled and demoralised, but their spirits were lifted when they were met not with glances of disapproval at their dirty state but instead with apparent acclaim. Clearly word of the robbers' capture was already out, and this earned them some generosity in the saloon from a throng of generous admirers.

Later, Jack and Ned sat alone again at their table near the fire, drowning their sorrows in the last of the jugs of ale kindly donated. 'Ned, forgive me for my stupidity,' Jack said contritely, examining Ned's bruised and battered face. 'I should've paid attention to your warning. First, the near drowning, and now both of us lucky to have escaped being beaten to death - what have I got you into? It was wrong of me to let you come.'

'Tis just as well I did, my friend,' Ned smirked, his face rosy with the heat and the liquor as he quaffed a mouthful of ale. 'I don't know what you'd have done without me!' he said, wiping his grinning lips with the back of his sleeve.

Jack realised that Ned was right, and smiled wryly; without him he would certainly have come off much worse on both occasions.

'And now I've lost all but a few farthings of my money, Ned, and my journey is therefore likely to end here. My only hope is that I can work my passage on the *Rebecca*; and if that's not possible, I fear that I shall have to return to the farm with you and think again.'

Ned flicked up his eyes to study his friend more closely, but was careful to keep his own expression neutral. For Ned, the two events had been omens, and now there was this talk of war - he felt himself becoming uneasy about his friend's venture. But despite his qualms, he could not bring himself to try to talk his friend out it; unnecessary as he believed Jack's mission to be, he did not want to be the one to pour cold water on what he saw to be his friend's honourable intentions. Jack was master of his own destiny and therefore should make up his own mind; and a matter of such gravity, where pride might be at stake, seemed far too personal to be interfered with by someone such as himself.

The following morning, Jack awoke stiff and bruised from his beating and immediately fell into a gloomy reverie as he calculated the few options that may now be left open to him. Perhaps he had taken on too much after all, and the setback had been sent as a sign. He knew himself well enough, however, to see at once that his pride would not let him so easily admit defeat; he had made so much of his mission to bring Smyke to justice, that he could hardly retreat from it so lamely. And he had only to think again of the man to realise that his bitterness was undiminished. He must not lightly allow himself to be deflected; that the devil might send his agents to place obstacles in his path must not weaken his determination to succeed, and he feared that if he turned back now, circumstances would conspire to deny him another chance. With a heavy sigh, Jack turned to gaze wistfully through the window at the rising dawn; he must try to find another way.

Shaking off his gloom over breakfast with Ned in the downstairs parlour, Jack suggested that they look around the town in the hope that some opportunity might present itself. And as they later set out along the main street, they found to their great surprise that they were greeted as celebrities. Of late, it seemed there had been numerous robberies around the town, and its citizens had seized upon the news of the captures as welcome retribution against the scourge. Jack was quick to capitalise on the opportunity to raise some sympathy for his predicament in the hope that it might lead to an offer of practical assistance. And wringing every last ounce of pathos from the tale, he claimed that not only had his money but also his travelling papers been taken, and that the robbery would thus force him to abandon his plans, leaving his grieving mother distraught by his absence. (By now, he had several of the town's womenfolk casting around on his behalf.) However, although he won much commiseration, little by way of concrete help was at first forthcoming. But later, surrounded by another cluster of well wishers in the town square, a man introducing himself as a member of the town Council offered to introduce him to a likely benefactor. Jack's heart leapt at this little glimmer of hope, and of course, he at once accepted.

It was back to the shipping office, adjacent to the scene of the previous evening's scuffle, that Jack was brought to meet the councillor's friend: a Thomas Harding Esq., the port's bona fide shipping agent (Jack remembered the name from the bulletin in the Ordinary a few days before he had set out). The pair shook hands. Harding was a stocky, round-faced man with sharp penetrating eyes and silver hair tied back into a short pigtail, tied with a black ribbon.

'Ah, our valiant visitors!' he said with exaggerated courtesy. 'The town is grateful to you, sirs. We were becoming rather weary of those marauding vandals. You have done us all a great service!'

'Thank you, sir, but the service was first and foremost to ourselves!' Jack retorted. 'And I am left wondering why they went for us at all, and not the shipping office itself – where there must have been more cash for the taking after such a busy day?'

'Travellers are their usual targets – easier pickings,' Harding replied in an off-handed manner. 'Besides, little cash passes hands here; we only issue letters of credit. The credit is realised by the plantation owners only when their consignment reaches its destination - where the price is set according to its quality and demand, which, I am afraid to say, is variable in both respects.'

'Yes, I suppose I should know that being a small-holder myself,' said Jack, slightly nettled. 'The planter takes the risk! Should his consignment become spoiled or lost en route, he gets nothing at all for his year's work; and he's already paid the shipping!'

'Indeed, sir, that is why they must find sound and dry ships to take it,' Harding countered testily. 'That is my task here – to act for the planters – to find them space on good ships bound for England,' he asserted. 'With winter approaching, however, there are few of those at present.'

'I know it, sir,' replied Jack, trying now to sound worldly, hoping to impress the man who seemed to have the necessary wherewithal to help him. 'My little crop will go from St Mary's when it is cured, but there is nothing scheduled to sail until Spring.'

'Most ships will over-winter here before setting sail, Mr Stone, the crossing at this time of year can be precarious.'

'Then the *Rebecca* is unusual?'

'Indeed, this is why she demands so much for tonnage. She is a sturdy ship – a former Navy sixth rate – and her captain appears to have no fear of the North Atlantic. He aims to get his cargo onto the European market when it will fetch the best price,' Harding replied, glancing at the clock behind the counter. 'But enough of this,' he said, smiling indulgently, and catching the eye of his councillor friend as he continued smoothly: 'My friend here has told me of your difficulty; your money was taken, I understand?'

Jack nodded. 'Yes, and my papers too,' he said quickly without batting an eyelid.

'Well now, obtaining papers should not be a problem,' Harding replied confidently. 'The magistrate is a good friend of mine and I am sure he will be able to help. Where did you say you were from?'

At this point in the conversation, it began to dawn on Jack that his pretences might be leading him onto dangerous ground. Under his real name, the St Mary's county register would record his criminal conviction and exile, barring him from travel, and his assumed name of 'Stone' would not match any address he could fabricate. Any enquiry by a Charlestown magistrate would thus quickly reveal him as a fraud. Jack began to realise that he should have given this aspect of his plan a little more thought.

'I fear that I am not of this county, sir,' Jack said hastily, as his mind sought to wriggle itself out of its earlier state of seizure. 'And so your magistrate friend may not be able to help me; but please do not trouble yourself on my account – I will return to St Mary's straight away to sort this out myself.' Jack glanced hopefully at Ned who stared back blankly; clearly he was not about to offer a way for Jack to extricate himself from his predicament.

Harding studied Jack curiously for a moment.

'But I understood from my friend here that you were desperate to return to England to visit your ailing mother, Mr Stone?' he said frowning, meanwhile shooting a puzzled glance at the councillor. 'You will not have time to return to St Mary's. The *Rebecca* will be underway before you could possibly return; and this will be the last sailing before Spring!' His voice had become firmer now. 'If you want to be aboard when she sails, sir, I would advise you to let me help you.'

Jack knew that he was cornered; there was nothing more that he could say without risking suspicion – even assuming that his equivocal manner had not already raised suspicion enough.

'Then I'm grateful to you, sir, and I would be pleased to accept your assistance.' Jack acquiesced graciously, but he knew that the stakes were high. At present, it might only be embarrassment that he risked, but discovery would not only stop him in his tracks on this occasion, it could also prevent him from using the port again.

'Good man! And as far as the passage is concerned, Mr Stone,' Harding continued with an enigmatic smile. 'I think that we might be able to help each other. Come into my office, won't you? Perhaps I could speak to you alone?'

An hour or so later, Jack returned to the hotel in better spirits and burst into the cramped bedroom to find his companion dozing in the armchair. Ned stirred at his friend's noisy entry and sat up, yawning.

'Well?' he asked, wincing in pain as his reawakened bruises made themselves felt.

'Interesting,' Jack replied mysteriously, kicking off his boots and throwing himself onto his bed. 'He wants me to keep an eye on his consignment – to check that it gets to England safe and sound. He reckons he's being short-changed in Cowes - either some of his tobacco is disappearing en route or there's some fiddling on the price. Anyway, he wants me to be his agent – and for that, I'll get my passage and our lodgings here paid!'

'Sounds too easy to me,' Ned said suspiciously. 'There must be a catch.'

'Hmmm! Maybe! I just hope that they don't find out who I really am before the ship sails. Still, since he has generously offered to pick up our bill in this fine establishment, I think it's time for some lunch, don't you?'

Chapter Seventeen

High up on the *Rebecca's* mainmast lookout platform, the solitary Captain Henry Auld braced himself against the rigging and peered through his telescope towards the Virginian shore. Zephyrs of breeze played upon his thoughtful face as the tall mast swayed gently to and fro with a rhythm that he found calming. A trim looking man dressed in navy blue uniform with captain's braid upon his sleeves and a gold band on the peak of his cap, he had a neat grey beard and moustache. He found it both exhilarating and liberating to escape the crowded confines of the decks to view the world from this lofty and precarious perch, a refuge that he often sought at anchor to clear his mind. But on this occasion it was his interest in the progress of activities ashore that brought him to this vantage point, having left the first officer below to ready the ship for departure. To be anchored so far from the quay was irritating but he could not risk getting his ship closer; at one time he could have taken her right up to the harbour side, but now, like so many of the Potomac estuaries, the channels were being silted up. Clearwater Creek was a wide expanse of water, a large natural harbour formerly of great commercial importance, but the shoreline was now littered with abandoned landing stages reaching out vainly towards the deeper water. Once, great tobacco ships might have sat alongside these relics, but only shallow-draught coastal craft could use them now.

Auld swung his telescope to scan the distant view. At the head of the Creek, in a shallow basin surrounded by low hills denuded by the encroachment of tobacco plantations, the harbour town of Dumper marshalled itself around the waterfront. It was a sprawl of clapboard buildings of odd shapes and unexpectedly bold colours that shone brightly through the rafts of wood-smoke that hung in the still air over the town. Auld focussed again upon the quay and was gratified to see the last of the ship's boats start back. As a consequence of his distant anchorage, his cargo of slaves and tools had been ferried ashore by the port's lighters; his men had followed them to assist in their offloading and were now at last returning. He watched them for a while, then shifted his field of view back towards the waterfront, and as he did so, the colour of the scene seemed to drain away as if suddenly a cloud had blotted out the light. Auld squinted through his eyepiece as an unexpected sense of unease gripped him. The slaves were being moved into pens of different sizes, sorted by age and gender, roped at neck and ankle, looking sullen and afraid as they waited for their fates to be decided. He had watched such scenes before, but never from this perspective, and never with the intensity of focus obtained through a telescope, so that now for the first time he began to grasp the horror of their plight. They were being brutally manhandled; young torn from their mothers, husbands from wives, brother from sister; beaten at the slightest hesitation to submit to orders that they could not possibly comprehend. The magnification of Auld's glass brought their images up close as if on a theatre stage directly before him, yet their tragic drama was enacted in mime. Auld looked into those haunting black and dusty faces as he had never done before and saw terror and despair in their eyes: men trembled visibly, women wailed, children screamed, babies clung to their mothers in wide-eyed bewilderment. Seeing in those frightened little faces the expressions of his own daughters in their childhood moments of distress, Auld felt a sudden wave of empathy sweep over him that brought a lump to his throat. He found himself unable to tear his eye away from the silent scene despite his vision blurring. In the foreshortened view of his telescope, the doleful faces seemed all at once to look in his direction; their glances were reproachful, condemning. Shot like accusing arrows, they found their mark in his conscience as if he had been struck. Staggering backwards against the rail, he slammed his eyeglass shut as if to close the lid on the shocking scene and stood in silent reflection. 'How have I come to this?' he wondered, 'that these free souls should by my own hand have been delivered to such a dismal fate?'

For some moments, he rested on the rail, staring at the distant scene with his unaided eyes. To his view, the figures were tiny now, hardly more than specks in the distance, reduced not only in their size but also in their apparent humanity. It was a drama no more, but merely a disturbance in the equilibrium of things which might draw passing interest - a swarm of some tiny species which could be shielded from view by an outstretched finger tip. Only in such a form, he realised with sudden insight, were men of power able to manipulate the fate of populations; but Auld could see now how he had become an instrument of such men.

Saddened by the revelation, he pondered on the path his life had taken to bring him to such a point. He remembered his rise through the ranks from master's mate to lieutenant in the Royal Navy, eventually serving as first lieutenant on several ships of the line. Not having the benefits of family connections in the upper echelons of the Navy, he was slow to attain command, but at last he was given the captaincy of a brig and orders to scout the Mediterranean. His tour of duty had been distinguished by several successful skirmishes with the Spanish that had won him mentions in Admirals' dispatches. After such recognition, it had hurt his pride subsequently not to be given a more prestigious vessel to command, since he believed that he had earned it, but he would not have admitted to being embittered at being passed-over. Nevertheless, when a Bristol trading company had offered him command of the *Rebecca*, a former Navy sixth rate, it had proved a necessary sop for a wounded ego. He would also have confessed to being attracted by the higher pay and bonuses and the permanence of his post.

His self-analysis was not deluded; he realised now that it had been pride and avarice that had brought him into slavery although at that time he would not have seen himself as so easily seduced. And if his new role as captain of a slaver had given him some qualms at the beginning, he had quickly rationalised it as a necessary and therefore respectable profession. But now, suddenly and belatedly at the age of fifty-eight, his conscience had been pricked; he had suppressed his misgivings for too long and now felt dishonoured by that very fact. He was filled with self-reproach. He had ploughed the 'golden' routes from England to West Africa and thence to America and back more times than he could remember, and yet the only measure of compassion for his fellow human beings that he could count as his own had been his introduction of an exercise regime that had reduced their death rate to *only* ten percent! What sort of man have I become, to calculate like this?' he wondered. 'And was it truly compassion that drove me, or my eye on my share of the profit?' He had thus begun not to like himself very much.

For a few moments more, he gazed ruefully down at his ship from his lofty perch seeing her now with different eyes. Where only minutes before he might have viewed her with pride, he saw her character as tarnished now, and the spreading stains that darkened her old timbers as a manifestation of her guilt. Long gone were her days of glory as a Navy three-masted frigate dashing about the seas like a filly; she was now more like an old mare, fallen on hard times, forced into a rag and bone trade to avoid the knacker's yard. She had been sold off when it was discovered that her structure could not take the heavier weaponry required to sink modern enemy ships, and a Bristol shipping company had bought her specifically for the tobacco and slaving routes, modifying her accordingly. In the conversion, the central hatches right down to the orlop deck had been enlarged to create a cavernous hold. From a distance, she still looked like a warship with her raked masts and long bowsprit, but closer to, her modified decks and the additional davits and derricks revealed her for what she had become. And her years of unremitting trading had also taken its toll; where once she might have boasted polished brass and pristine paintwork, she looked dull and weathered now. For the first time, Auld was seeing her as the tired old workhorse she had become through the years he had been her master, and he could not help but to reflect upon the symmetry of their fates.

Breaking out of his reverie, Auld looked down to check the progress of work below and saw that the stern mooring line had now been released and that the ship had begun to swing at her bow. A gentle breeze had sprung up from the south, and he watched as the hull slowly aligned itself into the wind like a giant weathercock. With all her gun-ports open to draw air into the dank and dismal reaches of her holds, she looked purposeful and menacing, but only eight of her twenty-eight gun-ports carried any punch. A nine-pound cannon sat behind each of the four forward hatches on each side of the cargo deck like old and forgotten soldiers, rarely exercised since the ship's conversion and now gathering dust. Auld had insisted that they be retained as useful insurance against piracy or French harassment, but he had waited in vain for an opportunity to try them out in action.

With a repentant glance towards the town, he lowered himself through the lubbers' hole and climbed down the ratlines to the quarterdeck. As he neared the deck, he spotted his new first officer with the boatswain amidst the clutter of the forecastle. Something about the nature of their conversation troubled him, although the distance prevented him from hearing what was being said. Rather than call the first officer to him immediately as he had intended, he held his tongue and watched the pair for a short time, noting the boatswain's apparently forthright manner. And there was also a certain conspiratorial air about the pair that made Auld uneasy at the casual nature of their relationship. Eventually, he called out:

'Mr Goddard, a word if you please!'

'Aye aye, captain,' Goddard shouted back, glancing quickly over his shoulder.

Across the distance, Auld could not see the boatswain's mean expression nor hear Goddard's uncertain voice, but he noted the undue delay before the latter detached himself and made his way along the deck.

'Mr Goddard,' the captain said evenly, hesitating while selecting the right words. 'I think that you allow the boatswain to be too familiar with you. You must try to put some distance between you and the men; you are a first officer now.'

'I understand, sir,' Goddard replied stiffly.

'Does Mr Judd have any problems below?' Auld persevered, hoping to draw out the young officer.

'Er, no sir. We were discussing the preparations for sailing, nothing more.' Goddard replied, seeming somewhat ill at ease.

Auld suspected some difference of opinion between the two and decided not to press the matter further.

'Well, remember what I said, Mr Goddard; as first officer, you will find yourself in command very soon, and to be effective, you must first command your crew's respect. You must therefore be their leader not their friend.' Auld's tone was kindly rather than admonishing, the voice of a master tutoring an apprentice.

'Well, we'll leave it at that for now, Mr Goddard,' he said in a tone that indicated that the matter was now closed. 'When you have the ship secured, make ready to depart; high water is at noon so we shall have ample depth to clear the bar by eleven and make sure to signal the ferryman in good time - he will need to lower his cable. You may pilot her to the Tobacco River entrance - we shall anchor there overnight and weigh at first light tomorrow morning for the trip up-river to the landing.'

'Thank you, sir.' Goddard's expression showed that he was pleased with his instructions.

Auld acknowledged this with a curt nod then glanced upwards to the mainmast top where the burgee fluttered lazily. 'I fear that the boats will have to tow us down river to the bend; in this wind we shall make little headway under sail alone.'

'That'll please the men, sir,' Goddard replied ironically with a thin smile; and with a touch of his cap, he turned on his heel to take up his command position at the quarterdeck rail. Auld retired to the stern and watched the young officer carefully from an unobtrusive distance as he and the boatswain called the crew through the ship's departure drill, reassured to see none of the earlier disrespect that he had previously observed in the latter's manner.

The boats were soon crewed up and manoeuvred into their towing positions, while the anchor was weighed and the ship got underway. Auld remained on deck for most of the day, pleased that Goddard could practice his piloting skills in relatively benign conditions and taking the opportunity to observe his competence in command. It was a faultless performance despite the difficulty of navigating the narrow channel out of the creek, and avoiding the unmarked sand bar outside the harbour mouth. Auld was quietly impressed with the man and he would write as much in his log, but it was no more than he than expected. He was well aware of Goddard's background from the confidential reports received on him when he reported to take up his new appointment on the *Rebecca* just two months before. The thirty-year-old officer had been at sea for ten years since moving out of the Company's administrative office where he had first been employed as a loading clerk. In his earlier seagoing appointments, he had shown himself to be a competent junior officer, passing his navigation and seamanship examinations at first attempt, and demonstrating sound practical ship-handling skills. He was assessed as a smart, personable, and intelligent young man, if possibly sometimes a little over-confident, showing good potential for leadership. And married to the daughter of a sea captain, it was felt that he enjoyed the necessary support at home for a long career at sea. This transatlantic voyage was his first aboard the *Rebecca* and also first as a first officer, and he had come to it highly recommended by his previous captain. If there had been any note of caution in that report, it was that Goddard was likely to take too relaxed a line in the discipline of his watch, preferring consultation and reasoning rather than the confrontational approach favoured by his last superior. When Auld had discussed this comment with Goddard at his embarkation meeting in Bristol, he had not wanted to be overly critical, thinking the approach possibly enlightened, but he had warned him that it could lay him open to manipulation.

Now, reflecting on his observation of the interchange between his first officer and Mr Judd, Auld recalled this warning and wondered if the young officer might need further counsel. Judd was a resourceful and experienced boatswain whose pugnacious and irascible character ensured that the crew jumped when he gave his orders, but he also had a shiftiness about him that made Auld wary. If the *Rebecca's* crew came under suspicion for the putative losses that Harding at Charlestown had reported on recent voyages, then Judd would be the first to come to Auld's mind as potential ringleader. But it had proved impossible so far, without making his concerns public, to identify where or how these losses were occurring, or indeed whether they were occurring at all and not some paperwork error. Thus it would be inappropriate, unjust, and possibly inflammatory for anyone on board to be challenged on the matter. He rather hoped that the thefts were occurring in Cowes rather than on his ship, since the latter would reflect upon his captaincy. But one way or the other, his private arrangement with Harding to put an independent agent aboard should soon bring matters to a head.

Chapter Eighteen

From the entrance of the Tobacco River on the Potomac to the main wharf at the naval port of entry at Neal's Landing measured some five miles, and the navigable channel, for large vessels of the draught of the *Rebecca*, was relatively narrow. In the still air of the early dawn, the river's cold surface was a gently winding avenue of feathery white mist. Now and then the hollow shriek of a moorhen or the double-syllable croak of a pheasant might break the silence, but to Jack, waiting on the quay for the *Rebecca* to arrive, it was so quiet that he could hear his own pulse beating out the time. He had awoken from a fretful dream in the early hours and, unable to slow his thoughts to a pace where slumber might have been regained, he had left the hotel to walk the mile or so down-river to the landing. Jack pulled up the collar of his long overcoat and watched the stars disappear in the emerging light. He must have stood there for half an hour before he became conscious of a new sound, faint at first and muffled by the mist; it was the steady rhythm of rowing oars splashing in the water. The first hint of blue had begun to colour the brightening sky, and in its light, Jack could now see the bend some quarter of a mile distant whose tall conifers restricted his view of the river beyond. The rhythmic sound grew closer, a fuller timbre now, and deeper tones had joined the higher notes to produce the unmistakable resonance of rowlocks twisting and straining in their slots. A movement above the tree line at the bend caught Jack's attention, and he lifted his eyes to see the slow procession of the *Rebecca's* three tall masts. Burgees and pennants hung limply from the mastheads to mark the ship's arrival; the sight reminded Jack of a military parade that, as a small boy, he had once craned to see over the heads of a jostling crowd. The vessel's dark bulk emerged from the bend, looking massive in the narrow confines of the river, its towing boats all but invisible in the mist. And by degree, she turned her long bowsprit towards the quay like an accusing finger, the procession then advancing in stately majesty.

Suddenly, the sound of a shifting foot on the gravely ground behind him alerted Jack to the fact that he was not alone, and he turned to find Harding standing a short distance away; how long he had been there Jack could not tell.

'Anxious to get away, Mr Stone? Or should I say Mr Easton?'

Jack frowned and made to protest, but was silenced as Harding continued evenly without a pause.

'Did you think you could deceive me? Sir Michael is a client of mine. We meet often to discuss business and we met yesterday in Chaptico. It did not take us long to work out who you were – your absence from New Hope could not possibly have remained unnoticed for long.'

Jack was taken aback and did not know quite how to react, and his spirits plunged as he saw his plans beginning to fall apart. *So near and yet so far*, he thought bitterly, as behind him the *Rebecca* slid alongside the quay, her men leaping noisily from her sides to make her fast.

'Mr Harding, forgive me,' he stuttered, 'it was foolish of me to try to deceive you when you were so helpful.' Jack was both embarrassed and crestfallen. He guessed that Harding's suspicions must have been raised by his clumsy subterfuge, a mistake that now seemed to have cost him his chance.

'I attempted to mask my identity for good reason, sir. I..' Jack started to explain, but Harding cut him off.

'There is no need to justify yourself - Sir Michael has told me your story.' Harding's tone was curiously ambivalent as he took Jack by the arm and led him away from the quay. 'You well know that you risk the gallows if you climb aboard that ship,' he said, confidentially. 'But I admit still to be disposed to help you - if you would risk your life, then that is your own business and I will not try to stop you. But you will have to go without official papers. I cannot, in all conscience, approach the Justice now.'

In the space of a few minutes, Jack's mood had bounced rapidly from one extreme to the other and back again.

'Mr Harding.' Jack spoke more lightly now, his tone one of relief. 'I'm truly grateful that despite my untruths you're still prepared to help.'

'You do not have me to thank, Mr Easton. Sir Michael spoke highly of you, indeed he persuaded me to do so - he hopes that you will find your mother well and that you will return soon to New Hope to meet your commitments to him.'

'Well then, sir, I'm grateful to both of you. You will no doubt be seeing him before my return, and you could perhaps pass on my assurances to that effect.'

'You may not thank me when you arrive in Cowes with no official papers, but I shall give you my own letter of authority as my Agency's employee, and perhaps that will be enough - the immigration procedures are a little haphazard there. If you are challenged, you may again be forced to depend upon your deception skills!' Harding said with a wry smile.

The following day, Jack set off early for Neal's Landing to meet Harding at the ship to have his duties explained; Ned, meanwhile, would deliver the bags to the town quay and start preparing Jack's boat for his own departure later.

When he arrived at the wharf, Jack found it a hive of activity. *The Rebecca* lay alongside, its hatches open for loading like hungry mouths, its decks strewn with the paraphernalia and disarray of preparing for a long sea voyage. At one end of the main deck, a chain of dusty black-skinned men climbed a shallow ramp, stooping under a variety of boxes and bales heaped upon their backs. At the other, gangs of stevedores sweated at the derricks, hoisting and swinging hogsheads of tobacco into the hold. The ship could be seen to lean first one way and then the other, as the heavy loads were lifted alternately from the quay and then from the lighters berthed alongside in the river.

Jack joined the line of men on the ramp and made his way up it to the deck. With no one there to receive him, he positioned himself out of the way near the edge of the main hold and watched the activity with interest. Deep in the gloomy bowels of the hold, a handful of men were manhandling the hogsheads and boxes and bales into numerous wooden compartments that extended laterally from the hull towards the ship's centreline. Between the compartments, running the length of the stacked cargo, a narrow alleyway had been left clear, evidently for inspection and access. Jack noticed a seaman crouching at the bottom of it, engaged apparently in close inspection of the hogsheads, moving from one to another, but before he could shift his casual glance away, the seaman looked up to catch Jack still looking down. The man seemed at first surprised to find himself under observation then stood up quickly and walked on. There was something secretive and surly about him that took Jack aback since he would not otherwise have given the man a second glance.

A strident voice from behind then startled him.

'You there, sir, come away from the hold if you please!'

Jack turned to see the first officer standing on the quarterdeck with a clipboard in one hand and waving him aft with the other, apparently in some degree of annoyance. The neat cut of the officer's uniform made

Jack suddenly aware of his own drab and crumpled appearance, the contrast making him feel immediately uncomfortable.

'I'm Jack Stone, sir,' Jack said as he reached the quarterdeck. If he was intimidated by the brusque manner by which he had been summoned, he hid it very well. 'I am to accompany you on your voyage as the agent of Mr Harding - you will have been notified I believe?' He extended his hand in greeting, but the young officer eyed him suspiciously and was slow to offer his hand in return.

'Ah, yes, Mr Stone,' he said, at last, 'the captain informed me that you would be travelling with us. But for the moment, sir, I must ask you please to confine yourself to the quarterdeck while loading is underway. It is potentially dangerous, you understand.'

There was suddenly a hint of nervousness in Goddard's manner that Jack found surprising, given that it was he who was the trespasser, but before he could reply, Harding's voice was heard to call out:

'I see you have met my new man, Mr Goddard,' he said panting as he reached the group still out of breath from his brisk walk from the town. 'And I trust that all ... Ah good! I see the last of my hogsheads going in.'

Goddard seemed to relax and greeted Harding with a fulsome smile; to Jack the transformation in his manner was puzzling.

'Yes, Mr Harding,' Goddard replied, glancing at the last hogshead which at that moment was being lowered gently into place. 'All is in order, sir, your consignment is now all aboard,' he said making a final mark on his clipboard.

'Then I'll take the manifest if you please,' Harding replied.

Goddard looked surprised.

'But surely you'll want me to look after the manifest, sir. I should lock it up for safekeeping until we arrive at our destination,' he said, looking slightly puzzled.

'Mr Stone will assume that responsibility on this trip Mr Goddard, thank you all the same.'

Goddard looked a little doubtful, but he rolled the parchment into a tight cylinder, slid it into a loop of black ribbon, and handed it over as requested.

'Thank you, Mr Goddard,' Harding said, looking satisfied with himself and slid the cylinder into his coat pocket. 'Now at your convenience, sir, perhaps we might be permitted a tour of the cargo deck? I would like to introduce Mr Stone to his consignment.'

Again the officer seemed uneasy but he visibly relaxed after glancing into the hold, apparently satisfied at what he had seen. The derricks had now fallen idle, and only the sullen line of stooping men still processed up the ramp carrying sacks upon their backs.

'Then follow me if you please,' he replied, turning to take the lead. 'Now is as good a time as any since the hatches will soon be battened down and there won't be any light below.'

Goddard led the pair down the companionways to the after part of the Orlop deck, the lowest working level of the ship above the bilges. The dank air brought a wrinkle to Jack's nostrils as he descended into these gloomy depths. There was another odour too, only faintly detectable above the stench of bilge water and sodden timber: it was the reek of human defecation, the unmistakable and enduring characteristic of a slaver - it instantly evoked uncomfortable memories of Jack's voyage six years before. The party passed the shadowy forms of casks and boxes stacked high on both sides of their route as they progressed, picking their footing with utmost care, and ducking to avoid the dark timbers that menaced at head height. Eventually, they entered the cargo hold, finding it better illuminated from the open hatch of the main deck above. Shafts of light shone down through the dusty air into the passageway between the rows of tobacco hogsheads piled on their sides five or six high. Goddard was already well ahead when Harding stopped alongside one of the containers, calling Jack to come closer:

'Now, look at this,' he said, bringing Jack's attention to the markings branded on its lid. 'These letters and numbers will tell you the batch number, the plantation name and the date of inspection in the Charlestown depot. They should tie up with the details that I recorded in the manifest and that Goddard should have checked as the hogsheads were loaded...I have it here, look.' Harding rummaged in his coat pocket and took out the roll of parchment. He slid off the retaining loop and unrolled it a few inches, holding it up for Jack to see, pointing at a list containing letters and numbers similar to those that he had indicated on the lid. Jack peered at the list; in the dim light it was difficult to see clearly, but alongside each of the coded annotations, he could make out the name of its origin and the number of hogsheads shipped. Harding rolled up the parchment again, replaced the ribbon and handed it to Jack.

'When you arrive in Cowes, give this to my agent so that he can check that the consignment corresponds with this list.' He glanced forward, apparently checking on Goddard's location, then lowering his voice almost to a whisper he continued: 'Goddard's predecessor used to carry it for me and, as I've said, there were often some discrepancies between the invoices that I received and what I thought had been dispatched. I'm afraid that my paperwork has not always been so careful however, and curiously, the losses only seem to have affected the larger batches where there is admittedly more scope for an administrative error. The differences have never been large either, perhaps half a dozen hogsheads in all. Nevertheless, I remain suspicious, and at around twenty-five pounds gross each, it represents a tidy loss of income. I therefore need to clear it up one way or the other.'

Goddard returned to join the pair, clearly interested to see what had delayed them.

'Ah, Mr Goddard! I was just showing Mr Stone our system of identification,' he said waving a hand airily at the casks, 'But we are finished now, so please lead on!'

Goddard led the party onwards towards the forward hold where more hogsheads were stacked at floor level. There was a great deal of noise above as bales and sacks continued to be hurled in on top and heaved into place, throwing volumes of dust into the air. In a sudden fit of coughing, Harding stopped to pull up his cravat and Jack waited behind him while Goddard continued on. Suddenly, there was an unusually heavy thud as one of the entering bales hit the edge of the stack above them and the top began to lurch precariously. Jack saw the danger as the column rocked and leapt forward to push Harding out of the way, both of them falling to the deck as several of the bales tumbled down onto the place where they had stood. It was difficult to get up in the tight confines of the narrow alleyway and Jack looked up in apprehension of a further fall. He was taken aback to see someone looking down who clearly found the spectacle amusing; it was the same man that Jack had seen acting suspiciously in the hold when he had first arrived on deck.

Goddard returned quickly to the scene.

'Mr Judd, what the devil's happened here?' he shouted angrily at the man above. 'Get some men down here right away to clear up this shambles! And have the restraining planks put in place if you please – these piles are unstable – they should have been put in place before.' He stooped to help the men raise themselves. 'Is anyone hurt?'

But other than to their dignity, neither of the visitors had suffered any injury, and after brushing off the dust the two men followed a strangely reticent Goddard back to the quarterdeck. As he climbed back into the daylight, however, Jack found himself wondering if the incident might have been mischief and not an accident at all. While there now seemed little point in recriminations, it nevertheless seemed odd to Jack that Goddard showed only passing concern about the potentially lethal episode.

As Harding had some private business with the captain to attend to in which Jack was not included, he suggested Jack return to the town without him. But the agent had a few private words of advice before their parting:

'Tread softly, Jack. Your presence itself should be sufficient for the purpose intended both en route and in Cowes. But watch your back. If there is mischief afoot here, whoever is responsible will not be pleased to have you aboard.'

The two men shook hands.

'You will be met by my representative, and he will send word to me in due course,' Harding continued, taking out a letter from his pocket. 'You have the manifest safely tucked away?' he asked.

Jack nodded patting his coat pocket in confirmation.

'Then give this to him as well,' Harding said, handing him the letter. 'It is a letter of introduction. Perhaps he can be of assistance to you in some way if you should find yourself in need of his help.'

When Jack arrived back at the town quay, he found Ned almost ready to depart, having already attached the boom and gaff to the mast so that the sail was now ready to lift on its halyard. His back was now bent to clearing the bilges of water with a leather scoop designed for the purpose. Jack watched him for a moment, silently contemplating without relish the imminent parting from his staunch ally and friend, wondering how he would fare without him. Ned soon finished his task and looked up in surprise to see Jack looking down. In their unspoken acknowledgement of each other, both saw the uneasy recognition that parting was upon them, but neither seemed willing to articulate their disquiet.

'Your bag's there,' Ned said pointing to where it lay.

Jack nodded. 'Thanks. You ready?'

Ned cursorily flicked his eyes around his boat. 'Think so.'

'Better be on your way then while you've got the tide.'

'Aye,' he said, with a sort of helpless expression on his face.

'Don't run into any ships on the way.' Jack forced a stiff smile.

'I'll try not to.' Ned did not return the smile, but he paused, and then added: 'You look after yersel, Jack.'

'I will.'

And with that, Ned hoisted his sail and cast off, pushing himself out into the river where his sail filled in the fresh breeze; and he was quickly borne away. For a long time afterwards, Jack stood on the quay watching the fast receding craft, fearing not to turn away lest he miss a backward glance or wave from his friend. But neither came. Even as the distant sail turned at the bend of the river, Jack could still make out Ned's form perched upon the thwart, leaning out against the wind. Jack raised his hand in a final farewell, and then the little boat was gone, suddenly hidden from view by overhanging trees. For some seconds, he stood staring at the bend wondering if the boat might come back into view; but hope died as it at last dawned on him that Ned had gone for good. With this realisation, a feeling of vulnerability overtook him and he shuddered as he contemplated the loneliness of his coming task. Until that moment, a simple logic had propelled him along his path from step to step without spending much time considering the entirety of his undertaking, but as each step had been taken so the next loomed into view seeming yet more difficult than the last. But if he had begun to doubt himself, he also knew that there could now be no turning back. With nowhere to go before returning to the *Rebecca* in due course, he found himself a place to sit in quiet solitude, quickly losing himself in thought, until the purple colours of the descending dusk turned to grey.

On his arrival on board, Jack was met and escorted to his cabin by the ship's boy who wore dirty baggy trousers and no footwear. He could have been no more than fourteen years old, with curly fair hair and pale blue eyes, and he greeted Jack with a broad grin and a cheeky salute.

Jack smiled, grateful to see a friendly face aboard, and followed the boy down the companionway to the officers' cabins located at the rear of the ship under the quarterdeck. The cabin allocated to Jack was little more than a six-by-four foot wooden box with headroom hardly enough to stand upright; and while Jack's eyes accustomed to the gloom inside, the boy fetched a taper to light the gimballed lantern mounted on the bulkhead. In its dim light, Jack could see that the tiny space had nothing in it but a hanging cot and a few wooden pegs and ledges on which to place his things. It felt as claustrophobic as a prison cell and instinctively he scanned it for escape. Above his head, a hatch had been let into the deck through which he reckoned he might just squeeze, and there was a smaller hatch in the curved planks of the hull wall that opened to the world outside. Both were firmly shut. Fighting a rising sense of entrapment, Jack threw his bag onto the bunk and reached across to open the latter to let in the air and the dwindling light of dusk. The sweet smell of the river poured in, providing some small relief from the acrid odours that permeated the ship's innards. The cabin would be cramped and uncomfortable for the long crossing ahead, and the rank smells and gloomy environment would be a constant and uncomfortable reminder of his last transatlantic voyage.

'And what shall I call you, young man?' Jack asked with an indulgent smile.

'My name is Matthew, Sir,' the boy replied in a faltering manner, 'but most of the crew call me Matt. I'm not sure I like it though, since I'm often treated like one!' he smiled coyly at his own joke.

'Well, I'll call you Matthew then, and I'll need a friend like you aboard to look after me,' grinned Jack, pulling from his pocket a few of his last farthings, which he then pressed into the boy's hand.

Matthew's eyes widened in delight at the sight of the coins. 'Thank you, sir,' he said brightly, touching his temple as he excused himself politely. But only a short while later, the boy returned with a message from the captain:

'Captain Auld sends his regards, sir, and hopes that you will join him and the first officer for dinner at six o'clock. I am told to call for you.'

Thus it was that half an hour later, dressed in his only presentable attire, now much the worse for its earlier tumble in the hold, Jack was led to the captain's stateroom. It was not ten strides from his own cabin, and Jack wondered why it had been necessary to send the boy for him at all, concluding that some arcane rule of maritime protocol demanded it.

By now dusk had faded to night, and the cabin was lit with candles and lanterns that reflected off its polished oak interior to give it a warm and comfortable glow. It was a spacious room, spreading itself across the entire width of the ship, with a lattice of windows running the whole width of its stern bulkhead. In daylight, the glazing would certainly provide a glorious panoramic view, but tonight only a cluster of glittering lights from the distant town could be seen penetrating the cabin's rosy reflections in the glass. Captain Auld and his first officer sat waiting, and both rose amicably to greet Jack as he entered. The officers' instincts to duck their heads when rising were well entrenched, but Jack's were not quite quick enough to avoid a resounding collision with a low deck beam as he approached to greet them. Jack winced and clutched his head, but the captain could not stop himself from letting out a snort of muted laughter.

'Oh, my dear fellow! I should have warned you. Are you quite all right?' he fussed, coming over to guide the stooping Jack to a chair.

Jack sat heavily, bringing his hand down from his head to examine it for blood. 'I think I shall survive,' he said with a wrinkled smile, 'but will the beam be weakened by the impact, I wonder?' At this, the captain shook with laughter.

'Many a noble head has made the same connection, sir. You are in distinguished company!'

And thus, what might have been a stilted evening got off to a good start. The ice broken, even the stiff Goddard managed some civil introductory conversation despite his earlier distance; no doubt his civility was partly in deference to his superior's observation, but it was welcome all the same. Once the preliminaries were over, however, the captain's tone turned more businesslike:

'Let us quickly dispose of the matters in hand before we entertain ourselves over dinner.' he said pleasantly. 'You of course know that I have agreed that you should accompany us in order to settle the concerns of Mr Harding who suspects some mischief with his cargo. By the way, I should tell you that Mr Goddard here is new to all this since this is his first round trip on *The Rebecca*; but I have taken him into my confidence and I am sure that you can depend upon his.' On saying this, Auld glanced at Goddard who smiled weakly in return, but Jack thought the first officer looked uneasy as the captain continued.

'Now in my opinion, Mr Stone, it is unlikely that there will be anything to occupy you until we dock at Cowes since it is there that any misappropriation will take place - such heavy containers can hardly go missing during the voyage can they!' he quipped. 'And of course, that also assumes that it is indeed misappropriation and not some administrative miscalculation that we are dealing with. And it is because of my doubts on this that I would not want to make your mission public - it might be taken as a lack of confidence in my crew's honesty, you understand. So, as far as they are concerned, you are a colleague of Mr Harding with some connected business in England, and that is all. Clearly, if we are to uncover any skulduggery, then we need to catch the perpetrators off their guard and not alert them beforehand. In short, I would like you to keep your head down until we arrive at our destination, and even then you must proceed with some considerable discretion.'

Jack agreed with Auld's assessment and began to reconcile himself to a long and tedious crossing with nothing to occupy his mind, but then he had an idea that might make the time pass more interestingly.

'Perhaps I may therefore take an interest in the sailing of the ship during our voyage, captain, otherwise time will move exceedingly slowly for me?'

Auld seemed amused. 'I'm sure Mr Goddard will accommodate you as far as he is able,' he replied, agreeably. 'Now, unless you have any questions, shall we enjoy our supper?'

In normal circumstances, such a social gathering would be unusual: on the one side of the table, two officers, educated, qualified and worldly-wise, and on the other, an ex-convict, smuggling stonemason of relatively humble origin having few of their finer graces. And so initially, Jack felt awkward, not able to make small talk and responding guardedly to the natural curiosity of his hosts. But later, with a glass or two of wine and a good meal inside him, conversation began to flow more easily. Indeed, Jack became quite open in a carefully selective way about his background, neither concealing his love of masonry nor the death of his father as the reason for his return to England; and his descriptions of the near miss on the Potomac and the robbery in Charlestown proved particularly entertaining. Naturally he concealed anything that might incriminate himself, and by and large he was successful in this.

But Goddard had reason to be worried by Jack's presence aboard the *Rebecca* as we shall see, and he was anxious to find out as much about his guest as courtesy permitted:

'And what then were your reasons for moving to Maryland in the first place?' he enquired in a deceptively light tone as the captain poured his guest another glass of wine.

Foolishly, Jack had not anticipated this question and at first he stuttered while his mind struggled to find a credible answer.

'Oh... adventure; ...a better life; ...a new start,' Jack mused airily, playing it off as a confident young man's wanderlust.

But the initial hesitation had been noted. To Goddard at least, it was clear that their visitor was holding something back; but in his anxious frame of mind, he misconstrued it as mysterious and threatening rather than something of which he might be able to take advantage.

Later that evening, long after Jack and the captain had retired and the crew had taken to their hammocks, Goddard made a stealthy visit to the boatswain's cabin in the forecastle. But if he looked anxious when he arrived at Judd's door, his face had completely drained of colour when he returned to his own cabin fifteen minutes later.

The following morning, Jack was woken early by the sound of running footfalls above his head and the scraping of heavy ropes and hawsers being hauled across the deck; it was a noisy commotion that resonated through the ship's timbers like a sounding board. The details of his tiny cabin were still invisible in the darkness, but the chink of light around the flanges of the hatch showed that dawn had arrived. Jack found that he could lift the hatch at its forward edge and through the gap so formed was able to gain a good view of the activity on deck. His cabin was located underneath the quarterdeck and his view thus captured almost the entire length of the vessel looking forward to the forecastle. Several men lined up along the starboard guardrail had hold of long poles with which they were fending off the timbers of the landing stage as the ship slid slowly forward. Jack assumed that her boats must be propelling her since no sails had yet been set. Some yards in front of him, Goddard stood looking about him attentively, betraying some anxiety in the quick movements of his head; clearly, he had been given charge of the vessel's departure. And alongside him a helmsmen stood at the wheel with Judd and another crewman standing nearby. At the larboard rail, his hands clasped behind his back, Captain Auld stood watching with a critical eye; his orders had evidently been given and now he marked their execution. The total complement of the vessel could not have been more than one hundred and fifty men, half that of a fighting vessel of the same size, and most of those not crewing the ship's boats now seemed to be on deck busying themselves as the ship moved slowly on its way. They worked in teams, moving from one task to another with little apparent communication between them, as if every man was familiar with his duty. Jack was impressed at the order and discipline of such an unlikely ragbag of men as Judd bellowed his instructions. If it was the boatswain's job to relay orders, it was Goddard's to tell him what he wanted from the crew; and he conveyed his orders to the boatswain in a clipped and measured voice, his manner somewhat stiff and formal.

From the shore it must have been a fine sight indeed to see this handsome ship glide down the narrow river, dwarfing the boats and buildings on either side. Even the tallest trees looked puny by comparison, and many ashore who were already about even at this early hour paused to watch the spectacle. Then, as if to signal the ship's departure, the rising sun's first beams, still hidden by the tree line from the view of those on deck, lit up the topmasts in a golden glow. It was at such times that the officers and crew felt proud to be seafarers - to be observed with such manifest admiration and interest from those along the river bank. Few of the mariners at that moment would have exchanged their lifestyles for the humdrum existences of their land-bound brethren. And Jack, who still observed from his hatch, could not help but feel the thrill of an adventure begun.

Aided by the slow drift of the ebb tide, the *Rebecca* was soon out of the river and into the Potomac where her rigging felt the first breezes that came unhindered across the water from Virginia. It was a fair wind, a soldiers' wind, a wind that promised a quick and easy passage to the Chesapeake and thence out into the open sea; and all the sailors on board recognised it at once and privately thanked the Lord.

Jack joined Auld and Goddard on the quarterdeck later, exchanging morning greetings as he arrived, but then found himself a position at the stern rail where he would not be in the way. The sun had climbed high into the morning sky by now; and stiff from an uncomfortable night in a damp and narrow cot, he revelled in its warmth. It appeared that he had arrived at an important moment for, to an accompaniment of belligerent shouting, crewmen seemed to rush into every segment of his view. He watched some winch the boats aboard while others swarmed the ratlines, spreading themselves along the yards where they hung poised as if awaiting some imminent spectacle. And then in an arresting crescendo of sight and sound, the huge canvases were let go, falling like avalanches from the yards and filling the air with thunder. The braces and blocks creaked and clattered as the rigging tightened under the strain of the filling sails. The wind tussled and buffeted the heavy fabric in a frenzy of whipping and cracking which seemed to go on and on, until, at last, the canvases snapped into shape with the percussion of artillery fire. And under his feet, Jack felt a surge of acceleration as the ship was picked up by the stern and thrust forwards on the wind. For better or worse, he was on his way to England.

Chapter Nineteen

Portland

At precisely the same moment that his older brother was setting off on his journey three thousand miles away in the Potomac, full of hope, Luke Easton was returning home from Weymouth somewhat down in the mouth. His meeting at the banking house had gone worse than he had feared, and reflecting upon it now, he knew that he was lucky not to be facing immediate foreclosure. The banker's terse words had come close to ridicule, leaving Luke feeling like an admonished schoolboy. But more particularly, he had begun to feel that he had let everyone down.

Luke's reluctant stewardship of the family business since his father's death could never have been called inspired, but somehow he had muddled through. Only a few months before, he had felt so pleased with himself for winning a new contract that he had confidently proclaimed a change in fortunes. The contract to supply stone for a large, prestigious London project had promised to be so profitable that it would allow long-needed improvements to the site. And so confident was he of this that he had taken out a loan on terms that could have been better negotiated had he been more careful. He now realised that he should not have been so impatient. With the stone already delivered to the capital, the project had foundered and the customer put into receivership with large invoices unpaid. With the great benefit of hindsight, he now saw that it had been naive to commit almost his entire production to this one contract - he should have held something back for sales to other customers and thus kept cash coming in - and it embarrassed him to remember that he had blithely ignored his wife's warning of the danger. As a result, he now found himself out on a limb. Potential customers had gone elsewhere, and with insufficient income, he had defaulted on his repayments, and the banking partners now threatened foreclosure. At stake was not only his tenure of the quarry and thus his livelihood, but also his home and that of his mother, since he had put up both freeholds as security. And there was also the pressing matter of his men's wages. It might be normal for them to have to wait for their pay until invoices were settled, but now they might not get paid at all, and some were already in desperate straits. He felt the responsibility towards them keenly, especially towards those whose names had been listed in the company's books for generations, fellows he had worked with man and boy. He now wondered how he could have been so foolish with so much at stake?

Standing morosely on the gravel beach near the Passage Houses at Smallmouth, he waited for the ferryman to bring his boat across the narrow stretch of water to collect him. A rumble of distant thunder turned his head westwards to examine the sky. It had been a clear day but tall clouds were now building in the west and an icy wind swept the expanses of Weymouth Bay to curl around his legs and reach its freezing tentacles through every opening of his clothing. Feeling chilled to his bones, he stamped his feet and pulled his coat around him tightly. Things could not get much worse, he thought gloomily.

Luke was as tall as his elder brother, but in the years since Jack's departure, his build had become fuller in proportion. Moreover, the developing paunch of his belly indicated a living standard very different from that to which his brother had become accustomed; his face tended towards flaccidity, his jowls rather more pronounced than might be expected of someone so young - an undoubted result of excess. Some in the Portland community would say that it had been a misfortune rather than a benefit to inherit his father's business, for it was already in a decline as a result of the old man's distractions. Yet Luke might also admit that he had been headstrong at the beginning, becoming so full of himself as master of his new domain that he had thrown caution to the wind. And after an injudicious early spending spree, the business seemed to have been hit by a run of unexpected difficulties culminating in this latest crisis. Disillusioned, Luke was fast coming to the conclusion that he had neither the temperament nor the acumen required to be a businessman, at last recognising that he had so deceived himself, feeling so flush with the borrowed cash that he had become careless with it.

Luke took a deep breath of cold sea-air, smelling the fishy odours of the decomposing seaweed stranded at the high-water mark behind him, and let out a long and listless sigh, his breath steaming briefly in his face before being whisked away on the wind. Idly, he watched an over-laden horse-drawn cart rumble its way towards the causeway opposite, its axles immersed in the slow-moving water which formed the ebbing outflow of the Fleet lagoon. On the far shore, the flat-bottomed ferryboat waited patiently while a single passenger embarked, then bent his back to the cable to haul the craft back across the stream. The boat moved sluggishly at first, the cable rising stiffly from the water at the prow and falling slackly at the stern with each heave; but it would not take more than a minute or two for him to cross the narrow stretch. As Luke watched the ferry's steady progress, a golden sun sank beneath the dark base of the approaching cloud, but its rays were soon submerged behind the Chesil Bank, lying ominously dark in its own shadow. Luke swung his gaze despondently across the bay to Portland, wondering how he might break the bad news to Mary. The Island seemed to be brooding darkly under the fading eastern sky.

The ferry grated on the gravel beach, announcing its arrival. The passenger stepped off, tipping his hat in polite acknowledgement as Luke climbed in, failing to notice the gesture in his preoccupation, and thrust the half-penny fare into the boatman's waiting hand. He crossed sullenly, and on the other side, strode out along the well-worn path along the causeway towards Castletown and the harbour of the Mere. Here, behind the idle wooden derricks on the quay stood the Castle Inn, and it was to this establishment that Luke now made his way.

The trying circumstances of late had driven him to seek solace in alcoholic refreshment, and his present low spirits made this a current fixation. He also sought company to distract him from his woes. He entered the inn, pleased to find it bustling. At first there was no one whom he recognised, but, after shouldering his way gently through the jostling and noisy crowd, he spotted a group of quarrymen at a table in the far corner. A few of them were his own men, but the others were journeymen, travelling masons and stone hewers brought in to work the quarries. Jack had employed some of the kimberlins himself from time to time and so knew them well enough.

'Can I join you, lads?' he asked, having to raise his voice above the din in the room to make himself heard.

Those in the group who recognised Luke acknowledged him coolly; and a few shifted along their bench to make room. As Luke seated himself, he saw one of the men opposite turn to his neighbour to whisper in his ear. There were some knowing looks in his direction that were hardly subtle, and Luke felt his heart sink, realising at once that his reception was not likely to be overly friendly.

'Come to drown your sorrows then?' one of the men called mischievously with a surreptitious wink at the others, but Luke brushed off the taunt with a non-committal smile.

'Can I offer you men a jug of ale?' he proffered in a bid to lift the mood. He managed to catch the inn-keeper's eye.

'We'll take a jug from you, Easton,' called someone, while another muttered under his breath, 'yes, and that's the least you owe us.'

'Come on, lads!' Luke entreated. 'Let's put all that behind us for a night and have a drink together. Maybe the morning will bring better times for all of us.' Luke's call must have sounded confident and optimistic to his audience and they seemed to rally to it, but in his own ears it was a lame and hollow ploy to curry favour. He wanted so desperately to be one of them again, to enjoy their unchallenging camaraderie as he used to, to chip away at stone as a simple mason and not to have the worries of management on his shoulders. The dull burden of responsibility as proprietor had taken all the fun away.

Eventually the ale arrived at their table and for a time the tensions seemed to ease as the group set themselves fervently to a bout of drinking and ribaldry. But the alcohol had an effect on Luke quite the opposite to the one he had desired, and it was not long before he became despondent again, once more sinking into gloomy introspection. One of those in the group, a large and brutish stone-hewer well known as a troublemaker, noticed Luke drooping and, seeming to take exception to his state, muttered some sarcastic comment to his fellows. But Luke was suddenly in no mood for sarcasm and, anger taking the better of him, he responded intemperately. The interchange quickly became inflamed, escalating into an argument involving several at the table, as aggression on one side was countered by attempts at restraint on the other. At some point, the burly stone-hewer, apparently becoming intensely frustrated, shook off a restraining arm and rose to his feet, from which height he poked Luke in the shoulder and shouted some derision. Spluttering for a moment like a piece of pinched fuse cord, Luke exploded in an inebriated rage at the affront, angrily pushing away the man's tattooed and hairy arm and swinging back wildly with his fist. By this time both men were on their feet, awkwardly straddling the bench as Luke's poorly aimed lunge knocked both of them off balance. With their legs restrained by the bench and thus unable to maintain stability, both fell backwards, bringing the bench and all those seated upon it sprawling to the floor. A crowd of nearby sailors leapt clear, roaring in amusement at the spectacle, as the hapless and infuriated quarrymen landed in an undignified heap. Still in an angry state, Luke sprung up and yanked his antagonist from the floor by the scruff of his neck and took another drunken swing as he did so. His aim was again wide of the mark, but its momentum propelled Luke into an impotent clinch with his opponent, in which pose they fell headlong into the others (still struggling to their feet) and knocked them all over like nine-pins. The sailors guffawed in delight at the entertainment while one or two bystanders attempted to pull Luke off. But he misinterpreted their efforts and reacted violently to the grip of these foreign hands, and there followed a wild and raucous melee of drunken punches, although it has to be said that little physical impact of any consequence actually ensued. The inn-keeper, a large and thick-set man with muscular arms long used to rough behaviour in his quayside tavern, now forced his way through the cheering crowd and picked upon Luke as the troublemaker nearest to hand. As has already been related, Luke was not a lightweight, but the innkeeper was able to lift him bodily by his coat like a sack of coal and throw him out onto the street.

The cold wetness seeping through his clothes sobered him quickly, and he brought himself unsteadily to his feet. Tasting blood, he raised his fingers to feel a swollen lip where his face had hit the ground and, resisting a momentary temptation to re-enter the inn to take his revenge upon the landlord, he turned to look about him whilst he simmered down. Moonlight glistened on the wet cobbles of the empty street but he could see the lights of several anchored vessels far out in the roads - the naval frigates he had spotted earlier in daylight as he had walked the causeway. Press-gangs often accompanied their presence in harbour and he would not want to meet one of these in his present state, despite his Portlander's immunity from impressment. Reluctantly and rather sheepishly, therefore, he made off quickly along the quay to find his way home.

His route took him past Portland Castle and up through the little hillside hamlet of Fortune's Well, passing the Dale's house standing conspicuously at the side of the steep track winding up the hill. The sight of it always drew his mind back to the celebration of the engagement of Elizabeth and his brother almost seven years before. He had passed the house often and always felt the same pang of indefinable sadness as he looked upon it, remembering that occasion. He reflected that it was probably the last time that he was truly happy; certainly he remembered getting very drunk and disgracing himself at the punch bowl. In retrospect, it seemed the point in time around which his life seemed to have turned; there was the time before it, and the time which followed; two quite different eras separated by the calamity which was to strike both their families soon after. He could not remember laughing a great deal since – at least not with the uninhibited joy he had once known.

And since the news had arrived of Elizabeth's death, a deep rift had alienated the families with angry recriminations and guilt coming between them like a wall - he would never forgive himself for being the cause of it.

Luke strode past the house without breaking his pace and pressed on up across the common land skirting the crest of Verne Hill. The cloud had passed, leaving a cold night under a clear sky. Wearied by the climb, his breathing was laboured as he reached the top, and so he paused for a moment to allow himself to recover, his breath forming a persisting milky cloud in the cold air. Nearly five hundred feet below, the lanterns of Chiswell and Castletown shimmered; and in his birds-eye view, a waning moon in the western sky threw its pale reflections across Lyme Bay so that Chesil beach was visible as a thin dark crescent reaching out as far as Abbottsbury, ten miles to the north. A stranger would have found the view entrancing, but Luke had seen it so many times before that he had grown indifferent to it and, suddenly impatient to get home, he pulled himself together with a despondent sigh and set off once again. Beyond the crest, his journey became easier, following a steady downward gradient that characterised the terrain all the way to the Bill. The flickering lights of the two lighthouses there helped to guide him in the darkness but, weary and still befuddled from the drink, he tripped and fell several times on the rutted ground.

The hamlet of Wakeham was notable because it occupied the head of the only verdant valley on the island which otherwise was almost treeless. It included the Saxon ruin of Rufus Castle and the now all-but-abandoned St Andrew's Church that still stood on the cliff edge overlooking Church Ope Cove - the foundations for its successor had already been laid in Reforne a mile or so away on safer ground. Above the old church, another ruin lay at the head of the valley, the old Vicars' House, a once magnificent oratory destroyed in the Civil War, its gothic arches and the fine tracery of its windows still standing majestically as its own monument.

Luke's home was a thatched cottage built from blocks of Portland stone, lying at the end of a row of similar humble dwellings that lined a narrow lane leading towards the Cove. The lane was deserted when Luke arrived, and he slowed his pace so as not to be heard as he approached his door. Lifting the latch carefully, hoping to avoid attracting his wife's notice until he could clean himself up, Luke stepped gingerly into the front room, ducking his head below the lintel. His heart sank as he caught sight of Mary sitting hunched over some papers at her desk, her back towards him. She lifted her head on hearing his entry to see his dishevelled form reflected in the mirror hanging on the wall before her. Sitting up, she turned to watch him fumble with the latch as he tried to close it securely. She knew instantly by his deliberate manner that he had been drinking and surveyed him with mild exasperation - this was not the fist time she had seen him in such a state. Luke caught her disapproving expression and shrank inwardly.

'It was dark, Mary, and I tripped and fell!' he said in lame explanation of his state, holding up his hands in a helpless gesture, his face flushing involuntarily at the half-truth. Suddenly aware of his throbbing lip, he raised his hand to explore the wound; the blood had congealed into a brittle shell and the swelling now extended to his mud-streaked chin.

'Luke, what in God's name have you been up to?' Her tone was admonishing.

'Er...I had a difficult time with Mr Chorley at the bank, Mary, so I called in at the Castle...' he started to explain in a pathetic tone of voice.

'Luke,' she interrupted impatiently, coming up to him to unbutton his mud-caked coat and pulling it from his shoulders, 'you'll find no answer for your troubles in drink. Now go and get yourself cleaned up,' she said, her voice softening. 'I'll bring you something to eat, and then you can tell me what he said.'

She took the coat to the outhouse where, as soon as the mud was dry she would brush it clean, and returned to the parlour some minutes later with some warm bread and hot broth from the stove. By then Luke had washed his face and smoothed his hair, making himself look a little more presentable; but, feeling like an scolded child, he avoided her eyes as she placed the food upon the table. He started to tell her of his meeting, but she silenced him, indicating that he should finish his meal first. An uneasy quiet thus fell upon the room, interrupted only by the clink of his spoon on the bowl; meanwhile she returned to her papers. The soft ticking of Mary's long-case clock, a treasured heirloom from her mother, marked the slow passing of time, and nothing further was said for a while.

The couple had been sweethearts since their time together at Mrs Primm's reading school in the nearby village of Easton, from which it was assumed that the family name was derived. Their relationship had progressed unchallenged into adulthood, and through courtship into marriage; if they had been brother and sister, they could not have been easier in each other's company. It was a relationship in which each accepted the other's foibles without quarrel or contest - and distressingly for them both, it was a marriage in which her pregnancies had miscarried. Of the pair, she was the more intelligent, brighter of eye and quicker of wit, and blessed with a sort of placid wisdom, unusual for one so young, which resisted fluster in a crisis. Some might unkindly consider her rather plain yet she was not unattractive and her height gave her an elegant air which she did not try to disguise. It was her style to wear her long fair hair drawn back and swept up; this evening, she had fashioned it into a neat bun held in place with an ivory pin. It made her look a little severe. It might be said that Luke had married the image of his mother, for she came from a similar mould.

Mary lifted her eyes from her papers and, resting her head on her clasped hands in quiet contemplation, she studied her husband's reflection in the mirror as he consumed his meal. Despite his shortcomings, she found that her tenderness for him had not diminished. Indeed, there was something in his simplicity that was endearing, and she wondered, ruefully, if perhaps it was this very quality that satisfied some inner need within her.

As he ate, Luke lapsed again into gloomy introspection. He knew that he was out of his depth. In business matters, his father, George, had been a brusque, hard-nosed and decisive man, wily and suspicious by character. Luke, by contrast, was an innocent dragged reluctantly into the unforgiving world of commerce, wanting always to see the best in others and thus easily taken advantage of. His strength was in his hands rather than in his head; he saw himself more as an artisan. While he had worked as junior partner to his father, the two men's characters and skills had complemented each other, but once he had been left on his own, Luke had found his father's shoes too big to fill.

The clock's soft chimes broke into the silence and brought both out of the thoughtful interlude.

'So then, what did he say?' she asked brightly, as if continuing the conversation without any interruption.

'He'll give us three months Mary, but that is all,' Luke replied, talking through a mouthful of bread.

Luke summarised his difficult meeting with the banker and its disappointing outcome but, whether through tiredness or the influence of his earlier drinking, he seemed unable to get his thoughts together as to what might be done to lift himself out of the financial hole he had dug for himself. Having unloaded his anxieties, Luke fell into a despairing mood despite Mary's attempts to raise his spirits with a more optimistic outlook.

She thus tactfully changed the subject.

'Your mother gets no better, Luke, I don't seem able to cheer her these days. Her companion tries so very hard to occupy her with distractions, but even she can't bring her out of it.'

Luke's mother, Eleanor, still unable to come to terms with her husband's suicide, had taken to her bedroom soon after the funeral and had remained there, more or less, ever since, with only occasional forays into the light of day. She lived in the family house just round the corner at the end of the winding path above the Cove and was cared for by a live-in companion whom Mary had arranged for her. As a dutiful and caring daughter-in-law, Mary attended to matters such as these with diligence and had made a point of visiting her mother-in-law every day since George's death. Luke had not been quite so attentive and had come to depend upon his wife's good ministrations to keep a watchful eye on his mother's state.

'She keeps talking about Jack,' she said evenly, flicking her eyes at his.

Luke met her glance and nodded knowingly. 'She would. He was her favourite,' he said morosely, 'and I've never quite matched up to his memory, have I Mary? In all the years since he was sent away, she's never given up the hope that he'll return. I so much wish he would – perhaps he would have the answer to my problems?' He shook his head in resignation. 'You are very good to visit her so much. I know that I should do more.'

'Luke, come with me tomorrow, won't you? It would please her so much to see you.'

'I will, Mary.' Luke replied with as much enthusiasm as he could muster.

With his own problems preying upon his mind, however, he found his mother's low spirits depressing and, while he felt it his duty to call upon her from time to time, he never looked forward to these events with any pleasure. 'It's not as if she is ailing in any way! Why can't she pull herself together?' he thought, uncharitably. But in his heart, he knew that his absent brother held the only key to lift his mother's spirits and he could not help but feel a touch resentful. It was as if his entire life had been spent in the expectant wake of his older brother's supremacy, and his parents' enduring distress after Jack's transportation, and then his father's suicide, had reinforced this perception and sapped his self-esteem. Now, he feared that he would fail another test - as custodian of the family firm, into whose unenthusiastic and inadequate hands it had been thrust.

Early the next morning, Luke dutifully accompanied his wife to his mother's house as he had promised, taking as an offering a few sprigs of the winter jasmine that had begun to bloom against the south facing wall of their cottage. They found her in her bedroom sitting in an armchair gazing through the window at the seascape that formed a large part of her view. An embroidered linen cap all but entirely covered her now completely grey hair, and she had wrapped a flimsy knitted shawl around her shoulders. The dowdy apparel did not suit her - it made her look much older than her years - but her downcast demeanour was not at odds with it. The pretty jasmine and the gentle tones in Luke's voice consoled and cheered his mother for a while, but she soon sank again into a preoccupation that both visitors found difficult to break. In the maddening silences interspersing the discourse, Luke studied his mother helplessly. Her once bonny complexion had paled through lack of sunlight, and her once sharp eyes had become dull, as if she had no interest in anything outside her head. Disconsolately, Luke remembered the gentle chiding with which she had often encouraged him as a boy when he had been ready to give up at some aspect of his schoolwork. He felt in dire need of that now, but she had abandoned him as she had abandoned herself totally to grief, and it distressed him to see his mother in such a state. He was glad, therefore, to find an excuse to depart as soon as an opportunity arose, leaving Mary to remain a little longer.

Luke had managed recently to secure some small local orders for stone and he walked to the quarry to confirm that work was progressing satisfactorily before returning home to give himself some peace to think. Mary came back later to find her husband pacing the kitchen floor, a habit he resorted to when fretting, and as Luke seemed eager to talk, she became his sounding board while preparing the evening meal. Not wishing to trample over her husband's sensitivities, Mary was nervous of offering advice, but when she heard him lapsing into a fruitless torment of self-recrimination, she knew that the moment had come for her to throw in some ideas of her own. She was not untutored on matters of business; she had been the firm's bookkeeper for some years. And since the old man's death, she had taken it upon herself to examine the ledgers – and his pricing work for estimates, to learn how this had been approached. It had not been difficult to see where Luke had been going wrong.

'The first thing that we must do, my dear, is to see the banker again and ask for more time. Three months will certainly not be enough.' Mary began. She rinsed her hands with a ladle of water from the pail, dried them on her apron, and turned to face her husband..

Luke stopped his pacing. 'Mary, I have argued with him as much as I dare! His mind seems to be made up!' Luke's tone was adamant, but Mary continued undeterred.

'But if we could give him some new evidence that his loan was secure, like any businessman, he must see the sense in it. Would he rather force us to liquidate and risk not getting all his money back?' Mary contended, '-when, by being more patient, he could instead get his full capital *and* good interest returned? Surely that is what he and his partners are precisely in business to do?'

'Yes Mary, but as you well know there is nothing on our order books save the small jobs I have just taken on, and you know how long we have to wait for payment. You have to understand that it is cash rather than promises he wants.'

'Then we must find a new customer who will give us an advance, my dear! You cannot sit back and wait for them to come to you. We have some of the finest white stone here; there are some who would fight for it at the right price!' Mary was in her stride now, and pausing only to check that her husband was still listening, she continued at full pace.

'And we must show him that we know how things have gone wrong and how we can do better. Otherwise, he will have no confidence that we can ever get it right.'

Luke knitted his eyebrows but nodded at the sense of this, as he followed his wife obediently into the parlour where she took some papers from her desk and laid them on the table.

'I've looked back through your father's books, Luke, to see how it was done in his time,' she said, turning up the wick of the lantern.

Luke nodded with a resigned sigh; he had always recognised his wife's common sense, and was quite prepared, perhaps even pleased on this occasion, to have her help.

'In your pricing and in the contract for this latest order, for example, you have been far too lax, my dear,' she continued, 'you should have tied payment in stages to the consignments of the stone to reduce the risk of late payment or default. That way, if the payments falter, you can react quickly to save costs.' She was lecturing, but her voice was kindly and understanding of his faults. 'I know that you accepted the loose wording because you did not wish to be held to deadlines yourself, but that reflects a weakness in your own management. You must learn how to deliver as the customer wants it, and build in some allowances for the things which can go wrong. If we can be better than the other quarries in this respect then we will gain the edge.' Mary paused to let Luke take this in. 'Also, in your pricing, you do not appear to have given yourself any leeway for slippage in production. So if things get behind, as you know they always do for one reason or another, your costs go on mounting without any reserve or contingency set aside. And you do not appear to have allowed enough even for your normal overheads and the time that you spend in administration.' She paused again, apparently awaiting some response.

Luke felt stultification creeping in. It was one thing to understand his wife's analysis but putting it into practice was quite another matter, and he felt daunted by the task.

'But if the price comes out too high Mary, we shall not win *any* contract,' he protested.

Mary nodded, but responded firmly: 'Luke, my dear, we must price properly for profit, otherwise the contract is not *worth* the winning!' she said, pausing to emphasise the point. 'And there are some other things which I have noticed.' Mary was now in full flood, encouraged by her husband's engagement. 'You and your father often kept your men turning up for work when there was clearly not enough to keep them fully occupied. I know that this is because you are kind and do not want to see them suffer by being laid off. But if the company fails, they will suffer even more, and so your first responsibility must be to keep the quarry on a sound financial footing.'

'I have not paid the men even for the work that they *have* done, Mary,' Luke said lamely.

'And they will blame you more for that than for being laid off in the quiet periods, when they have at least the chance of finding other work! But there is one more thing that we can put into our proposals for the future which might convince the bankers to extend our loan, or at least to hold off until we can win another contract.'

Luke was interested.

'We have some of the best stone and good transportation access to the Cove and the other piers nearby, but we need to organise the moving and the loading better. Getting the stone to the piers takes too long and there is too much damage done by rolling the blocks down onto the

Weares - this lowers the value of the work we have already done. And we waste too much time waiting for the weather and the tide to load the barges - so our deliveries are unreliable for the architects – remember, they have costs of their own to think of.'

Mary hesitated; she had some final thoughts to convey but, wanting her husband to be part of it and not brow-beaten by her confident assertions, she now contrived to get him involved.

'If there were some way of making our operations here more efficient...' she said, pausing to give him time to think, 'we might well even beat Isaac Grant on reliability and price!'

Isaac Grant operated the biggest quarry on the island and was ruthlessly acquisitive and competitive. A mainlander employing local labour, Portlanders regarded him with suspicion, but he paid good rates and, for most men, that was enough. There were also several other smaller quarries on the Island like their own jostling for custom, and the rivalry between them was keen.

'Yes, yes, I know you are right Mary, I've thought this myself before,' Luke said, a trifle nettled. 'We could build out the piers to provide for bigger barges to load up, and we could lay in a sled-way to speed up moving the stone, but all that would take time and money, and I can't put my men to work without first paying what I owe them. Credit at the stores has dried up for most of them, and those whose women can't earn something on the side will be destitute before long.'

'Then we shall have to persuade your Mr Chorley to help us Luke, won't we, and that Exeter enquiry might yet become the break that we're hoping for. At least, that is what we shall have to make him believe!'

But without an appointment, they would have to wait a long time to see Chorley the following day, and after some considerable time waiting in the oak-panelled opulence of the banker's anteroom they began to feel less sure that they would succeed.

It was not until early that afternoon that the Easton's turn in the queue of clients waiting upon Chorley would come. But preceding this, the banker would first accompany his previous client through the anteroom on his way out. Luke nudged Mary as Chorley appeared from his office, leading the way. As round in face as figure and wearing a light grey long-tailed coat, he walked briskly ahead of his client to open the outer door. He caught Luke's eye in brief acknowledgement as he passed, but his face remained set in an inscrutable mask. A few paces behind came Isaac Grant, a tall, gaunt and darkly dressed man of middle years. Luke had recognised him earlier as he had been ushered deferentially into the banker's office, but there was no acquaintance between them. The two men talked in subdued tones for a moment at the outer door and then shook hands as Grant took his leave. After some brief words to his secretary, Chorley returned to Luke and Mary who were by now standing expectantly.

'Ah! Mr and Mrs Easton!' Chorley greeted them coolly. 'Please forgive my not being able to see you earlier, I am afraid that I have had rather a busy day,' he said curtly, a little puffed-up with his own importance, and with a slightly disdainful air.

Chorley led the couple into his sumptuous office, waving them to sit in chairs arranged to face a splendid pedestal-desk, while he circumnavigated it to seat himself in a throne-like chair which had the emblem of a merchants' guild carved ostentatiously upon its high back. Luke saw straight away that their own chairs had been arranged to put them at a relative disadvantage of height and, in an attempt to reduce the man's lofty superiority, he shifted his position to sit more upright, perching on the front edge of his seat. Mary was not much bothered by the psychology at play, and sat herself down, looking serenely self-assured as she calmly arranged the folds of her long velvet dress. A buff-coloured file lay squarely in the centre of the desk, and Chorley now opened it and studied its contents with slow deliberation. There was a certain theatricality in his posturing, Mary thought, but Chorley's face remained deadly serious, and he was clearly playing to Luke's apparent nervousness. The banker then frowned and shook his head wearily as he appeared to find some detail of special interest, lowering his head to peer at the papers more closely.

'Hmmm!' he grunted, as if to the file. He did not look impressed.

At length, he looked up and, as if to make the point that time for such unplanned meetings was given grudgingly, he took out a silver timepiece from his waistcoat pocket, glanced at it cursorily, and put it back with a sigh. But if Chorley gained any satisfaction from Luke's obvious unease at the gesture, he was careful not to show it.

'Well, Mr Easton, are you going to tell me that in the two days since I saw you, you have inherited a fortune?'

Luke ignored the jibe and launched immediately into the proposals for improving the profitability of the business that he and Mary had rehearsed several times at home. He spoke confidently, having been persuaded by his wife's arguments, and he faltered only a little from time to time under Chorley's sceptical gaze. But Luke deliberately avoided any mention of the possible new contract, as it had been agreed between them that Mary would try to employ her business acumen and her femininity to better tactical effect later in the discussion.

'These points you make are all well and good, Mr Easton,' the banker said, as Luke sat back in his chair, 'but is it not a little late for bright ideas.' He shook his head as he spoke, shrugging his shoulders helplessly as if to indicate that it was beyond his power to assist further. 'Your repayments are so far behind, that I shall have my partners at my throat if I don't soon put a stop to your running up further debt.' He smiled condescendingly, and then continued: 'It would seem to me that your company is in a perilous state, Mr Easton, and that you'll have insufficient time to put your proposals into place before you become insolvent. You'd be better advised to obtain a valuation and find a buyer quickly; otherwise we could well be forced to put matters into the hands of the receivers. And if that happens, there will certainly not be much left for you after the disbursements are paid. And I do not need to remind you that your homes could be forfeit.' Chorley's expression was more one of disdain than of compassion, and he leant back against the ornate carving on his throne as if awaiting some reaction from Luke.

But then, after a moment of uneasy silence in the room, Mary took her cue and spoke up, taking the banker clearly by surprise.

'Mr Chorley,' she said pleasantly, but contriving to sound a little tentative, 'I - I well understand what you say, and of course you must keep your partners content; but may we – please may we - beg you to give us a little more time - perhaps twelve months rather than the three months that you have given us?' She made a confirming gesture to her husband and he nodded a confident response.

'We have been obliged to keep it secret until now but in the circumstances it seems right to tell you - in confidence of course - that we are close to finalising an agreement with an Exeter architect, which promises to be very profitable indeed. And if we are able to take action on some of our ideas for improving our operations in the meanwhile, I know we shall quickly be in a position to settle our debt with you in full measure.' Mary lied smoothly, elevating the recent enquiry to the status of a firm order, and Chorley was clearly as intrigued by the revelation as taken by her charm.

Chorley sat forward in his chair. 'And who is your customer?' he asked, trying to make his enquiry sound casual.

'Not wanting to give offence, Mr Chorley,' Mary replied, mustering the most tantalising of her feminine smiles to light up her face, 'we'll have to keep that information to ourselves for the present.'

Mary's intervention proved decisive, and fifteen minutes later, standing in the front lobby of the banker's house with a somewhat bemused husband beside her, she was inwardly congratulating herself. They had got what they had wanted - Chorley had been enticed by the hint of a profitable return, and had extended the repayment deadline initially to nine months. She knew, nevertheless, that there would be much to achieve if the extension were not merely to become a stay of execution - but now was not the time to talk further on the matter.

Outside on the street, the heavy folds of dark cumulus looked threatening. And so, their business finished later than expected and not wanting to risk a soaking, Mary suggested that they remain in Weymouth overnight in the nearby home of her sister, Anna. With her new husband, Edward, Anna had lately moved into one of the customs' apartments overlooking the waterfront, he being employed as a junior tide surveyor recently recruited by the despised Captain Smyke. Luke had hopes that he might cultivate a friendship with his new brother-in-law, not blind to the possibility that something useful might one-day come of it, and so he was happy to agree to Mary's proposal.

As they made their way through the narrow streets, conversation returned to their meeting with Chorley, with Luke acknowledging gracefully that Mary had rescued it from near disaster. However, while they had won themselves more time to sort things out, no further credit had been extended, and so, as Luke was at pains to point out, they were living on borrowed time. Moreover, Chorley's suggestion that they should seek a valuation and contemplate selling the business had frightened him, making him realise how precarious the situation had become.

It was at this point in their conversation that something about the meeting struck Luke as suspicious. He had noted it at the time but had not realised its significance until now. How was it that the folder with details of their account had laid on Chorley's desk when they had entered his office, when he and Grant had been in that room until moments before? Grant was known to be predatory as far as quarry operations on

Portland were concerned; was it possible that Chorley had told him of their predicament? Would Grant now also be told of the enquiry from Exeter? If so, they might have less time than they had reckoned on.

The following day, having slept poorly, troubled by thoughts of Grant's possible acquisitive interest in his business, Luke left Weymouth early to walk back to the quarry via the ferry at Smallmouth. Mary would come on later by chaise after spending the morning with her sister.

It took him less than two hours to reach the cliff path that would take him down into to his quarry and he paused to survey the familiar scene below him. In the distance, he could see two figures standing outside the little wooden shack that served as a site-office at the northern end of his workings. Even from this distance, he recognised them as William Coley, his foreman, and Jack Pearce, his longest-serving and most loyal masons. Luke hailed the pair with a shout and started down the precipitous zigzag path that would take him to the foot of the cliff and thence on to the shack. From this elevation, his view took in the full extent of the works; it stretched from Durdle Pier at its northern boundary, to the ruins of Rufus Castle at its southern edge, a strip of just over half a mile. On a sunny day, the rocky coastal scene would be spectacularly colourful, but today a grey sky merged turbidly with a greyer sea in a dreary monotone, save for the small disturbance of whitecaps swirling over the Shambles Bank.

Luke smiled a greeting as he strode the last few yards towards his men, but he could tell instantly from their perplexed expressions that something was wrong. With sudden foreboding, he cast his eyes around the works and saw immediately what it was that troubled them: the quarry was eerily and unexpectedly still.

Chapter Twenty

The pale loom of dawn's new light severed a leaden sea from the grip of darkness to reveal a desolate scene. Line after line of heavy black combers harried by an icy wind bore down upon the *Rebecca* as if directed with malevolent force. Ominous walls of dark water rose up behind her scurrying stern in regular procession, drawing her upwards with sickening gravity to meet their breaking crests. Like flotsam in the surf, the ship was swept along giddyingly for long moments in the boiling tumult, exposed and vulnerable in the howling wind. Then, as each racing crest moved inexorably onwards, eventually releasing its grip, the ship slowed and slewed, plummeting into the silent chasm that followed in its wake as if some protecting hand had suddenly cupped it. But the respite was transitory, for the succeeding wave was already looming monstrously behind even as the last was hurrying away.

Below, even the hardiest seamen cowered at the storm's violence, most having taken to their hammocks where they swung in an uneasy harmony enduring the torment in sufferance. On deck, only the lookouts and the two helmsmen fighting the wheel remained to accompany the officer of the watch – all of them miserably cold as they squinted into the stinging spindrift scanning for danger ahead and counting the long minutes until the end of their watch. The ship ran before the wind under bare spars with only the fore course set to give her steerageway and trailing a tangled raft of sea anchors in her wake, without which she would already have broached for sure.

Jack clung to the sides of his cot exhausted, his heart forced into his mouth at every shuddering impact and sudden lurch. The storm had battered the ship for two days without relent. With each crashing blow, the tormented hull writhed and squealed as if in throes of agony. Brine spurted at high pressure through the cracks between its yielding timbers, filling the cabin air with saline vapour that gagged his throat and stung his eyes. His bedding was sodden from the steady drip of ice-cold water from the hatch above his head, while shadows from the swinging oil lamp danced around him like demented phantoms. The relentless onslaught on all his senses had brought him almost to the edge of reason.

And then, almost as suddenly as it had begun, the wind died, the waves subsided, and the scudding cloud swept away as the front raced eastwards leaving the weather-beaten vessel giddy in its wake. Soon, the rising sun ascended the high and wispy anvils of the retreating storm clouds, and puffy white cumulus moved in behind to take their place.

It was a long time before anyone stirred below decks as the ship began to wallow in a lumpy sea with only a limp fore course to steady her uncomfortable rolling. But an exhausted Captain Auld fortified himself with a discrete swig from his hip flask and sent word for Goddard and Judd to join him on a survey of the damage. And soon others began to emerge from their quarters in twos and threes, peering wide-eyed at the devastation that confronted them. Two of the ship's boats had been torn from their mountings. One of them swept overboard taking part of the starboard main deck bulwark with it, the other lying upended in the forecastle, its keel buckled, its rudder squeaking incessantly on its pintles with the rocking of the ship. Remarkably, the sturdy mizzen gaff spar and boom had been wrenched off their mountings and broken like matchwood - the torn spanker now lay in a heap alongside the splintered segments on the quarterdeck. Tangled rope and debris littered the ship from stem to stern. And long fragments of ripped sailcloth flapped indolently from the mainmast topgallant yard like shrouds, lending the ship a funereal air.

Auld's party picked its way down the companionway to the old gun deck, now used as quarters for the crew - it was little better there. Under sagging hammocks in which some men still lay groaning, the deck was in a frightful state; several casks and sacks had broken loose from the ship's stores and these lay scattered, smashed or torn, their contents disgorged and intermingled in a glutinous mess. A sickening mixture of viscous fluids and spoiled foodstuffs had been washed into the bilges by storm water, and the rank solution now sloshed about audibly as the ship rolled. Even the ship's manger had been breached by a canon sent careering from its blocks by the storm's violence; and the chickens and the two remaining sows, quick to take their chance to flee, now rummaged contentedly amongst the debris. The single casualty, an unfortunate goat, lay panting on its bed of straw with its rear quarters at an odd angle, its back apparently broken. But if the animal's certain demise heralded the end of goat's milk for the officers, then at least fresh meat might be served up later for the men.

Eventually, repair parties were mustered and work put underway, and soon the whole ship became a hive of noisy activity with the entire crew working in a sort of measured frenzy born of an impatience to be home -

after nearly five weeks at sea, the men already had the scent of land in their nostrils.

By nightfall, all the damaged sails and rigging had been exchanged or repaired, and the whole ship checked over and declared ready to be put back into action. Then, with the topmen once more in their positions along the yards and in the ship's top, orders were shouted and the ties let go. One after the other, the huge square canvasses fell in a furious and noisy cascade; topsails and topgallants first, then mainsails and fore courses; while simultaneously, the staysails, jib, and spanker were being hauled up from the deck. For a time, there was a great deal of flapping and whipping as the loose sails were sheeted home and made fast, but then the yards were braced up and the sails quickly blossomed into their full and pregnant shape. With a shudder, as if shrugging off the bruises of a fall, the great ship leant before the wind and began to accelerate. At last, the *Rebecca* had come back to life.

By joining the work parties involved in the repair, Jack had earned further respect from the crew, consolidating the position he had established earlier in the voyage. From the beginning of the journey, he had taken a keen interest in the workings of the ship, trying his hand at many of the sailing tasks, even climbing up the ratlines and perching on the horses to reef sails. His interest had amused the crew; some were even flattered by it, and the activity had helped to pass the time during the long and tedious passage before the storm had hit. The complicated web of rigging lines controlling the huge sails had fascinated Jack; a sailing man himself, he had often watched awestruck, as the crew had brought the ship onto a new tack. The result of his involvement was that, while always inevitably an outsider, he was at least tolerated with good humour. Jack's friendship with young Matthew too had become almost paternal, the pair often teaming up to work together, since both were accorded the status of apprentice; and both were given an equally hard time by their generally good-natured if mischievous comrades. Only the curiously hostile Judd, always wary and curt in his manner when encountered, had kept his distance.

As for Goddard, Jack had warmed to him. Put under his wing by the captain, Jack had joined the first officer's watch and had come to respect the young officer. They often dined together, and, although conversation between them was rather stilted at first, a friendly relationship had developed - indeed, first names had been exchanged and were now used in private. Nevertheless, Jack could never quite rid himself of the impression that his new acquaintance was holding something back. Something in the man's manner that Jack detected just occasionally in conversation triggered this feeling - Goddard's sudden lapses into thoughtfulness, a curtailed sentence here and there as if suddenly the discourse had strayed onto forbidden ground. Occasions such as this usually occurred when conversation touched upon Goddard's future in the merchant service, for example, whether he saw himself attaining captaincy in due course, or whether he aspired to a commission in the Royal Navy. Such subjects would normally engage young ambitious officers, a breed not usually given to reticence in talking about themselves, but Goddard had been strangely quiet on this. And Jack had thus quickly learned to avoid such delicate areas. But he had also begun to think that there must be something troubling the man, some embarrassment in his past perhaps, that made the young officer so sensitive.

By comparison, Jack had enjoyed little contact with Captain Auld, speaking with him only in passing. On these occasions, Auld had always shown polite interest in Jack's activities, but nothing more. He seemed to prefer to maintain a distance from his officers and crew, leaving Goddard to run the ship; and when he was not on deck, he spent the majority of his time in his cabin, taking most of his meals alone. Jack saw a certain sadness in the captain's self-imposed isolation from the day-to-day activities of the ship, often seeing him standing alone at the stern rail gazing at the horizon. He found himself wondering if something troubled the man.

For several days, repair work on deck continued as the *Rebecca* sailed on at full speed, and by the end of the fourth day following the storm's abrupt end, a casual observation would reveal little of the former disarray. Yet, for all the skills on hand, the broken-backed boat had proved beyond repair and its timbers thus put to good use in patching up the railing swept away.

It was now nearly six weeks since leaving Charlestown, and with the work all but complete above decks, Jack decided on an impulse to make an inspection of his cargo. Considering the battering the ship had suffered, it seemed somehow neglectful of his duty to Harding not to show a little interest. Thus, collecting the manifest from his cabin, he made his way to the hold, picking up a lantern to illuminate his way. To his surprise, he found all the containers still firmly in place despite the violence of the storm, and with time on his hands, he fell to examining the brand marks on their lids out of idle curiosity.   From a quick inspection, he could see immediately that the hogsheads were grouped in batches belonging to individual plantations, and he took out the manifest to see if he could identify any by name.   In the dim light of his lantern it was difficult to see clearly, but here was one, SCM - St Clement's Manor, and another CHP – Chapel Point, the plantation below the high bluff that he and Ned had passed on their entrance to the Tobacco River.   As he proceeded along the corridor, he identified other batches, and it soon became a sort of collector's game to see how many different markings he could find.   But adjacent to one of the larger consignments, there were a few barrels at the lowest level whose identifying letters he could not locate on his list.   The dim light made further investigation difficult and eventually tiring of his detective work, he decided to return to his cabin to look again in better light.   But as he turned to make his way aft he was startled to find Mr Judd watching him silently from the gloomy reaches of the corridor.

'Ah, Mr Judd!' he exclaimed in some shock.   'You gave me a fright!   I did not hear you coming,' he said, embarrassed to have been observed occupied so intently in his trivial pursuit.

'Aye, Mr Stone,' Judd said with a curiously ambivalent air about him. 'I saw you coming down and came to see if I could be of assistance.   You should not be here, sir, it could be dangerous - the cargo could shift with the movement of the ship, especially in this sea.'

'Yes, of course Mr Judd, it was wrong of me not to ask permission.   I had nothing useful to do and merely wanted to see if Mr Harding's tobacco had survived the storm.'

'Come now, sir,' Judd interjected.   'I think that you could leave that task to us,' he said condescendingly.   'The containers are hardly likely to run away!'

He turned and made to leave, beckoning Jack to follow and clearly anxious to draw him away, but Jack did not like the man's manner and so was slow to move, feeling some slight had been conveyed which he thought unwarranted.

'Mr Judd,' Jack called, trying to reassert himself.   'Some of the codes on these lids do not seem to appear on my manifest; is it possible that I am mistaken?'

'Indeed it is, sir,' Judd said smoothly as he strode on. 'But I'll gladly assist you further in Cowes when we see them in the daylight. Some of the brands will be difficult to see clearly down here, and sometimes they are hastily done and may confuse outsiders, such as yourself. Now sir, if you would follow me.'

If Judd's short manner had been designed to obfuscate then it had failed, for it stimulated Jack's suspicious nature. And so later in his cabin, with his hatch opened fully to let in more light, he scrutinised his manifest more closely.

The list comprised more than fifty lines, each line annotated with the name and code of a plantation, with the number of hogsheads carried for each written alongside. He checked each code carefully, wondering if the letters of the missing code may have been inadvertently juxtaposed; it was the letter-group EBP that he sought and so he tried various combinations of the letters. But none came even close. Then Jack remembered that the hogsheads bearing the unidentified initials had lain adjacent to those belonging to the Ferry Point plantation; perhaps if he looked there, he might find a clue? The Ferry Point plantation was one of the largest consortia in the Charlestown area and the list showed it consequently to have one of the largest consignments, over one hundred hogsheads in all. But the mysterious initials seemed to have no relationship with any of the plantation names, even allowing for the scrawl of the quill pen that had written them. Jack was completely stumped and eventually grew tired of the puzzle as he began to wonder if he had perhaps misread the markings after all.

Feeling suddenly quite weary, Jack tucked the manifest back into the bundle with his other letters in his bag, threw himself upon his cot, and gazed lazily through the hatch at the waves roaring past just a few yards from his head. By the rate of their passing, he estimated that the ship must be making close to ten knots and, recalling his last look at Goddard's chart, he fell into a mental estimation of when they might arrive, concluding after some tiresome arithmetic calculation that they would be in Cowes within ten days or so if the wind held. But it was a soporific exercise.

Jack must have fallen asleep, for it seemed to him that the very next moment he was being rudely shaken awake, and forcing his eyes to open, he found himself staring straight into the rather sombre face of Philip Goddard.

'Get up Jack,' he said, speaking almost apologetically.

Obediently, Jack clambered from his cot wondering what on earth must be afoot. Standing behind Goddard, Judd hovered in the doorway, and over the boatswain's shoulder, shadows of others could be seen in the gloomy gangway outside. Through the open hatch Jack noticed that the sky was already black and he realised that he must have been asleep for several hours.

'What's going on,' he asked, bewildered, running his hands over his face and stretching himself awake.

'Mr Judd here has evidence that you are not who you say you are,' Goddard said evenly. 'And moreover, Jack, that you are an exiled convict!'

Jack froze, a frown passing across his face as he wondered how he should react: whether to protest his innocence angrily or make a clean breast of it, throwing himself upon the mercy of the captain. But then he saw that Judd was holding a bundle of letters in his hand that he recognised immediately as his own; the bundle contained his mother's letter and Rose's letter to her parents, and Harding's letter of introduction to his agent in Cowes. All of the letters would contain something that could incriminate him if not directly then by inference, but his mother's letter had openly lamented his conviction and exile and that would be proof enough of the truth of the accusation. He knew then that it would be futile to protest.

'Is this true Jack?' Goddard persisted.

'Yes, Philip, but I can explain..' Jack replied, alarmed at the sudden peril he was in, but Goddard held up his hand to silence him.

'I'm sorry to say that it's too late for explanations, Jack,' Goddard said almost sadly. 'You must know that it is the captain's duty to hand you over to the authorities; it will be they, I'm afraid, who must now be the arbiter.' Goddard's voice became harder now. 'And you must also know that there is likely to be a price upon your head which Mr Judd has already claimed as his reward for his...' Goddard seemed to be searching for a word, '...for his investigative work,' he said, with barely concealed contempt.

Jack was suddenly furious and shouted angrily: 'You've been in my bag, Mr Judd; you've no right!'

'I'm afraid that it is you who have no rights now, Jack,' Goddard said with an air of finality.

Jack also saw the look of triumph in Judd's eyes, and it occurred to him that somehow the two men might be acting in some sort of uneasy conspiracy in which Goddard might have his hands tied. He decided to try a bit of pleading:

'Philip, listen to me. I'm returning to England because I seek to put right the injustice done to me! I was wrongly convicted, and would otherwise not have been transported. I have a wife and property in Maryland; I'm hardly likely to be returning with other than this honest intent. Have compassion, let me complete my task, I beg you.'

But Goddard seemed impervious to his words.

'I'm sorry, Jack. You'll have to save your explanations for the authorities, '

'Then can I speak to the captain?' Jack persisted. But as he spoke, he caught Judd's quick touch of the first officer's elbow and the latter's hesitation, and he wondered again at the boatswain's undue influence.

'I will inform him in due course, but I am in charge for the present,' Goddard replied rather stiffly, beckoning in the two burly men waiting outside the door. 'Take him below,' he said, but with some uncertainty his eyes. 'I'm sorry, Jack,' he said more softly, dropping his gaze to the floor.

Jack allowed himself to be taken hold of and led out, but as he ducked his head to pass through the doorway of his cabin, he overheard Judd say to the two escorts in a low voice, 'Keep him away from the captain.'

Chapter Twenty-One

During her operational days as a Royal Navy frigate, the *Rebecca* had been equipped with a large copper-lined magazine in which to store her stock of gunpowder. The magazine was buried in the bowels of the ship below the waterline to protect its explosive contents from enemy cannon fire; but during the ship's conversion, most of its copper lining had been stripped out and sold off, and the magazine split into two sections. The smallest of these retained its former use as a store for the depleted quantity of gunpowder and shot more appropriate to the protection of a merchantman; while the other, a slightly larger space approximating a cube of six-foot sides, had been converted into a ship's brig. Although the magazine's solid timbers had been designed to protect its contents from external fire and blast, they were also ideally suited for their new purpose. It was this second space that now accommodated the dejected and disorientated prisoner from Portland.

Jack had lost track of how long he had lain on his damp mattress in this dark and airless room, insulated from all sight and sound due to the thickness of the timber surrounding him and with only the ship's movement to give him any sense of where he was. Without light, he was also, to all intents and purposes, blind, and therefore forced to perform every act by feel and touch. For his ablutions, Jack had been provided with a chamber pot which, due to the ship's motions, sometimes slid around the floor sending him on all fours on a game of blind-man's bluff to find it whenever nature called. His meals had been inserted, (and his chamber pot removed), through a small hatch at floor level let into the bottom of the four-foot door. By the number of the meals he had received (and the number of chamber pots passed in the opposite direction), Jack reckoned that his stay now amounted to three or four days.

In solitary confinement of any duration, the mind can gradually turn inwards upon itself, and when also deprived of external stimulus, it can become detached both from body and reality. In the worst cases, this delusion can attain a level at which a victim might feel as if mind and body are floating independently in some ethereal soup in which even the pull of gravity seems to lose its orientation. This is the way of hysteria and madness. Some men are more resistant than others to this dementia, and some devise strategies to defend themselves against it. Jack's strategy, whether consciously applied or the beginnings of an obsession, was to set his mind determinedly to solving the riddle of the casks, bringing into his mind every line of the vellum document that he had so carefully studied. The letters EBP floated into his view so clearly that they seemed illuminated; something about the letters and their proximity to the batch from Ferry Point plantation drew his thoughts. But even after several hours of concentrated effort over several days, no clue had emerged to shed light on the faint inkling that nagged him tantalisingly from some hidden corner of his brain. But then the letters FPP were conjured up as if rising from the imagined list of their own accord, and at last he saw the connection. The pieces of his puzzle fell into place and instantly he realised what had caused Judd to react so quickly to his inspection of the hold. Jack knew at once that there must be two manifests - one that he had held for Harding's tobacco consignment and another for other cargo carried aboard the ship that the boatswain would normally hold; and he speculated that items might move from the former to the latter with a few strokes of a pen. Jack smiled to himself wryly. It was a nice little scam; one which would have amused him in his former days of smuggling. He also guessed that somewhere on the ship, a few simple branding irons with curious ends must be stashed away; with shapes required to change the letters F to E and P to B. There were not many characters in the alphabet that could be altered undetected, but FPP for Ferry Point had been an obvious candidate, and Judd had plenty of other codes to choose from that contained those characters in various combinations. It was no wonder Judd had needed to get at his manifest; he would have to alter some of the numbers to conceal his fraud. And while searching for the scroll, he would have seen Jack's letters since they were attached to it in one bundle. It seemed an irony that the very task for which Harding had given him this passage had apparently contributed to his downfall. And despite some satisfaction at cracking the conundrum, Jack realised gloomily that his investigative deductions could now well come to nought, for he doubted that exposing the thievery could do him any good. Disheartened and wearied by his thinking, he once more drifted into a troubled sleep.

Something in the ship's motion pressed into Jack's consciousness and brought him quickly out of his slumber. Above his head, muffled by the thickness of the heavy timbers that incarcerated him, the quick percussion of men's feet running on the deck drummed amidst the resonating clatter of tackle and blocks. Even in the darkness of his cell, he sensed the ship turn and was momentarily puzzled at the need to change course so abruptly. He wondered if the shift in course signalled that the ship was already closing on its destination, becoming suddenly frightened by the prospect. If this were the case, there was little that could save him now, and his heart sank as he contemplated the certain fate that would await him. Fond lamenting thoughts of Rose and his Maryland homestead, of Ned and Sebi too, drifted through his mind; he so much longed to be with them all now, and he understood why they had been so cool about this foolhardy adventure - the odds against it succeeding had simply been too high.

But then came the sound of bolts scraping, and the door to his cell was pulled open with a shudder. There in the low doorway, silhouetted in the dim lantern light of the orlop, crouched Goddard on his haunches peering in.

'The captain would like you on deck, Jack,' he said. 'But I need to talk to you first.'

Jack swung his legs off his mattress, and squinted at the dark form in the doorway.

'Come on, Jack, we've not got much time!' Goddard urged.

At this, still suspicious of his senses, Jack took his weight upon his legs. They buckled under him weakly from lack of use, and finding himself on hands and knees, he crawled through the low opening and struggled to his feet - with a helping hand from the first officer.

'Say nothing to the captain of the matter with Judd, Jack, and we may yet be able to help each other,' Goddard said in a low voice. 'Until then, there is a little problem with a Frenchman on our heels, so count yourself lucky that Captain Auld does not want you locked up below when there is action in the offing.' He turned and started to lead on.

'Wait, Philip,' Jack said quickly. 'Before we go up, tell me: what is it between you and Judd? He seems to have a hold over you.'

'I can't tell you the whole story now, Jack, there just isn't time,' Goddard said, impatiently. 'But suffice to say that I've got myself rather stupidly into a real mess, and you may be the only one who can help get me out of it in one piece. The rest will have to wait for a better opportunity, I'm afraid, – assuming we get one that is! Now, come on!' he said, offering his arm to Jack as a prop to lean on. 'And remember, say nothing to anyone until we have had time to talk again.'

By the time Jack reached the quarterdeck, he had regained some of his balance, but he leant upon the larboard rail to steady himself while he accustomed himself once more to daylight and fresh sea air. The ship had all sails set and was making good way in a fresh southerly breeze. Scanning the deck, he saw Captain Auld standing at the opposite rail, his telescope raised at the horizon in the starboard quarter, and following his gaze, Jack spotted the object of the captain's interest. On the southern horizon, its sails dark against the pale grey of early dawn, a ship could be seen heading directly for them.

'She's a two-master, sir!' came a call from the lookout platform high above. 'A French brigantine, by the look of her, and making straight for us!'

'Then let us hope that we can reach the English coast before she catches us, Mr Goddard!' Auld called to his first officer. 'Have the stuns'ls set, if you please, and steer northerly a point off the wind to starboard to keep the courses filled. We must sail as fast as this wind will drive us!'

Auld lowered his glass and turned to see Jack standing at the other rail and walked calmly across the deck towards him, seemingly unconcerned with the flurry of action on deck and aloft that his orders had just provoked

'Ah, Mr Stone, or rather, Mr Easton, I should say. Your gamble does not appear to have paid off, does it? I am sorry for you - but I could not in all conscience object to my first officer's decision to have you locked up. I will do what I can for you in due course, but for the moment, as you can see, we have other matters to attend to.' Auld looked genuinely concerned for Jack's plight.

'Thank you for releasing me, captain, and I would be grateful for the opportunity to explain myself at some more convenient time. But for now, how can I be of assistance?' Jack asked.

'Could you load and fire a musket in anger if your life depended upon it?

'I could fire a cannon if my life depended upon it, sir!

'It may well come to that,' Auld grimaced. 'We may need every man fighting tooth and nail if she catches us. The *Rebecca* may once have been a fighting ship, but without her proper complement of crew and armament, she is a paper tiger. The Frenchman will have sixteen guns to our eight!' Auld glanced upwards for a moment to watch the activity aloft as the studdingsail booms were extended from the main and foremast yards.

'Mr Goddard!' The captain's call brought the first officer quickly to his side. 'Every man on the starboard watch except the designated gun crews is to be issued with a musket and reminded how to use it, if you please! And that includes Mr Easton here,' he said. 'But I want no weapons to be seen on deck for the moment; they will undoubtedly be watching us as they close and I do not want them thinking that they might be in for a fight.'

'I understand, sir,' said Goddard.

'And will you also have the gun crews open up the magazine and set to rehearsing their drills,' continued the captain. 'No firing, of course, and use only the forward larboard-side gun ports for practice at present; with our stern quarter towards her, the Frenchman will remain blind to our preparations!'

'Aye-aye, sir!' the first officer replied smartly and strode off towards the wheel where a cluster of men had already gathered. There was an air of anxiety about them as heads turned to meet his approach, and the group fell immediately into a conference around him.

The captain glanced at the approaching sail, now a point off the stern as a result of the *Rebecca's* recent change of direction; to Jack's eyes, it did not appear to have closed significantly.

'How long before she catches up with us, captain?' he ventured.

'She's a good five miles behind us, but she's fast, perhaps a knot of overtake, maybe a little less. If she doesn't change her mind, there'll be action before mid-afternoon. And she won't be put off easily; a former British frigate would be quite a prize.'

'And how far to the coast?'

'Just a little too far I fear - the shore batteries will be of little help to us. Our only hope is that we spot a friendly warship that we might enlist to scare her off. '

'Then we are for it, captain?' said Jack, scanning the empty sea ahead.

'I am afraid so Mr Easton. Even if the French have been swept from the North Atlantic for the moment, they still harry British vessels here in the Channel. It is all that they can do for the present, but they do it with a fury!'

Auld broke off the inspection of his pursuer to examine the sky. Dawn had broken upon a clear day with good visibility in all directions. Only the mare's tails of cirrus high up in the stratosphere heralded any change of weather, and this too far away to offer hope of refuge. Neither would the present wind give them any advantage - a stronger blow might have decreased the Frenchman's rate of closure, giving the *Rebecca* more time for escape.

'There's nothing for it, Mr Easton!' said Auld emphatically at last. 'Our only recourse is a good breakfast - perhaps you'd care to join me? I'd like to hear your story. And afterwards, I would like you to join the starboard watch in their firearms instruction. It is as well that we prepare for any eventuality - I don't believe that any of us relish the idea of a summer locked up in a French gaol, and we may be able to deter them.'

At noon the captain and his first officer stood on the quarterdeck, sextants in hand, comparing their readings of the sun's elevation from the midday sun shot. Jack had for the moment finished with his musket instruction and had returned to the deck. He watched the pair, impressed that they could appear so calm with the brigantine breathing down their necks only a few miles behind and clearly closing quite fast. He had been aware of the *Rebecca's* course adjustments during the morning as the wind had shifted; and that the Frenchman had matched every change precisely, had dashed any lingering hopes that the crossing of the two ship's paths might be coincidental. There was still no sign of the English coast nor of any rescuing sail, but to Jack the drama was unfolding so slowly that it hardly felt real. For all their musket practice, he found it hard to believe that these new skills would soon be put to the test.

Seeing Jack watching, Auld moved aft to speak to him.

'She will know by now that we are not a fighting vessel or she would not chance her luck to come so close,' he said calmly. 'My guess is that her captain intends to board us rather than risk damaging his prize.' He dropped his voice so as not to be overheard. 'Her crew will certainly outnumber ours in fighting spirit if not in number and be eager to fight for a share of the reward. I fear that few of ours would be prepared to die for a consignment of tobacco and sail cloth, since they know that they will not be harmed if they surrender. I do not have a company of marines to keep them at their posts, and I begin to wonder if, in the end, they would not be right in that approach.'

Jack made to protest, his hopes surmounting the captain's dismal view.

'Surely, you underestimate them captain?'

'Mark my words Mr Easton, they might be full of bravado now, but they would be different men faced with a hoard of screaming Frenchmen pouring over the rail. I'm afraid that they would all perish within five minutes in hand-to-hand fighting. The odds against us are too great. I begin to fear that to escape unscathed now, we would have to deal them such a blow that it stopped them dead in their tracks.' Auld's tone was unruffled despite the hopelessness of his words, and Jack felt his confidence slipping away as a shiver of alarm ran up his spine. Until now he had neither contemplated defeat nor imprisonment in France, and ignorant of the grim realities of naval warfare, his instinct was still to fight. Perhaps this was his reckless streak emerging once again, but, now that his cover had been blown, it seemed to him that he might anyway have nothing to lose.

'But what of the cannons, captain; surely we can bring them to bear and blow them out of the water? She may be fast but she is small by comparison to the *Rebecca*.'

'I cannot risk a broadside engagement; we only have four cannon on each side. And despite their practice loading and running out this morning, my amateur gun crews will not reload under fire in less than ten minutes. The brigantine could get two or three shots off for every one of ours,' Auld replied patiently. 'And if we tried to tack to bring our second side to bear, our manoeuvring could stop us dead in the water at our weight. We simply do not have the fire-power to win a gun battle - we might get one salvo off, but if we didn't finish her off with that, the Frenchman would have us for supper with his sixteen guns and the nimbleness to run rings around us!' The captain shook his head. 'I am afraid that the burden will fall to me in due course to decide whether to fight and risk annihilation or to strike our colours to save our lives.' He paused, thoughtful for a moment. 'What would you do, Mr Easton?' he asked, with a note of resignation in his inflexion; but Auld's question was rhetorical, and he turned and walked away thoughtfully to stand alone further up the rail.

Jack's mind raced. As a sailor himself, albeit of smaller boats, he understood the problem. Coming up fast from behind, the brigantine had the advantage, especially as the *Rebecca's* few guns were located forward in her hull and facing to the side. 'But what if...?' Jack had a flash of inspiration.

'Captain!' he called urgently to Auld, and strode after him. 'How long do we have before she reaches us?' Jack's voice was excited.

Auld glanced back at the Frenchman, now perhaps one and a half miles astern.

'Two hours at the most,' he said quizzically, reacting to the urgent tone of Jack's voice. 'Why? What have you got in mind?'

'Your cabin, sir, will its deck take the weight of four cannons in a row?'

By two o'clock, the French brigantine had closed to within two hundred and fifty yards of the *Rebecca's* stern and was inching closer by the minute. On the *Rebecca's* quarterdeck, Captain Auld and his first officer made a show of looking nervously behind. No longer were they dressed in merchant navy uniform, but had clothed themselves in more humble attire. A cluster of men stood at the wheel in their customary positions similarly dressed down. Here and there on the main deck, a few crew went about their tasks in studied indifference. To the Frenchman, every indication would be that the *Rebecca* was a cargo ship going about her business, albeit in some consternation at the pursuit. And indeed, that is exactly what she was. Except that now she had a bit of a sting in her tail - the carpenters and the gun-layer having been hard at work in the captain's cabin for the past two hours.

Auld watched as two flags were run up on the Frenchman's flag halyard. 'Two signals, sir!' called Goddard. 'They read: "You are running into danger" and "You should stop your vessel immediately" sir.'

'Thank you Mr Goddard,' Auld said calmly. 'Send the reply "I do not understand your intentions" - let us draw him in as close as we can. When you have done that, check on readiness below. Walk slowly mind, I do not want to give them the slightest hint of what we have in store for them.' Auld took out his telescope and looked astern. Standing in the prow of the brigantine, a blue-coated officer held a speaking horn to his face, but the sound of the waves rushing past at speed drowned out his voice. Auld lowered his eyeglass and shrugged in an exaggerated manner at the man, raising his upturned palms to the sky in simulated bewilderment; he knew that eyes would be trained upon him. For all their inspection of his vessel, they could not know that behind the curtained windows of the *Rebecca's* stern cabin, the muzzles of four cannon stared them in the face.

Goddard returned to the quarterdeck. 'The guns are ready, sir. Three are loaded with canister as you ordered, the other with double chain. The

gun layer has set the elevation for fifty yards to rake her deck and rigging.
- the aiming line runs along our keel line exactly.'

'Good man. And the four forward guns ready with chain?'

'Aye, sir.'

'Good! Set those at maximum elevation. Our second salvo will be
aimed at their rigging from about one-hundred and fifty yards if we get
the chance.'

Goddard acknowledged keenly, 'Aye-aye, sir!'

However much Goddard's ways had concerned him in the past, Auld
saw a different man in his first officer now. The man's earlier somewhat
diffident manner had been replaced with assured confidence, responding
to his own decisive command in the emergency. Auld saw too that by
ordering the reconfiguration of his guns rather than simply abdicating to
fate, he had seized the initiative and this had clearly impressed his
subordinate.

'Mr Judd!' he called over to the cluster of men at the wheel.
'Assemble the musketeers on the main deck out of sight. On my order, I
shall want them up here quickly to pick off any who are still firing after
our first salvo. We must not let them regain the initiative if we are
successful. Instruct them to shoot at the officers and helmsman as a
priority, but beware, they may have marksmen in the yards and in their
fighting top.'

Moments later, hidden from the Frenchman's view in the lee of the
quarter deck balustrade, twenty musketeers crouched in a line, bandoliers
of extra shot and powder strung across their chests, their weapons at the
ready. Jack was amongst them. While the larboard watch had manned
the sailing rig, the starboard watch had rehearsed their musket drill for
hours under the instruction of the quartermaster, firing from the forward
hatches where they could not be seen. Their average re-loading time was
now down to about one minute, but this had been in the safety of the
lower deck - under fire it would be a different matter entirely. These
were not war-hardened fighting men fighting for their country; they were
merely plucky patriots ready to have a go to save their ship from falling
into an enemy's hands. Where before it may have seemed that resistance
against such odds would mean almost certain death, Jack's idea had
inspired them to think they now had a real chance of escape. But as they
crouched waiting for their orders, a few hands could be seen trembling at
the imminence of action.

It was similar below as the cannon crews crouched waiting nervously for the order to fire. As they sweated in the airless confines of their two compartments at either end of the ship, young Matthew, doing a sterling job as the ship's powder monkey, delivered the last of their limited supply of gunpowder from the store. Perhaps the boy's youth and innocence diminished his perception of the danger, but his careless whistling as he went about his task had cheered the men and eased the tension.

The distance closed to one hundred yards as the brigantine inched inexorably forwards along the *Rebecca's* wake. At some point soon, she would have to decide on which side of her quarry's decks to board. Her gun ports remained shut on both sides giving no clue as to her intentions, but with all four of the *Rebecca's* forward guns located on the starboard side, it was vital that the Frenchman go to starboard herself if Auld's tactics were to work.

His plan was simple. First, he must lure his adversary close into the *Rebecca's* starboard quarter giving every outward impression of surrender. Then he would turn his stern towards his adversary in a manoeuvre which would be seen as evasive, even panicky, rather than provocative. If he got his timing right, this would require a turn of only thirty or so degrees and thus not require any serious trimming of the sails in the following wind. His guns could then open fire at very close range and at just the right angle to send the blast sweeping down the Frenchman's deck. Immediately, he would then alter his course to bring his forward guns to bear, opening the gun ports as he turned. Again, if he had calculated correctly, his turn would not need to be prolonged nor require any sail adjustment for the short time he intended to hold his new heading. In the favourable wind, it should be possible to repeat this sequence quickly at least once more without losing too much way, reloading the cannon during each change of direction. In this manner, Auld would make maximum effect of his limited firepower and gain best advantage from surprise. But his plan hinged on forcing the brigantine to move to starboard as it overtook.

The Frenchman was now approaching seventy-five yards astern, still solidly in the *Rebecca's* wake. Even without his telescope, Auld could see that her deck was now crowded with armed men jostling at the rails. He could feel Goddard and Judd becoming restless at his side. The moment to put his plans into action was approaching.

'Mr Goddard, I think that the time is upon us. Are we ready below?' he said calmly.

'Aye, sir, as ready as we'll ever be,' came Goddard's reply.

'Good man. I shall control the ship from the quarterdeck, giving my instructions directly to the helmsman - you and Mr Judd will control the firing of the cannon. Please ensure that you position yourselves where you can receive my orders to fire, but should I fall after the first volley, you must act quickly at your own discretion. The quartermaster will, of course, take charge of the musket party on deck as rehearsed.' Auld paused briefly in a moment of thought, as if checking items on some mental list. He then took a deep breath. 'Now, everyone to their positions if you please,' he said firmly. 'And may the Lord God preserve us all.'

Goddard and Judd left to take up their positions below, and Auld walked over to the helmsman as casually as he could. Then, turning to face astern, he leant on the rail directly forward of the wheel. From here, he would use the base of the mizzenmast as his aiming mark for the first salvo.

The helmsmen shifted nervously - perhaps realising that he would become a target when the firing started. A second helmsman stood nearby at the ready.

'A touch of port wheel, helmsman if you please, and stand by to reverse it' Auld said softly, and then waited and watched as, slowly, very slowly, the ship started to respond. The change of direction was slight, almost imperceptible, but it was enough to place the brigantine some yards to the starboard side of the *Rebecca's* wake as she continued to close. The *Rebecca* then resumed her original course. It would look as if the helmsman had had a lapse of concentration, nothing more. There was some subtle psychology here; the brig's captain - hopefully unaware of the ruse - would now favour coming along the *Rebecca's* starboard side for it would become his natural preference. At this close range and with his high rate of overtake, it would require a marked change of heading now for him to change to the larboard side. The subterfuge seemed to have worked, for a moment or two later, the brig's boarding party, until now dispersed randomly around her foredeck, moved quickly to her larboard side and now faced their quarry expectantly.

The Frenchman's bow closed to seventy yards - then sixty. Both ships were ploughing through the waves at a good ten knots, their sails full and taut in the increasing wind. The narrowing stretch of water between the two racing hulls boiled in foamy turbulence. Spray leapt up and rained down upon the pursuer's decks, as the gap closed further yet. Auld could see the French captain gesticulating at him now, pointing at the *Rebecca's* sails and drawing his hand across his throat in a cutting motion - he was demanding that the *Rebecca* drop her sails. Auld looked up at his sails in apparent confusion; then, feigning belated understanding of the Frenchman's demand, he nodded his head vigorously.

'Quartermaster!' he shouted to the chief musketeer still hidden in the lee of the rail. 'Have a few of the deck crew run up and down the deck if you would. A little frantic activity is called for here,' he called.

Auld saw the Frenchman acknowledge his action and then turn to address an officer standing nearby, but his French musketeers had already raised their guns to aim. The brig was now fifty yards in the *Rebecca's* starboard quarter and still closing.

'Mr Goddard, are you ready?' Auld shouted.

'Aye, sir!' Goddard shouted from the officers' door on the main deck, from where he could relay the captain's orders to the gun crew.

'Helmsman, wheel half to larboard.' Auld spoke his order without emotion, all his former naval experience and battle training now coming to the fore.

'Mr Goddard, fire when the guns bear! Quartermaster! Musketeers quickly to the starboard rail if you please! Open fire when in position!' The *Rebecca* answered her helm quickly taking the Frenchman completely by surprise. The brigantine's gun ports still remained firmly closed, and as the *Rebecca* swerved away, Auld saw the look of consternation on the French captain's face. He had not anticipated a fight and it took some seconds for the man to respond, but even then Auld could see that he had not fully appreciated the meaning of the *Rebecca's* manoeuvre. Puffs of smoke and the sounds of ragged musket fire exploded from the Frenchman's deck, and a volley of shot zipped through the air clattering into the *Rebecca's* superstructure. One of Auld's musketeers fell clutching his breast just as he reached the top of the companionway in his dash to the rail.

'Helmsman, wheel amidships,' Auld called to slow the ship's turn, anticipating its inertia even before the guns had fired. The helmsman spun the wheel. Auld saw the French captain call more orders to his crew. A second round of musket fire rang out from his deck, but the guns were wildly aimed and this time found no human target. The range between the two vessels started to open up again as their courses began to diverge. Auld's aiming marks came slowly into alignment. It was now too late for the French captain to respond. Even as the man shouted, the

Rebecca's four cannon fired simultaneously in a thundering volley, and three canisters and one double chain-round ripped through the *Rebecca's* stern windows in an explosion of splintered wood and shattered glass. Instantly released from their containment, four hundred pistol balls and two flailing chain rounds splayed out in a deadly arc and sped towards the brigantine at sonic speed. Three of the brig's mainmast shrouds were severed instantly and thirty Frenchmen were mown down where they stood, their looks of startled disbelief still frozen upon their faces as they fell. With the following wind, the *Rebecca's* quarterdeck was quickly enveloped in canon smoke just as the musketeers settled their aim; they fired blindly through the obscuring mist in a rattling volley without seeing its effect and quickly ducked behind the balustrade to reload.

'Wheel half-a-starboard!' shouted Auld to the helmsman, the cannon fire still ringing in his ears. 'Mr Judd!' he called forward. 'Run out your guns and fire when they bear!'

'Aye, aye, sir,' came the distant reply as Judd, waiting alertly half-hidden in the forward hatch, disappeared below to ready his crew. As the smoke began to clear from the *Rebecca's* quarterdeck, the brigantine could be seen two points off the stern at a range of about one hundred yards. The *Rebecca's* musketeers opened fire again – this time in an untidy volley. A body fell from the brigantine's yards – *A lucky shot*, thought Auld. Strangely the Frenchman's course had not changed; he expected her to have turned sharply to starboard to bring her own guns to bear on his stern, but the vessel ploughed on in a straight line, its mainsail creased and sagging. The vessel seemed to be losing way. But the *Rebecca's* starboard turn continued steadily with her wheel held over, and the courses of the two ships first paralleled and then started to converge. At that moment, the range between them was at its maximum at about two hundred yards, but would now start rapidly to close. The *Rebecca's* musketeers were firing again at the brigantine, but most of their shots were seen falling short. Auld had noticed Jack's steadying influence earlier in the thick of fire, and now saw him prompting his comrades to raise their aim; the Portlander had more about him than met the eye, he thought.

'Midships!' Auld shouted as he saw his firing solution approaching, and the helmsman once more spun the wheel to bring the rudder back to centre. In a few seconds, his target would be in the line of fire, but he must be ready to reverse his course again quickly to put the Frenchman astern for a second salvo from the rear. For Auld, the blood was now up.

His tactic had worked; and he was amazed how effective the improvised gun configuration had been - but it was the element of surprise that had really won the day; the Frenchman had simply not recognised the danger. The captain congratulated himself, he could not have hoped for a better opening. But it was not over yet.

He raised his telescope to his eye, and his mood changed in an instant.

The brigantine's deck was a scene of utter devastation. Not one man remained standing. The French captain, his blue and cream tunic turned crimson by his own blood, sprawled lifeless on the quarterdeck; the first officer, his face half shot away, lay dying beside him. From bow to stern, the ship's topsides were littered with corpses heaped in hideous contortion, flesh ripped from their bloody bodies by the deadly wall of lead from the *Rebecca's* cannonade. The helmsman lay slumped across the wheel in a macabre embrace, and with no one to steer her, the ship was losing her grip on the wind as her heading fell off slowly to starboard. Here and there on the main deck a few men stirred, crawling amongst their dead and wounded comrades, dazed and bewildered, their faces blackened and splattered with blood. Auld was awe-struck as he surveyed the terrible effect of his point-blank volley, but, as he watched, he saw one of the survivors stagger to his feet and make his way unsteadily towards the stern. It took some moments before Auld realised that the man must be running to strike the ship's colours. The sheer horror of what he had seen through his telescope had slowed his thinking; it should have been obvious to him straight away that the brigantine was in no state to continue the fight.

'Cease fire!' shouted Auld, suddenly galvanised into action. 'Cease fire!' he called again in dread.

But his call came an instant too late for the forward cannon crew who, as instructed, opened fire the moment their guns came to bear. The explosions sent four double chain-shot spinning on their way, irretrievably bent on destruction. Auld watched sickened as they arced over the hundred and fifty yards which now separated the two vessels. The single second that it took for his missiles to complete their deadly journey was the longest in his life, and he prayed desperately that they would miss their mark. But his gun-layers had been too good. The tops of the brigantine's two masts were severed like matchwood by the flailing chain and ball and they crashed splintering to the deck in a tangle of sailcloth and rigging. Many of those lying on the deck below who until that moment still clung to life could not have stood a chance. The brig slewed and broached across the waves as the helmsman's anchoring body fell to the deck, sending the wheel spinning. The *Rebecca's* second volley had made the brigantine a floating wreck.

'Cease fire!' the captain called again, 'the battle is won!' But there was no trace of triumph in his voice.

A loud cheer erupted from below as the call was relayed to the lower deck, and men leapt up the companionways eager to get a look at their floundering prey. Just minutes before they had reconciled themselves to death; now a surge of victorious relief had gone straight to their heads, and they shouted and danced and threw up their caps in a tumultuous celebration of lives regained. Even Jack, who had played but a small part in the action, joined in the cheering with as much excitement as the rest. Only the captain, who had seen at close quarters through his telescope the terrible destruction that his guns had wrought, remained pensive; and while the crew still celebrated, he suffered a terrible moment of remorse.

'Mr Goddard, Mr Judd! We'll heave to until she's drifted ahead then come alongside; to your stations if you please,' Auld ordered. 'Quartermaster, have the weapons stowed and clear some space below for the wounded.'

Chapter Twenty Two

The jubilation died as the *Rebecca* closed on the brigantine and the crew got their first look at the carnage on the Frenchman's deck. The stricken craft wallowed helplessly, the motive drive of her tattered sails dissipated and confused after the collapse of her mastheads to the deck. Auld's crew stared in awe at the tangled mass of lacerated and bloody bodies that lay strewn along the Frenchman's larboard gangway. The French crew had fallen where they had stood readied to board the *Rebecca*, so confident of an easy victory, so totally unaware of their impending death. The hail of canister shot which had exploded in their faces had reaped a devastating toll. Torn flesh and shredded broken limbs protruded from the bloody mass of dead or dying men in a gruesome pose which, for some of the horrified onlookers, would be the stuff of their nightmares for years to come.

Coming alongside another vessel even in the slight swell that existed, courted crippling damage from collision or entanglement. Captain Auld knew this very well, but in view of the urgency to get help aboard to tend the wounded, he decided to chance it nevertheless. He also realised that the scale of repair work required would be greatly facilitated by having the two vessels rafted up side by side, at least while the sea remained kind.

Auld took charge of the manoeuvre from the start, not trusting Goddard with so hazardous a task, and, judging his approach with precision, he ordered the sails shortened progressively to adjust his rate of closure. His target lay across the waves at that angle of uneasy stability where the vectors of sea drag and windage conspired to trap her. She wallowed impotently, the remnants of her ripped sails flapping noisily in abandoned surrender to the elements. His approach path was therefore chosen to bring the Frenchman into the calming shelter of the *Rebecca's* lee, and Auld conned his ship immaculately almost to a complete stop abeam some five yards off. A dozen rope and sailcloth fenders now dangled from her bulwark to protect the hulls as they came together, pressed closer by the wind. From the masthead platform, a lookout watched as the gap narrowed with remarkable gentleness until contact was made. But even as the gap closed, men were already leaping from the *Rebecca's* rail into the brigantine's ratlines, and they scrambled aboard dragging lines with them to bind the two jostling hulls together as if one.

Only after this task was complete, in the relative calm that then ensued, were the men able to take stock of the terrifying consequences of their actions. To some of the younger crew, it was too much to comprehend, and they stood about with mouths agape not knowing quite where to start. A few, nauseated beyond measure at the sight of the blood and gore, staggered to the side to hurl the contents of their stomachs into the sea. But many of the older hands, steeled by past naval service, immediately set about the grim work of separating the wounded from the dead, and laid them out to receive the rudimentary attentions of the *Rebecca's* two cooks doubling as their surgeons.

Essential repair tasks were also quickly put in hand, and Jack found himself soon allocated to assist with the erection of jury rigs on the brigantine's shattered masts. This was perhaps the most urgent of the work required if they were to save the valuable vessel from foundering. Fortunately for him, others had been allotted the gruesome work of dealing with the bodies of the dead whose putrefying remains had quickly to be disposed of. But the funeral protocol was as meticulous as it was swift. As the thirty-three bodies were solemnly committed to the deep, the *Rebecca's* crew ceased their work and stood together with the brigantine's survivors in silent salute as if members of a brotherhood. The single victim from the *Rebecca*'s decks - the unfortunate musketeer who had fallen under the Frenchman's opening fire - was treated no differently, save for the union flag instead of the French tricolour under which his body had been laid out.

For a full two days after the battle, repair work on the brigantine's masts and rigging continued at such a fevered pitch that time passed quickly. The first imperative was to make the stricken vessel seaworthy enough to be put quickly under tow so as to detach her from *The Rebecca's* side where it posed a threat of damage and entanglement should a sea come up. Like most of those aboard, Jack lost himself in the work, but as time wore on, he could not help his thoughts returning to a contemplation of his fate. Despite his contribution, he still feared that he might find himself again under arrest. Auld had been sympathetic towards him on hearing his story over breakfast before the battle, but Jack had been left uncertain, and nothing had been said of the matter since. Goddard's tantalising words kept recurring in his mind: 'Say nothing to the captain of the matter with Judd, and we may yet be able to help each other'; and Jack was thus desperate to hear how, hardly daring to believe that Goddard may have the key to his salvation. He was therefore most anxious to arrange a meeting with the first officer, but it would, of course, have to be in the strictest privacy.

They eventually met in the first officer's cabin, choosing a time when it was unlikely that they would be observed. At first, Goddard was a little evasive and in some evident embarrassment about the situation in which he found himself, but he overcame his discomfort and was soon in full flow. He spoke ardently, as if needing to purge himself through confession, as if by exposing every detail of his thoughts, he might not lose Jack's respect. Clearly, it seemed important to him that Jack should understand.

'It all started when I caught Judd hiving off some tools from the consignment we delivered in Dumper,' he began. 'He'd altered the identifying markings on one of the boxes and was in the process of selling it off separately when I spotted him – actually he was rather brazen about it and didn't seem too bothered that I'd seen him, either. Anyway, it was only a few tools and I knew their absence wouldn't be noticed in the thousands we delivered, and so I let him get away with it. I know I shouldn't have, but at the time it seemed a small price to pay for keeping him on side - I needed his cooperation to manage the crew, and if he'd turned against me, I knew I'd have had a hard time, especially as a new number one.' He paused, as if marshalling his thoughts. 'Well, I thought that would be the end of it - that maybe he'd have been embarrassed that I'd seen him and wouldn't do it again. He even treated me to dinner ashore one night to thank me for not reporting him!' Goddard paused, then frowned. 'But then in Charlestown he changed, threatening to make more of my collusion if I didn't help him do the same with some hogsheads of tobacco. Only this time it would be much bigger, and he'd need access to the tobacco manifest in order to make some alterations to cover the loss. He said he'd make things difficult for me if I didn't co-operate. He also said he had others aboard working with him, so I believed that he could – make it difficult for me, I mean. Again, stupidly, I acquiesced, thinking that somehow I could extract myself later and maybe even turn the tables. But then I realised what I was getting myself into and told him that he should put a stop to it there and then otherwise I'd report him. That's when things got really frightening because, among other things, he threatened to pay my family an unpleasant visit next time I was away if I didn't cooperate. I worked in the company's shipping office for some years before I came to sea, so it would not be difficult to find out where I live - and frankly Jack, I was terrified of what he might do.'

Jack was privately astonished at the first officer's naivety in letting the affair go so far. 'So you went along with it.' he said, trying not to sound too judgemental.

'Well, yes, I'm afraid to say I did,' Goddard admitted with a guilty look, but then added rather lamely; 'but I like to think that in the end I'd have done the right thing, despite his threats. Anyway, when you arrived unexpectedly on the scene - unexpected by me at any rate - you were given the manifest instead, and everything suddenly became more complicated. From that time on, I felt trapped between the devil and the deep blue sea – threatened by both of you simultaneously. All that time you and I spent together before the storm, I kept on thinking that I should tell you what was going on, but it never seemed quite the right moment, and I was afraid that if it all came out I'd be ruined. I just kept on hoping that somehow I could sort it out in Cowes. But then Judd went looking for the manifest and he found your letters, and... Well, you know the rest! Your arrest was just what he needed to keep you out of it too, and he gave me no option but to have you locked up. He must have been afraid that you'd find out what he was up to.'

'He found me in the hold after the storm. I must have worried him then,' Jack mused. 'But I wonder, Philip,' he added in a speculative tone, 'do you think that he might have set you up from the beginning? I mean, do you think it's possible that he let you see him hiving off that box of tools, and then later compromised you by repaying your silence with that apparently innocuous dinner? Your familiarity could have been misconstrued, and he would certainly have turned it against you.'

'God, I never thought of that! I suppose it's possible.' Goddard's jaw went slack as he turned the thought over in his mind, then he slumped visibly, as if suddenly realising that he'd been played for a fool. 'I never thought of that,' he repeated absently, and shook his head in disbelief. Still looking rather shocked, he opened a drawer in the small dresser by his bunk and pulled out a bundle of letters that Jack recognised immediately.

'Here they are, by the way,' Goddard said, handing over the bundle. 'I'm sorry he did that. I've got the manifest too, but I'd better hang on to that for a while, at least until we know what's going to happen to you. But if he's altered any of the entries, he's done a good job - I couldn't tell.'

'Let me have a look.' Jack took the manifest, unrolled it, and studied it carefully, looking at the quantities annotated against the Ferry Point Plantation in particular. 'He's done it,' he said at last. 'Look!' Jack pointed out the numbers that had been so neatly changed that they would not have drawn the attention of an unsuspecting eye. 'At worst, it might look like some scribing error that would leave the agent and Harding unsure exactly what was loaded - especially since you've signed it off! It's clever. He's done this before hasn't he?'

'Yes, undoubtedly. And the missing hogsheads will already have been switched to Judd's other manifest - to be sold off separately,' said Goddard plainly.

'What do you think he'll do now?' Jack asked.

'We haven't spoken on the matter since your arrest,' Goddard replied. 'Your release may have unsettled him but I believe he still thinks he's safe. He's certainly his usual cocky self, especially since the action. He probably thinks, even if you suspect him, that you won't have any evidence. Anyway, he's under the impression that you'll be taken permanently out of the way when we arrive in Cowes. He also believes that he still has me in his pocket, and that I won't report him. So I'm pretty certain that he'll carry on with his fiddling just as he has done apparently for some time. It's worth a lot of money to him and he'll certainly have become used to it.'

'I worked it all out for myself, incidentally - when you gave me that nice break in the brig!' said Jack, looking slightly smug. Then after a moment's thought, he added: 'All right, let's assume that he'll go ahead with his scheme either this time or at some future time. If I help to protect you from him, how can you help me get out of the pickle I'm in?'

'I'm going to speak with the captain about the brigantine and how we get her back. I have a proposal that might help you, but I can't predict how he'll react. Leave it with me for a while,' Goddard said, firmly. 'And as far as Judd is concerned, I'm not sure yet how to handle him. I want him brought to justice but clearly I also want to protect my family from any later recriminations. His sort will have a long and vindictive memory even if he is put away for a while, and I don't want it preying on my mind while I'm at sea. And of course, I would prefer my criminal stupidity not to go down on my record if I can avoid it.'

'A bit of thieving is one thing, Philip, but his threats and blackmail are another,' prompted Jack. 'And you can't pretend it isn't happening and hope it'll go away. It won't,' he said emphatically. 'And you'll go down with him if you let it continue. We must simply make sure that he's caught by the agent, and indisputably in the act, both so that he doesn't connect you with it and so that he can't wriggle out of it. That way, you won't become the target of his revenge, and with a bit of luck, the captain will also never know of your involvement. That's where I think I can help you, Philip, but first, I'm hoping that you'll be able to help me.'

When the repair work was eventually completed, the captain called a meeting of his officers on *The Rebecca's* quarterdeck, and Jack was expressly invited to attend. Being the first to arrive, Jack waited patiently at the stern rail gazing at the brigantine, now trailing some fifty yards behind on her towline. He thought her name, *L'hermine, 'The Stoat'*, appropriate for a diminutive predator of the seas, only on this occasion its prey had turned the tables just as the stalker had been about to strike. Jack reflected on the change of fortunes that had seen victim turn victor in a moment of terrible reckoning (recognising some uncomfortable parallels with his own plight) and he continued to speculate what would become of him now that the crisis was over. So much had happened, yet nothing had changed in this respect; the issue on which the course of his future life might hinge, still lay unresolved. Auld had probably been too busy attending to the grim aftermath of the battle to think of such diversions.

Jack leant on the rail heavily and watched the brigantine skipping along in the *Rebecca's* wake like a skittish greyhound straining on its lead. After four long days of attention, *L'hermine* at last looked seaworthy enough to face the homeward voyage alone. Two new forestays now ran between the foremast and the sprit onto which a jib and staysail would be hanked; all of the damaged standing rigging had been repaired; the surviving mainmast and foremast yards now sported new braces and rigging; and the wrecked mizzen boom and sail looked almost like new. But both masts were considerably truncated with the loss of the topmasts and the topgallant yards that had been severed by the cannon fire. It would win no prizes for elegance, but it would get her home, Jack thought. And despite her stunted look, the comely lines of her hull and the graceful upsweep of her fine stem threw up a clean white bow-wave that mesmerised his wistful gaze.

Eventually, the captain, Goddard, Judd, and the quartermaster, arrived on the quarterdeck to rouse Jack from his quiet reverie.

'Ah, Mr Easton!' said Auld leading his party to join Jack at the stern rail. 'I am sorry to have kept you waiting. With my cabin still in tatters, it was rather difficult to lay out my charts in the draught,' he said, with an ironic lift of his eyebrow. 'I am afraid that it will be some time before I can entertain my guests attired in anything but oilskins!'

Jack returned the captain's smile uncertainly, unsure of what would come next, sensing that the light remarks would be leading up to more serious talk about his fate. He rather hoped that he might have earned some clemency but had not let himself become too optimistic in this respect. He glanced at Goddard to gauge what might be coming, but the man's expression was difficult to interpret, giving nothing away of their earlier conversation. Judd stood behind him looking smugly inscrutable.

'Mr Easton, I shall come to the point without beating about the bush,' Auld said cheerfully, his face flushed. 'Firstly, we all owe you a debt of gratitude. Without your idea to move the guns aft, we would all by now either be at the bottom of the English Channel or on our way to a French gaol.' Auld glanced at the others, who nodded their agreement. Even Judd looked grudgingly impressed as the captain continued:

'It was a brilliant piece of tactical thinking and I find it difficult to admit that in all my years of naval service, no one has apparently thought of it before!' He laughed and shook his head disbelievingly. 'Their Lordships might be slow to learn the lesson of this little scrap but, mark my words, warships of the future will be equipped to fire in all directions. May I shake your hand, sir, for your contribution to the development of naval warfare?' This was a command rather than a request, and he reached out with both hands to pump Jack's arm vigorously, the others following suit in turn in a more modest fashion so that at the end of it, Jack felt well and truly fêted - as well as shaken.

'And as for Mr Goddard and Mr Judd here,' Auld continued in the same hearty vein, 'they'll both be receiving my commendation. No doubt the shipping company will reward them for their exemplary service in the face of aggression, and I would not be surprised to see Mr Goddard a captain before long. The men too will share our success when the prize money is shared out – I'm proud of them all!'

Jack caught Goddard's meaningful glance that told him that there was more to come, while Auld brimmed visibly with pride. *It takes a fight for vital causes for men to learn to pull together,* Jack thought. *Without a common mission, our petty rivalries and silly tricks create islands of us all.*

'Now, I come to the point of your return from exile,' the captain continued turning more serious. 'I have decided to put you aboard the *L'hermine* this afternoon with Mr Goddard and a small crew who will sail her back to the naval anchorage at Spithead. We have just plotted our respective courses and have drawn his track to pass by Portland Bill in order to set you ashore there. As far as the authorities are concerned, I shall make no mention of you in my log, and you have my word that we shall not speak of you when we are ashore. We have agreed on that, have we not gentlemen?' At this point, Auld turned to catch the eyes of his colleagues, and each acknowledged the captain's glance with a nod. 'I cannot do fairer than that,' Auld finished.

Jack was still aware of his responsibilities to Harding for the safe arrival of the tobacco, and while elated at the captain's proposal, he was now unsure how he would honour his undertaking if he did not see the journey through. And he now had a new commitment to consider – his promise to help untangle Goddard from the mess that he was in; he would not want to let either of them down. He knew straight away what he must do.

'I am most grateful, sir,' said Jack, modestly. 'That will give me a head start, but could I therefore ask you please to take charge of the manifest to hand to Mr Harding's agent personally in Cowes in order that I can fulfil my obligation to him. And perhaps you would be kind enough also to deliver a note in which I shall carefully explain my absence?' Jack flashed a glance at Goddard that was acknowledged with an almost imperceptible nod. Meanwhile Judd's attention had visibly wandered. Indeed, it appeared that the boatswain was entirely at ease as he gazed carelessly about him.

'Of course Mr Easton,' the captain replied gracefully. 'But now perhaps a private word with you?' he said, dismissing the others to their duties and taking Jack aside.

'You were gracious enough to tell me your story, and I wanted to wish you well with your quest – you are pitting yourself against the authority of a corrupt administration which is riven with self-interest and privilege. Tread carefully, I know myself how spiteful these people can be. I do not know how I might repay you for what you have done for us, but I would stand up and speak well of you in court if that became necessary.' The captain produced an envelope from his pocket and handed it to Jack. 'Here, take this with you; it contains my address ashore. Please do not hesitate to contact me if you find yourself in trouble.'

'You do me an honour sir, I am most grateful,' Jack said respectfully, pocketing the envelope, 'but the kind of assistance I am likely to need will not be of the sort which you so generously offer!' Jack grinned. 'I fear that some rougher forces may need to come to the fore when I arrive in Portland!'

'Then let me know where I may contact you,' Auld replied after a moment's thought. 'We are sure to receive a handsome prize for the brig as she will undoubtedly be put into His Majesty's service, and as captain, I shall receive a large proportion of it. I would like to share it with you. I plan to retire at the conclusion of this voyage since I have had enough of this slaving - and even half of my due will provide an unexpected boost to my pension! Without your quick-thinking sir, I might instead be languishing in a French prison and my family forced into penury - I hope that you will do me the honour of accepting it in due course?'

'Why, Captain Auld, I'm speechless!' Jack replied, incredulously.

As Jack returned to his cabin to prepare for his departure, he caught young Matthew's eye, indicating with a flick of his head that the boy should follow as soon as he could. It took a little time for Matthew to break away from his duties, but when the boy arrived, Jack was still scribbling furiously.

'Matthew, I'm going aboard *L'hermine* shortly so I wanted to say good-bye. I've written down details in this note of how you can find me in Maryland.' Jack handed over the note. 'Can you read it?' he asked. Matthew read its contents aloud falteringly but accurately, and then thrust it into his trouser pocket. Jack continued: 'If you should get tired of the sea, you'll find a home there on my farmstead if you want it.'

'Thank you, sir,' said Matthew. 'A new home in a new land! That's a prospect indeed; I shall think it over, for I am very tired of being a skivvy! I shall miss you, sir.'

'And I you, Matthew, but now be off with you!' said Jack with a grin, chivvying the boy out with a playful punch to his chin. 'And I hope that we shall meet again very soon in America! Should you want to take up my offer, show the note to Mr Harding in Charlestown; I shall ask him to look out for you and help you on your way.'

With that farewell, Jack set himself quickly to finishing his letter to the Cowes agent in which he would alert him to Judd's scheme. It would contain the warning not to act in any way until the hived off hogsheads had been put up separately for sale. Only then would Judd's intention permanently to deprive their rightful owner be demonstrated under the law and conviction thus assured. And to cover the case of Judd getting cold feet on this occasion, Jack would also advise the agent to bide his time until the next.

Chapter Twenty-Three

Jack stood at the wheel of *L'hermine* staring at the compass binnacle, his face aglow in the amber light of its lamps, concentrating on holding his course due East. Under his feet, he felt the vessel lift bodily and surge forward with the passing of every roaring wave under her hull. A following sea was surfing the ship up the Channel, driven on by a brisk and steady wind from astern. The jury rig had proved sound and easy to control, but the reduced sail area made the ship roll uncomfortably, especially on this point of sail. He braced himself again as the ship lurched and plunged headlong into the darkness. The sky jet black, still half an hour before the first inkling of the dawn, his world was confined to the sphere of faint light which illuminated the rocking compass card. No moonlight, no stars, no phosphorescence from the sea - he steered the ship blindly through an inky void, feeling disembodied and adrift in space. But at least he was on his way home!

Separation from the *Rebecca* the previous afternoon had taken place as planned with the brig being cast off her towline under the command of her new captain. Only fifteen deck crew had been transferred with Goddard to man her – all that could be spared from the mother ship, and Jack was thus required to play his part as second-in-command - as well as take his turn at the helm.

Goddard came running up the companionway out of breath to join Jack at the wheel.

'You should soon see Portland off to larboard,' he shouted, raising his voice against the roar of the sea, 'about five miles by dead-reckoning - our last fix by sextant was by yesterday's mid-day sun-shot so my navigation may be a bit out.'

'And our speed?' Jack shot an anxious sideways glance at his companion.

'We were making eight knots at the last throw of the log-line. Quite fast enough for this rig! And we're on the east-going Spring tide at its peak, so we're probably closing at ten to twelve knots overall!' He looked a little apprehensive. 'I've plotted our course to bring us south of the Race, so we should be well clear of the rocks.' His voice sounded hopeful rather than assured.

Jack detected the uncertainty in Goddard's voice and shared it - these were dangerous waters; the Isle of Portland stuck five miles out into the English Channel at the very end of Chesil Beach like a giant trap reaching into the darkness to scoop up the unwary in its rocky embrace. But this was not the only danger. Portland Bill was where the current's rip reached its maximum speed, churning itself into a terrifying frenzy that could swamp a ship or even tear it apart. On spring tides, when the tidal flow was at its strongest, the Race extended two miles or more south of the Bill and was as feared by mariners almost as much as the rocks. It was wise to steer well clear - the seabed around the island was littered with the scattered wreckage of those who had already succumbed to one or the other, and Jack did not want *L'hermine's* name to join the long list of wrecks lamented on the commemorative plaque in the nave of St Andrew's church.

Goddard stood silently alongside Jack as *L'hermine* ploughed on relentlessly into the blackness, but his lips were clamped in a tight line across his face as he shifted his weight uneasily from side to side; he was clearly perturbed. Then, seeming to come to a decision, he strode over to the ship's bell and rang it urgently.

'All hands on deck!' he shouted twice through the deck hatch, then returned to Jack's side. 'With the dawn, we should be able to see where we are, and I want to be ready to alter course quickly if we need to. If my navigation is in error, we may need to act fast!' he added, still peering into the unremitting darkness ahead.

Both men stood together in silence for some minutes cocooned in the dim glow of the compass light, waiting, hoping, praying for the dawn.

'I can't understand it. We should have seen the upper light by now!' Goddard's voice was tense.

'Don't depend upon it!' shouted Jack shaking his head. 'They're idle scoundrels, those lighthouse keepers – they'll sometimes let the fires go out at this time of the morning to save the cost of coal! I've been caught out by their penny-pinching before.'

The minutes passed agonisingly as the two men became more anxious in their blindness; and all the while the little ship pressed on full-pelt. It was Jack who called the first sign of dawn. He saw it as a line of grey between the two hemispheres of blackness that met on the horizon. But cross-checking his compass against its direction, he became suddenly concerned; the loom was much too far south for the time of the year. *The compass is in error*, he thought in alarm, as the possible consequences of such a fault flashed through his mind. He checked the compass again, and was about to call Goddard's attention to it when the real cause of the anomaly hit him. The compass was not at fault at all! Something must be obscuring the dawn's light dead ahead! He forced himself to crane his head upwards, and saw what he had at that same instant begun to fear. Well above the horizontal and directly in *L'hermine's* onward racing path, the ominous wedge-shaped outline of the Portland's land mass stood etched by the dawn light. Its invisible black shape had blotted out the dawn and now rose threateningly before them like a sea monster emerging from the depths, silhouetted by an evil yellow hue. Jack screamed a warning at Goddard as he instinctively spun the wheel to starboard. Still unable to gauge the distance from the invisible rocks in the dim light; his flesh crept in fearful anticipation of an imminent collision. He expected at any second to founder – to feel the sudden jar - to hear the splintering of the ship's fragile timbers upon the rocks. Jack saw the ship's head start to answer, but the mainsails began to fold as they came off the wind. Goddard appeared not to be reacting to his warning, so Jack pointed upwards into the rigging and shouted again:

'The yards, Philip! We must come hard up on the wind!'

Goddard at last saw the danger and reacted immediately, calling the mainsail crew quickly to the braces and sheets.

Jack shouted at the few men left with him on the quarterdeck: 'Sheet the spanker in tight, men, then get forward to the jib and stays'l as quickly as you can, and do the same! Look lively now!'

The spanker and the foresails would give good drive even close-hauled, whereas the square sails would struggle to provide propulsion with wind much forward of the beam. In a tight situation like this, therefore, the fore-and-aft sails could make the difference between life and oblivion.

The little ship was nimble and responded quickly to the turn of the wheel, but with the unfamiliar rig and too few men to control it, Goddard's crew took too long to bring the yards around. Suddenly, the huge square sails lost their grip and broke into a frenzy of thunderous flapping as they started to back; the ship's turn slowed immediately as drive was lost and her head started to fall off the wind. Jack could just make out the surf of the shoreline now in the increasing light of dawn; it was so close that he could hear the waves breaking on the rocks. *L'hermine* was less than half-a-mile from disaster and still a good mile north of the Bill which she would have to navigate in order to reach safety on the other side. Unless they could get the mainsails filled again quickly, Jack knew that they would not weather it. He watched on tenterhooks as the crew struggled wildly with the snaking rigging lines on the main deck while he fought to keep the ship pointing as high he could, searching for the best balance between heading and speed. If he brought her up too high, the brig would lose way completely and they would fall to the mercy of the wind and the sea. Jack was steering the ship as he would his own boat, and she was reacting just the same. But even at the best he could manage, *L'hermine* was still on a collision course with the towering cliffs. He knew there was not much time left; if the yards could not be brought round within the next few seconds, it would be too late.

Goddard's barked orders cut through the crew's turmoil, quelling the increasing alarm that was already turning into panic. The men responded sharply as he rushed them from block to mast and back again with brisk and incisive discipline. Jack eased the helm as the sails came round to help them fill, and one by one, they ceased their flapping and cracked into their proper taut shape. Jack felt the ship lurch as they bit on the wind. With the main and foremast yards now braced for the tack, and the fore-and-aft sails already pulled in tightly, he coaxed the little ship to point as close to the wind as he dare. *L'hermine* leaned yet further and then surged forward as he found the right point of sail. He glanced at the compass; they were making south-by-south-east, and her bow was at last pointing clear of the Bill by a good margin.

Goddard ran back to the wheel to watch her progress; there was nothing more that he or his crew could do now except pray to the Lord for deliverance. He drew a deep breath and exhaled loudly in relief, catching Jack's eye; they had come close – far too close – the cliffs were but a cable's length away. *L'hermine* was perilously embayed, but now at least she had a chance.

Both men watched anxiously, measuring the ship's track as the minutes ticked away, willing the distance from the cliffs to open. The bow was still pointing clear of the Bill, but the ship's course over the seabed remained stubbornly parallel to the shoreline - the Bill's strong currents had taken *L'hermine* into a fierce and tenacious grip. Despite her apparently safe heading, the ship was being swept bodily down towards the rocky promontory at a high angle of drift. The realisation of their plight slowly dawned on the two men as they stood transfixed. And relief turned to dismay.

'We've lost her,' said Goddard evenly at last. 'So much for my first command.'

Jack was still deep in concentration, studying the relative movement of the Bill against the ship's bow. By playing the wheel carefully, he could hold the bearing of the Bill steady. If he could maintain this course, they would miss it by a hair's breadth.

'We might make it yet, Philip. Look!' he called. 'I'm holding a steady bearing just off the Bill. Our current track will take us clear.' Jack pointed, beckoning Goddard to confirm it with him.

It took a moment for the two men to be sure, their gazes meanwhile locked unblinkingly upon the jagged point which now rushed at them from no more than five-hundred yards ahead. But it was true.

'Yes, by God, you're right,' Goddard said, curiously downbeat. 'But a lot of good it'll do us; look at those white caps on the Race. The rig will never take it!

'Wait!' Jack shouted urgently. 'Have you any idea what we draw?'

'A good ten to fifteen feet,' Goddard replied despondently. 'Just look at the way the land falls, there can't be enough depth………'

'I know these waters, Philip!' Jack interrupted sharply. 'Trust me! There's an inside channel which'll take us between the Bill and the Race, but we'll have to swing her around within fifty yards of the point. Get your men ready to swing the sails! First we'll run, then we'll quickly come onto the opposite tack. It'll be critical. If we miss the entry point, we'll be swept into the Race and that will be the end of us!'

Within less than a minute, the brig's path had converged to about one hundred and fifty yards of the craggy shoreline. By this point in their southerly course, the towering height of the cliffs had declined, and from the deck, Jack could already see their grassy tops. It seemed unreal; he recognised those fields! He was almost close enough to jump ashore, and yet he knew that he would be swept away mercilessly if he tried - *so near and yet so far*! The gap closed rapidly and *L'hermine* accelerated with the current as it entered its slingshot course around the Bill; the little craft was now being swept at terrifying speed.

'Ready?' Jack shouted to Goddard and his crew, now poised anxiously on the braces and already taking the strain. 'We'll jibe onto the larboard tack as soon as we're abeam the point – with luck, the current should do the rest!' he cried, his voice almost lost against the thundering roar of the approaching surf.

The moment approached. Jack swung the wheel hard to larboard, anticipating the turn by half a cable.

'Helm-a-lee! Yards a-beam!' he shouted at the top of his voice, and Goddard's men bent their backs on the trimming lines and pulled with all their strength - and in absolutely no doubt that their lives depended upon it.

The helm was slower to respond than Jack expected. Swept along by the strong current, the craft's relative wind and thus the sails' driving power had decreased dramatically, steerageway reducing as a consequence. But eventually, at full larboard wheel, the rudder seemed to bite and the craft began to turn. *L'hermine* was now being pressed sideways, her curving course around the Bill leading the heading of her bow by as much as thirty degrees of drift. Jack could hear the ominous crashing of stone upon rock as the mighty torrent hurled loosened shingle against the sub-marine ledges below his feet. He held the wheel hard over, frustrated by the slowness of her turn. The sea became a maelstrom of ferocious vortices as the racing tidal flow squeezing past the promontory collided with the step-like layers of shoaling ground beneath the waves. The ship slewed and bucked in the whirling brew. She was a projectile now, almost completely at the mercy of the sea.

'Jibe-Ohhhhh..!' Jack shouted as he felt the wind direction swing across the stern with the ship's continuingly ponderous turn. 'Fores'ls and yards onto the larboard tack as quickly as you can, Philip!' he shouted as the spanker boom slammed across above his head so violently at the point of jibe that it almost ripped itself off the mast; Jack ducked instinctively as it passed. Goddard responded quickly to Jack's call, dispatching two men forward to reset the foresails for their new course, and simultaneously took their place in the line of men already heaving on the main yard tackle.

The roar of the waves crashing upon the fast approaching rocks became deafening as Jack coaxed the vessel through the neck, the rocks to his left the Race to his right, spinning the wheel first one way then the other as he fought against the swirling currents. He felt the hairs on the back of his neck stand on end, expecting at any second to feel the first judder of impact on the keel as the ship surged under his feet. The blackened rocks of the Bill were now only yards away from the larboard rail; Jack could hardly bear to look at them as they hurtled past.

But no impact came, and after a few seconds more, as *L'hermine's* slow turn continued onto a north easterly heading, she suddenly broke free of the current's grip.   There was a rustle of sailcloth overhead as the sails shook themselves into shape on the new tack, and Jack felt *L'hermine* lean to starboard with the wind as she began to claw herself into the clear smooth water in the Bill's lee.   And the panic was over.   The craggy coastline was still ominously close - literally a stone's throw off their larboard side and slipping by at speed as *L'hermine* was taken by the less vicious north-running current - but they were through.   Jack had steered the craft through the eye of a needle; he had navigated the narrow passage between the rocks on one side and watery oblivion on the other.

And as the speed of *L'hermine* slowed and the roar of the Race diminished in their ears as they left it behind in their wake, a curiously hollow feeling descended on the crew.   There was no celebration, no throwing of caps into the air; it was if they had been cheated of the necessary climax; deprived of some final and decisive act of triumph needed for elation to kick in.   The victory had been so narrowly won that it had left them all rather in a state of shocked disbelief that it had been won at all.   Their reaction was unspoken; it was an intense and private relief that left them reflecting quietly on the stealth with which unseen perils creep up and threaten those at sea.

Goddard stood quietly at the larboard rail staring thoughtfully at the shore; he turned, and for a moment he and Jack exchanged relieved and acknowledging glances in mutual regard.   For Jack, still standing at the wheel, his hands still locked in a fierce grip upon its spokes, it took some minutes more before the involuntary tremor in his legs and the tingling of his flesh subsided.   It was not the excitement of exhilaration that he felt, but more a sense of profound gratitude that he had survived.   He knew how close he had come to death, so nearly thrown into a wild sea amongst the splinters of a ship that had so nearly foundered.   Of all deaths he feared, it was the fear of drowning which haunted him most; and this time the spectre had been so slow in the unfolding that the terror had sprung upon him only at the end, even as he had sailed the ship free. *My stock of good luck's being spent too fast!* he thought, grimly. *Surely it can't last?*

Several more minutes passed thus in quiet introspection as men slowly resumed their tasks before it suddenly dawned upon Jack that he must very soon depart, for there, just a few miles ahead was Church Ope Cove. With a few crisp words of instruction, he quickly handed over the wheel to a nearby crewman and slipped below, and a few minutes later he had returned with his bag to join Goddard on the quarterdeck just as the ship's boat was being swung out on its davits.

'Ah, Jack, I see that you are ready; good, we have very little time. I will have one of the men run you ashore shortly,' he said. 'I shall shorten sail but do not intend to anchor, and so the boatman will have no time to dally if he is to catch me after dropping you.'

'Thank you, Philip, I shall not keep him longer than necessary to prevent my feet from getting wet, I assure you!' Jack replied with a chuckle.

Goddard smiled, then suddenly became serious as he offered his hand. 'I shall remember how you have helped me, Jack, and also what you have done for us today,' he said. 'And I believe that I shall be a better man for knowing you. It'll certainly be a relief to put this regrettable business with Judd behind me.'

Jack took his hand and shook it warmly. 'If my letter to the Cowes' agent has its effect, Judd will get his just deserts. But remember, Philip, when you rejoin the ship, leave everything to the agent; you must act as if nothing has changed.'

'Yes, I understand. And thank you. Captain Auld told me of your situation and what you hope to achieve here in Portland, and I wish you well. If I had had your courage, I would not have got myself into this mess in the first place. I shall endeavour to live up to your example in the future.'

'We've travelled different journeys, Philip, but our paths have converged along the way, and I think that we now know each other and ourselves better for it,' Jack said with an appraising smile. 'And from this new starting point, may God take us both where we deserve to go - I believe that we've both earned a fair wind, don't you?'

'Well said; I do indeed. Perhaps we shall sail together in less trying circumstances one day,' said Goddard, breaking into a smile.

'I shall look out for your sails in the Potomac. But I have a final request to make: would you take this letter back to Charlestown for me when you return, and ask Harding to see that it gets to my wife? It is hastily written, but it will relieve her to know that I have at least arrived at my intended destination.'

Chapter Twenty Four

Wakeham

From the window of her bedroom, Eleanor Easton had a fine view of the sea over Church Ope Cove. Her arthritis was always worse during winter, and in the debilitated state into which she had allowed herself to descend since the death of her husband, she spent much time sitting at the window gazing out. This morning followed the pattern that she often adopted when there were no pressing household duties to attend to, and she had seated herself there to receive her breakfast. Her companion, Mrs Edith Holmes, a plain and mousy little lady thrown onto her uppers by the sudden departure of a philandering husband, had just entered the room behind her carrying it on a tray, when a strange-looking vessel hove into view at the entrance to the Cove. It was oddly proportioned, Eleanor thought – its masts seemed stunted and misaligned - and then she noticed that a little sailing boat trailed in its wake. She watched the boat cast off and turn towards the Cove to head in while the ship glided onwards at a sedate pace. The boat moved swiftly inwards, and soon it was close enough to see the forms of the two men sitting in it. Such craft were not unusual in these waters, but something about this scene caused her to sit up and look more closely; some element within it was tantalisingly familiar yet she could not identify what it was. Strangely, the picture evoked fond memories of her young Jack sailing there long ago as a boy; and the thought of him caused a pang of sweet sorrow to brush her heart like the soft caress of the curtain caught by the breeze - a gentle wistful memory of a favourite son. She gazed on as the boat come closer, leaning forwards in her chair - eventually lifting herself up to maintain the boat in sight, until it was lost behind the cliff edge shielding the beach from her view. For a moment or two longer, she hovered at the windowpane gazing out to sea; the oddly-shaped vessel had passed out of sight and the view from her window was empty again - but the memory of her son lingered on. Where moments before she had been in her usual melancholy state, she now felt a curious, almost electrifying sense of unease. Nothing within her comprehension had alerted her, but her subconscious mind had triggered some alchemy in her veins, throwing her into such confusion that, even after it subsided, she was left wondering what in heaven's name had happened to bring her to such a state.

Sloughing off the mood crossly, Eleanor turned stiffly from the window to find her companion still standing uncertainly at the door with the tray in her hands.

'Edith, why on earth are you waiting?' she snapped.

'I saw you watching that boat, Eleanor,' Edith replied, appearing somewhat taken aback at the brusqueness of her companion's attitude. 'I thought...'

'It was nothing,' the old woman said testily. 'Bring me my tray, I'm hungry.'

The little boat's keel grounded on the shingle beach and Jack jumped ashore, immediately turning to grab hold of the prow and push the craft back through the surf into deeper water. He watched it turn and sail away on a direct interception course towards the *Rebecca* now drifting under shortened sail; he guessed Goddard would be watching through his eye-glass and so gave a wave before turning to clamber up the stony beach towards the cliff path.

'There'll be no parties for my homecoming,' he thought ruefully, as he climbed the familiar winding route towards St Andrew's church whose gothic windows looked down on him kindly like an old indulgent guardian signalling him to pass. He remembered the last occasion he had descended from its parapet on that fateful night so many years ago. The intervening time had taken its toll on the crumbling stone walls that now lay in the grip of encroaching ivy, and when at last he reached the ledge on which it so precariously perched, he crossed to the wall to look down into the Cove. In a melancholy turn of nostalgia, he chose to stand at exactly the same spot that he had last stood with his father. The memories of that night and its terrible aftermath were suddenly so vivid that they could have happened yesterday, and he was seized with grief that welled up so palpably that he almost choked upon it, clasping his mouth to stifle his muted cry as his eyes filled with tears. He pictured his father sitting astride the wall, taking out his time piece and telling him gruffly to be on his way; he remembered the old man's parting words and their final embrace - and his heart ached to claw back the years and have that moment again - just one more time, *just one more time*. But this time he would not go down to the boats, and therefore he would not be captured, or wrongly convicted of murder and sent to America, and he would not lose Elizabeth and his unborn child. Instead he would remain behind with his father and he would be with him still, and everything would be all right again. Everything would be as it should be.

Wouldn't it?

But even as he let his mind be taken by the fantasy, he knew that it would never be thus. It would never be all right again; what was done was done; the vessel of his life had hit the rocks and he must keep patching up the damage in order to remain afloat, or else ground again and never be able to move on. And so he let his wistful gaze drift around the horizon as he brought himself back to the reality of his homecoming and the mission he had set for himself, and let out a long lamenting sigh.

The little sailing craft had now rejoined the *Rebecca,* and Jack remained at the wall watching her sails unfurled again as she was turned to head for the Solent. The Isle of Wight was just visible as a grey smudge on the eastern horizon beyond the bluff cliffs of St Aldhelm's Head. 'She'll be in Spithead before sunset,' he thought, and turned to move on, scanning the wooded valley of his route up to the village for signs of anyone about. The trees were bare, and so the path was visible all the way up to the village edge; he could see some of the lower cottages between their thin trunks and branches. Bluish smoke issued from their chimneys and caught the breeze as it rose above the cover of the higher ground behind, wafting down towards him as it thinned; the smell of wood smoke was never so evocative of his youth. He saw no one, but pulled his sailor's cap over his brow and put his collar up, before realising that his beard and whiskers were all the disguise he would need against casual observation. Even his friends would have trouble recognising him without a second glance.

Jack bounded up the steep path from the churchyard and entered the familiar village lane, where he paused to catch his breath and savour for a moment the mixed emotions of his homecoming. Directly in front of him, his mother's cottage was the nearest of several similar stone cottages standing in a line. Nothing had changed in the narrow rutted thoroughfare - it was as if he had never been away, but was returning instead from some fishing trip of short duration. Jack looked up to the main bedroom window of the home in which he had spent his childhood, half expecting to see his father standing there waiting for him like so often in his rebellious boyhood when he had come home late. The windowpanes reflected the bright sky and so he could not see inside, but his mind conjured the clouds' passing shapes into his father's form and, for an instant, he imagined him clearly. In his mind's eye, he looked upon his face as he had done in the days of his youth, seeing his father as a younger man, his hair dark not grey. He wanted to race inside to embrace him just as he should have done then – but his mind too quickly intervened to remind him that it was far too late.

A muted crash of breaking china and a clatter of cutlery somewhere near at hand, brought him quickly to his senses. He rushed into the cover of his mother's front porch, a solid stone arch erected to shield her door from the Portland winds. Hidden now from any onlooker further up the lane, he tried the latch and found it unlocked, but as he slowly pushed the door ajar, he heard an excited cry and the sound of footsteps running down the wooden stairs inside. The door was pulled out of his hand as he stood there dumbfounded on the threshold and, before he realised what was happening, he found himself wrapped tightly in his mother's arms.

'My boy, my boy, my boy!' she sobbed into the nape of his neck, repeating it again and again, tears flooding down her face. 'I knew that you would come.'

For several days, Jack spent much time resting himself in the quiet privacy of his old bedroom, preserved as at the time of his departure by a mother unwilling to let her son's memory fade. He retired early and woke late and took naps during the day, his sleeping sometimes curtailed by his mother's too attentive peeping around the door. He had heard her careful lifting of the latch and the soft slow creaking of the hinge, but had lately pretended to be asleep when she looked in. Jack had already spent many hours with her, locked in long and often tortured conversations that had already given him enough to think about, and for the moment he did not want any more. Much as he loved his mother, she had a terrible habit of going over the same ground again and again, which even understanding her need to mourn her loss, was becoming quite trying. Instead, he allowed himself a little longer each day in that luxurious state of dreamy comfort that preceded full wakefulness, while his bed heaved gently under him in some imagined swell.

On the morning of the third day he awoke with the dawn at last fully refreshed, and propped himself upon the bedstead while he considered his next moves. As far as he knew, his arrival had remained a secret on the island; only his mother and her companion were privy to the information, and the latter had been dispatched quickly to stay with a distant relative to get her out of the way. He had thus had the peace and quiet he needed to consider a few possible schemes by which he might achieve his objectives. But his mother's reports of his brother's precarious financial state had become somewhat of a distraction to his planning. This had inhibited him greatly, especially since his mother's home was at risk if the bank foreclosed, for he could not in all conscience proceed with any scheme to bring Smyke to justice with this concern unresolved in his mind. While he was at a loss as to what might be done to extricate Luke from the apparent mess he had got himself into, he resolved that he must see his brother without further delay. It sounded as if they needed each other's help – and urgently!

Luke called at the house later at the request of his mother on the pretence of some errand she wished him to perform; and she said nothing by way of explanation as she led him into the parlour to find Jack waiting there. At first, Luke showed no sign of recognition. He had certainly not expected to see his brother and he was no doubt put off by his brother's beard and long hair. A wrinkle of puzzlement passed fleetingly across Luke's face as he recognised the waistcoat and jacket that Jack now wore. They had belonged to his father. Luke turned to his mother uncertainly, expecting an introduction, but instead she simply stood there smiling, her delighted and expectant gaze switching alternately between the two men. Luke frowned, bewildered, the more so because of his mother's surprisingly buoyant mood; she looked as if the prodigal son had returned, (which, as yet unknown to him, he had of course). Smiling uncertainly out of politeness, Luke studied the stranger more closely, but was none the wiser until Jack's face broke into a grin. Luke remained baffled only for an instant longer before a startled look flashed into his eyes as recognition dawned, and the two men burst out laughing simultaneously.

'Jack, it's you!' Luke yelled through his mirth as he leapt towards his brother and took him in his arms.

The joyful reunion of the two brothers was shared by their mother, and for a time the mood in the parlour remained bubbling and full of happy banter, made happier yet with the news of Jack's marriage to Rose and of their expectation of a child. In response, Luke was delighted to tell his brother of his marriage to Mary in terms that took Jack quite by surprise by their tenderness. He found himself both incredulous and impressed at the same time to see his previously wayward and headstrong brother so miraculously transformed, and was fulsome in his congratulations for a younger brother apparently grown to maturity during the years of his absence. Luke's curiosity then got the better of him in his impatience to hear of Jack's adventures, bombarding his brother with questions, and chattering on excitedly almost as if intoxicated. But conversation became more strained as he clumsily trespassed onto the more sombre ground of Elizabeth's death and of their father's suicide. On both subjects, Jack prevaricated, heading his brother off those still delicate subjects sharply with a warning glance. He found himself unable yet to speak openly of Elizabeth without choking on his words, and he knew from his experience over the last few days that his mother equally would clam up at the mention of her husband's tragic death. Indeed, it had seemed to Jack that she had thrown a veil over the event as her way of inuring herself from the obvious pain it had caused. Fortunately, Luke took the hint and checked himself; and predictably, Eleanor broke the short but uncomfortable silence that ensued by changing the subject.

'And the Dales, Jack?' she said, as if the thought of them had suddenly entered her mind. 'They will not yet know that we are now in-laws after all – surely you will have to see them soon? They'll be desperate for news about Rose.'

Jack caught his brother's eye knowingly, but responded calmly. 'I can't risk it yet, mother, much as I would like to see them. I must wait until it is safe for me to do so - I can't afford yet for word to get around that I am back.'

Luke planned to visit again during the afternoon and Jack decided to take the opportunity to talk business with his brother whilst their mother was out of the house renewing her acquaintance with a long neglected friend. But when Luke ducked through the front door, his manner was hesitant and in such contrast to his earlier ebullience that it was clear that something was on his mind.

'Jack, I've been thinking back to the time of ...of your capture, and..,' he faltered, dropping his glance to the floor as he fumbled with his cap. 'I wondered if you blamed me?' he asked rather meekly. 'For Elizabeth's death, I mean?' he said glumly. 'If I hadn't bragged about our run and agreed to her coming that night...'

Jack cut in swiftly, 'Luke, I don't blame you for anything,' he said, surprised. 'It's Smyke I blame for all of this! You mustn't blame yourself; and that's the last we shall speak of it!' Jack gave his brother a reassuring pat to his arm at which Luke perked up a little. 'Thank you, Jack,' he said, smiling lamely, 'but I do blame myself, and I'm sorry. I don't know what you've got in mind, but if I can help in any way...?'

'Well, first, you'd better bring me up to date on your troubles at the quarry.' Jack led his brother by the arm into the parlour and gestured for him to sit beside him on the high-backed wooden settle adjacent to the window which overlooked a stone-walled courtyard in which washing could be seen hanging out to dry.

'Mother has given me the background as far as she knows it, but I need to hear it from you.'

Luke held nothing back about the dire situation in which he now found himself, wringing his hands as he spoke with anxiety and self-recrimination. He told Jack too of his suspicions that the banker, Chorley, might be in collusion with Isaac Grant to acquire the quarry and that half of Luke's men had already gone to him on promise of work and better wages. While just enough money was now coming in from some small contracts to keep the business afloat from day to day, he said, it was not enough to pay off the loan when it became due, and the back-pay for his men for earlier work was still outstanding. Luke told his brother of his wife's new role as business manager bidding for new contracts, while his was now to concentrate on making operations in the quarry more efficient. He was hopeful that they would win a large contract in Exeter, but even if they won it, he said, he doubted that they would get enough payment in advance to pay off the loan in full. For the moment, therefore, they lived on hope and prayers with goodwill strained and time running out.

'How much do you need?' Jack asked, resisting sympathy and cutting quickly to the core of the problem. He knew his brother was never suited to the subtleties of business, but at least he had not sought to excuse himself from blame.

'That's the problem, Jack. One thousand pounds!' Luke said, his tone already helpless.

Jack thought of *L'hermine* and his part of the prize money. If Auld were true to his word, Jack might expect to receive a sum that might approach this amount, but, even so, it was unlikely to reach him within the time that Luke had indicated.

'A tidy sum!' Jack said at last, pursing his lips.

'And as mother will likely have already told you, Jack, both our houses are included as security for the loan. We could lose everything if I can't pay it off.'

Jack began to realise that within the time that he had allowed himself to attend to Smyke and his crimes, he would also have to try to find a solution to his brother's problems for he could not return to Maryland leaving the situation as it was. At the same time he did not want to renege on his promise to Rose to be back before their baby was born. With seven weeks already gone since leaving New Hope and allowing a similar time for his return journey, only two months or so remained before he must depart; 'it'll just have to be enough!' he thought.

'Still involved in free trading, Luke?' Jack asked.

'I took over from father when he became ill. We don't do much now and it's a smaller gang, but we bring in a few hauls each year.'

'D'you still work with Captain Pritchett and the *Alice* out of Alderney?'

Luke nodded. 'Yes, but it's relatively small beer. I haven't got the cash to risk making bigger hauls. And with the costs of buying the stuff up front, and everyone getting their share of the profit at the end, each run doesn't clear more than a hundred pounds.'

Jack considered for a moment, the beginnings of a plan coalescing in his mind from the different possibilities he had already considered as ways of ensnaring Smyke.

'I'd like to meet Pritchett in secret as soon as possible, Luke. Can you arrange it?' he asked. 'I think that I might have a scheme that could attend to both our problems at one and the same time if we can pull it off.'

The next meeting with Luke took place late the following morning in Jack's bedroom to give the pair some privacy. From now on, Jack wanted his mother to have no part in the discussions; 'the less she knows the better, for her own sake,' he thought. He had rearranged the furniture in his room to place the table near to the window, and he and Luke now sat at it as the sunshine beamed in. Since their last meeting, he had had time to put more flesh on the bone of his plan of action, the different parts of which were still bound together with a fair amount of wishful thinking. He had decided to use a smuggling run as the bait with which to draw Smyke unwittingly into Jack's domain where Jack could set the rules; just as Smyke had set the agenda seven years ago. But to pull off the plan he now conceived, he would need help, not only from those like Pritchett whom he trusted, but also from others whose help or discretion could not be so easily guaranteed.

Luke greeted his brother and seated himself at the table, sounding pleased with himself as he announced:

'I've already been down to the harbour this morning Jack, and have sent word to Alderney in the usual way. Pritchett normally responds quickly and he should anyway be here by the end of the week on his regular run, weather permitting – it's only a ten or twelve hour trip as you know.'

'Good. Now, tell me everything you know about Smyke.'

Luke related developments at the Customs Office since the deaths of Middleton and Hayes. After their funerals, Smyke had been given acting rank to take over Middleton's role temporarily, but the commissioners had made his rank substantive two years later and had simultaneously made his appointment permanent. Luke surmised that this was probably because of the absence of applicants brave enough to challenge Smyke's position.

'Apart from that, things seem to have continued much as before Middleton's time,' he said. 'And the demand for goods is stronger now than ever, with taxes on imports higher than they've ever been,'

'And yet you keep your operations modest?' posed Jack. 'Why not just increase your activity to increase your take?'

'I dare not risk it, Jack. The Revenue keeps a cutter based in Weymouth now and you never know when they'll come sniffing about. We're right on their doorstep, and we've too much to lose if we get caught. You at least should appreciate that!' Luke said meaningfully. 'I recall that you weren't too keen on the game, either!'

'What's his intelligence like?' said Jack, ignoring the remark.

'Seems to be quite good between here and St Aldhelm's. If we planned anything big, he'd certainly get to know about it,' Luke lamented. 'And yet in Lyme Bay the Chesil gang don't seem to have any trouble with him at all. Word amongst the other gangs is that Smyke has his sticky fingers in the Chesil pie and he protects them; but it's only a rumour and the likes of us can't very well accuse him, can we?'

'I wouldn't put anything past him, Luke; he's a nasty piece of work,' said Jack. 'Somehow we've got to put all that to our advantage - and for that we'll need someone on the inside. We need to catch him in the act to make it stick and to expose him for what he is. D'you know anyone in the Service who might help us?'

'Why yes, actually,' Luke responded brightly. 'Mary's brother-in-law, Edward Mawdsley, is a tide-surveyor in Weymouth - that's where Smyke has his office.'

'D'you think that he'd be willing to listen to what I have to say?'

Luke looked doubtful. 'We'd need to take Mary and her sister Anna into our confidence, Jack,' he said cautiously. 'We'd have to communicate through them initially. With my connection to you, he seems a bit wary of me, and we might need Anna to twist his arm. He doesn't know I'm in the game either, so I'd be a bit wary of him too.'

Jack gazed through the window at the sea, losing himself for a moment in thought as he considered his options. His risk of exposure would undoubtedly increase with the number of people knowing of his presence, he thought, especially if they were officials; but on the other hand it would be impossible to make progress without help. Nor was it in his nature to dither on the remote off chance of a better option. 'Better a bird in the hand...' he thought. Anyway, at present he seemed to have little choice - if he wanted to get closer to Smyke, this sounded like the best chance he'd get.

'Then I think it's time that you brought your good wife to see me!' he said at last.

Jack had met Mary before, though he scarcely remembered her from their brief encounter seven or more years ago. At that time, she had been merely a young girl he had seen attached to Luke's arm from time to time and he had not taken much notice of her. But when she walked into his room later that day accompanied by her husband, Jack was struck by her presence; she had grown tall and confident, and her bright eyes, sparkling with reflections from the window, engaged him straight away. She smiled a greeting, stooping slightly to remove her bonnet whose feathery attachment brushed the ceiling. Her fair hair was swept up and back behind her head to fall as a clump of lustrous loose ringlets held together with a bow of crimson silk which she had put on especially to meet her brother-in-law. She reminded Jack of his mother as a younger woman.

It was clear from the beginning that Mary was eager to help, especially since one of Jack's objectives was to try to find a way of helping the quarry out of its troubles. Mary agreed without hesitation to act as a discrete broker in making the connection through her sister to her brother-in-law to establish the possibility of a confidential meeting between the men; indeed, she seemed intrigued and excited to play a part in the unfolding drama. It was agreed that she was to say merely that a contact of Luke's had information that would be of assistance to the Customs Service and to say nothing more; and she would certainly not mention Jack by name or reputation.

Chapter Twenty Five

Things began to move quickly after the meeting with Mary. With her sister's ready collusion as intermediary, Mary established that Edward would not be at all averse to a meeting, and she had therefore taken the bull by its horns and set it up in the knowledge that for Jack time was of the essence. She had thus arranged for the meeting to take place two evenings hence on neutral ground, about half way between their two residences, at the inn at Smallmouth, a small hamlet sitting on the Wyke side of the ferry crossing to the mainland.

Jack would make this first outing in the company of his brother to affect the introduction; and thus, as darkness fell on the appointed evening, the pair slipped out of the house to make their way to the rendezvous. Nervous of being seen in the streets, their chosen route was through the quarry and the wears, initially following the winding pathways along the eastern shoreline then crossing the common land to reach the causeway. It was familiar ground to both brothers, but it took them over an hour to reach their destination, their progress being slowed by the difficult terrain and the relative darkness of a new moon. The causeway was also shrouded in drifting sea mist as they walked its length towards the ferry, a mist so dense that it would hide them from the view of any passer by. But by the time they reached the ferry, the damp air had chilled them to the bone. Fortunately, the boatman came quickly to their urgent ringing of the calling bell, no doubt eager for his penny fare, and some minutes later they entered the inn, grateful for the warmth.

Finding themselves the first to arrive, they chose a table from which they could observe the door. Candles and oil-lamps of varying intensity lit the parlour, and the room had the cool and tidy expectancy of an early evening, with the blaze of the newly lit fire not yet died back to embers. Jack ruffled his beard and encouraged his hair into unruliness to cover the greater part of his face; in the dim light he looked surly under his seaman's cap, and to a casual observer he would have appeared like any of the many disgruntled seamen around the bay that night whose shore leave was about to expire.

The door latch lifted with a loud clack and the door was swung inside; a head appeared rather tentatively at its edge a moment later. Luke recognised it immediately as Mawdsley's even in the dim light, and with an impatient wave, he called the young officer over. Rather stiff handshakes were then exchanged, with Luke introducing Jack simply as a 'friend'. Mawdsley seemed somewhat wary at first, taking Jack's hand as if frightened that it might bite; and his fresh-face, bright-blue eyes and fair tousled hair, lent him a boyishness that his awkwardness did nothing to dispel. But he had complied with the instructions earlier relayed to him through his wife to wear nothing that would label him as an official of the customs service, and there was certainly no deviousness in his manner.

A rotund landlord arrived at the table carrying a large jug of ale and poured the frothy liquid into three pewter tankards he had placed presumptively upon the table. It seemed that there was a certain expectation on his part that ale would be required, but none of the three men objected. Luke settled the bill and the landlord departed. And there then followed a short period of uncertainty, during which neither brother seemed quite sure how the conversation might be started. Luke cleared his throat and began:

'Edward, my friend here thinks that he may have some, er, some important information that, er..' Luke was making a faltering start so Jack cut in quickly, silencing his brother with a sharp look.

'Perhaps I should bring us to the point,' he said, leaning forward and pitching his voice low. 'It is possible that your Captain Smyke is protecting one of the smuggling gangs and lining his pockets with a cut of their profits. Would that surprise you?'

Mawdsley tightened of his lips and took a sideways glance at his brother-in-law as Jack continued:

'And you will no doubt know of Luke's brother's conviction for the murders of two of your officers in Portland some years ago for which he was transported.'

Mawdsley nodded slowly. 'Yes, I do know of it,' he replied cautiously. 'The story is that he killed both of them trying to evade capture.'

'Well, I have a witness who would swear that it was not Jack Easton who was the killer but Smyke, and I am looking for an honest officer who would help bring him to justice. Luke thinks that you might be that man,' Jack said, flatly. But in examining the immature features of the young man who stared so guardedly back at him across the table, Jack was now not quite so sure.

Mawdsley swallowed silently, seeming to study Jack's shadowy features carefully for a moment. He took a mouthful from his tankard and placed the vessel back upon the table with slow deliberation, then let out a sort of toneless whistle as if taking time to think.

'I'm new in the Service,' he said slowly, 'but I have heard and seen things which have given me cause to believe that there is something underhand going on. And I am not alone in that. There may be something in what you say, and you see from my reaction, sir, that I have not rejected it. But Captain Smyke is an intimidating man who has gathered around him officers who are as fearsome as he. There is an inner circle from which all us junior officers are most definitely excluded, and I don't think that I could penetrate it to get any closer to the truth. I'm certain that I'd put myself in danger if I tried.'

Jack was pleased not to have received an angry rebuttal, but the young officer's suspicions would not be enough. Mawdsley took another mouthful of ale while Jack and Luke exchanged uncertain glances. But then the young officer leant forward and spoke again:

'There is one officer I might trust,' he said thoughtfully. 'He's one of our more senior officers, a Lieutenant White; I've watched him in the company of Captain Smyke, and I don't believe that he is entirely well disposed towards him. He's certainly not one of his cronies. I could try to arrange a meeting?' he suggested, sounding unsure yet watching for his listeners' response. Seeing Jack nod, he continued more boldly:

'I would not tell him of your suspicions in case I have misjudged him and he links me to them; I'd have to say simply that I have a contact who has some information on a smuggling run, and that he - you that is - will speak to him and no one else. You'd have to feel your way once you had him before you. But for heaven's sake be careful; we could all be for it if he *is* loyal to the captain.'

Jack considered for a moment; Mawdsley was wiser than he looked.

'Then do it,' he said quietly.

Word came of the proposed meeting with Lieutenant White two days later through Anna who visited her sister in Wakeham especially to convey it. The meeting would take place at the same inn in Smallmouth the following evening, but Jack decided that on this occasion he would go alone, not wanting to endanger his brother in any way. And he would take his pistols with him.

Jack arrived an hour earlier at the rendezvous than arranged, and as a precaution against entrapment, he concealed himself in the shadows of a nearby outbuilding to await White's arrival. In due course, two cloaked figures, one of them unmistakably Edward Mawdsley carrying a lantern, emerged from the direction of Wyke and entered the inn. Jack had watched their arrival to ensure that no one followed; and after a few minutes of further careful observation, he followed them inside.

As he closed the door behind him, Jack saw that the officers had seated themselves and that the presumptive landlord was already pouring them their first draught of ale. The man's large back partially obscured Jack's sight of the pair and so he hovered uncertainly until his view cleared. Jack was alert and apprehensive, and while he waited, he scanned the room nervously checking for other exits in case he should need them in a hurry. The candles had flickered in the draught of his entry, throwing the shadows in the room into turmoil for a moment, but they had now settled. A log fire smouldered in a wide inglenook and wisps of lazy smoke rose from a large heap of ashes and embers that had spread themselves untidily across the hearth. Apart from the door through which he had entered, there was one other possible way out. Behind a rectangular table on which a pile of dirty plates and tankards had been stacked, there was an opening that led off apparently into some sort of scullery. Light flickered in the doorway with the shadows of someone moving about inside, but this seemed of no importance - probably a helper in the kitchen, thought Jack. There was one other opening - a shuttered window behind the table at which the two men sat, but it offered no easy way out. If this were a trap, Jack thought, he would find himself hard pressed to escape.

Eventually the landlord moved away from the table and lumbered back towards his scullery, flicking an enquiring glance at Jack as he passed. By way of answering, Jack pointed at the seated men, and with a nod of understanding, the man continued by. Jack's line of sight was now unobstructed and for the first time he could see young Mawdsley's companion. As he saw the officer's features, he froze.

The name of Lieutenant White had meant nothing to him when Mawdsley had mentioned it two evenings before, but now Jack recognised the man as the officer who had sat so prominently in the gallery at his trial. He had filled out somewhat since then and looked more at ease with himself; a mature and confident individual, Jack thought, rather than the lanky subaltern he had been at that time. But there was no mistaking him. Jack's first instinct was therefore to retreat, not confident that his beard and unkempt hair would be sufficient disguise; and he turned for the door, not wanting to press his luck. But at that moment Mawdsley called out:

'You there at the door! Wait!'

Simultaneously, the door latch lifted and a crowd of uniformed men pushed in, sending a shock of alarm through Jack's strained nerves as he was forced back into the room, his hand still outstretched in the act of reaching for the handle. His heart raced as he thought of making a dash for the other door, but Mawdsley called again, this time, standing at his table:

'You at the door! We're over here. Come on over!'

Mawdsley's strangely incongruent call came at just the same moment that Jack saw that the incomers wore sailors' garb and not the Customs uniforms that he had first thought, and he realised at once that this was not the trap that he had feared. And with his way blocked by the high-spirited crowd, Jack realized that he would have no option but to brazen it out.

'This is the man, sir,' Mawdsley said quietly, as Jack approached the table, but the two officers remained seated and no courtesies were offered. With a cursory flick of White's hand, Jack was invited to take a seat, but his expression revealed disdain rather than politeness.

'Tell me what you've got to say and be done with it,' White said dismissively, his expression inscrutable.

Jack took a deep breath, knowing that the imminent conversation might become one of the defining moments of his entire expedition and that he must therefore choose his words carefully.

'Your young colleague will have told you to expect some information about a smuggling run,' Jack started, with his heart in his mouth. 'But I have something more important to talk about concerning your commanding officer. Are you prepared to listen to what I have to say?' he asked, coming straight to the point.

White brought his elbows onto the table, clasped his hands under his chin, and threw a calm glance around the room as if to confirm that no one could overhear.

'Who are you, and what do you know?' White's reply was measured.

'I knew Captain Middleton. I tried to help him once,' said Jack mysteriously, assessing White's reaction to gauge how far he could go without revealing himself too soon.

The lieutenant blinked, but his expression remained unchanged. 'Tell me how the likes of you could have been of any assistance to a gentleman such as he?' He paused, then frowned. 'Were you his informer? That I could believe!'

Jack said nothing, but instead held his interrogator's steady gaze for some moments before replying:

'I know how he died - and the young officer with him,' he said, eventually.

White's eyes narrowed. 'Go on,' he said calmly.

This is it! Jack thought, knowing that the words that he was about to speak would lead White inevitably to realise who he was speaking to. And if he had misjudged the lieutenant, Jack would need to be ready for a hostile reaction. His right hand strayed to the pocket of his coat where his fingers found the pistol waiting there. He wrapped his hand around its stock and carefully pulled back the cocking arm; the feel of it gave him comfort.

'Your captain was pushed to his death over the cliff above Church Ope Cove and a young officer was shot in cold blood. A petty smuggler by the name of Jack Easton was accused of those crimes and was exiled as you know, but it was Smyke not he who committed the acts.'

'How could you know this, there were no witnesses,' White reacted with derision.

'There *was* indeed an eye-witness who saw the whole event,' said Jack quickly, stilling his interrogator's evident disdain.

'Then why did he not come forward at the trial?'

'He did,' said Jack, leaving his statement hanging in the air.

'Easton, you mean?' White looked puzzled. 'His evidence was not believed. Captain Smyke convinced the jury otherwise.'

'Did he convince you?' asked Jack quietly.

White did not answer.

'Were you there that night?' continued Jack.

Again, White did not answer. Instead he stared intensely into Jack's face, his eyes suddenly alive.

'Smyke had two pistols in his belt when he set out that evening, didn't he?' Jack pressed.

White remained passive, but Jack could see that his eyes remained fully alert as he continued:

'He said that one of them had been taken from his belt by his attacker and used to shoot Hayes - and that Hayes had fired his own weapon against Easton as he fell.'

Jack was recapping for White's benefit but as he did so, his mind was taken back to that moment on the cliff when Smyke's second shot had been directed at him even as the echoes of his first still reverberated from the cliffs. The picture was suddenly vivid in his mind: when Smyke had raised his second weapon the first was still held firmly in his other hand. The blinding flash and searing pain had come an instant later as Smyke had fired, but the image of him standing with both weapons in his hands as he had taken aim was clear.

White still said nothing, but a furrow had begun to crease his forehead. Jack knew he might be on to something but did not quite know what; something prodded at his memory but it was still just out of reach. But then suddenly it was obvious what Smyke must have done to cover his tracks. He wondered why he had not thought of it before.

Jack spoke with more urgency now: 'At the trial, Smyke said that he observed both killings from the ground because he'd been beaten up so badly, and that he therefore didn't use his second weapon. Yes?'

White nodded. Jack continued:

'But according to Easton, it was Smyke not Hayes who shot him. If Easton was telling the truth, the unspent pistol in Smyke's belt must have belonged to Hayes. Did anyone think to check the identity of the weapons found at the scene?'

White nodded.

'We found two fired weapons on the ground, one alongside each of the bodies,' he answered slowly. 'They were both service weapons by their markings, and so it was assumed that...' He stopped suddenly in mid sentence, his mouth stilled following his last syllable, and sat expressionless, apparently in thought.

'Now I see it!' he said emphatically at last. 'He did take Hayes' pistol after all! I thought saw him with it later – at the funeral - but was not sure.' White's features were animated as he spoke but now his face became more serious as he fell into a moment's contemplation. 'Smyke couldn't have realised that it was different from the other weapons, otherwise he wouldn't have been so stupid as to wear it.' He shook his head sadly. 'Hayes was my friend. He let me use his pistol once or twice at firing practice; it was his father's - handed down.' He seemed suddenly to become angry with himself. 'Damn it! I should have pursued my suspicions!'

The three men sat in silence for a while. Jack uncocked the weapon still gripped firmly in his hand; he would not need it now. Mawdsley sat transfixed, his eyes wide, staring at Jack intensely as if he had been struck by a thunderbolt. White sat back, dropping his hands into his lap, and levelled an appraising gaze at Jack.

'Thank you, Mr Easton,' he said evenly, as his eyes narrowed. 'And it was he who pushed Middleton off the cliff? You told the truth?'

'Just as I said it then. I saw the fight between them as I reached the top of the cliff making my escape from your boys. And I would have got away had I not stopped to try to save him. Instead I became the convenient scapegoat for his acts of murder. Hayes must have been killed to silence him; and that would have been my fate too had Smyke's aim been better.'

White nodded. 'If I had put these pieces together before, I might have saved us all some trouble,' he said. 'But I doubt that I could have proved it then even if I had been sure about the weapon; and Smyke will have disposed of it as soon as he realised what it was - if he is not entirely devoid of sense.' He paused for a moment, his eyes seeming to search the air, then continued, frowning:

'I remember thinking then that the information that I had received about your operation that evening came rather too easily and too inaccurately into my hands.' White shook his head despairingly. 'I'm afraid that I played an unwitting part in the affair. It was an episode which, to my eternal shame, I have all too conveniently forgotten as the years have passed.'

'The consequences of that injustice, sir, have been harsh indeed!' Jack said, his voice now taking on a bitter edge. 'I have not been able to forget so easily. But will you help me now?'

'I will, sir,' said White offering his hand, 'if it is in my power to do so; but we shall have to find some other way to bring the man to justice - he is surrounded by powerful friends.'

Jack took White's hand and gripped it tightly. 'Then isn't it about time you offered me a drink from your jug?'

The room had filled in the meantime, and, becoming uneasy at the press of people, the lieutenant eventually suggested that the conversation continue in more privacy. The landlord helpfully offered them a small room at the back and led them to it through the scullery, picking up a pair of candlesticks to light their way. It was a bare room with only a table and four chairs located in the centre of its stone-flagged floor, and in contrast to the warmth of the parlour, the room felt chilly and damp. With some huffing and puffing and a cursory flick of his cloth across the table, the heavy man at last departed, leaving the candlesticks flickering at its centre. The three men then sat down.

'But what in heaven's name could Smyke have been up to, sir?' Mawdsley posed the knotty question that must have been troubling him since the earlier revelations. 'The whole thing sounds too evil to be true – to kill two fellow officers like that, I mean. Why would he have wanted to kill Captain Middleton - what could possibly have been his motive.'

'It's difficult to understand,' agreed the lieutenant.

'The word from my contacts in the harbour, sir,' Jack ventured, 'is that Smyke has a foot in both camps, turning a blind eye to contraband if someone makes it worth his while. And I also hear that he may be protecting one of the gangs for a cut of their profits - is that possible?'

'Hmmm; possible,' said White, thoughtfully. 'But it would have to be one of the bigger gangs. None of the smaller gangs is organised enough; they'd rather take their chances with the law than have someone like Smyke holding them to ransom. Only the Chesil gang would be big enough to cut in someone like Smyke, but it's a very secretive organisation. Captain Middleton, Hayes and I had a lucky success against them once, just weeks before the Portland killings actually, but we didn't get anything useful out of those we captured, and we still know very little about them.

'I crossed their path once or twice before I got myself caught,' contributed Jack, helpfully. 'They'd operate on this side of the Bill occasionally. They had their own vessel - always seemed to prefer running it directly into landing places where they could shift the stuff by wagon - much larger loads than the likes of us who brought our stuff ashore by rowing boat and carried it away by hand. They must have had inside information of your boys' whereabouts because they were pretty brazen about it too; never seemed to worry much about noise anyway - if we saw them about we always reckoned we'd be safe! My guess would be that there is someone behind them; someone with the resources necessary to operate at that large scale, and pay for inside information to keep themselves out of your way.'

'Middleton seized their contraband a couple of times,' said White, 'which must have knocked them back a bit. He had quite a few successes against the bigger gangs in his early days. He was a good organiser; the one who enlisted the help of the local regiments to give us more cover on the ground.'

'Then perhaps he needed to be put out of action?' suggested Jack, 'and Smyke was the instrument.'

'That would explain a lot,' said White, nodding slowly.

The men fell into a reflective silence while the candles sputtered in the draught. The flickering light threw dancing shadows of three pensive heads upon the walls behind them. The silence endured, but then Mawdsley sat up.

'Pettigrew!' he exclaimed, as if the thought had suddenly occurred.

White inspected him quizzically.

'Pettigrew,' said Mawdsley again, more confidently this time. 'Pettigrew runs a shipping company and he often calls on Smyke. I've seen him in Smyke's office frequently. Perhaps he's our man behind the scenes?'

'No, surely not,' said White, shaking his head disbelievingly. 'He's a magistrate and one of the local Customs Board commissioners. Anyway, he was on Smyke's appointment panel and so would naturally have an interest in Smyke's work; I'd be surprised if he *didn't* have to meet him from time to time,' he protested. But as soon as White had uttered these words, he frowned. Mawdsley was clearly crestfallen, but Jack thought the young officer might be on to something.

'Well, it must be possible to look at the pattern of his shipping movements,' Jack suggested. 'You must keep records of departures and arrivals – perhaps we'd find some clues in the lists to help us - especially if we looked for a match between his ships' movements and the dates of your counter-smuggling operations.'

Given the task of carrying out the study, Mawdsley reported back two evenings later at a meeting in the same place. It seemed that Pettigrew operated several vessels into or out of Weymouth on a regular basis, but only one, the brigantine *Marguerite*, might be worthy of further attention, he suggested. She was a coastal craft that regularly operated as a packet ship between West Bay, Weymouth, and the Channel Islands. The records of her movements seemed innocent enough on the face of it, but her route would take her regularly along the length of the Dorset coast - most convenient, he thought, for making unscheduled deliveries. But Mawdsley had made another interesting observation: by matching the *Marguerite's* movements with records of counter-smuggling operations, there was a significant correlation by date, too frequent an occurrence to be mere coincidence over the several years' movements he had examined.

Pritchett did not arrive from Alderney until Monday the following week, and Jack met him at an alehouse in Castletown that evening. It was a convenient rendezvous between Wakeham and the harbour at the Mere, where Pritchett berthed his vessel. And its booths offered some privacy for a discrete conversation.

Jack's first task was to acquaint Pritchett with the situation and to enlist his help, but he was careful not to mention his new connection with Andrew White and Edward Mawdsley; Pritchett would be nervous of any liaison with the customs service and, for the moment anyway, he most certainly did not need to know.

'Aye, I heard all about your troubles from Luke, Jack.' The Scot nodded his bearded head dolefully. 'It was a sorry business all right. That was the last time we met – off the Shambles I believe - a perfect night if I remember it correctly, and an excellent rendezvous! A pity it all went so wrong for you afterwards, laddie – I'm sorry.'

Jack told him of his suspicions of Pettigrew's possible involvement and of his deductions regarding the brigantine, *Marguerite*, as the only vessel that seemed to be a candidate in his fleet. As far as Jack was concerned, this was merely a pebble in the pond to find out whether Pritchett might know more, but it proved not to be such a long shot, and he was surprised to have his suspicions confirmed straight away. It seemed that the community of masters operating out of Alderney was relatively small, and each was well known to the others.

'Aye, I know her well, Jack! She comes into Alderney as regular as clockwork. Her packet duties provide good cover; I wish I had it so easy with my *Alice*.' Pritchett was amused.

'So she *is* in the game!' Jack exclaimed, his mind already racing.

'Oh, aye; no doubt about it; I know her master, Tregaskis - we share information when it suits us. I've watched her load up many a time.'

And with this, Jack had luckily stumbled upon the link between Pettigrew and the Chesil gang, and it was then not much of a leap of his imagination to guess Smyke's possible role in it. The evidence was only circumstantial, he reminded himself, but something told him that his hunch about Smyke would prove correct, and he decided that he should act upon it. With the skipper of the *Alice* already a willing ally, it did not take long for a plan to form in his mind, and his heart began to race with excitement at the prospect of its fulfilment. He smiled inwardly at its audacity, gaining malicious pleasure imagining Smyke and his paymaster falling into the trap that he would set. But he would need the co-operation of Andrew White and the most loyal of his men to implement it.

'I think I may need your help to ferry a few of my new friends to Alderney, Captain,' Jack said at last. 'Can you be back here a week today?'

Chapter Twenty-Six

A particular tavern on the waterfront at Weymouth had a reputation of being the meeting place of the most disreputable personage in the town. It was there, in a shadowy corner of its dim and smoky parlour two days after Jack's meeting with Pritchett, that another kind of meeting took place. This time, one of the participants was a scruffy individual with unkempt hair and a stubbly chin who Lieutenant White would know as the 'Chandler'. Alongside the 'Chandler' sat another man whose bearded face was shrouded by the shadow of his wide-brimmed leather hat. To anyone observing them casually, the two men were simply drinking ale rather uncommunicatively together, but a careful onlooker might have noticed a small purse pass surreptitiously from the 'Chandler' to his companion before the latter stood up quietly and departed. A few minutes later, after scribbling a note on a scrap of parchment (and downing the remnant of his drink), the 'Chandler' also departed and stepped briskly out into the hustle and bustle of the busy quayside. The same careful observation might have revealed that on passing the Customs office a few doors down from the inn, the 'Chandler' slipped the note into a receptacle mounted on its wall which had inscribed upon its lid, under the impression of a king's crown, the initials *G II R* .

Only a short time later that day, a burly man with dark side-burns and down-turned moustache dressed in the uniform of a Customs and Excise captain, would be seen to emerge from that same building in some haste, and stride off quickly in the direction of the courtroom.

From either direct or distant vantage points, all these observations were indeed made and reported on with satisfaction, and they confirmed to Jack that the first part of his plan had been accomplished. And to Andrew White, who was complicit in the plan, the report of Smyke's hasty call upon the courtroom in particular, put a malevolent smile upon his face; if the outcome of their joint plotting was as anticipated, it would be a pleasing parallel with that of his own experience seven years before. Revenge, both thought, would be very sweet indeed.

Smyke found Pettigrew in his retiring room alone, sipping an amontillado wine before taking his seat in court. Instead of his usually rather ostentatious style of dress, today he wore his more sober business attire -

a modest grey top coat with broad lapels, dark trousers, and shiny black buckled shoes - in deference to his duties as a magistrate. In front of him on the table at which he sat a file lay open, but he did not seem to be reading it.

'Ah, Captain Smyke' he said languidly. 'And what have you got for me today, I wonder? But be quick can you, I am just about to go in.'

'I've just received some interesting information,' Smyke said smirking conspiratorially. 'The Portland gang is mounting another run, sir. Is it not time for us to do another for ourselves – this would make excellent cover.'

'Really now! When and where?'

'Next week – into Church Ope Cove. We don't usually bother with them, but it should be just enough to keep White and his men occupied for a day or two.'

'Captain Smyke, my confidence in you grows daily,' said Pettigrew, with a complacent and condescending air. 'Arrange to meet with Tregaskis straight away will you, and get him to set it up – he's scheduled to take the *Marguerite* to Alderney next week on his monthly packet run. Tell him to come to me for the money before he leaves; I think a big one this time, don't you? And better warn Bolton and his boys to be ready; we'll give him the details later.'

'It's almost too easy, isn't it?' Smyke said with airy conceit, while helping himself uninvited to a glass of amontillado from the cabinet. 'And the irony of it is that my record for the seizure of contraband is the best on the south coast this year, and I'm constantly praised for my excellent performance by your fellow Commissioners!' he chuckled, gazing smugly through the window at the scene outside, his back now turned to Pettigrew as he sipped delicately from the glass in his hand. 'We make a good partnership, don't you think?'

The magistrate glanced disdainfully at the back of Smyke's head as he spoke. *The man's insufferable,* he thought. 'I prefer to call it a business arrangement, Mr Smyke, if you don't mind. And it's an arrangement that happens to suit me at the present, but don't forget yourself, sir,' Pettigrew's voice took on an edge intended to put the captain in his place. 'You're where you are today entirely through my patronage, and its continuation depends entirely on what you can do for me. Now if you've finished taking your ease, I think it's time you got on with attending to my instructions, don't you?'

His peremptory dismissal had its desired effect. Smyke put down his glass still half full and excused himself with a deferential glance. And for a few moments, Pettigrew sat alone in silence, smiling contentedly as he finished his wine, before eventually rising to his feet, stretching himself lazily, and stifling a yawn. Catching sight of himself in the mirror, he stopped to admire his new peruke, adjusting it carefully and smoothing the strands of its silvery horsehair into place with a wetted finger. His image clearly pleased him for he gave out a little sigh and smiled admiringly at his reflection.

A week later, Captain Pritchett's *Alice* sat on her mooring in Alderney harbour in the lee of the long breakwater that protected it from the wind and the waves of the open Atlantic. Her decks were deserted and dark except for the riding light swinging gently from her mizzen boom in the light swell. The rigging creaked softly like an old man's snore. The crew were in their quarters. The ship was at rest.

Below in her hold, illuminated by an odd arrangement of lanterns hanging from the beams, seventeen men, some uniformed, some in civilian clothes, sprawled untidily in various states of casual untidiness. A few swung in their hammocks asleep or resting. Others played cards in groups using upturned casks as tables. And a few more smoked pipes contentedly in quiet corners. The clutter of an evening meal lay scattered around their feet amidst boxes of pistols, powder flasks, and lead shot, the closed lids of which had been used as temporary tables.

By their different attire, it would be immediately clear that there were two quite different groups of men assembled in that uncomfortably tight space. Yet from the way they now intermingled, it would also be apparent that the two groups had merged into some sort of alliance. Ten of Luke Easton's toughest and most loyal quarrymen and seven of Andrew White's most trusted officers now shared a common objective with their differences temporarily set aside. For the Portland quarrymen, this was their chance at last to repay Smyke for the deaths of Ben Proctor, George Easton and Elizabeth Dale, and for all the strife and anguish that his treachery had caused amongst friends and families in their small island community. For White's men, it was a just cause to put an end to Smyke's arrogant, bullying, and corrupt activities. And, to a man, their blood was up for revenge.

Above their heads, in the small enclosed area below the main hatch that served as the navigation room, Jack and Luke Easton, Captain

Pritchett, Andrew White and Edward Mawdsley despondently rested their elbows on the chart table. It had been a long and fruitless day's wait since they had arrived early that morning in the quiet of the dawn.

'Perhaps they'll come tomorrow,' said Jack wearily, stifling a yawn.

'Aye,' said Pritchett. 'They'll come all right; Tregaskis has already assembled his consignment. I use the same suppliers as he does, so I get to know these things,' he said, tapping the side of his nose. 'I got word of it this evening; and it's a big one too, by all accounts - but then perhaps you already knew that,' he added, lifting an eyebrow.

Jack said nothing in reply and his expression was ambiguous; but Pritchett noticed the meaningful glance that then passed between the two brothers.

In the early hours of the following morning, Pritchett shook Jack awake urgently, leaving the others asleep.

'They're here!' he whispered into Jack's ear, beckoning him to follow as he roused himself from his slumber.

Jack had slept fully clothed for the second night running to be ready for action, and so he climbed out of his hammock and followed Pritchett straight away. The two men ascended the companionway and poked their heads through the open hatchway from where a clear view of the harbour could be gained. At its head, the village of Braye lay all but invisible in the darkness, with only a few dim pools of light marking the quay. The *Alice* lay approximately in the centre of the protected anchorage, and all around her, a score of other vessels of various sizes swung similarly on their moorings. The reflections of their riding lights snaked across the glassy surface of the almost still water that was otherwise an inky black. The gentle lapping of the swell upon the multitude of swinging hulls and the lazy frapping of loose halyards from their masts, combined to create a sort of harbour lullaby that often sent the men of the graveyard watch to sleep. But no one had been on watch aboard the *Alice* except her skipper.

Pritchett caught Jack's eye and pointed. Not much more than a hundred yards from the *Alice's* stern, partially hidden behind the hull of a fishing boat anchored nearby, the *Marguerite* was tied up to the extended arm of the harbour wall, lit up by a host of lanterns. She had slipped in silently during the night and had already been turned to point her bow to seaward, ready for departure. Along the narrow wharf leading from the town, half a dozen horse-drawn carts piled high with barrels and casks of various sizes were being led. One was already alongside the vessel's larboard bulwarks, its contents being unloaded into rope cradles suspended from derrick booms swung out from her two masts. Jack and Pritchett watched from the cover of the hatch as the bulging loads were swung aboard the *Marguerite* and lowered into her hold. It looked a slick operation. No sooner had one cart been emptied than the next would be drawn up to take its place; and by the time the others aboard the *Alice* had awoken to join Jack and Pritchett at the hatch, the loading was already complete. And just as quickly, the empty carts were led away, leaving the quayside with the abandoned appearance that it had had before they arrived.

'She'll leave this afternoon to get the benefit of the north-running tide around Cap de la Hague, and she'll plan to arrive in darkness on the other side of the Channel,' Pritchett surmised. 'It's what I'd do myself. And my guess is that Tregaskis and his crew will want to get some rest after last night's crossing, especially with another night crossing to come. They always sail short-handed and every man will likely have been on watch - so they'll be knackered! Give 'em a couple of hours and they'll all be flat out, if my crew is anything to go by!' Pritchett ducked his head below the opening and led the group back to the chart table. He took out his parallel-rule and placed it on the chart.

'You've not yet told me what you're up to, Jack, 'though I can guess. Will you take her?'

'Yes, that's my plan, but you've done all that I shall ask of you, captain. From now on, it's better that you and your crew stay out of the way.'

Pritchett nodded. 'Thank you, Jack; it would not do for me to be seen assisting your new friends against a fellow master. This community is too close, and memories are long.'

Pritchett paced his parallel rule carefully across the chart to line up with the compass rose. 'You're on neaps, so the currents will not be strong. Once you're clear of the breakwater, steer one point west of north. You should pick up the Portland lights dead ahead after about eight hours' sailing, and from there you'll know your way, I think. The Race won't be a problem for you tonight.' He paused to think for a moment. 'What will you do with Tregaskis? – from what I know of him, he's ready to retire and he'll be glad to be rid of his employer, but I would not want him to be hurt or find himself destitute. Like most of us, he does what he does to live.'

'He's not our target, captain. Actually, we have an important role for him to play. If he co-operates with us, he'll have nothing to fear, and we may be able to help him in his retirement.'

Pritchet nodded, satisfied.

'Then, if you no longer need us, I'll muster my crew and take them ashore. If someone would kindly row us to the quay in one of the boats, it can be returned so that you'll have all three at your disposal. You'll probably need at least two of them later to get all your men across to the *Marguerite* in one go. By the way, there are some tarpaulins in each boat to give you some cover if you need it. I would suggest that you tie up in front of *Marguerite's* bow where you'll not be seen from the town quay — there's a ladder up the wall there.'

By mid-day, the *Marguerite's* decks lay deserted, while elsewhere in the harbour, boats and sailing craft of every sort came and went in a scene typical of any busy port. Hidden in the seaward lee of the *Alice's* hull, out of the sight of any prying eyes from the harbour wall, seventeen men quietly boarded two of her boats and pulled away. In the first boat, Jack and Luke, and in the second, White and Mawdsley rowed side by side from the forward thwarts with their men hidden under the tarpaulins. By the time they came into view crossing the narrow stretch of water separating the *Alice* from the *Marguerite*, it would appear to any onlooker that the boats were conveying a load of some sort to the quay for off-loading. And no one would guess what crouched uncomfortably beneath the covers, armed to the teeth.

Unseen and unheard arriving at the harbour wall, and now hidden from view under the *Marguerite's* overhanging prow, the unlikely cohort clambered up the rusty rungs of the iron ladder onto the quay and slipped quietly aboard. Treading deftly on silent feet, the men assembled on the main deck to listen out for any sign of movement from the crew. All was still. Dividing themselves between the fore and aft companionways, the two groups then descended and moved quietly along the lower deck to approach the crew's sleeping quarters from both ends of the vessel simultaneously. At each careful step and as each corner was turned in the dingy and cluttered confines of the ship's innards, Jack expected to encounter a watchful guard or hear the sudden shout of alarm. But the *Marguerite* seemed to be fast asleep; hardly a sound could be heard; even the soft creaking of the resting hull sounded like a muted snore. The two groups entered the cramped crew deck from either end at the same time to find half-a-dozen sleeping bodies hanging motionless in their hammocks, cocooned like chrysalises suspended in metamorphosis. Jack caught White's eye, pointing a finger to indicate the slatted door of the master's cabin that lay off to the starboard side. With mouthed instructions, the party was divided and allocated to their quietly slumbering targets; Jack and Mawdsley would attend to Tregaskis, while White would oversee the capture of the others, assigning several men to each sleeping form. Each man moved with great stealth to his allotted position and waited, poised with weapon raised, for the signal to act. In the half-light, the scene evoked the worst of any nightmare.

It was an almost silent coup as each recumbent man was awoken to the click of a flintlock being pulled back onto its catch. One of the crew fell out of his hammock in a panic, a few struggled to resist, but despite their startled mutters and curses, all were quickly subdued. Tregaskis, a light sleeper however, was already on his feet as White and Mawdsley burst into his cabin to find him facing them nervously with a pistol in his hand. There was a moment of tension as Tregaskis raised his weapon, but he saw immediately that he was outnumbered and had the good sense to submit. While the six-man crew were escorted in a sullen and somewhat chagrined mood to the forepeak where they could conveniently be secured out of hearing, Tregaskis was led up to the main deck for a parley.

It was explained to the bewildered and frightened Cornishman that his options were limited - either he could co-operate with the customs service and retain his freedom, or he could resist and lose it. This was at first apparently a bit of a dilemma for the confused man, for he clearly feared the consequences of betraying his employer and his gang as much as he feared prosecution and punishment. But when it was explained that Captain Smyke was the principal target of the operation, and that Pettigrew was the next in line, he seemed mollified. Perhaps he recognised that these two individuals were the principal causes of his concern, and with them out of the way, he would have little to fear by way of retribution. And when finally it was put to him that he might, at the end of it all, be allowed to return secretly to Cornwall with a sum of money in his hands to aid his retirement, he seemed persuaded. Although still clearly uncomfortable in the company of White and his uniformed officers, Tregaskis would really have no choice but to play the part mapped out for him, for it was made clear by some of Luke's burly quarrymen what discomforts he would suffer if he did not. Jack felt some sympathy for the man. Tregaskis seemed to be a decent chap with loyalties, like many in his profession, built upon a necessity to eke out a living from the sea; and Jack therefore wished him no harm. But such is the course of life, Jack thought, that it proceeded sometimes in unexpected directions, and Tregaskis would have to adapt or face the consequences.

By mid afternoon, Jack and others in the group who had some experience of sailing had worked out between them how they would crew the ship. Tregaskis had offered his advice and it was accepted, but neither Jack nor White would trust him to take command; while the captain's apparent conversion to their cause had been quick and inevitable in the circumstances, it could not as quickly be guaranteed to be secure. He would be confined to his cabin under guard until his services were called for, and his crew would not accompany him on this voyage.

Fortunately, the rig was relatively light – designed for the minimum crew of a packet ship – and only the square-rigged sails of the fore and mainmast would require work aloft from the yards, all the others - the brigsail, the staysails and the foresails - were rigged fore-and-aft and thus would be hoisted and trimmed from the deck. As long as the weather stayed fair, they would manage her without too much difficulty, Jack thought and, after studying the sky and the glass for signs of change, he was hopeful of a smooth and speedy passage.

At three o'clock that afternoon, the mooring warps were cast off from the quay and the *Marguerite* slid slowly out of the harbour using the two foresails alone. In her wake, like a puppy on a leash, one of the *Alice's* boats trailed obediently behind. The purpose of this trailing craft soon became clear. As the brig cleared the sunken breakwater about a mile and a half north east of the harbour, Tregaskis' crew was brought up from the forepeak at gunpoint and invited into it to row themselves back to the quay. This was Edward Mawdsley's bright idea to avoid giving them any opportunity for immediate retaliation that might have presented itself had they been let go ashore. It could be days before the disgruntled men could work a passage back to Weymouth, by which time it would be far too late for them to raise the alarm. And they were unlikely to do this anyway; as far as they were concerned, the *Marguerite* had been confiscated and her captain arrested by Revenue men and taken back to England for prosecution.

An hour before midnight, guided by the lights of Portland Bill, the *Marguerite* nosed silently into Church Ope Cove and dropped her sails and anchor - carefully laying out a kedge and line in the last half cable of her inward drift.

'I think that we have now arrived at the point where my men and I should look the other way, don't you Mr Easton?' White said, with a theatrically quizzical look in his eye. 'I don't think that the Commissioners would approve of our connivance in denying the State her rightful benefit on confiscated booty. But be quick, we must be anchored in Weymouth by two o'clock if our plan is to have a chance of working.'

Jack had taken the *Marguerite* in to the beach as close as he dared without grounding; it being a neap tide, he would not have much of a fall to reckon with and so the minimal depth he had allowed under the keel would not be too critical in the shelter of the Cove. And when the time came to depart, the kedge line would be used to haul her out stern first.

Enjoying an unusual confidence that customs men would not tonight disturb them, Jack and his brother had come up with a novel scheme for rapidly getting the contraband ashore; they would simply float it in. The idea had come from the rope cradles that Jack had seen used earlier during the ship's loading. And throughout the eight hours or so of their short voyage across the Channel, Luke and his men had been put to the construction of several more of these using other coils of rope found on board. It was a necessary innovation, for with so few men involved, it would have been impossible otherwise to get the load ashore in the short time available.

With the boats in the water crewed by Luke and five of his men, the cradles of casks were lowered into the sea by Jack and other quarrymen using the derrick arms. Meanwhile, White, Mawdsley, and their customs men looked on bemused, restrained from their urges to assist by White's sense of propriety as an official. But it soon became clear, as Jack and his men struggled with the heavy loads, that the rate of progress was far too slow; and with a weary sigh of resignation, White eventually conceded, ordering his men to pitch in. They did so cheerfully and with relish and within an hour, the entire load, bound by a dozen nets each cradling ten to fifteen floating casks, was jostling in the gentle swell like apples in a water butt. Gazing down from the rail, watching Luke sort out the tangled mess, Jack reckoned that he must be looking at two-thousand guineas worth of liquor bumping about in such an unruly shambles. It looked chaotic, and Jack began to fear that the nets might unravel, thus setting the whole load free to roam the seas, but as the boats started to head in towards the shore, the lines straightened and a sort of untidy order was restored. Fortunately, it was not more than fifty yards for them to row, and in the dim light of the half-moon, Jack could already see a dozen men waiting at the water's edge to help them in; Luke's shore party were already there as pre-arranged, alerted by a lookout as the *Marguerite* had neared. The boats beached amongst a flurry of foam as the men jumped ashore, and quickly all hands were set to the nets allowing a boat to be sent back to ferry the remaining quarrymen ashore. And soon twenty or more men were on the water's edge, rolling the barrels onto waiting stone-sledges to be hauled up the beach by the winch lines already hooked on. Luke would have the casks spirited away into hiding places well before any idle constable lifted his head from his pillow.

But Jack, White, Mawdsley and the uncertain Tregaskis had other important work to accomplish in the five hours remaining before dawn, and no sooner than the boat had returned, than the capstan-bars were already turning to wind up the anchor. The brig was then drawn out by her stern to leave the shelter of the Cove; and even as the kedge broke the surface, the jib and the brigsail were already flapping in the breeze. Jack sent two men forward quickly to back the foresails, and watched as the *Marguerite* rotated on her keel, calling for the sails to be set as her head passed north. Next the large brigsail boom was sheeted in and the foretopmast staysail pulled up and set to match the jib for a larboard tack. This would be enough for the few miles that they had left to sail, thought Jack, as he took up a course for Weymouth; with his now depleted crew, there were not enough hands to manage more.

It was just before three o'clock when the *Marguerite* slid quietly into the harbour and rafted up against the customs cutter already sitting at anchor in the deep-water basin a short row from the quay. A few lanterns hanging from the houses on the waterfront threw pools of light here and there. The scene was like a composition of little cameos painted in shades of pale yellow in flat perspective; still-life studies of house fronts with arrangements in their foregrounds of fishing nets, lobster pots, and carts and trolleys abandoned at odd angles. Reflections of the lights streaked the black water in yellow flashes, rebounding off the ripples that the *Marguerite* herself had caused by her entry; but other than the waves' gentle slip-slopping against her hull, the harbour was utterly quiet.

The first task was to deliver Tregaskis, Mawdsley and two officers ashore to the custom's compound where the three officials would change into civilian clothes to assist in their disguise. They would be dispatched urgently to the house of Mr Pettigrew, using the customs' post chaise as far as the state of the bridle-way would allow them; this being the fastest route, if rather a rough ride. The vehicle was a rugged four-wheeled carriage especially equipped with steel springs, procured recently by the Service for just this sort of mission – that of carting a small posse of armed customs men around the rough tracks and bridleways of Dorset. The chaise would be found waiting ready to hitch up to its horses in the stable block behind the customs office where it had been left on White's instructions two nights before. Mawdsley had been put in charge of this part of the plan because his face would not be so familiar to Pettigrew; but in the darkness it was most unlikely that he would anyway be recognised. Meanwhile, Jack, White, and the remaining officers would remain on board until this first task - that of entrapping Pettigrew and bringing him back to custody - had been accomplished. Once the magistrate was safely out of the way, and thus not able to call out the constabulary, the next stage of the plan could commence.

The carriage was left some few hundred yards short of Pettigrew's grand residence so as not to alert him to its approach, and the four men got out to walk the rest of the way. Mawdsley checked his timepiece in the moon's light - half past three – so *far so good*, he thought. The group made for the cover of a nearby yew tree and crumbling dry-stone wall, and while his officers charged their weapons, Mawdsley surveyed the scene. Ahead of him, the pale outline of the house stood a field's-width away, standing in a gap between several stunted and windswept trees. There were seven upstairs windows on the front façade and six larger windows on the ground floor divided equally by a large porch and door; all were dark against the moonlit pallor of the walls. There was no sign of life.

The group crossed the field in silence except for the sound of boots brushing the long grass. Here and there, the pale shapes of sheep lay huddled in clusters on the dark ground; Mawdsley was careful not to disturb them, deftly steering the group to give the dozing animals a wide berth, not wanting to lose the element of surprise. One or two of the creatures looked up lazily, but none of them seemed inclined to move. Tregaskis identified Pettigrew's bedroom window and the group assembled silently beneath it. Mawdsley took out his pistol, cocked it, and thrust it firmly into Tregaskis' back.

'You know the plan; stick to it or you'll never see the dawn!' he growled into the Cornishman's ear in the most threatening voice he could muster, then threw a handful of gravel from the path up to the window. The stones hit the glazing with a clatter, shattering the silence like an explosion, and setting off a chorus of discordant bleating in the adjacent field as a score of sheep leapt up and bolted in alarm. It took just twenty seconds, as the thunder of their stampeding hooves receded into the darkness, for the light of a candle to appear inside. The light could be seen moving erratically within the room through crimson curtains, flickering and growing in intensity as it approached the window. Moments later, the heavy drapes were yanked aside, the sash-window pulled up with a loud scrape, and the angry face of Mr Pettigrew Esq. JP, bedecked in nightcap, poked out like Punch without his Judy at a show on Melcombe beach.

'What the devil! What in God's name are you men doing here at this time of night? Who is it?' he harangued, irritably peering into the darkness and apparently unable to see anything other than the dark shapes of the four men standing below him on the path.

'It is me, sir, Tregaskis! We've had some trouble,' the Cornishman uttered nervously. 'Smyke has double-crossed us. He and a few of his cronies boarded us in Alderney; I didn't realise until too late what he had in mind but, just south of the Bill, he put a pistol to my head and forced me to bring the *Marguerite* to Weymouth instead of to the planned landing place. I think that he intends to unload her there and keep it for himself. These men and I escaped. We came to tell you, sir. I'm not sure what to do.' Tregaskis was convincing, but then he was telling a story that was not very far from the truth.

It was not often that Pettigrew lost his composure, but on this occasion his jaw dropped visibly. He was both furious and incredulous at the same time and he puffed with affront.

'The money-grubbing son of a whore! Don't I pay him enough for his services already! The bastard would have got his share once we'd sold it – was that not good enough?' he ranted.

'The man is so arrogant, sir.' Tregaskis tone was smoothly obsequious towards his master, despite his present betrayal. 'He believes that you cannot touch him without incriminating yourself. I think you've trusted him too much, sir.'

'We'll see about that! We need to stop him, Tregaskis. Where are Bolton and his men?'

'Still waiting at the landing place, sir, as far as I know,' Tregaskis replied managing to get some urgency into his voice as he felt the barrel of Mawdsley's pistol pushed into his back. 'They're too far in the wrong direction and we'll not have time to alert them if we're to get to Smyke before daylight. He can't start unloading until he's assembled more of his men from the morning watch. We would have a chance of re-taking the ship if we acted right away. If you were there to confront him with us behind you, sir, he couldn't resist us - you being the magistrate and all.'

'And these fellows with you, are they prepared to fight to get it back?' asked Pettigrew flicking his head at Mawdsley and his companions.

'They are loyal to you, sir, and I've some more men still waiting at the quay who would join us if you led them.' Tregaskis was playing his part superbly.

'Then they'll have to do for the present,' said Pettigrew finally, 'we must get there straight away. Are you armed?'

'Aye, that we are sir, and have a post chaise waiting in the drove.'

'Wait there - I'll get dressed.' Pettigrew ducked his head inside the window and the curtains swung closed behind him. But an instant later, some new thought apparently occurring to him, he stuck it out again and shouted down. 'How much did you have aboard, Tregaskis? Did you buy all that I asked you to?'

'Aye, sir, all three-thousand guineas worth – I filled the hold just as you asked.'

'Good God man, I'll be ruined if he takes it!'

He withdrew his head again in such haste that the curtains dislodged his nightcap and Mawdsley caught it with a flourish as it fell.

'I think we have him!' he whispered with a wink, clutching the cap in his hand.

Pettigrew's continued fretting marked their hurried journey back to Weymouth as the carriage shuddered and rocked along the rough and winding tracks. Even in the light of day, he might not have recognised Mawdsley in civilian clothes and cap, but with hardly a glimmer of the moon's light penetrating the carriage, there was no chance at all. And so preoccupied was he with Smyke's putative deceit that he also failed to notice the coach turning abruptly into the stable yard of the customs compound instead of continuing further along the quay. So that when the vehicle at last came to a halt and he alighted, he was confused to find himself surrounded by stables instead of a harbour scene. But seeing the magistrate's hesitation, Mawdsley stepped in quickly.

'The men are in here, sir,' he said gruffly pointing at a stable door, immediately quelling his captive's bewilderment in the nick of time. And apparently reassured, Pettigrew followed tamely as Mawdsley purposefully led the way towards the stable door, politely deferring to the magistrate to allow him first entry.

No one knew how the magistrate reacted when the door slammed shut behind him and he found himself locked alone in total darkness on a bed of wet straw and horse droppings, for the door was so solid and the walls so thick that no sound could penetrate to reveal it. But they could well imagine his fury, and to a man, their faces broke into wide grins of triumph. Even Tregaskis chuckled in amusement to see his pompous ass of an employer so beautifully brought down.

Leaving one of his men to guard the door, Mawdsley then led the others quickly back to the quay where they found the boat waiting to take them back to the *Marguerite*. It was a little after five o'clock, when Mawdsley and Tregaskis reported their astonishing success to the others waiting patiently in the hold.

'Right, now it's Smyke's turn,' White said, sounding slightly apprehensive as he buckled the belt of his uniform tunic and thrust his pistol into it. 'Let's hope that this bit goes just as sweetly!' He pulled on his officer's cap and glanced at Jack and the others now gathering around him expectantly. He held his timepiece to a lantern then nodded as if satisfied.

'A quarter past five,' he said. 'Give me forty minutes at most; I'll try to have him here well before dawn, but keep only one of these lanterns alight so that he'll not see too clearly.'

Jack interjected: 'Before you go, Lieutenant!' he said quickly, stepping forward into the circle of men. 'Let's all be clear. Smyke must incriminate himself regarding the murders of Captain Middleton and Hayes before anyone precipitates anything, or I'll have no proof of my innocence. And as far as his dealings with Pettigrew are concerned, we must trick him into admitting to that too, otherwise you may find yourselves locked up with me for apprehending a magistrate and making off with his property!' he said with a wry smile, to which a few chuckling glances were exchanged.

'Yes, I hope that's clear to everyone,' said White emphatically. 'Anything can happen, so let's be prepared, but you, Mr Mawdsley, will play a leading role, so play it well!' Then turning to address his men, he said: 'Now, Smyke must believe that you are Tregaskis' crew. Remember, you've been locked up for fourteen hours in the forepeak; I don't want you looking too neat and tidy when you emerge. And Mr Tregaskis: you must join them I'm afraid; you've done well so far this evening, so don't let us down now.'

Not more than ten minutes later, White stood alone with his lantern at Smyke's front door under the overhang of a first-floor bay window. He paused for a moment, looking up and down the quay to settle his resolve as his lips subconsciously rehearsed his opening words. There was not a soul about; even the night-soil men had finished their dirty business and gone home to bed. The lieutenant tentatively lifted the brass knocker and tried its action, wanting the measure of it before he struck. Then, putting his shoulder behind it, he hammered the solid implement against its plate repeatedly with such force that its rattling percussion sounded like a volley of cannon fire. There was an instant yell and a heavy thump from the bay window above his head, followed by the sound of rapid footfalls reverberating on bare-wood floors. The sound grew louder as the footsteps evidently descended the stairs into the front hall, and then the door was flung open with such violence that it banged the inside wall as it slipped out of the opener's hand and bounced back to hit him on the shoulder. Glaring out of the dark void, his face full of fluster and made to look grotesque in the oblique light thrown up by White's lantern, Smyke stepped forward in a rage.

'White! What in God's name are you doing here at this time of the night?' he said in astonishment.

'Good news, sir! We have captured the Portlanders' brig,' said White, feigning breathlessness. 'I went out with the cutter to scout in the Channel last night and by chance we came upon her. She looked suspicious so we boarded her. The captain tried to tell us she was a packet boat bound for West Bay but we found her full of contraband. Mawdsley and I have brought her back to the harbour, sir! Her crew are locked up on board.'

Smyke looked a little puzzled, even piqued, but in no way alarmed. 'You should have obtained my authorisation to deploy the cutter,' he said testily, 'I thought you were watching Portland?'

'I was sir!' said White, sounding a little affronted. 'I sent my men to stake out Church Ope Cove as you instructed; but when nothing happened, I authorised the cutter to go out. I didn't want to bother you.' He paused. 'Surely you're pleased by the news, sir; it will be a major success for us – and I thought that you should know of it before daylight comes and the word of the capture gets about.'

'Yes indeed! Good man White; well done!' Smyke's praise was fulsome, but he could not hide his impatience. 'But now that you've done so, it will surely wait until the morning. Keep everything under control and we'll talk again then.' He stepped back into the doorway, taking hold of the door, and started to close it.

White realised that his oblique references to the packet boat and West Bay had not been enough for Smyke to make the required connection with Pettigrew's operation; perhaps he was not thinking clearly having just awoken, he thought, and decided that he would have to be more obvious.

'Yes sir,' said White apparently deferring to his senior's wishes, but then he broke into a triumphant smile as if delighted by his own success. 'That captain, Tregaskis, is mightily displeased to have been caught red-handed,' he added, excitedly. 'Our records show his vessel to be one of Mr Pettigrew's fleet and so *he* won't be much pleased either when we confiscate it!' White turned to leave, but Smyke's closing of the door had stopped the instant the names Tregaskis and Pettigrew were uttered as if hitting an obstruction, and the door was now rapidly reversing its course.

'Er, White!' Smyke called abruptly, stepping out into the porch. 'Perhaps I have been hasty in dismissing you. You'll probably need some help - I'll come back with you after all.'

'Yes, of course, sir,' replied White sounding pleased, but he was careful not to betray his pleasure at success of his manipulation. 'Shall I call out more men to accompany us, sir? – I'm afraid that I have left myself rather short-handed with only Mawdsley aboard to guard the captured crew; 'though they are, of course, securely locked up in the fore-peak. Perhaps you think that unwise?' White's tone became deferential: 'The cutter's crew had had a long night, and I thought it safe to let them go off duty.'

'Perhaps, White, perhaps.' Smyke had become patronising now. 'But let me be the judge of that when I'm aboard. Wait here if you will; I'll dress and be with you in a moment.'

It did not surprise White when Smyke returned to the doorway dressed in his civilian clothes rather than in his uniform. 'The man's intentions are quite predictable,' White thought – 'he won't want to be conspicuous on the quay in his captain's uniform.' And protruding from the captain's leather belt, the shining stocks of two pistols caught the light of White's swinging lantern as the pair strode down the quay at a pace.

Back on board the *Marguerite,* White led Smyke down through the forward hatch and onto a narrow area of lower deck separated from the main hold by a bulkhead; it was cluttered with boxes and casks and coils of rigging cord. There was not much headroom here, and both men needed to stoop to avoid hitting their heads on the deck beams. White removed his cap and reached over to the single hanging lantern to turn up its wick. Flickering through smoke-blackened glass, its weak light revealed the sleeping body of Mawdsley, once more in uniform, propped up against the bulkhead with his pistol in his lap. There were two large hinged hatches leading off the narrow deck: one, adjacent to the entry companionway behind them, led into the main hold; the other, on the opposite bulkhead, led into the forepeak, the triangular storage space in the ship's bow. To Smyke, both hatches would have appeared firmly closed in the dim light, but closer inspection would have revealed that the hatch into the main hold was slightly ajar. And through the narrow crack left open between it and its frame, Jack Easton watched and listened in total silence.

'We've got them in here, sir,' said White pointing at the forepeak door.

'How many?' Smyke asked scanning the deck.

'Six men, and their captain, sir, we've stowed their weapons over there.' White pointed at a chest that sat open under the companionway down which they had descended. 'Just a moment, sir, I'll wake Mawdsley,' he said stepping towards his junior.

'No, wait!' said Smyke rather too abruptly. 'Leave him be for the moment; he's obviously had a long night; I think that we can manage this between us,' he said, patting the two weapons in his belt as reassurance. 'But, I think we'll take this from him so as not to tempt our captives when they emerge.' So saying, Smyke removed the weapon from Mawdsley's lap and stuck it with the others in his own belt.

'Now, open the hatch, I want to see Tregaskis for myself,' said Smyke.

'We should call for some support sir, surely?' White made himself sound apprehensive.

'Damn it man! Do as I say. I'll have you covered,' said Smyke pulling out two pistols, cocking them, and aiming them at the hatch. 'Unlock it, and call Tregaskis out.'

White looked hesitant but withdrew the bolt. Then, stepping back as the door swung open, he took out his weapon and shouted for Tregaskis to come out. There was a moment of evident uncertainty within, as the two men stared into the dark void so revealed, but eventually Tregaskis' s anxious face appeared.

'So it is you, Tregaskis! I wanted to be sure,' said Smyke calmly, stepping back to position himself alongside the companionway. Until this point, Smyke's aim had remained steadily on Tregaskis as he had emerged into the dim light, but now he turned his pistols on White instead. White managed to look suitably surprised as he raised his hands.

'Take his weapon, Tregaskis!' Smyke growled and Tregaskis quickly complied. 'Now Mr White – I must ask you to get back against the bulkhead if you please!' he said, stepping forward to kick the feet of Mawdsley's sleeping form. 'Wake up, you lazy blackguard!' he shouted, angrily.

Through the crack, Jack watched Mawdsley feign his waking, cringing at the man's ham act of shocked bewilderment which was thankfully not noted by Smyke who saw him only from the corner of his eye. Seeing the threatening flick of Smyke's pistols, Mawdsley quickly staggered to his feet and backed over to join his colleague against the bulkhead at the far side of the deck.

Tregaskis, now armed with White's pistol suddenly looked menacing, and Jack, still secretly observing, wondered for a moment if the man's new loyalty would hold. If the Cornishman changed sides now, the situation could unravel quickly and someone could get hurt; between them, they now had the advantage with four weapons at their disposal. He closed his hand around his pistol, withdrew it from his belt and cocked it. In the silence of the empty hold, the echoing click of the flintlock was piercing. He froze, holding his breath, expecting some reaction from the other side of the hatch, but Smyke was already talking to Tregaskis and clearly had not heard it.

'You must get the ship back to sea before dawn to save the load, Tregaskis. Get your men on deck and get her underway as quickly as you can,' said Smyke urgently. 'I'll go ashore before you depart and get word to Bolton. Go out into the channel, then return to the landing place after midnight tonight and you'll find him waiting.'

Tregaskis glanced nervously at White and Mawdsley.

'What'll become of them?' he asked.

'This old packet boat of yours can drop off two more packages in the Race on your way past the Bill.' Smyke curled his lip in a sneer. 'Now, get your men on deck and get the ship ready; you must be out of here before daylight!'

Tregaskis hesitated for a moment, glancing in the direction of Jack's hatch, apparently unsure of how far to take his act. At his glance, Jack recoiled from his spy hole, terrified that Smyke would follow the Cornishman's eyes; and for a dreadful moment, it seemed that Tregaskis' odd behaviour might inadvertently alert Smyke to the trap. Jack held himself motionless in the darkness of the hold, hardly daring to breathe, his finger moving to the trigger of his pistol as he readied himself to act. But then Tregaskis seemed to snap out of his indecision.

'Aye, all right Smyke, but I hope you know what you are doing,' he said, in a show of reluctance.

Smyke was contemptuous. 'Do as I say and be quick about it, man!' he said irritably, 'you'll get what's due for your work, and be glad for it, I don't doubt.'

'Oh aye, the good Lord will see that we'll all get our due in the end, Smyke,' Tregaskis muttered ambiguously.

Jack let out a long silent sigh of relief as he heard Tregaskis call the officers from the forepeak and order them onto the deck. But he quickly tensed again as one by one the men filed past their putative rescuer, coming within inches of his shoulder on their way to the companionway. If Smyke recognised them as his own officers, Jack's tidy plan could quickly turn to bloody chaos, but in the dim light and preoccupied with his two captives, Smyke failed to notice who passed him by, remaining completely unaware of the snare closing in around him. 'We've got you Smyke, you loathsome bastard!' thought Jack; but he needed the captain to say a lot more before he could act, and he prayed that White would get the opportunity to draw the man out without putting him on his guard.

'Collect your weapons, men,' ordered Tregaskis, as the officers approached the foot of the companionway. But Smyke still had his eyes on White and Mawdsley as the men stooped to collect their pistols from the box.

'Leave two of your men behind, Tregaskis;' Smyke called over his shoulder. 'I'll want these officers gagged and bound.'

Two of the departing men took the initiative to hang back, relieving Tregaskis of the need to make a choice, while he and the others continued up the companionway onto the deck and out of sight. Tregaskis was apparently thinking himself into his part with a penchant for realism, for soon his shouted orders and the noises of running rigging lines and the clatter of deck machinery could be heard coming through the open hatchway; it seemed that the *Marguerite* was indeed about to get underway.

At the sound of the activity above his head, Smyke threw a triumphant smile at his captives who still stood at the bulkhead facing him in studied intensity. Meanwhile, the two officers left behind by Tregaskis began to untangle some rope from the heap lying untidily on the deck. It was then that White evidently decided that it was time to play his hand:

'You'll kill us like you killed Middleton and Hayes to protect your treason!' he called out defiantly, shifting his feet as if about to spring.

'Yes, and like them you're expendable,' Smyke spat, cocking his weapons to deter White from making a move. 'Only I shall have a tidier way of dealing with the situation this time,' he leered menacingly. 'You'll never point a finger at me in court like that quarryman, Easton. You'll never get the chance. You two are about to abscond with the contraband, and I'll have been asleep in my bed all night completely innocent of your treachery,' he taunted. He flashed an irritable glance to the officers behind him who were still rather deliberately untangling the lengths of rope. 'Get a move on!' he rasped. 'And make sure they're bound up nice and tight. They're about to take a plunge into the Race, and we wouldn't want 'em to swim ashore, would we?' he leered.

'You're a fool Smyke!' White said angrily, keeping up the pretence. 'The cutter's crew I sent ashore will testify that I came to get you. They'll know this vessel is the *Marguerite,* and it'll not be difficult to find out that she's one of Pettigrew's fleet. Neither you nor he can possibly get away with it.'

Smyke laughed. 'It's you who are the fools, White! Other than Tregaskis and his crew, no one actually saw you with me, did they.' His tone was mocking now, and his dark features twisted into an evil smirk. 'One of my most loyal officers will plant the thought that you sent the cutter's crew away so that you could steal the contraband for yourselves. And then a trusted informer will report seeing you in Alderney setting off for France. After that neither you nor the *Marguerite* will ever be seen again. Pretty conclusive I'd call that, wouldn't you?' Smyke was laughing now, full of heady bravado.

From his hiding place, Jack had listened to every word on tenterhooks, his heart pounding with mounting satisfaction at Smyke's almost unbelievably brazen candour. 'The man is so arrogant that he thinks himself untouchable!' he thought incredulously. But he smiled grimly. Smyke had said more than enough. At last it was time to act.

Jack pulled the hatch slowly open to give him a full view of the deck. Smyke now stood with his back towards him, his legs spread, and with his two pistols pointing unwaveringly at White and Mawdsley. The two other officers still fussed with the coils of rope, apparently attempting to extract a piece of suitable length. One of them saw Jack's entry and quietly nudged his comrade to make him aware of it; they made some clumsy noises to cover his approach. Jack crept ever closer towards his target, treading silently on the balls of his feet, focussing on Smyke's back, watching intently for any sign of detection. But Smyke seemed totally unaware of his approach.

But then Smyke suddenly turned his head, apparently losing patience with the two officers making such a meal over untangling the rope; and glaring fiercely, he shouted: 'For God's sake, get on with it! I can't stand here all night!'

With Smyke's head now half turned towards him, Jack froze, suddenly petrified that he would be seen. Smyke must be taken by surprise if bloodshed was to be avoided - the man had two cocked pistols in his hands and another ready in his belt; someone, most likely Jack himself, would go down in any shoot-out. But seeing the danger, White called out quickly:

'No one will believe you, Smyke, you haven't got a chance!'

Smyke turned back towards his captives with a withering smile.

'D'you think I'm alone? Smyke was exultant. 'My friend the magistrate will find the evidence against you compelling; and the Commissioners are dullards – they'll believe anything I tell them,' he sneered. 'Anyway, you won't be around to object, will you?'

At that moment, Jack sprung the last two yards, grabbing Smyke roughly by the neck in an arm lock, and simultaneously thrust his pistol hard into the man's ear. At the same time, White, Mawdsley, and the two other officers leapt forward to grab Smyke's wrists, smashing them up into the deck beams to disarm him of his deadly weapons. One of the pistols went off inches from Jack's head. The shattering explosion rang out in his ears and the shock of it nearly caused him to let go his grip. But Smyke was well restrained by now with five pairs of arms holding him fast, although he struggled with the strength of an ox to free himself. Then, with a desolate cry of frustration, he finally submitted to the overpowering force and let his weapons fall clattering to the deck. At that moment, Tregaskis and the other officers came stampeding back; some leaping down the companionway, others bursting through the hatchway from the hold, all of them with their pistols at the ready. But the struggle was already over. Less than a minute after his last callous and triumphant remarks, Smyke found himself surrounded by a posse of armed and angry men.

Jack removed the barrel of his pistol from Smyke's ear and released his grip as White and Mawdsley turned Smyke to face him. Smyke's face was screwed up in an angry contortion as he strained against the firm restraint, his eyes darting from left to right at last recognising the half-dozen officers who now stared at him with such contempt from all sides. Then he turned his gaze on Jack, now standing before him, his pistol lowered to his side, his lips held tightly in a fierce grimace. For a moment, Smyke failed to recognise the bearded man who stared back so intensely; but then a look of consternation came into his eyes as recognition dawned.

'You!' he spat. 'I should have let you die in the castle like your friend Proctor when I had the chance!'

At the mention of young Ben's name, a wave of loathing and revulsion swept through Jack's being as he glared at Smyke's sneering and ugly face. This was the man who had wreaked havoc on his life, the man who had taken Elizabeth and his father from him, the man who had let Ben die from his beating in the Castle. Jack wanted to batter the living daylights out of him there and then, to inflict such pain upon him that he would sink to his knees and beg for mercy – a mercy that Jack would deny. He lifted his pistol and pointed it directly into Smyke's face, its barrel only inches from the narrow space between the man's weasel eyes. Smyke struggled vainly against his restraint, desperate to move his head from the pistol's deadly aim.

White shouted: 'No, Jack, don't be a fool! We'll need him in the dock to face a jury – otherwise you'll get no acquittal. '

The smell of urine and the dark wet patch appearing in the crotch of Smyke's trousers revealed the man's stark terror. Jack tightened his finger on the trigger as he struggled to control the hatred that now raged inside him like a furnace. White and the others looked on transfixed, rooted to the spot in the tension that had enveloped them. But then White's words began to register in Jack's ears; at first they sounded distant like an echo, not penetrating his consciousness to any depth, but then their meaning became clear. Slowly, almost reluctantly, he released his flintlock and lowered his weapon to his side, his face losing the evil look of revenge that had momentarily disfigured it.

'You're right, Andrew. And he'll suffer for his crimes before the gallows takes him!' he spat. 'Much more than he would with a quick bullet in his head to send him into oblivion,' he added calmly, and turned away.

Chapter Twenty Seven

Coincidentally, a few days before the trials of Smyke and Pettigrew an editorial on crime and punishment appeared in the January 1758 edition of a London gazette. In it, the editor lamented the careless indifference of the Government to corruption in the public services and criticised them for their poor oversight of legal processes in particular. Alongside the piece, a cartoon in the style of Hogarth's popular series caricatured a courtroom scene in which a corpulent blindfolded judge administered justice while the prosecutor dozed and the defendant (depicted as a gentleman) offered a purse to the constables apparently as a bribe. In the witness box, an individual holding another purse behind his back stood carrying a case on which the words "Evidence for hire" was written, while on the jury benches sat twelve gentlemen identical in appearance to the defendant. It is not impossible that these words and images had some effect upon the outcome of the trials in Dorchester that took place a few days later.

The courtroom was packed with members of the public as well as officers of the Customs service come to see the dishonour that Smyke's deeds had brought upon their Service duly expunged by the process of law. Amongst the crowd, there were many inhabitants from Portland, including Albert and Jane Dale, Eleanor, Luke, and Mary Easton, and the long grieving parents of Ben Proctor, all of whom sat together in the front row of the mezzanine gallery. They had had the courtesy extended to them of being conveyed to the courtroom by post-chaise from Smallmouth, paid for from public funds by Lieutenant White, now acting senior Customs officer at the Weymouth office. The lieutenant himself, Mawdsley, and Jack Easton would of course be appearing as witnesses for the prosecution in due course along with some of the other officers who were present on the occasion of Smyke's capture, and so they all remained in the waiting room below. The immediate families of Captain Middleton and Clifford Hayes, both still resident in Wyke, were also present, choosing, in a touching act of solidarity, to sit adjacent to the Portland families. Since this was also to be the day of Pettigrew's trial, a member of the town's council and the chairman of the bench attended to see justice done, but there otherwise seemed to be an official disinclination to flatter the disgraced man's ego with attention.

The first matter of business in the court was to set aside Jack's conviction for the murders (on the strength of the new evidence against Smyke), and announce the retrial. This was done with such little ceremony that it hardly dented the expectant chatter that persisted in the public seats in anticipation of the entertainment to come. Jack was not even present at the time since he waited in the witness room below, and the news was relayed to him in such matter-of-fact tones by a court usher that it took several seconds for its significance to hit him. It was a mere formality, of course, but it did not seem enough that after all his trials his conviction should be set aside with such little immediate opportunity for celebration. Nevertheless, with an inner surge of quiet pride at what he had accomplished, he accepted the handshakes and congratulations of his fellow witnesses with alacrity and good grace. On hearing the announcement in the courtroom above, the Dales and Eastons, already partially reconciled on the basis of Jack's earlier relayed reports of Smyke's apprehension, turned to each other and smiled with satisfaction, even though it had been a foregone conclusion. But the quashing of the convictions of Elizabeth and Rose Dale on grounds that the evidence against them was similarly tainted was a source of bitterness, since nothing could bring back a lost daughter or the years of Rose's life of servitude. (That Jack had not yet visited the Dales meant that they did not yet know of his marriage to their daughter or of Rose's pregnancy; and he had also forbidden his family to speak of either until he had done so himself as a free man.)

When Smyke was brought up from the cells, he at first refused to plead on the multiple capital charges that faced him. In a display of bruised and condescending affront, he asserted that the charges were contemptible, that they were all trumped up, and that he would not dignify them with a plea. It is also possible that he hoped by not pleading to avoid a guilty verdict and thus the confiscation of his property and the resultant catastrophic reduction of his wife's residual estate. That her over-bearing personage had been seen haranguing the man during her several visits to the prison as he awaited trial, suggested that wifely pressure might have influenced him to attempt this ploy. But this was not the only pressure he faced. To break the impasse caused by Smyke's obstinacy, an impatient judge threatened to invoke the law of *piene fort et dur*, under which Smyke could be stretched naked with weights placed upon his body until he succumbed (or changed his mind). It was not surprising therefore that, when shown the deadly apparatus, he quickly dropped his recalcitrance and indicated his plea, clearly preferring to risk the quicker mercy of the hangman's noose instead.

The trial lasted a full day; but unlike at Jack's trial seven or so years before, when the jury's prolonged deliberations had been swung by Smyke's unfettered rhetoric and tainted by the furore in the press, this time there was quick and unanimous agreement in the jury retiring room. Jack's eyewitness account of the shooting of Hayes, and his descriptions of events preceding the deaths of Middleton and Proctor would probably have been enough to secure conviction unsupported. But importantly, White, Mawdsley, and two other officers, all of whom had heard Smyke's incriminating admissions in the *Marguerite's* hold, corroborated Jack's evidence. This left absolutely no doubt in the jurymen's minds as to Smyke's guilt, and he was thus convicted on all charges. And in view of the heinous, almost treasonable nature of the offences, the judge was not inclined to be lenient. For the three killings and one attempted murder (the latter on Jack himself), Smyke would be hanged in chains from the gibbet on the Nothe at the mouth of the Wey, where he would be left to rot as a visible warning for all those who might be tempted to abuse their civil power. Amidst the jubilation of those spectators who had crammed themselves into the courtroom, the judge was hardly heard as he made his final pronouncement – that Jack was exonerated and his sentence revoked.

By contrast, Pettigrew's trial was an anti-climax. There was, however, a certain poetic justice in his sentence, which provided some amusement to his peers. Not unexpectedly he objected to the charge, and to refute it he produced several referees who propounded the impeccable nature of his character. But the evidence against him was too strong. Mawdsley and his two colleagues gave convincing testimony as to Pettigrew's incriminating remarks spoken from the window of his bedroom, but the large quantity of contraband found stored in his cellars was unequivocal. Pettigrew was consequently convicted of conspiracy to defraud the State on a grand scale, for which he was sentenced to transportation to the American colonies, and penal servitude for a period of sixteen years. Needless to say, he was also stripped of his office, and the *Marguerite* and all the contraband found in his possession confiscated by the Crown. In addition, his company accounts would now be subject to a full-scale investigation by the Board of Customs and Excise with a view to establishing if any back payment of taxes was due. Short of capital punishment, the ignominy and hardships of penal servitude were the cruellest penalties that could have been meted out to someone so used to power and privilege. Moreover, the confiscation of his property and the fear that irregularities in his accounts would be revealed must have filled him with absolute dread. Even the rosy make-up on his cheeks could not hide the sudden draining of colour from his face as he listened in to the judge's condemning remarks. And the haughty disdain that he had exhibited from the dock until that moment collapsed in a display of righteous histrionics that made some of those present turn away in disgust.

The outcome of the trials was widely reported in the London press and also in the provincial editions in Dorchester and other major towns of southern England. In *The Gentleman's News* published a few days later, Mr Justice Rogers, the presiding judge at the trial, called for a wide-ranging overhaul of procedures in the legal process. In his article reviewing the miscarriages of justice on Jack Easton, and Elizabeth and Rose Dale, he ventured the formal adoption of a controversial principle that a defendant should always enjoy the right to legal counsel and representation, rather than be forced to defend themselves. He also urged that the prosecution case in court would more safely come from independent prosecutors rather than from the complainant himself, who would then no longer be able to avoid cross-examination. In his closing remarks, he made two further suggestions: firstly, that there should be some restraint on press reporting before any trial took place, and secondly, that juries should be drawn from a wider cross-section of the community more representative of those whose guilt they judged. Both of these measures, he suggested, would have reduced the prejudice that had clearly been a factor in the miscarriages of the Easton case. This was revolutionary stuff indeed.

As far as Tregaskis was concerned, White chose to bring no charges against him, and the Cornishman's testimony at the trials of Smyke and Pettigrew was not called for since the evidence was quite strong enough without his contribution. His collaboration had thus not been exposed, and the rest of the gang would therefore never know of it. However, with the hiatus in Pettigrew's shipping operations, Tregaskis would lose his income as well as any pension he might have secured from his employer. This was unfortunate, since he had been an honest and hard-working employee of Pettigrew's father for many years before being led astray by his avaricious son. Perhaps he should have been stronger in resisting the coercion, but this was easier said than done in a land where there were more people seeking employment than work available. But Jack and Luke had kept to their part of the bargain too; Tregaskis's one-hundred pound share of the proceeds of Pettigrew's hijacked contraband would buy him and his wife a cottage in Cornwall where they might be supported by family and any casual work he might find in the peninsula. At least he and his wife should avoid the poor house.

For his leading part in bringing Smyke and Pettigrew to justice, Andrew White was made acting-captain and appointed as the county's senior customs officer. In his subsequent restructuring of the organisation, several men, principally those who had been Smyke's cronies, would lose their jobs peremptorily and with no pension, and young Mawdsley would be promoted to lieutenant.

And Luke and Mary's dire financial situation would in due course be salvaged by the sale of the 'free goods' that had been delivered so helpfully by the *Marguerite* into Church Ope Cove. With the duty paid, a matter upon which the incorruptible White would eventually insist, the sale would raise sufficient funds even after the fair shares for the participants had been allocated, for Luke to pay off his bills and settle his debt to the bank. This would confound Chorley and Grant who still quietly conspired to take over the Easton's quarry should Luke default, and it would save Luke, Mary, and Eleanor from forfeiting their homes. But it would not be all plain sailing from now on. Although Mary would secure the Exeter contract in due course, it would be won in the face of such fierce competition from Grant that practices at the quarry would need drastically to be improved to ensure a profit. This, however, would be the very spur that Mary needed to force the business to become more efficient in its ways; and with her now in charge and Luke concentrating his practical skills where they would be put to best effect, the prospects of the quarry looked better than they had for years.

The day after the trial, Jack called upon Albert and Jane Dale at their home in Fortune's Well. Jack always remembered the house as immaculately kept, but as he waited for them in the hallway, it now looked rather tired and unloved, with dusty surfaces and clutter scattered everywhere, as if the home had not been given the attention it had once received. He was aware that his mother had spoken briefly with the Dales on several occasions since Smyke's arrest, but he had expressly forbidden her to tell them of his marriage to Rose, wanting to convey the happy news himself at an appropriate time. With this thought in mind, Jack had preferred to await the trial's outcome before meeting his new parents-in-law, having an ardent desire not to speak to them until he could do so as a free man. Although he had caught their glances in the courtroom, this visit would be Jack's first proper meeting with them in seven or so years, and one bound to be highly charged with emotion and the damaging residue of all the trauma they had suffered in that time.

As the couple came down the stairs to greet him, their faces already betrayed the mixture of powerful feelings that his visit would inevitably evoke. There were tearful hugs and fulsome congratulations on his acquittal as they led him by the hand into the parlour, but there was no hiding their anxiety to speak of Elizabeth and Rose, for they mentioned them straight away after. They seated themselves together on a chair-back settee in the centre of the comfortable airy room and leant forward expectantly as Jack seated himself opposite. Out of the corner of his eye, Jack saw Jane Dale reach for her husband's hand and bring it into her lap. He glanced hesitantly at the couple as he wondered where to start; they had a certain stoic air about them as they waited, but their faces seemed drawn. It was at once evident that the couple still grieved over Elizabeth's loss, and Jack decided therefore to save news of Rose until he had spoken the words of commiseration and sympathy that he felt necessary. He knew that it was likely to be a painful catharsis, perhaps for all of them, to speak of their dead daughter, surrounded by such bitter-sweet memories of her, but he recognised their need to discuss her death in greater detail than had been possible in the short and circumspect note that Rose had written some years before.

Jack found it hard to relate the story of Elizabeth's suffering and eventual death, but he did so knowing that it might bring the grieving pair a sense of closure. He chose to spare his weeping listeners from the worst images of their youngest daughter's horrible death and the manner of the disposal of her body into the sea, telling them instead that the headstone on his Maryland farm now marked the grave of her remains, and that he and Rose visited it often and laid flowers there. And in due course, everything that needed to be said was uttered with such careful sensitivity that the pair eventually seemed satisfied. Although Jack felt himself inadequate, and his words sounded sometimes trite and facile in his ears as he spoke them, he eventually came to feel that the couple might now be able to put their dear daughter to rest in their minds. And with this, the mood lightened quickly as if some terrible burden had been lifted; and suddenly, it seemed an appropriate time for tea.

By the time Jane Dale returned to the living room with a tray tinkling delicately with china cups and saucers, Jack had handed Rose's letter to Albert and he was reading it avidly with an expression of mounting amazement.

'Jane, my dear!' he said joyously, glancing up with a tear in his eye and the broadest possible grin upon his face. 'Jack is our son-in-law after all! And what's more, we shall have a grandchild in the Spring!'

Jane Dale nearly dropped the tray in astonishment, just managing to put it down on the low table.

'Let me see, let me see!' she said excitedly, snatching the letter from her husband's hands and scanning her eyes over its pages as if devouring the sentences line by line. Albert looked on, his face brimming with vicarious enjoyment as his wife's eyebrows lifted in pleasure as she read.

'Jack!' she said at last. 'This is such wonderful news!'

As Jack left the house to return over the hill to his mother's home in Wakeham, his mind was drawn back inevitably to that last occasion when he had passed through the wicket gate, and to that strange feeling of finality and melancholy that he had felt at that time. Had it been a premonition, he wondered, as he looked up to the window where Elizabeth had stood silhouetted by the lantern light? Now, only the reflections of the sky glanced back at him from the glass, but in his mind's eye, he saw her there again. Her face was full of joy and youthful optimism, and in her belly, their child had shared that moment too. He had resisted an urge to rush back to her then, and he wondered now whether, if he had given in to it, things might have turned out differently, the trajectory of subsequent events somehow altered? That evening had been the last time they had shared happiness together, and his mind flashed back so that he was with her again, re-living the fond moments repeatedly like a sad tune which goes around and around in your head. He stood there almost in a trance allowing himself to sink into its dark embrace. Something in its essence seemed to be telling him that this was the drawing of a line, the expurgation of the ghosts of the past. Only now, at this moment and after all that he had been through, could he at last feel the closing of the final chapter of his loss. He stood there lost in thought for what seemed like minutes; but after a while the sounds of the street pressed in on him again and he found himself once more standing in the light of the sun. A weight had been lifted. He would remember Elizabeth as he had seen her then, and his mind would blot out those terrible images that had haunted him since their nightmare had begun. He took a deep breath and exhaled sharply to signify his resolve, and then he turned and stepped out up the hill with a determined stride - he had said his last good bye.

The following week, a letter arrived from Captain Auld who had read of Jack's exoneration and wrote to congratulate him upon it. This was gratifying indeed, but it was the content of the subsequent paragraphs that drew his greatest interest. It seemed that after delivering Jack's letter and the manifest to the agent in Cowes, Auld had immediately departed for Portsmouth to see the arrival of *L'hermine,* leaving Judd in charge of unloading the ship's cargo. Reunited with his first officer there, the captain had spent some time negotiating with the naval authorities on an appropriate settlement of prize money for the captured ship. To Jack's astonishment, it appeared that his own share would amount to the sum of nearly one-thousand guineas, and a draft to this amount would be paid into an account of Jack's naming as soon as it could be arranged. Jack was overwhelmed by the news and had to read the paragraph several times before he could let himself believe it. In passing, it occurred to Jack that Auld's swift departure from the *Rebecca* would have left Judd with a free rein, and he could only speculate as to whether the boatswain had already hanged himself with it or decided to change his thieving ways. That information would have to come from Goddard in due course, but for the present he let himself be taken by the heady fancies of his new wealth.

Jack had not yet fully adjusted to his new freedom to come and go as he pleased; but now, on top of all this, he had become prosperous beyond his wildest expectations, and suddenly everything in his life had changed. He realised at once that he was not only free in the eyes of the law, but also that he could now be released from all the restraints and hardships that had bedevilled him since his capture. For hours he paced his room, his mind dancing dizzyingly from one scheme to another as he contemplated the prospect that he could now do almost whatever he might wish.

To clear his mind, Jack took a walk across the Island to the west cliffs where he stood for a while looking down on the rocks on which he had so nearly met his end on *L'hermine* only a few weeks before. Behind him sat the squat tower of the higher lighthouse whose extinguished fire had not warned him off, as if it meant for him to finish there, his mission uncompleted. But he had succeeded then as he had succeeded against all the challenges that he had faced along his way, and now he was strangely restless for more. He gazed westwards to the horizon across Lyme Bay and imagined that his extended line of view over the countless horizons that lay beyond it would end at New Hope farm, and that the sea below his feet would connect him directly to it like an uninterrupted thoroughfare. He thought longingly of Rose and their new baby, due to be born, God willing, in just two months or so. He thought of Ned and Sebi, who he had come to look upon almost as his brothers. He thought of his farmstead; of southern Maryland and the Potomac creeks; and of all the new possibilities that would now await him there. And he knew then what he wanted more than anything else in the world - as soon as the prize money arrived, he would race home as fast as the winds would carry him.

THE STORY CONTINUES...

Jack Easton's story continues in the author's second novel, **Fortune's Hostage**, published 2009 by Arima (ISBN 978-1-84549-381-3), which is available through Amazon and good bookshops.

Printed in the United Kingdom by
Lightning Source UK Ltd., Milton Keynes
141438UK00001B/114/P